THE GATES OF BYZANTIUM

BOOK 2 IN THE BABYLON SERIES

SAM SISAVATH

The Gates of Byzantium

Published by Road to Babylon Media LLC
www.roadtobabylon.com

Edited by Amanda Sumner, Samantha Gordon & Wendy Chan
Formatting by BB eBooks

ISBN-13: 978-0615961149
ISBN-10: 0615961142

AUTHOR'S NOTE

The *Babylon* series was conceived and written to be read in order, starting with the first book in the series, *The Purge of Babylon*, and continuing with Book #2, *The Gates of Byzantium*. It is highly recommended you begin the series with *Purge*. Don't say I didn't warn ya.

Man is no longer at the top of the food chain.

The Purge has devastated the globe, turning much of humanity into night-dwelling, bloodthirsty creatures (dubbed "ghouls" by the survivors), while small pockets of remaining humans have managed to carry on.

With the loss of their sanctuary, Will and his small band of survivors are forced to seek shelter elsewhere. Following the call of a mysterious radio broadcast, they make the treacherous journey to Louisiana, where an island might hold the key to survival.

Along the way they meet new survivors, clash with new enemies, and renew old acquaintances that have been forever altered. Collaborators—humans working with the ghouls—are more dangerous than ever, and the ghouls have begun a new phase of their domination.

Will learns that a larger war between survivors and ghouls is raging in the rest of the country, but before he can join the fight, he must first ensure the continued survival of his group at all costs.

Where The Purge ends, the Gates beckon…

PRELUDE

"HELLO. IF ANYONE can hear me out there. This is Song Island in Beaufont Lake in Louisiana. We are broadcasting on the FEMA frequency to any survivors. We want you to know there is hope. There are survivors on Song Island. We have food, supplies, electricity, and protection against the darkness. If you are receiving this recorded message, we encourage you to make your way to us. I repeat: we have food, supplies, electricity, and protection against the darkness. Hello. If anyone can hear me out there. This is Song Island in Beaufont Lake in Louisiana. We are broadcasting on the FEMA frequency…"

BOOK ONE

THE ROAD AGAIN

CHAPTER 1

JOSH

PROS AND CONS: What were they?

Pros: Finally, after crushing on Gaby since the sixth grade and following her adventures throughout middle school and high school, he was finally spending quality time with her. Best of all, she wanted to spend those times with him.

Cons: They were surrounded by undead creatures, some of which might very well be their relatives and friends and neighbors and even, God forbid, teachers. That forced them to hide at night and move in the day. The creatures wanted them. Or, more specifically, the blood pumping through their veins. Another big con: The world had gone to hell, so there was no help coming from the state or the government or whoever was still out there. Which meant they were, for all intents and purposes, on their own.

Conclusion: The pros win by a landslide.

He guessed others might see it a little bit differently; but then again, others weren't Josh. They didn't live next door to Gaby. Of course, it could just be the hormones talking. The hormones ran wild when Gaby came up, and she came up often in his mind. He would be horrified if she ever knew that, but Josh took some comfort in the very real fact that there were more dangerous things out there than his unbridled desire for Gaby.

"Jesus, you're gone again," Matt said.

Josh knew he was daydreaming as soon as Matt's deep baritone voice reached him. He tried to play it off. "So are we doing this or what?"

Matt chuckled. "Okay, kid, whatever you say."

Kid?

That was rich coming from Matt, who was exactly seven months older than him. Not that being eighteen going on twenty, thanks to that unshaven jawline of his, mattered in the brave new world. Still, Josh wished he could sprout hair like that. It was genetics. His father couldn't grow a beard to save his life, and neither could any of his cousins.

"I feel kind of bad," Matt said. "Someone spent a lot of time on this."

"Seriously?" Josh said.

"Yeah, don't you?"

"Nah."

Matt laughed. "Man, you're cold. Were you always this cold before?"

They were standing in front of a Thanksgiving mural, part of a corner grocery store window. Josh stared at a big pumpkin clutched dangerously tight in a young girl's hands. The girl was wearing a one-piece Sunday picnic dress with a blue bow in her hair. People were serving meals and shaking hands and laughing around her. It was actually a pretty nice mural, drawn in some kind of watercolor that stayed on the glass. He didn't know how that worked. How did watercolor even stay on glass months later?

Matt picked up a rock from the sidewalk. He was a big kid, almost six feet tall, with a shaggy haircut getting longer every day. To look at him, you would think Matt played football, basketball, or maybe baseball. But he didn't. No on all three. Matt wasted his size and spent his time…doing whatever the heck he did before all this. Josh didn't even know Matt existed until eight months ago.

"Well, sorry, window, but you had a nice run," Matt said, and flung the rock.

The window shattered into hundreds of pieces, taking half of the girl's face with it. Matt picked up his baseball bat and batted down the rest of the girl's face, along with other jagged shards clinging to the edges of the window frame.

There was enough sunlight that they didn't have to be afraid of what lurked inside the store. You always had to be careful with the shadows, even in broad daylight. The bloodsuckers were good at hiding. They usually slept in the daytime, but you couldn't really count on that.

They climbed inside, crunching glass underneath their sneakers. Josh slung the empty backpack over his right shoulder, hoping to find something to fill it with this time. Lancing, Texas, was not the biggest city in the state, but it was bigger than the podunk no-name town they had raided for food and supplies two months ago. There were enough stores and houses here to keep them happy for a while, but as always happened, they had to go farther and farther out of their comfort zone to find more.

Josh headed straight for the back room. He could hear Matt moving around behind him, going through the shelves, grabbing bags of snacks and anything else that hadn't expired yet. Josh could smell rotten vegetables and fruits to his right.

The greens aisle, I presume.

Greens weren't going to be of much use now. It was all about non-perishables, and as much as grocery stores kept those on the shelves out front, they kept even more in the back. He wouldn't have known that before; but then again, he rarely went into grocery stores looking for food in the "good old days."

He gripped the steel prying bar tightly in his right hand. The thing was bright blue, over fifty-six inches long and three and a quarter inches wide, with a slight angle at the end that made it easy to slip into tight crevices for prying. Thus, the name "prying bar." It also served as a defensive or offensive weapon in a pinch.

Josh didn't need the bar on the back room door. It wasn't locked, so he turned the doorknob first, then pulled it open slowly, revealing blackness inside. Just his luck, there wasn't a single window in the whole room. Not even a tiny skylight to brighten the place up. It was pitch-black, and there was no telling what was hiding in there.

Darkness had ceased being their friend a long time ago.

He fished out his flashlight from one of the pockets of his cargo pants. He switched it on and moved it around the back room. Empty boxes on the floor, a mop and cleaning supplies, and what looked like a stack of used overalls.

And there, way in the back, two shelves filled with thick, bulging boxes. His heart leaped in his throat.

Jackpot.

Josh thought about calling Matt over. Matt had the baseball bat and he was bigger, and if he went in first, well, they could find out if there really were any bloodsuckers hiding inside. Josh could stay outside and wait for the all-clear signal. If push came to shove, Josh could back away from the door, into the sunlight and safety. Matt, on the other hand…

Shit, it's not like I know the guy.

He sighed. Yeah, like he could really do that. The lonely part of him, the one who spent all his nights at home surfing the web, might have been able to use Matt as bait. But the new him, the one who had befriended Matt and Gaby and escaped their shitty cubbyhole of a small town together, couldn't.

God help him, he had become fond of the big doofus.

"Matt!" Josh shouted.

"Yeah?" Matt called back.

"I'm going into the back room."

"Be careful, man."

"If you hear me yelling like a little girl…"

Matt laughed. "I gotcha back."

Josh leaned into the doorway and banged the bar against the wall, then listened to the echo waft through the room.

"That you?" Matt, alarmed, shouted from behind him.

"Yeah," Josh shouted back. "I'm making sure there's nothing in here. Maybe I can lure them out."

"Good luck with that. They're not that stupid."

"Yeah, well, you never know."

Matt was right. The bloodsuckers weren't stupid. Josh had seen them up close, seen the way they pounced and attacked, always relying on their numbers. Then again, stupid creatures wouldn't have been able to take over the world in one night. At first, Josh had thought it was just their little corner of the universe—Ridley, Texas, population 4,100 in a good year—but he had learned the truth quickly enough.

No, the bloodsuckers weren't stupid at all.

Josh took a breath and stepped into the back room, gripping the cold steel rod tightly in his right hand, ready to swing. He swept the room again with the flashlight. The backpack felt light and empty behind him, and his sneakers did what sneakers do—they squeaked ridiculously loud against the cheap, tiled floor.

He made a beeline for the shelves in the back, careful not to move too fast, running the flashlight along every inch of the room for signs of occupancy. Corner to corner, around the empty and opened boxes on the floor, the piles of clothes nearby, an old raggedy couch, a bucket, and a mop. Nothing. Just the sound of his movements, the sound of Matt tossing things around in the store beyond the opened door.

Jesus, Matt, you're louder than my grandma without her meds, man.

Then he was suddenly at the shelves. Josh grinned at the first box he saw, labeled "Canned Fruits."

Jackpot, mofos!

Josh leaned the prying bar against the shelf and stuck the flashlight between his teeth. He reached for the nearest box, but before he even touched it, the shelf wobbled and Josh froze.

And he heard it (*and smelled it*) and alarms began ringing inside his head. In the second or two it took Josh to pull back his hands and reach for the bar, the shelf wobbled again as the bloodsucker leaped down from the top of the shelf—where it had been hiding all this time—and crashed right into Josh.

The force of the impact threw Josh back to the floor. The flashlight flew from Josh's mouth, the lens shattering against the concrete floor, even before Josh crumpled nearby in a heap of blinding pain. The creature was on top of him, gripping him with long, slender fingers, and Josh's nostrils flared at the pungent smell of the thing's breath, the unmistakable odor of death that seethed from the gnarled flesh and the rotting muscles underneath.

He let out a scream before he could stop himself *(Oh, man, Matt's going to have fun over that one*), and the adrenaline rushed through him, pumping him full of urgency and somehow, somehow, Josh was able to throw his right elbow into the bloodsucker's cheek. He felt the bone underneath what was left of the creature's flesh breaking, and the thing flopped off him. Josh scrambled to his hands and knees, saw the bright blue prying bar nearby, the color giving it away in the blackness.

He leaped for it and got the bar by the middle section just as he landed, feeling another massive stinging sensation ripple through his body as he crashed back against the floor. Josh could feel it coming—*smell* it getting closer—and he spun around and saw the creature flying through the air. He swung on instinct and caught it in the head. It jerked off course and landed on the floor three feet away from him, bony arms and legs making a hell of a racket against the hard concrete.

Josh fought for his footing, managing to get up on his knees before the bloodsucker beat him to it. There was a big gash in its left cheek, thick clumps of coagulated black blood dripping free. There wasn't a lot of it because the bloodsucker was small and frail, and it looked miserably weak, almost malnourished, though it was hard to tell with them. This one looked especially pathetic, as if it hadn't eaten in a while, and Josh wondered pointlessly how long it had been in here, just waiting for some idiot to stumble cluelessly inside. Some idiot like him.

The creature opened its mouth and bared its teeth, revealing filthy, dirty, brown- and yellow-stained teeth, chipped and crooked and twisted. *"Meth teeth,"* he remembered thinking the first time he saw a bloodsucker, on the night everything changed forever.

They were hairless creatures, more animal than man, with pruned flesh and skin that hung loosely over bones underneath, like ill-fitting clothes. Their dark black eyes, lifeless and pale, gave away that they were no longer human. There was a thick, overwhelming smell about them that reminded Josh of his dog Sally, especially after she had gotten into the trash cans.

The bloodsucker leaped into the air again. It was fast—so much faster than Josh had expected—and Josh was staggering backward even before he had completely risen to his feet. He felt the edge of the metal shelf dig into his back as he bumped into it, and boxes tumbled down around him. One box hit him on the head and Josh thought, *Oh, great, now I have a concussion, too. Can this day get any worse?*

But it did, because soon Josh was on the floor again, and the bloodsucker was on top of him. It glared down at him, emotionless eyes like the pits of some hell Josh used to read about on the Internet while everyone else was out having fun. He felt skeletal fingers digging into the flesh of his shoulders through his T-shirt as it pinned him down and opened its mouth. Josh stared into the cavern of ugly, twisted, disgusting teeth, like something out of a nightmare. His stomach twisted into knots, the disgust of being this close to the creature overcoming even the fear of the moment.

The bloodsucker grabbed his head and turned it, lowering itself toward his exposed neck. Josh felt weak and stupid and useless under its grip.

Thick, sticky black blood dripped down from the gash in the creature's cheek. The blood caressed Josh's temple and he winced. It didn't hurt or sting, but the reality of coming in contact with their blood was enough to make him want to retch.

He closed his eyes and stopped fighting the bloodsucker and thought about other things, of Gaby. Lovely, lovely Gaby. He hadn't been sure she could possibly get any lovelier than when he had seen her that first time in sixth grade. She got prettier as she grew up, and now that she was eighteen, he was certain she was the most beautiful girl in the world. It was too bad he never had the courage to tell her, even before all of this. And now he never would.

Regrets. He had so many regrets.

Oh fuck it, just get it over with, you smelly piece of shit.

Sticky saliva dripped down on him as the bloodsucker put its mouth over his neck, and it was about to take a bite when Josh heard a loud, bloodcurdling scream that sounded very familiar coming from behind the creature. Josh's eyes snapped open at the same time the bloodsucker lifted its head away from his neck and turned just as *ping!*—and the bloodsucker looked like it was levitated up into the air by some unseen force, off of Josh, and flung sideways. Josh swore he could hear the creature's bones clattering as it landed roughly in a pile across the room.

He saw Matt—big, muscular, handsome Matt—standing over him, the bright, open doorway perfectly framing him in some kind of heroic pose.

Oh, come on, he saves my life and *gets the heroic profile, too? This is too much.*

Matt stood with the aluminum baseball bat in his hands, and he was changing up his grip on the shiny weapon when the bloodsucker sprang back to its feet like nothing had happened. Of course the creature hadn't felt anything. What was Josh thinking? He had caught the thing twice in the face and it kept coming. And he had a steel bar. All Matt had was an aluminum baseball bat.

Josh scrambled to his feet, groping the semi-darkness for the prying bar, even as he heard a loud scream behind him. He looked back, afraid Matt was getting the worst of it, only to find Matt wading into the creature, swinging the bat like it was some toy, tiny in his big hands. Matt was connecting with every swing, and Josh heard the loud, almost sickening *ping! ping! ping!* every time Matt hit pay dirt and crushed flesh and broke bones.

But the bloodsucker kept coming, and coming...

Josh finally spotted the prying bar. It had slid underneath the metal shelf. He dived to the floor and stuck his hand underneath and grabbed the bar and pulled it out. He was back on his feet again, turning, just in time to see Matt letting out another wild scream as the bloodsucker clamped down on his left arm with its teeth and blood splattered again. Thick, bright red blood.

Matt's.

Matt, in a fit of rage, dropped the bat and grabbed the creature and pried the undead thing off his left hand with impossible brute strength.

My God, he's strong.

The bloodsucker stumbled back and obscenely licked the corners of its mouth with a long, reptilian tongue. Most of its lower jaw was covered in blood.

"Fucker!" Matt shouted, and scrambled for his bat.

The bloodsucker looked back at him with dead, pale eyes and kept licking at the blood coating its mouth. It wasn't paying attention to Josh at all, and Josh took the moment to rush forward and *thwack!* got the bloodsucker in the back of the head. The blow sent it stumbling to the floor. Josh thought he might have even heard the creature's skull breaking into a million pieces when he landed the blow, but when the bloodsucker lifted its head and looked back at him, utter annoyance on its face, Josh wasn't so sure anymore.

"Fucker!" Matt screamed again, attacking, swinging a mighty blow that caught the creature in the face.

The Herculean strike obliterated the creature's nose—or what was left of it, which wasn't very much. The bloodsucker stumbled backward, dazed by the blow, reminding Josh of a drunk. It eventually lost its footing and tumbled to the floor as its feet came undone underneath it. It wasn't dead, but it was hurt. It was still trying to get back up when Matt stood over it and began smashing the bat down into its face.

Over and over and over again, all the while shouting, "Fucker! You fucker!"

Josh was suddenly very sick as he watched Matt turn the bloodsucker's head into squishy pulp, a puddle of thick black blood (*God, that looks like Jell-O*) that now coated every inch of the aluminum baseball bat. And Matt was still swinging, still raining blows down on what was left of the head, even though there wasn't much left of the head at all.

Josh thought about telling Matt to stop, that the bloodsucker was dead, but that wasn't true. Even with its head bashed in and looking like something that resembled ground beef, the creature's arms and legs were still moving. Then the creature's hands groped at Matt's legs.

Matt felt the tugging and finally seemed to snap out of his momentary insanity. He stopped swinging and staggered back, pulling himself free from the bony hands. The creature was already starting to stand up again, and Josh and Matt found themselves staring, wide-eyed, more shocked than afraid at the moment, as the bloodsucker pulled itself back up to its feet. It did this, even as lumps of flesh and blood and what was left of its head flopped down to the floor around it in thick, disgustingly messy clumps of flesh and bone and muscle.

"Matt," Josh heard himself say. "I think we should go."

Matt looked over at him and Josh thought Matt was going to scream *"No!"*, that he wanted to finish this, but instead Josh saw fear in Matt's eyes. "Yeah," Matt said, and stumbled toward the open door.

Josh hurried after him and they staggered their way back into the bright store, back to safety.

Matt was out of breath, his chest heaving. Josh's heart was pounding at a thousand beats a second, and he didn't think he remembered how to breathe. They didn't bother to pick up Matt's backpack, stuffed with bags of chips and unopened beef jerky sticks. They also stepped over a plastic bag filled with warm Gatorade and water bottles, its contents spilled out on the floor.

Josh didn't know why, but he looked back and saw the bloodsucker—or what was left of it—standing just inside the darkness of the back room, "looking" after them. Though of course it couldn't really look anymore. Its eyes were gone, along with its entire face, now pooled on the floor behind it in a puddle. Pieces of skin and what remained of its head hung grotesquely behind its body like a hoodie, something it could pick up and pull back on.

The creature didn't come out of the back room. It stayed in the shadows, beyond the open door, just beyond the reach of the stretching sunlight. Josh knew the creature would die if it stepped into the sun's rays. He had seen it happen. Watching the bloodsuckers vaporize before his eyes in sunlight, leaving behind only piles of bones, had been almost as surreal as realizing that the world as he knew it was gone for good.

Josh stared back at the creature, or as much as you could stare back at something that didn't have eyes or a head anymore. It was a sight he would never forget, and it occupied his entire world, even with Matt wheezing next to him, bleeding all over the sidewalk as they stumbled out into the bright, sweltering Texas heat.

"Oh God, oh God. It bit me, Josh, it fucking bit me!" Matt said. "Oh God, what's going to happen, Josh? What's going to *happen* to me?"

CHAPTER 2

BLAINE

"THIS IS SOME kind of bullshit right here," Deeks said.

Blaine laughed and tried to blink away the sweat dripping into his eyes. It was hot, but hot meant day, and day was good. "You always say that."

"This time I'm right."

"You always say that, too." Blaine finished cranking the jack when he had the Jeep high enough to pull out the blown tire. "Grab the spare, old man."

Deeks grunted and walked back to the Jeep, slinging the Mossberg shotgun over his shoulder. Blaine carried a similar Mossberg model, except his didn't have the elaborate camouflage pattern of Deeks's.

Blaine pulled off the flat tire, careful to avoid the big metal chunk sticking out like a sword, sharp enough to cleave his flesh from his bone without effort. It looked like something from a car, probably shredded in some kind of high-speed accident. The tire blew almost immediately after running it over, and it was a miracle they didn't careen off the road and into the ditch the way the steering wheel was fighting him.

It was stupid, and all his fault. He was going too fast. Fifty miles per hour on a road filled with debris, cars, and God knew what else was a stupid way to travel. He should have known better, but the road down here, far from the Dallas-Fort Worth area, opened up, and there were so few cars that he had let it lull him into a sense of security.

He heard footsteps and looked over at Sandra, walking back toward them along the flat, empty road. She played with her blonde hair, cut short to combat the smothering Texas heat.

She smiled at him, the sun glinting off deep green eyes. "Look at you staring. Like you've never seen a pair of tits before."

"You know I can't help it."

"Of course not. That's the point. Or points." She put her hands on her hips and posed for him. She wore jeans, cowboy boots, and a Dallas Cowboys T-shirt that was probably a size too small. "Let's go, let's go," Sandra said, clapping her hands for effect. "*Vamos, amigos*!"

Blaine tossed her a crooked grin. Sandra was probably the whitest person he knew, but she liked to throw in some Español every now and then for his benefit. Not that she knew more than a few words.

"We'd be done by now if this asshole would hurry up," Blaine said.

Deeks grunted and rolled the spare tire over, his face glistening with sweat. He stood back to catch his breath. Deeks was only about fifty years old, but those were hard, city years. His eyes drooped, and Blaine sometimes wondered how much longer the old man would last out here.

"Where are we?" Sandra asked, looking around them.

"About ten miles out of Lancing," Blaine said.

"What's in Lancing?"

"Hell if I know. We'll grab whatever supplies we can, then keep on trucking down south."

"'Keep on trucking?'"

"What, you don't think a Mexican knows what 'keep on trucking' means?"

"Half-Mexican," she corrected him.

He grinned. That was technically true, but he had the dark complexion, and one look at him and all anyone ever saw was "Mexican." He never corrected them, because it didn't matter. Blaine was always good about taking what God gave him and running with it. Like the end of the world. While people were getting turned and eaten, Blaine was surviving. He was good at that, too.

"Correctamundo," Blaine said.

"That's definitely not proper Spanish."

"Close enough."

Blaine was halfway to putting the lug nuts back into place over the spare tire when he felt the road underneath him tremble slightly. It came from behind them, back up the highway. Approaching vehicles.

Blaine quickly spun the fifth lug nut into place and tossed the crank into the back of the Jeep, then unwound the jack. When all four of the Jeep's tires were touching the asphalt road again, Blaine stood up and unslung the Mossberg.

Deeks glanced over. "What is it?"

"Cars coming down the road," Blaine said.

"I don't hear anything."

"You can't feel them?"

"No."

"Damn, you're old."

Deeks grunted back.

"I hear them," Sandra said.

She walked over to stand beside Blaine. She was a foot shorter than him, even in boots that gave her an extra three or four inches. But then, most people were short next to Blaine. Sandra wore a gun holster with a .32 Smith and Wesson in it. She put her hand on the handle of the revolver now, her body stiffening noticeably, the way it always did when she was scared.

"It's okay," he said. "We'll be fine."

She looked over at him and tried to smile, but it came out badly.

"It'll be fine," he said again.

"What's happening?" Deeks said, nervously unslinging his Mossberg.

Three vehicles, little more than black dots, materialized out of thin air down the flat road behind them.

Blaine quickly went over his options.

They could take off now in the fixed Jeep, try to outrun them. But if they decided to pursue, then what? Sooner or later, they would have to stop and seek shelter for the night. That was the problem. Sooner or later, they always had to stop for the night...

Blaine glanced at his watch: 4:16 P.M.

They were cutting it too close. It was June, and summer in Texas meant 8:15 P.M. sunsets. That was four hours away. Usually that was more than enough time to look for shelter, but the flat tire had thrown his schedule out of whack.

"Who are they?" Sandra asked.

"I don't know," Blaine said.

"What do we do?" Deeks asked anxiously.

"Jeep's fixed," Sandra said. "Maybe we should go before they reach us?"

Blaine shook his head. "They've already seen us. They'd just follow."

"So just stand here and say hi?"

"Maybe they're friendlies," Deeks said.

Like the last three groups we ran into? Blaine thought, but said instead, "Maybe. But grab the rifles anyway, just to be safe."

Deeks came back with two AR-15 assault rifles. He tossed one rifle and a spare magazine across the Jeep to Blaine. Blaine stuffed the extra mag into one of his cargo pants pockets.

"Do you really think we're going to need those?" Sandra asked.

"Just to be safe," Blaine said.

"Never hurts to show them we have firepower, darling," Deeks said.

"I know, but still," Sandra said. "It might give them the wrong impression."

"Deeks is right," Blaine said. "Show of force."

Blaine watched the vehicles get larger as they drew closer. The road was a four-lane highway, flat and low to the ground. A thick wall of trees separated the north and southbound lanes, and there was green wherever you looked, with woods to both the east and the west. It was a long, flat corridor, with the road extending north-south for miles.

Out of the blue, Blaine caught a whiff of Sandra's perfume settling in the air next to him. Chanel something that had been sitting around in an expensive mall in Kilgore. They had found a lot of useful stuff there, which was why both Sandra and Deeks had hated to leave.

Blaine could make out a Jeep moving up the road. It looked similar to the one they were driving, moving at the front of what looked like a mini caravan. A GMC SUV and a Ford F-150 truck trailed the Jeep. Blaine would know those vehicles anywhere. Gas guzzlers. He hoped the people driving them at least had hand cranks for siphoning gas, because they probably had to do a lot of gassing up on a regular basis to keep those two monsters on the road.

But he hadn't seen anything yet. Coming up behind the first three vehicles was the towering cab of a big rig, pulling a large trailer behind it.

Jesus, where do they find the diesel to run that monster?

He felt Sandra tightening up next to him. He reached over and squeezed her hand. She smiled back, putting on a brave face he easily saw through. Sandra didn't scare easy, but she was scared now.

"It'll be okay," Blaine said. "Just follow my lead."

"Okay."

"Deeks," Blaine called.

The older man glanced back at him. "Yeah?"

"Get back here."

Deeks had absent-mindedly wandered twenty yards up the road, and he quickly jogged back to the Jeep. By the time he reached them, he was huffing and puffing, his cheeks flushed red, sweat caking his forehead.

"Go to the front of the Jeep," Blaine said.

Deeks nodded and hurried over to stand behind the hood of the Jeep.

"Shouldn't we get back there, too?" Sandra said.

"You should. I'll stay here. I don't want to give them the impression we're afraid of them."

"But we are."

"They don't have to know that, babe."

Blaine listened to the sound of Sandra's cowboy boots as she hurried back down the length of the Jeep. Blaine remained standing where he was, near the rear tire. He unslung the Mossberg and put it on top of the Jeep, making sure the handle was turned toward him for an easy grab. Shoot-outs weren't something Blaine knew a lot about, but he wasn't a total idiot.

He spent the next few seconds checking the AR-15's magazine. If shit hit the fan, he would unload with the rifle, then switch over to the Mossberg as a last resort. He wasn't exactly the best shot in the world, but the simple red dot sight on top of the rifle helped with accuracy. Mostly. If all else failed, he would make up in quantity what he lacked in quality.

The three vehicles were fifty yards away now, and Blaine could just make out two men in the front seat of the Jeep. His initial instincts about the Jeep had been correct—it was an older, more beat-up model of theirs. Blaine looked past the Jeep at the GMC. The front windshield was tinted, and so was the F-150's. He was sure there was more than one person in both trucks. Counting the two in the Jeep, that made at least six people.

At least.

The vehicles finally came to a stop forty yards up the road. First the Jeep, then the two trucks. The big rig was next, stopping behind the other three vehicles, its brakes squealing loudly, the highway groaning underneath its efforts. They turned off their engines, and Blaine saw the man in the passenger seat of the Jeep talking into a radio. Blaine was too far away to hear anything, but he could make out the man's large shock of white hair.

"Blaine?" Sandra said behind him. "Maybe you should come back here with us..."

"I'll be okay," Blaine said. "Just stay calm and follow my lead."

The man with white hair stood up in the Jeep, waved over at them, then shouted, "Hello over there! You folks have car trouble?"

"Not anymore!" Blaine shouted back.

"I'm coming over," the man said, and started to climb out of the Jeep.

"Not necessary!"

The man didn't seem to have heard him. Or if he did, he didn't care, because he climbed down to the road anyway.

Shit.

The man with white hair began walking toward him. He wore a sweat-stained white T-shirt, cargo pants, and a gun belt with the holster tied low around his right leg like some kind of gunfighter's rig. Blaine thought that was amusing, but not enough that he cracked a smile. Instead, he scowled at the guy, hoping to intimidate him into stopping.

It didn't work, and the man with white hair kept coming.

"Maybe he didn't hear you?" Sandra asked nervously behind him.

"He heard me," Blaine said.

"This is trouble right here, Blaine," Deeks said.

Tell me something I don't know, old-timer.

"That's far enough," Blaine shouted, even though he didn't have to.

The man stopped twenty yards away. Closer now, the white hair looked more pronounced, like a dye job. How could hair be that white? The man looked to be in his fifties, but it was hard to tell with all the white hair.

"What's with the hostility?" the man asked.

"I don't know you," Blaine said.

"And I don't know you. But that's no need for all this aggressive behavior."

"Sorry. But it's a dangerous world out here."

"That's true. Which is why we're offering help. Nice Jeep, by the way."

"Yours don't look so bad."

The guy looked back at his Jeep. "Not as nice as yours. Got a lot of wear and tear on it. You folks came out of Dallas?"

"Around there, yeah."

"Us, too. Took a while to get down here. Looks like it's the same for you guys. Dangerous out there, especially at night. But that's why we're together." He indicated the mini-caravan behind him. "Safety in numbers."

"We're doing just fine on our own."

"We have supplies. Maybe we can trade. I'm sure we have something you might need, and I'm sure you have something we might want."

"We don't have anything to trade, and chances are you don't have anything we want."

"You sure?"

"I'm sure. You should go back to your Jeep and keep heading down the road."

"We don't want any trouble," the guy said. And he held his hands up in surrender, then casually smiled at Blaine.

"There won't be any if you just go back and—"

Blaine never finished, because at that moment someone popped up behind the roof of the F-150, the sun glinting off the steel barrel of a rifle as the guy laid it across the roof and took aim. Blaine saw it two seconds before the guy fired and he felt the bullet chop into his left side, exit, and bury itself in the asphalt highway behind him.

He heard Sandra's voice: "Blaine!"

Blaine didn't think, didn't try to figure out what the hell was going on, and instinctively lifted the AR-15 to open up on the guy with white hair. But the guy was anticipating it and was already running sideways, and he leaped into the ditch before Blaine could fire. Suddenly without a target, Blaine swiveled the assault rifle back to the F-150 and fired off two quick shots. His bullets stitched the front windshield of the truck, and the sniper ducked back behind cover.

Blaine saw the Jeep's driver scurrying behind the Jeep. Meanwhile, two men had rushed out of the GMC, both armed with rifles.

"Blaine!" Sandra screamed behind him again.

He turned and began running back as the two guys at the GMC opened up on him with full-automatic rifles. The highway around him exploded into big, scorching chunks of asphalt, and Blaine swore there was no way he was going to survive this. He could hear bullets ricocheting off the sides of the Jeep and zipping past his ears.

Sonofabitch!

He and Deeks were stuck with semi-automatic rifles while the bad guys were unloading on full-auto. That was some shitty luck right there.

Deeks was at the hood of the Jeep, shooting back with his AR-15. Casually, like he had all the time in the world. The old man was either delusional or didn't realize how much trouble they were in.

Sandra was crouched next to the Jeep's front grill when Blaine reached it. Her eyes, wide with relief at the sight of him, quickly turned to horror. "Oh my God, you're bleeding!"

"I know, I know." It was all he could get out.

He knew he was bleeding because he had felt the throbbing pain all the way from the back of the Jeep to the hood. The bullet had gone clean through, which he thought was a good thing—not that he knew anything about getting shot. He was sure of one thing, though—it hurt like a sonofabitch.

Blaine popped up from behind the Jeep and fired off four quick shots at the guys at the GMC. They had retreated behind the vehicle now and were firing back from safety. Blaine saw the Jeep's driver hiding behind his own vehicle, shooting with an assault rifle. Blaine thought it looked like an AK-47.

Suddenly, the driver of the F-150 opened his door and dived out and ran for cover behind the truck. As he did so, the sniper in the bed of the truck popped back up and fired over the roof. Blaine felt the bullet zip past his head, an inch from taking it clean off at the shoulders. He ducked back behind the Jeep, thankful he still had a head to duck with.

He became aware of Sandra fumbling with his waist, trying to stanch the flow of blood. He had no idea when she had started doing that, but he didn't stop her. He was bleeding too badly and he was already feeling light-headed from the blood loss. At least it wasn't a gut shot. He wouldn't be dead right away from a gut shot, but he wouldn't get better, either. A bullet that went clean through his side meant he could survive it. Probably.

Then Blaine heard a loud *pop* and turned and saw Deeks falling to the highway behind Sandra. There was a hole in Deeks's left temple and one side of his head was completely gone. His AR-15 clattered to the hot asphalt next to him. Sandra saw the body and clutched her mouth to keep from screaming, though her eyes screamed plenty for her.

The guy with white hair! That fuck!

It had to be. The gunshot had come from up close, and it was from a handgun. No one was going to hit Deeks with a handgun from forty yards away. But the guy with white hair was closer, and the last time Blaine had seen him, the man was diving into the ditch beside the road.

Blaine leaned out from behind the Jeep's grill in the direction of the ditch and saw white hair moving steadily up the highway, crouching low. The guy saw Blaine a split-second after Blaine saw him, and the man fired—too fast—and the bullet ricocheted off the Jeep's hood and burrowed into dirt along the ditch, but it kicked up enough paint and metal that Blaine felt the heat against his face even as he pulled his head back.

"Nice shotgun!" the guy shouted.

The sound of the Mossberg being racked from the back of the Jeep.

He looked over at Sandra and saw her staring back at him, one hand still clamped over her mouth, eyes wide and afraid.

Save her, you idiot. Find a way to save *her.*

He looked toward the woods to his left. It wasn't too far away. Thirty yards, maybe. Probably a little bit more. Sandra was a runner, had been her entire life, from high school to college, where she got a scholarship to run track and field. So she could run. She could *really* run. All she needed was a chance, and he could provide that.

He stared at her, willing her to listen to him. "When I give the word, you run into the woods. Understand?"

She shook her head furiously back at him.

"You have to!" Blaine hissed, putting as much force into his voice as he dared without white hair overhearing. "You can make it," he said, calmer this time, trying to be convincing. "You're fast enough. Remember? You're *fast.* On the count of three…"

She was still shaking her head.

"I'll be right behind you," he lied.

She finally nodded, though he could tell she didn't completely believe him.

"I promise," he smiled, and before she could say anything, he said, "One, two…*three*!"

Blaine lunged out from behind the Jeep, moving to his right. In the two-second advantage that the sudden, unpredictable move allotted him while the shooters adjusted, Blaine saw the guy with white hair hiding behind the back of the Jeep, the top of his head just barely visible. Blaine took aim, but before he could fire, the guys up the road began shooting first and Blaine felt his right leg buckle slightly.

At first he thought he had stepped into something, maybe a pothole in the highway and twisted his leg, but no, he had been shot in the left thigh.

Blaine pulled his aim away from the guy with white hair and squeezed off as many shots as he could at the three vehicles. That got most of them running back behind cover. Even while he was shooting, Blaine saw from the corner of his eye Sandra running out from behind the Jeep and racing into the ditch, then up and over it and toward the woods.

She was running fast, his Sandra, like the wind.

Faster, girl, faster!

He was afraid they would start shooting at her, but they didn't. Instead, they concentrated all their fire on him, and Blaine kept moving to his right, drawing their attention away from Sandra.

She was halfway to the woods now, and she was still moving fast. He smiled. She would make it. If nothing else, at least she would make it.

He felt a burst of happiness that was short-lived when a third bullet tore through his right shoulder, and suddenly he could no longer hold the AR-15. Blaine crumpled to the highway on his knees and lowered his head, and waited for the fourth and final bullet to find its mark.

He waited, and waited, but the final bullet never came.

Instead, the shooting stopped, and he heard the guy with white hair shouting. "That's enough! Hold your fire!"

Blaine couldn't find the strength to lift his head. He wasn't even sure how he was still on his knees. Shouldn't he have fallen by now? He was bleeding pretty badly. Not just from the wound in his side, but the one that had taken a big chunk out of his thigh, too. The third one, in the shoulder, had hurt the most, and the bullet had probably shattered a bone or two. It had to be his right arm, too. What the hell was he going to do without his right arm?

Nothing but die.

Footsteps approaching, then the guy with white hair crouched in front of him, the Mossberg shotgun draped lazily over his lap. "I know what you're thinking, but don't you worry about the girl. We'll find her for you. Hell, you didn't think we chased you down for you and the old man, did you?" The guy laughed. "Nah. It was always for the girl. How did a bum like you land her, anyway? Must be pretty slim pickings for a ten like that to voluntarily go with a two—generously speaking—like you. No offense."

Sandra, run like the wind, girl, run like the wind...

More footsteps approaching along the highway, then a new male voice said, "Should we put the poor sucker out of his misery?"

White hair stood up. "No point. Look at him. He's not going anywhere. If he makes it to tonight, then what?"

"Tasty treat," someone else said.

Another voice: "What about the girl, Folger?"

The guy with white hair, Folger, said, "We got plenty of daylight. Spread out and start looking. She couldn't have gone far."

"She took off like a fucking deer," another guy said, and there was laughter. "That girl can run."

"First guy who catches her gets dibs," Folger said.

"She's mine, boys!" someone shouted.

Running footsteps all around him. Into the grass. Or maybe already in the woods. No, that was impossible. They couldn't move that fast. Even Sandra hadn't been able to move that fast.

He heard Folger's voice, coming from somewhere very far away now: "Don't worry, amigo, we'll treat her nice. We treat them all nice. At first, anyway. Guys get bored easy, you know?"

Then Blaine couldn't hear anymore, because everything became dark and he must have finally toppled sideways. Suddenly the side of his head was pressed into the hot highway surface, and the only sensations were heat and hardness and the sound of blood pumping free.

His blood. Who knew bleeding to death could be so damn noisy?

Run, Sandra, run…run like the wind, girl…

CHAPTER 3

WILL

THEY SHOWED UP sometime around ten at night. He guessed between 300 to 400, maybe more because his vantage point was limited. Grime, Texas, like most small towns around the state, was surrounded by trees, and you never knew how many of them were in the darkness of the woods.

He watched through night-vision goggles as they spread out across the street below him. Darting, hunched over, black-shaped moving things—*ghouls*. Already preternatural, they looked even more so in the green phosphorus.

Through the earbud in his right ear, Danny was, of course, making with the jokes.

"So this businessman has an extremely important trip coming up. It's make or break for the company, depending on whether he gets the client to sign on the dotted line. The guy is desperate, and during his presentation, he starts sweating and knows he's not making much of an impression. So he makes a decision to just go for it, starts undressing, falls to his knees in front of the client, and begs, 'Please, sir, give me this contract and I swear I'll suck your dick!' The client gives him a pitying look and says, 'I'm sorry, son, but that's just not how the Church rolls these days!' But then the client leans down and in a hushed voice adds, 'But would you happen to have a younger salesman you could send over?'"

"Oh, a Church sex joke," Will whispered into the throat mic. "Really? That all you got?"

"It's funny because it's true."

"Are we speaking from experience here?"

"Hey, that's between me and Father Al. He had very soft hands."

"Oh, Danny," Carly said, and Will could picture her rolling her eyes at him back in the basement a few streets over.

Will was alone, crouched against the edge of the clock tower along the side of the town's Main Street. He was twenty-five meters up, high enough that anyone on the streets below couldn't see him. The clock tower looked more like a church steeple, and getting to the very top required climbing some rickety stairs he hadn't been confident wouldn't shatter the first time he put pressure on them.

Grime was a small town that used to house around 2,000 people, and like most small towns, it was squeezed into a few square miles. Will figured he was somewhere in the center of town, with Route 69 about eight hundred meters to his right.

"Speaking of which," Danny said in his right ear, "how's the show out there?"

"I see about 300 to 400 ghouls. Maybe more. They're searching the city, so keep your heads low."

"It's as low as it can go, buddy. I got the girls covered. You just keep from getting dead."

"Will do."

He heard Lara's voice: "Don't do anything stupid."

"I'll try my best."

"I mean it, Will," she added, and he could hear the burden in her voice. "I have too much invested in you."

"Yes, ma'am."

Danny made the sound of a cracking whip.

"Shut up, Danny," Lara said.

Will smiled, and watched a couple of the creatures peering into a bright red truck parked at the curb below him. They spent no more than a few seconds on it before bounding up the street to join the swarm flowing southbound, so many that they swallowed up the roads and streets with their vast numbers.

Maybe 400, maybe more…

"So what's the verdict?" Danny asked. "You just out for a walk, or is there something worth watching out there?"

"They're definitely looking for something."

"Aren't they always looking for something? What else is new?"

"It's been eight months since The Purge. I'm pretty sure they've cleaned out every small town like this one. And even if they were just looking for survivors, they wouldn't need 400 to do it. No, they're looking for something specific."

"Us," Lara said.

"Yeah," Will said. "I think they're looking for us. And have been since we left Starch."

"You sure you're not just indulging in your paranoia again?" Danny asked.

"It's not paranoia if there are blood-drinking creatures chasing you."

"I saw that coming from a mile away."

"I'll radio back if something happens."

"Roger that."

Will laid the Remington 870 tactical shotgun on the concrete floor behind him. He only carried the shotgun and a Glock in a hip holster with him, having left his tried and true M4A1 assault rifle back at base. His weapons were loaded with silver ammo, the only thing besides sunlight that could kill the ghouls. Silver, even a tiny amount, once exposed to the creature's bloodstream, caused a kind of chain reaction that destroyed it almost instantly. Because of that, his group collected silver like junkies, smelting and recasting it into bullets whenever they got the chance. Sunlight was the only thing the ghouls feared more, but it was a little harder to wield the sun as an offensive weapon.

Night hadn't done a lot to temper the heat around him, and Will was already sweating underneath the black T-shirt and stripped-down urban assault vest. He reached down and touched the handle of the cross-knife, in a sheath strapped on his left hip, just to make sure it was still there. The knife's double-edged blade was covered in silver, and it was a reminder of that very first night when all of this started—The Purge, as they had come to call it. That was when Will had discovered the killing properties of silver, the main reason they were still alive to this day. He hated to think it was superstition, but he did feel naked without the knife on him at all times.

He heard glass breaking from somewhere behind him and moved to the other side of the clock tower. Two dozen ghouls streamed up the driveway of a house. They had accessed the residence through the windows—their usual M.O.—and gaunt figures flitted across the second-floor windows, briefly visible in the moonlight. After a while, the ghouls came rushing back out, down the same driveway, then spilled back out into the night, spreading out in different directions.

They're definitely looking for something…

Will had suspected it, but he had become convinced when they had stopped for a few days at a small incorporated community called Village Mills about six kilometers back. There was no reason for the ghouls to be there. The place was barely a blip on the map, and Will made sure to keep their vehicles away from the main roads. Over the months, they had become good at hiding their tracks. And yet, there they were, about a hundred or so of the creatures, scouring through the few buildings in the area.

Looking, searching for something.

Someone.

This wasn't a ghoul scouting party in search of random survivors. He was convinced of that now. This was a ghoul hunting party. They were being hunted. Will, Danny, Lara, and the others. And they had been ever since they had abandoned Harold Campbell's facility in the town of Starch, Texas, three months ago.

In the back of his mind, Will wondered if *she* was down there, too…

HE BLOCKED OUT the rickety noise as he climbed down. He hopped the last couple of meters to the floor below just to be safe, and as soon as the soles of his boots touched the hard concrete, he breathed a sigh of relief.

Another day, another dollar.

He clicked the Push-to-Talk switch connected to the radio clipped to his vest. "Danny, I'm headed back now."

"Grab some breakfast, will ya?" Danny said.

"McDonald's or Burger King?"

"You even have to ask? Mickey D's all the way. Grab me one of their world-famous Big Breakfasts. The one with hotcakes."

"You want syrup with that, too?"

"What are you, high? Of course I want syrup with my hotcakes."

"I'll grab a dozen on the way back."

"My man."

Will pushed at the heavy display case in front of the clock tower's glass doors, just enough to squeeze through. He stepped outside, blinking under the bright sun, then glanced down at his watch: 7:11 A.M.

He passed the red truck from last night, then jogged up Main Street. He turned left farther up the street and kept walking for a hundred meters or so until he came to a big, white two-story building at the end of the street. The Miller Hill House was surrounded by white picket fences that looked tiny next to its huge, towering frame. More importantly, it had a solidly built basement with only one way in.

By the time Will reached the house, Danny and Carly were outside with the girls, Vera and Elise. The eight-year-olds were racing around the overgrown lawn snatching up flowers and sticking them in each other's hair, blades of grass rising as high as their chins. They looked happy, oblivious to the empty world around them. Vera was Carly's sister, but Elise had come to them from Dansby, Texas, back when they still had the safety of Harold Campbell's facility to fall back on. It seemed like another lifetime ago.

Danny glanced over. "I don't see my Big Breakfast anywhere."

"They were fresh out."

"Ugh. That's the last time I send you on a breakfast run."

Carly said, "Lara's fixing breakfast in the dining room."

"Great idea," Danny said, "keeping radio silence all night. Lara was real happy about it, too."

"Be quiet, Danny," Carly said. "I'm sure Will feels bad about it already."

"I hope you're wearing a cup," Danny grinned.

"Oh, Danny," Carly said, and punched him on the shoulder.

Danny feigned pain as Will walked past them.

They made for an odd couple. Tall, lanky Danny, with his blond hair and California surfer looks—though he was as Texan as Will—and the smaller Carly, with her darkening red hair. When they were together, it was hard to tell Carly had only turned twenty recently and Danny was ten years older than her. The end of the world tended to age you. Or in the case of Danny, kept you exactly the same.

Will climbed up the steps of the Miller Hill House and slipped into the foyer. The place had that overwhelming old home smell about it and had been blood-free when they had arrived yesterday. Which made sense. Who was going to flee to an old historical home when bloodthirsty creatures attacked?

Lara was walking past the open kitchen door, her blonde hair tied back in a ponytail. Haircuts were in short supply these days, and his own hair was getting noticeably longer. He felt the stubble along his chin and made a mental note to take the time to shave in the next few days.

"Morning," he said.

Lara looked back at him. She was wearing cargo pants and a T-shirt like everyone, opting for practicality over fashion. The cargo pants had pouches that were useful for carrying supplies, and the T-shirt was, well, it was hot out there. She had a bundle of silverware in her hands.

"Hey," she said back. "I almost have everything ready."

She had laid plates for the six of them, with the day's rations spread out along the length of a table big enough for ten diners. The windows were open, and sunlight filtered into the room. The world looked and sounded different from in here. He could almost believe everything was fine outside.

Lara and Carly insisted on this whenever they could. It was their way of holding on, and Vera and Elise seemed to appreciate it just as much. He could have done without breakfast at a table, but then again, he and Danny were trained to sleep in mountain caves and survive on Meals, Ready-to-Eat rations. Eating off a plate was gratuitous, but it made Lara smile, even if she wasn't smiling at him now as she went around the table laying the silverware next to the plates.

"I'm sorry," he said.

"For what?"

"Carly said you were waiting to hear from me last night. I didn't..." He was going to say, *"I didn't know,"* but thought better of it. Instead, he said, "I'm sorry. I should have known you would be worried."

"Of course I'm worried, Will. I'm always worried. I love you. That's what we do when we love someone and they're hiding out in a clock tower at night by themselves. We worry."

"I'm sorry," he said again.

"Stop saying that."

He reached for her arm as she walked past him. She tried to jerk it free, but he held on tight and pulled her against him.

"Let me go, Will," she said, gritting her teeth at him. "I'm not in the mood."

He held her against him and sought out her mouth and kissed her deeply. She fought him for a moment, but then gave up after a while and kissed him back.

He had forgotten how good she smelled, even if it was just water and soap. It didn't matter how much sweat and dirt she had on her from the constant moving, the constant living in someone's abandoned home or dank, confined basement. Lara always smelled like home.

She softened after the kiss and pressed her body against his. Will stroked her hair, then blew playfully at her forehead.

"Don't do that again," she whispered. "Last night. Ever."

"I won't."

"Promise me."

"I promise."

"I'm always worried about you," she said softly.

"I know. It wasn't fair of me to do that. I'm an idiot. I know that."

She laughed softly. "No, you're not. You're just...you."

"That doesn't sound like a good thing."

"It is. But it can also be frustrating, because you're not aware of it. You and Danny. You don't know how Carly and I worry when you guys are out there on your own. One of you out there alone is hard enough, but sometimes, I think it's harder when both of you are together. You know why?"

"No."

"Because you numbskulls think you're invincible when you're together. It's annoying."

He laughed. "Sorry."

"Just don't do it again," she said, and pulled away and smiled at him, and he thought the sunlight reflecting off her crystal-blue eyes was the loveliest thing God ever created. "I love you, Will."

"I love you, too," he said, and kissed her again.

"Yuck, get a fucking room," Danny said behind them.

Danny and Carly came into the kitchen, Elise and Vera rushing past them, joined invisibly at the hip like always. The girls hopped into chairs at the table and scanned the food.

"What are we having today?" Vera asked.

"Vienna sausages, canned fruits, and turkey MREs," Lara said. "And oh, maybe some SPAM for later if you're both good. Dig in."

"Yum, SPAM," Danny said. "It's like home all over again. If by home you mean hell."

Carly punched him in the thigh.

WHILE THEY HAD made the Miller Hill House their base last night, their vehicles were stashed in a garage two streets away. After breakfast, while Lara and Carly and the girls got their supplies ready to move, Will and Danny walked over to fetch their trucks.

They carried M4A1 assault rifles, their old weapons from Afghanistan. The M4A1s were their weapons of choice in the daytime, when spreading power took a backseat to distance and accuracy. There was also the fact that if they had to shoot something in daylight, it was usually some*one*, and they didn't need to waste silver bullets for that.

Grime, Texas, in the morning was eerily quiet and devoid of activity, like every other small town they had occupied for the night since Starch. Will would have been satisfied with spending however many years he had left within the facility's gray concrete walls with Lara, but the decision was never his.

"So, they're following us," Danny said.

"They're hunting us," Will said. "As far as I can tell, they've been on our ass since Starch. We're going to have to shake them sooner or later. One of these nights, they might catch us in a bad spot, and it won't be pretty."

"Just to let you know, I only have enough C4 left to blow up a house or two, so whatever crazy Plan Z you come up with next, be advised."

"I'll keep that in mind."

Danny's mastery of C4, a skill he had learned during their time serving in Afghanistan, had been invaluable since The Purge. First in

Houston, then later on the road to Starch. But they were running out of C4, and it didn't look like they were going to find more any time soon. Unlike guns and ammo, which were lying around everywhere, military-grade explosives were impossible to find, even in Texas. Go figure.

"We might not have to do anything drastic," Will said. "We know they're hunting us, but they don't know that we know. We can take precautions. Double our alertness. Now, instead of putting the vehicles two streets down, we do four. Et cetera."

"That sounds like a plan. A very convoluted one, but a plan nonetheless."

The radio clipped to Will's vest squawked and he heard Lara's voice: "We're done, guys. Whenever you're ready with the trucks."

"Roger that," Will said. "ETA five minutes."

"See you then."

"Tough girls," Danny said. "I have to admit, they're handling this pretty well. The kids, too. I thought there would be more freaking out. More second-guessing. It must be my Captain Optimism rubbing off on them."

"That, or your bad BO."

"Either/or," Danny said.

THE BLUE AND black Ford Rangers were in the same garage of the two-story house where they had stashed them last night. The Rangers were roomy four-door vehicles that got great gas mileage, a major consideration when they had found them at a used car lot some months back. The fact that the trucks were also called Rangers made them serendipitous, even though Will didn't particularly put stock in that kind of thing.

The plastic moving crates filled with their expendable supplies were in the back of the trucks underneath heavy tarps. Their main supplies, like weapons, ammo, and enough food and water to last a month, were back at base.

They drove the Ford Rangers back to the Miller Hill House, where Vera and Elise were waiting outside on the front curb amidst a pile of backpacks, carry-on luggage, and a pair of red crates with their emergency ration of food and water. The girls were dutifully clinging to a pair of ammo bags, each one weighing almost as much as them put together.

Carly and Lara came out of the house with more carry-on luggage as they pulled up to the curb.

"Silverware?" Will shouted over at them.

Lara held up one of her luggage bags and jingled it. "I cleaned the place out. The Millers will be super pissed when they get home."

"It's a good thing they're all dead."

"Sucks to be them," Danny said.

THEY TURNED RIGHT off Main Street and headed south on Route 69/US 287, and before long, Grime, Texas, faded into their rearview mirror. Will drove the black Ranger up front with Lara in the passenger seat, while Danny followed in the blue Ranger with the girls. They kept twenty meters between them in case Will had to make an emergency stop.

Months after the end of the world, there were signs other survivors had begun using the roads again. They saw it in the dwindling cans of non-perishables in store shelves, empty boxes of beef jerky, and suddenly empty store refrigerators that used to be piled high with warm drinks. There were also more obvious signs, like cars recently pushed to the sides of roads or old pile-ups untangled in order to get big vehicles through.

Lara was engrossed with the ham radio in her lap. She was making minor adjustments to the dial, honing in on the familiar Federal Emergency Management Agency frequency, where they had first encountered the looped message. She stopped only when the soothing female voice drifted through the speakers. Like all the other times, they found it while the message was in the middle of its prerecorded loop:

"...Song Island in Beaufont Lake in Louisiana. We are broadcasting on the FEMA frequency to any survivors out there. We want you to know there is hope. There are survivors on Song Island. We have food, supplies, electricity, and protection against the darkness. If you are receiving this recorded message, we encourage you to make your way to us. I repeat: we have food, supplies, electricity, and protection against the darkness."

There was a pause of a few seconds, then the message resumed from the very top:

"Hello. If anyone can hear me out there. This is Song Island in Beaufont Lake in Louisiana. We are broadcasting on the FEMA frequency to any survivors out there..."

The message was broadcasted day and night, every day. It was unchanged from the time they had originally picked it up four months earlier. It was probably appropriate that Elise had been the one to discover the message while showing Vera how to work the ham radio. Elise had, after all, come to them because she was playing with a ham radio.

Beaufont Lake was not on Will's radar, but finding it on a map was easy enough. It was about twenty-five kilometers from the Texas-Louisiana border, past Sabine Lake and close enough to Interstate 10 that they would be able to take the long stretch of road once they joined it off Route 69.

They were traveling cautiously, like they always did, with the Rangers moving at a steady thirty miles per hour—sometimes forty if they were feeling especially brave that day. Speed was not an option here.

Slow and steady survives the darkness.

And besides, Song Island was advertising safety and protection. If it really was safe, the island would still be there a week or a month from now. And if wasn't, then it was never as safe as the people broadcasting claimed in the first place. Either way, Will wasn't going to be hurried. Not now, not with so much at stake.

Lara turned the radio off and put it back down on the floor. "Is it possible? Can an island be that safe?"

"It could be. We've never thought about ghouls and water. Maybe they can't swim."

"Why wouldn't they be able to swim? Nothing about their physiology indicates an adverse reaction to lake water. I think they might even float better than us. They're mostly just skin and bones."

"Why do they melt in sunlight? Why do they fold up and die if you prick them with a little bit of silver?" He shrugged. "Eight months later, what do we really know about them?"

"You're right," Lara said, and she leaned back against her seat.

"We should know more about them by now. *I* should have discovered more. I feel like I'm the one dropping the ball here."

"Take it easy. You've done pretty well for a third-year medical student."

"Ah, to be a fourth-year medical student," she said wistfully, and allowed herself a rare smile. "I wonder how Song Island is broadcasting the signal?"

"There could be a radio tower on the island or nearby that they're bouncing their signal off. It doesn't have to be that strong of a signal. Without all the usual traffic, you could probably contact someone on the other side of the world these days and get a perfect connection."

"It has to be someone who knows about the FEMA frequency."

"That makes sense. Maybe military, or ex-military. A former government official. They did promise protection, so maybe they even have a standing army on the island. Or a civilian army of some type."

"That would be nice, wouldn't it? An army?"

"I wouldn't mind one."

"Maybe you can finally make captain," she teased.

"I've always wanted to be a captain."

"Why stop at captain? How about General Will?"

He laughed. "I'll settle for major."

IT WAS A body in the middle of the road, and Will almost ran over it.

He was maneuvering around a beat-up Jeep parked in his lane when he saw it, popping up out of nowhere not much farther up the road. It looked like a big lump of road kill rotting in the sun, but he had seen bodies before—too many to mention—and he knew instinctively it was a man.

Will jammed on the brake and fought the steering wheel. Lara let out a shocked gasp as the seatbelt clenched against her body. Will quickly glanced at this side mirror and saw Danny pulling up behind him. If he had been going any faster than thirty-five, he would have easily run the body right over.

Slow and steady survives the darkness…

Will put the Ranger in park and grabbed the M4A1 resting against his seat. "Stay here and keep low."

"Be careful," Lara said, catching her breath as she pried the seatbelt free.

He hopped out of the truck but stayed behind the open door. He heard another door opening behind him, then Danny's voice from his vest radio: "Don't tell me you almost got us into a wreck over a squirrel."

"Body," Will said. "Make that bodies."

There was a second body nearby, closer to the side of the road. An older man, face up, sun-beaten white face staring at the bright, cloudless sky. Congealed blood underneath his head, and the telltale signs of a bullet hole in his left temple.

"Dead?" Danny asked.

"One for sure. The other one undetermined."

"Well, let's determine it, then."

Will scanned the areas to his left, then right. The highway had four lanes, with the north- and southbound lanes separated by walls of trees to both sides. He instinctively flashed back to the early days after The Purge, when they had been caught in a road ambush.

Never again...

He glanced back at Lara, crouched low in front of her seat, clutching her Glock in one hand. She mouthed, *"What now?"*

He shook his head, then looked back at Danny standing behind his truck's open door, M4A1 at the ready, eyes scanning the road and trees. Carly was crouched low in the passenger seat of the second truck, and the two girls were invisible in the back, just the way they were trained.

"I don't see anything," Danny said.

Will looked down the road at the bodies again. He focused on the one in the center. Big, about six-two, with a thick, shaggy beard and dark curly hair. The man lay on the road with his face toward Will. He had been shot. More than once, from the placement of blood underneath his body. A hole in the man's leg, another one somewhere along his shoulder. Dull black eyes were staring back at him—*dead?*

"I see two bodies," Will said into the radio. "Gunshots. One's one hundred percent dead. The other one is probably dead. Wait—"

He saw movement from the big man. It hadn't been much—just

enough to get his attention. He focused on the man's right hand, waiting—*there.* The man had moved his pinky finger. As Will watched, the finger moved again, then a third time.

"Looks like the second body's still kicking," Will said.

"I see bullet holes in the Jeep behind us," Danny said. "Shell casings along the shoulder. Looks like a firefight."

Will scanned the trees to his left and right again, then made up his mind. "Cover me."

"Go for it," Danny said.

Will slipped out from behind the door and rushed toward the man in the middle of the road. He passed the first body, which didn't move as he glided past it. As he moved forward, he heard a truck door slam farther behind him, then quick footsteps chasing—Danny, moving forward from his truck to take over the position at the door of Will's Ranger.

Will moved quickly, keeping low, toward the survivor in the road.

The man looked worse up close, though not by much. The hot sun had been baking him for a while. Amazingly, he was still alive, chest moving, if just slightly. Will crouched next to him and felt for a pulse. There. It wasn't very strong, but it was enough.

The man's eyes fixed on Will. Cracked lips struggled to make a sound.

"You don't look like a decoy," Will said, smiling down at the man.

The man moved his head side to side. Or tried to, anyway.

No.

"You sure?" Will asked.

The man nodded. Or something that resembled a nod.

Yes.

Will watched the man for a moment, trying to read his soul through dull brown eyes. He was in his mid-thirties, but there was a lot of mileage there. Will saw a stubbornness that bordered on being impressive.

His radio squawked and he heard Lara's voice: "Will, if he's still alive, we can't just leave him out here."

Will considered his options. Saving this man's life didn't fit into his priorities, which were simple: stay alive, and keep everyone else alive, too. Will could leave him now and not think about it ever again. Smart people with medical degrees called it triage. Will called it practical survival.

His radio squawked again, and he heard Danny's voice this time: "What's the call, Kemosabe?"

"I'm trying to decide," Will said.

"Decide faster. I hate standing out here with my nuts in my hands."

"Uh, great visual, babe," Carly said through the radio.

"I love you, too," Danny said.

Will realized the man was saying something. Or trying to. He was drooling blood, and would have been coughing up blood, too, if he had the strength.

How was this guy even still alive?

Will leaned in closer. "I can't hear you. Say again."

"Sandra," the man said, with as much life as he could muster. "Sandra..."

CHAPTER 4

JOSH

HE REMEMBERED THAT night vividly. How could he forget? It was the night the world as he knew it died. Oh sure, the planet kept turning and the sun kept rising in the east and setting in the west, and the oceans certainly kept lapping (or whatever it was that oceans did), but everything else was irrevocably changed.

It was Thursday, which meant Date Night for his parents. He was left home alone—because it would be Family Night if he went along, and that defeated the purpose of Date Night—which was fine with him. He didn't feel the need to see his parents canoodling or exchanging baby talk over a meal...and in public. No, thanks.

It didn't happen right away.

At first there was the news about police actions from the Dallas-Fort Worth area. As soon as night fell, the news seemed to just shut down, and Josh resorted to following reports on the Internet, which was blowing up with rumors of crazy stuff happening around the world. Twitter, Facebook, and guys uploading videos onto YouTube. The word "impossible" kept coming up over and over again.

Josh remembered sitting in his room, staring slack-jawed and taking it all in. It was almost like watching a movie, because things like that didn't happen in his small town of Ridley, Texas. And if it didn't happen outside his window, then it didn't feel real.

Then it got real, *real* fast when he heard police sirens start up around town. It wasn't like Ridley had a big police department. They had a sheriff and five deputies, and even that was overkill. So it was a rarity to hear police sirens, especially one that didn't seem to ever end.

But it still didn't *feel* real until he heard the loud pounding on the front door. He ran down, expecting to see his parents, but instead there was Gaby, all five-seven and long blonde hair of her, screaming, makeup smeared and bawling her eyes out, and yet somehow still managing to look like the most beautiful girl he had ever seen. She stood in his doorway and the rush of information came between spurts of crying and hysterics. Her parents were dead—or dying—and something, some *creature*, was in her house.

That was when Josh saw it.

This *thing*, all black pruned skin, hairless, racing across the street toward his house. The street lights were still on then, and the sight of the bloodsucker made Josh freeze in place. It was such an anomaly, like one of those bad B-movies he sometimes caught late at night suddenly come to life.

Gaby must have seen the look on his face, because she turned and saw the bloodsucker. She rushed inside the house, almost pushing him out of the way. "Close the door, Josh! Close the door!" she screamed at him.

Josh didn't close the door. He couldn't move. He was frozen and he couldn't take his eyes off the bloodsucker as it bounded across the street toward him. Gaby was the one who grabbed him by the arm and dragged him away, then snatched the door and slammed it shut and pushed the deadbolt in place.

Almost right away, the creature crashed into the door and they felt the wall shaking against the impact. It was then Josh snapped out of it, just in time to hear the living room window shattering.

Josh saw Gaby's face, even more terrified than his own. Then something must have kicked in and he knew what he had to do. He grabbed Gaby's hand, stunning her for a moment, and led her toward the back of the house.

She might have asked him where they were going, but he couldn't hear anything at the moment. His ears were pounding and his heart was rampaging against his chest. He thought he might have heard glass breaking behind them. He wasn't sure. But he was sure of where to go, and that was the basement. He saw the door coming up and pushed at it and it opened, because his dad never locked it.

"Go down the stairs!" he shouted, and turned and slammed the door shut behind them and locked it.

The basement door was solid steel, and the basement was built with reinforced concrete. It was his father's idea, his old man's emergency plan in case of a tornado. God knew there were plenty of those things around the area whenever it got too warm. The basement was built to withstand a tornado, so it stood to reason it could withstand one ugly, skinny *thing*, couldn't it?

Josh took an involuntary step back as something crashed into the door on the other side, but the steel door didn't move at all. It held solidly, the way it was supposed to. Almost just as quickly, the thing seemed to give up, as if it just knew it wasn't getting into the basement in a million years. Josh heard quick, rabid footsteps racing away.

Josh turned, numbed, and looked down the stairs at Gaby, standing at the bottom looking back up at him, arms clutched around her chest. Their faces were illuminated by soft, yellow-tinted lightbulbs that had come on automatically, activated by motion sensors as soon as they had entered the basement.

They stared at each other in silence, and Josh realized, quite suddenly, that this was the first time he had ever been this close to Gaby for longer than a few minutes. Her family had moved in across the street almost eight years ago, and in all that time, he had always watched her from afar, too shy and too afraid of rejection to approach her. Even when they passed each other in the streets, or in school hallways, they always just exchanged a courteous "hey" and went on their way.

But he stared at her now, into those green eyes. Eighteen-year-old Gaby was the loveliest thing Josh had ever seen, from afar or up close, but it wasn't love or lust he was feeling at the moment. It was gnawing, growing terror, because he could hear it, too.

Screams, and the sounds of gunshots, from the world outside the basement.

He thought they both knew, at that very instant, staring at each other in horrified silence, that everything had changed forever.

HE SAW THAT same look of horror on Gaby's face now as Josh hurried inside the basement with Matt hanging onto his arms. It was all Josh could do to keep his knees from buckling, because Matt was so much bigger and goddammit, he was really *heavy.* Josh hadn't realized how much heavier Matt was until he had to drag the guy back to their hideout.

Gaby had opened the basement door immediately when he had pounded on it, as if she had been waiting for them all this time. When she saw the blood-soaked shirt Josh had wrapped around Matt's left arm to stanch the bleeding, Josh expected her to start screaming, but instead she reached for Matt to help him stay upright.

Together, they carried Matt down the creaky wooden steps, Matt's body a limp, useless thing hanging between them. They were both out of breath and sweating in the swelteringly hot basement by the time they got Matt down and carried him over to his bedroll in the corner.

The basement wasn't particularly big, but it had everything they needed, including no window access and enough comfortable space for all three of them. Portable LED lamps hung from a couple of hooks, with two more on top of boxes in the corners. The LED lights were godsends—surprisingly bright despite weighing almost nothing, powered by lithium batteries that could be recharged every day by putting them outside in the sun.

They laid Matt down on his bedroll and Josh stumbled away, finally able to catch his breath. He wiped at Matt's blood clinging to his shirt and pants but only ended up making more of a mess.

Gaby kneeled next to Matt, tightening the shirt around Matt's left arm. She was wearing khaki shorts and a cotton undershirt with a long-sleeved plaid shirt over it, and Matt's blood had already gotten on them during the short trip from the door. Matt shook violently on the bedroll, like he was suffering through a seizure. He was covered in sweat and had been since they left the grocery store.

"What happened?" Gaby asked. She grabbed a towel from her backpack and dripped water from a bottle onto it, then placed it over Matt's head.

"One of them bit him," Josh said.

"Oh my God. How?"

"It was hiding inside a back room. I went in and it attacked me. Matt came in to help, and I guess during the fight it bit him. I don't know how it happened, it was so fast."

"Josh, Jesus." He could hear the disappointment in her voice. "I told you to be careful about that. How many times did I tell you? You never listen to me."

"I know, but ..."

"What was so important in there you had to risk your life and Matt's?"

"There were canned fruits inside," he blurted out.

"They're not worth this, Josh. God, you have to know better!"

"I'm sorry..."

Gaby continued dabbing the wet towel against Matt's forehead and wiping at the blood clinging to his face. Josh stood quietly behind her. He felt like a little kid again, hoping his parents didn't notice he was still there and wouldn't remember how badly he had messed up.

"He's lost so much blood," Gaby said softly.

"I didn't know what to do. I just grabbed a shirt that was on the ground and tied it around his arm."

"You did good." She looked back at him and smiled. He knew she was making an effort, and he could feel pity in her eyes. Somehow that stung even more than when she was chastising him a moment ago.

"I'm sorry," he said again.

"You didn't mean for him to get hurt."

"I didn't..." *Though I thought about it.* "I didn't," he repeated.

"I know." She picked up another rag and the same bottle of water and held them out to him. "You have blood on you."

He clumsily took the rag and bottle.

Gaby went back to stroking Matt's head. She had that deep, worried look on her face that always made her appear older than her eighteen years. "He's really burning up, Josh. I don't know what to do. The towel isn't helping..."

He walked over to his corner and sat down on his bedroll, feeling heavy and tired and thankful to finally be off his feet. Josh wiped at the blood on his neck and cheek with the wet rag, then realized he had blood in his hair, too. It was while he was pulling at the sticky clumps of hair that Josh realized what he had done.

"I shouldn't have brought him back here," he said softly, not even realizing he had said it out loud.

"What?" Gaby said, looking over at him. "What did you say, Josh?"

"I made a mistake, Gaby. I shouldn't have brought Matt back here."

"Of course you should have. He's Matt. He's one of us."

"*Look* at him, Gaby," Josh said, trying to make her see. Didn't she understand? "He's already infected. The blood… That's how it works. They bite you, get their blood into your system somehow. That's how they turn people. It usually happens faster, but the bloodsucker at the store, it looked weak, maybe that's why it's taking so long for Matt to…turn."

"You don't know that," Gaby said.

"You know I'm right, Gaby," he insisted.

She shook her head. "No, Josh."

"Gaby…"

"No!"

She looked back at Matt, as if afraid she had woken him up. She hadn't. Josh didn't think anything could wake Matt up now.

Gaby went back to dabbing Matt's forehead with the wet towel, as if she expected him to wake up at any moment and prove Josh wrong.

But he didn't. He didn't…

PROS AND CONS: What were they?

Pros: He liked Matt. Gaby liked Matt. Matt was their friend. *Is* their friend.

Cons: Matt was bitten. He was probably infected. That was how it worked. Josh had seen it up close, more than once. When they bit you, they turned you. Wasn't that how it worked? Though he didn't understand why it was taking Matt so long to turn. Did it usually take this long?

Conclusion: Uncertain, because Matt hadn't turned yet. He was still Matt. Mostly. Maybe Josh was wrong after all? Shouldn't Matt have turned by now if he was infected? Could he risk it, though? Could he risk Gaby's life on a hunch? What if he was wrong about everything? But what if he was *right* about everything?

Matt hadn't gotten better since Josh had brought him back to the basement an hour ago. If anything, he looked worse, and even Gaby, sitting by his side, seemed to realize that. She continued wetting the towel and wiping the sweat off Matt's forehead and face, but Josh knew it was pointless. There wasn't a whole lot they could to do help poor Matt now. The bloodsucker's tainted blood was inside him, coursing through his veins this very moment.

But why hasn't Matt turned yet?

Gaby finally looked over at Josh, and he was struck by how tired she looked. "Why didn't you guys take the truck?"

The question surprised him, and it took him a moment to understand it. "We didn't think we would be going out that far. By the time we were a block away..."

She nodded. "Did you get anything from the store?"

"No. I was about to, but ..."

"This happened."

"Yeah." Josh paused. "Matt was throwing a bunch of stuff into his backpack, but I forgot it at the store when we ran out. I can go back for it. It's probably still there."

"No. Not today. Maybe tomorrow, once Matt's feeling better."

"Yeah, once Matt gets better," Josh said, not believing a single word of it.

Neither one of them said anything for a while, and the basement felt as if it were squeezing Josh. He started to perspire and wiped at a bead of sweat on his forehead.

"But just in case," Gaby said.

"In case of what?"

She didn't answer him. Instead, she got up and walked over to where they had stacked a half-dozen brown moving boxes filled with supplies. Whenever they found a new place to hide out, they always transferred their supplies from Matt's pickup truck, which they had been using since Ridley. It was better than leaving the food outside, where anyone could just take it. And besides, it saved them the trouble of going back and forth, especially since they usually spent a lot of time in one spot anyway.

Gaby rifled through a backpack on top of the boxes. He recognized it as another one of Matt's backpacks. She took something out. When she turned around, he was surprised to see her holding a gun—a silver chrome revolver.

"Is that yours?" he asked.

"It's Matt's," Gaby said. "I think it's his dad's. He showed it to me once. I don't think he's ever actually used it."

"What are you going to do with it?"

Gaby walked over and held the gun out to him. Josh stared at it like it was some third arm Gaby wanted him to have.

"Why me?" he asked.

"You're the guy," she said, as if that answered everything.

He stared at her for a moment, then back at the gun. Then over at Matt.

I'm the guy...

Josh took it. The gun felt big, unwieldy, and cold, and he didn't think he could wrap his fingers around the handle, but when he tried, he found that he could. Josh looked down at the steel object and couldn't shake the very alien feel of it against his skin.

"There's a safety," Gaby said. "My dad showed me. He had a gun for home protection, and when he bought it, he had us all gather in the living room and showed it to us. He wanted us to know what it was, how to hold it if we had to—if he wasn't home and someone broke in—and things like that. Here." She took the gun back and showed him a switch near the trigger. She flicked it with her thumb. "It's the safety, see? And the red button? If you switch it there, that means the gun is ready to fire."

She offered the gun back and looked at him, as if to say, *"Here's your second chance to turn it down."*

Josh hesitated. It was always Matt who led the group and made the major decisions. Matt was bigger, stronger, and older. It was Matt who went into the rooms first when it was too dark, or took risks that freaked Josh out. It was always Matt...

But Matt couldn't do any of those things now, and Gaby was giving him Matt's gun.

He understood what she was doing. She was *trusting* him. The very idea horrified him, and at the same time made him swell with pride.

I'm the guy...

Josh took the gun for the second time.

"It's loaded," she said, "so be careful with it."

"Do I have to pull this back?" he asked, his thumb on the hammer. It was heavy, and he had to exert a lot of strength just to pull it back even a little.

"No," she said, "but it makes shooting easier." She looked at him closely for a moment. "Maybe I should keep it…"

"No," Josh said quickly. "It's a gun. Guns are simple things, that's what makes them so deadly. Anyone can use them."

She didn't look entirely convinced, but nodded anyway.

Josh sat back down and placed the gun on the floor next to him. "Matt will probably be fine," he said.

"Yeah, probably," she said, and smiled back at him.

He could tell she was lying, too.

AROUND THREE IN the afternoon, it seemed like Matt was getting better. Or at least, he stopped shaking, and for a moment Josh was afraid he had died. But no, he wasn't dead. Matt had simply gone to sleep. His face, already pale for the last few hours, now turned an almost opaque shade of white. The only movement was the steady rise and fall of his chest.

Gaby felt Matt's forehead. "It's so much hotter than before. He's really burning up."

"What does that mean?" Josh asked.

"I don't know, Josh. But it's probably not good."

"But look at him," Josh said. He stood up and walked over to stand beside Gaby. "He just looks asleep."

"He shouldn't be this hot, though. This isn't just a fever."

"Maybe we should—" Josh started, but stopped himself. He looked down and saw he was holding the gun in his right hand.

When did I pick the gun up?

"What is it?" Gaby asked. Then she saw the gun. "Josh…"

He looked over at Matt, and he could feel Gaby watching him closely.

"Not yet, Josh," Gaby said.

"When?" he asked, not even sure he wanted to know the answer.

"I don't know, but not yet. He's still…Matt."

"But he won't be for long. Look at him. You said it yourself. He's not getting better, he's getting worse."

"I'm not a doctor, Josh. I could be wrong. I probably am

wrong."

But he didn't buy it. She wasn't committed to the answer. She wanted to believe. So did he. But he had eyes, and it was hard to believe when his eyes told him something completely different.

"Gaby," he said, "you should step back."

"Why?"

Because I'm the guy, he thought, but said, "Just in case."

She seemed to think about it, then got up and began moving away from Matt.

She had gotten three steps before Josh shot Matt in the head.

He expected the gun to buck a little harder. There was a kick—a big kick—but not big enough to knock his aim completely off. Maybe he had actually expected it and was able to absorb it. Or maybe he felt so numbed by what he was about to do that when the kick happened, he hardly felt it.

There was a lot of blood. Or something that looked like blood. It was thick and clumpy, and it was splashed across the bedroll and the concrete floor around Matt's head and on the wall behind him. There were thick gobs of it everywhere.

Gaby turned back around and looked at what was left of Matt. She didn't say a word.

I'm the guy...

"What should we do with the body?" he asked.

"I don't know."

"Maybe we should put it outside."

"I guess."

"It's still light outside. We could take him farther away—"

Josh suddenly lost his voice when Matt sat up on the bedroll. Gaby let out a loud, bloodcurdling noise and stumbled backward, her hands clamping over her mouth.

Josh didn't know what was happening, but found himself back-pedaling with her.

Matt was dead. He had to be dead. But then dead people didn't sit up and stare back at you. And Matt had done exactly that. *Was* doing exactly that. Which should have been impossible, because Matt didn't have a brain anymore. Josh knew this because he was the one who had splattered Matt's brains all over the bedroll and wall and floor.

So how was he still moving?

Like the bloodsucker at the store...

Josh lifted the gun, and that was when Matt seemed to notice him for the first time. Except Matt's eyes had changed. They were black now. Like a bloodsucker's. His skin had started to harden, and strands of his hair fell free as he sat up.

Then he heard Gaby's voice behind him, filling the basement, shouting, "Shoot him! Shoot him, Josh!"

Josh shot Matt again.

This time he actually felt the gun kicking, and it was all he could do to hold on to the revolver with both hands.

He shot again.

Both bullets hit Matt in the chest. Except Matt didn't go down, didn't even seem to feel the gunshots. Both bullets had gone clean through Matt and embedded in the wall behind him, leaving two small holes in his shirt.

Matt was almost on his feet when Josh shot him again, and again, and again.

He kept squeezing the trigger until all he heard was the *click-click* of the hammer striking down on empty chambers.

"Run!" Josh screamed.

Gaby turned and raced to the stairs. Josh ran after her, and he was halfway to the stairs when he saw Matt's backpack on the crates in the corner. Josh stopped at the last second and ran over and grabbed the backpack.

He heard Gaby, from the top of the stairs, shouting after him, "Josh, come on! What are you doing?"

"I'm coming!" he shouted back.

Josh ran back to the stairs and took the first step, then the second, then a third—and risked a glance over his shoulder. Matt had stood up and was looking at him, and as he tilted his head—in some kind of curious pose—something solid but also wet dropped out of the hole in the back of his head and plopped to the floor behind him.

"Josh!" Gaby's voice, pulling him back to the present.

Josh turned and ran, taking the next few steps two at a time until he was at the top of the stairs, where Gaby was waiting for him. Her eyes met his and for a split second he recalled that first night in his basement.

He slipped through the door and grabbed it and slammed it shut.

There were no locks on this side of the basement door, but that didn't matter. It was still afternoon, and there was sunlight outside. He could feel the heat in the air. He fled through the living room after Gaby, kicking aside a chair and knocking free a vase along the way but not giving a damn.

They burst out into the sunlight, racing down the porch, and stopped only when he could feel the harsh rays against his face. Gaby lowered herself into a crouch next to him, gasping for breath. Josh looked back through the open front door. He could see easily through the house, down the hallway, with the basement at the very end.

The basement door opened a fraction, and a dark, blackened hand with prune skin peeked out from the other side, feeling along the frame. Josh waited, but no one (no *thing*) came out. Instead, the door closed again, softly, and there was only silence.

He looked down at the gun in his hand. He didn't know how he had held on to it the entire time. But it was empty now, and the gun felt lighter. He looked at Matt's backpack in his left hand and wondered if there were more bullets inside, or if he had risked his life for nothing.

Please, God, let there be more bullets inside.

They stood silently next to each other and stared back at the house, down the hallway, at the closed basement door on the other side. For some reason, Josh expected the door to open again, for Matt to come bursting out and scream that it was just a joke, that he had planned the whole thing as a gag.

They waited for something to happen, and nothing did.

Finally, Josh said, "We should go. We need to find another place before nightfall."

"Just leave?" Gaby said. Sweat dripped from her face.

"We can't stay here. We need to find somewhere else before nightfall."

They heard the sound of a vehicle braking loudly behind them, and they both spun around. Three men were climbing out of a Jeep parked twenty yards away, dust still swirling around the vehicle.

One of the men had a full head of white hair. The other two men walked closely behind the first, both wearing military-style clothes over plain white T-shirts and combat boots. They were both armed with assault rifles that looked ugly and dangerous.

It had been such a long time since he had seen other people besides the three of them that for a moment Josh was paralyzed with indecision. By the time warning bells went off in his head, the men were already ten yards away and getting closer. Josh was also suddenly very cognizant that he had no more bullets left in Matt's gun.

"Don't shoot," the man with white hair said, grinning at them and lifting both hands in mock surrender.

"What do you want?" Josh said.

"Right to business, huh?" He looked away from Josh and over at Gaby. "My name's Folger. You have a name, miss?"

Gaby didn't answer. Josh could feel her body tensing up into a ball of nervous energy next to him.

Josh didn't realize when exactly he made up his mind, but suddenly he was standing protectively in front of Gaby and pointing Matt's silver chrome revolver at Folger's face, even cocking back the hammer for effect. "Stay back," he said, trying to inject as much menace as he could muster into his voice.

The two men behind Folger raised their assault rifles and aimed them at Josh, but for some reason Josh wasn't afraid. He didn't know why, maybe it was stupidity, or maybe it was even courage. He could sense Gaby behind him, trembling slightly, and he realized all of a sudden that he would do anything—do *everything*—to keep her safe.

I'm the guy…

He expected to see fear in Folger's eyes, but there wasn't any. Instead, Folger seemed almost amused by the situation. "Are you sure you have any bullets left in that thing, young fella?" Folger asked.

Josh felt his heart miss a beat.

"I heard you firing it a number of times before we pulled up," Folger continued. "How did you think we knew you were here in the first place? Sound travels these days, you know. Heard that first gunshot from a few streets down. From my count, you fired at least five times. Is my math right, Del?"

One of the men behind Folger, a big man with a bald head and almost no neck, grunted out, "Five sounds about right."

"What about you, Betts?" Folger asked.

The third man said, "Five, maybe six. I don't think the kid has any bullets left. I think he's just playing hero."

Betts towered over the other two like a scarecrow. He sported a big, ugly scar that ran from the corner of his right eye all the way down to his jawline. Josh found himself wondering how anyone had managed to get high enough to put that scar on Betts's face.

"You think so?" Folger said. "You just playing hero, young man?"

"Take one step and you'll find out," Josh said.

"Oh, that's dangerous talk," Del said.

"Kid's dangerous," Betts chimed in, though he said it without any trace of humor.

Josh's eyes darted to his left and right. There was nowhere to go. There was the house behind them, but Matt was in there. The good news was, Matt was in the basement, which still left the rest of the house. If he and Gaby could make it back inside, he could open the backpack and grab more bullets. *If* there were more bullets to be grabbed. He wasn't even sure about that.

It was a plan. It wasn't a great plan, but it was a plan. He only knew he couldn't let these men get their hands on Gaby. He saw the way all three of them were looking at her, and he didn't like it one bit.

"Five bullets," Folger was saying. "At least. The way you were firing it, over and over again, my guess is you didn't have time to reload before the two of you bolted out of that house. So, I'm willing to bet you either have one bullet left in that gun, or none."

"You don't want to find out," Josh said.

"I think I do," Del said.

"No, you don't—"

But he never got the chance to finish before Del walked forward and snatched the gun out of his hand with such swiftness for a man of his size that it stunned Josh. He was still trying to come to terms with what had happened when Folger drew his gun and stepped forward and hit him across the face.

Josh felt a massive stabbing pain, like someone had thrown ten tons of rocks on his head, and he was aware of falling. Then darkness.

From somewhere in the blackness, the sound of screaming cut through.

It wasn't him screaming, though, it was Gaby…

No, no, I'm the guy… I'm the guy…

CHAPTER 5

LARA

WILL CONSIDERED CONTINUING on to Lancing, a city farther down the road, before stopping for the day, but eventually they decided to pull off Route 69, turning into the driveway of a sprawling estate on the side of the road. It was an impressive house and looked relatively new, with a huge surrounding yard filled with something they had seen plenty of recently—an overgrown lawn that in a year or two would probably end up covering half of the house. They went up a concrete driveway, and Lara saw an attached two-car garage.

She looked back at the man they had picked up, literally, from the road, just to make sure he was still alive. She hadn't been sure he would even survive the short trip, but he had. The man looked back at her through a mask of pain.

"Man's got something to live for," Will had said when they carried him off the road.

She had done the best she could with his wounds, but she didn't give him much of a chance. The man had, after all, been shot three times and was lying on the road for God knew how long. Fortunately, there was only one bullet still in him—in the right shoulder, about half an inch from shattering his humerus bone, which would have completely taken away the use of his right arm. He was lucky, or as lucky as any man could be with three bullet holes in him.

"Will says you've got something to live for," Lara said to the man.

He looked back at her, and she could tell he wanted to respond, but he couldn't. His lips quivered and he blinked once, twice, but even that seemed to take a lot out of him.

"Don't try to speak," she told him. "We're going to stop for the day and I'm going to sew you back up. You've already survived this long, stay with me for a few more hours and I promise, you'll live through the night. Do you understand?"

He moved his head. *Yes.*

Tough guy. Let's see if he's tough enough to last the night...

LARA WAITED OUTSIDE the house with Carly, both of them armed with shotguns. It wasn't just for show. They were trained on the weapons—had been ever since the ghouls had laid siege to Harold Campbell's facility in Starch. During the first few days of training, she had gone to sleep with throbbing pain in her shoulders, which wasn't too bad since every other part of her body from the waist up was also aching. If she thought the Glock had a kick, the shotgun was like getting body-slammed by a mule.

Slowly but surely she had gotten used to it, and though she still felt it every time they did target practice, the ear-shattering blast didn't surprise her anymore and she was able to hit her target. Most of the time, anyway. That was the point of a shotgun. It had spreading power, which made it invaluable in close-quarters battles.

Lara and Carly stood watch at the trucks, with the girls still inside Danny's Ranger. The man from the road was in the black Ranger, unconscious in the back seat. Lara kept her eyes on the road behind them, a good fifty yards away. The house was big, and she could see at least three bedrooms from the front. She guessed there were probably more inside. Five, maybe six in all.

She glanced down at her watch: 2:11 P.M.

Will and Danny had gone inside ten minutes ago, and she considered it a good sign that they hadn't fired a single shot. It never took them more than twenty minutes to clear a building, depending on how many rooms they were confronted with.

Lara found herself staring at two Labrador dog statues perched on their hind legs, standing guard at the front doors like dutiful sentries.

"Cute dogs," Carly said. "If I ever get a house, I'd like one of those. Or maybe one of those weiner dogs. What do you call them?"

"Chihuahuas? I don't know my dogs."

"Sounds right."

"Not much of guard dogs, though."

"Danny with a shotgun should make up for that."

Lara smiled at the image of Danny standing permanently outside a house with a shotgun, boyish blond hair fluttering in the breeze. "Now that's an image."

"I know, right?" Carly looked over at the black Ranger. "Has he said anything yet? Like his name?"

"He's trying."

"Danny said he was shot three times."

"He was."

"How do you survive being shot three times?"

"Determination. Guts. A reason to keep living…"

"Who do you think Sandra is?"

"Probably a girlfriend. Or a wife. Someone he met on the road after The Purge, maybe. There's a lot of that going on."

Carly chuckled. "Tell me about it."

Lara's radio, resting on the hood of the black Ford Ranger, squawked and they heard Danny's voice: "All clear. And I call the master bedroom."

"That's my man," Carly said.

SHE WAS CLOSE. The house had five bedrooms—one on the first floor and four more, including the master bedroom, on the second floor. Will and Danny carried the wounded man inside, putting him into one of the smaller rooms on the second floor before heading back downstairs to move the trucks into the parking garage next door.

There was a fenced-in section at the back of the house, with two trucks parked in the dirt and a third with lumber stuffed in the back. The ground was flattened and trees chopped down to make room for whatever grand plans the family never got to put into action. For once, they didn't find any blood or signs of struggle inside the house.

The front door was unlocked and the windows intact. There were also no cars in the garage. It all pointed to the family abandoning the house in a hurry.

Like she always did whenever they took over someone's house for the night, Lara wondered where the family had gone. Were they still alive? Maybe they were even on Song Island in Beaufont Lake. Wouldn't that be something?

Lara and the girls brought in their personal carry-ons first, stuffed with clothes and personal items. The big plastic crates with the emergency rations came next. After that, they lugged in the thick, heavy bags of guns and ammo.

And finally, they brought in the four portable fans they carried with them everywhere, dividing them up between rooms on the second floor. The fans were the only things keeping the Texas summer at bay and made whatever room they were bedding down in for the night mercifully breathable. All four ten-inch oscillating fans ran on a ridiculous eight D cell batteries and could, conceivably, work continuously for forty straight hours. Fortunately the D cells, like all of the batteries they carried, were rechargeable using solar-powered adapters. Even with the fans, it was still always too hot, but that was Texas.

Lara left Elise with Carly and Vera and found her medical bag. It was a black bag filled with medical supplies and reminded her of old movies where small-town doctors went from house to house.

A simpler time, when creatures from the darkness didn't try to eat you.

She went to check up on the wounded man upstairs. He hadn't moved from the bed where they had deposited him earlier. He was still dangerously pale, and his eyes opened and closed intermittently, as if he were afraid to fall asleep.

It was a small room, and she guessed it was for one of the family's children. A teenage boy, from the looks of the *Call of Duty* and gaming posters along the walls. A baseball bat lay among a pile of sports toys in one corner and discarded clothes in another. Tidiness hadn't been the kid's modus operandi.

She put her medical bag on a chair close by. Before they had left the facility, she had stocked up on everything she thought she would need for a portable MASH unit. The items in the bag were just a small sampling—her emergency supplies. The rest were in the trucks Will and Danny had hidden inside the garage.

She pulled out a syringe and a bottle of morphine and leaned over the man. "Can you hear me?"

His eyes darted, seeking out her voice. Finally locating her, he managed to nod—or as much as he could.

Yes.

"This is morphine," she said, showing him the syringe.

His eyes widened in alarm.

"You need this," Lara said, "or you're going to die when I pull the bullet out of your shoulder. And it has to come out, you understand?"

Yes.

"Good. Is Sandra your wife?"

No.

"Girlfriend?"

Yes.

"Did someone take her? The same people who shot you?"

Yes.

"How many were there? More than one?"

Yes.

"More than five?"

Yes.

"Do you know where they went?"

No.

"Okay. Enough with the twenty questions for now. You're going to see Sandra again, but you need to trust me first. Understand?"

He looked uncertainly at her.

"If we'd wanted to kill you, we would've left you on the road, don't you think?"

He paused.

Then: *Yes.*

"Don't fight the morphine. You've fought enough, and it's got you this far. You don't need to keep fighting. I'll keep you alive, but you'll have to let me. And that means taking the morphine and sleeping through the day. Agreed?"

Yes.

"Good."

She gave him the shot and watched him slowly drift off.

Lara took out a small portable IV bag and looked for a place to put it. She saw a framed picture of a good-looking teenager, about twelve or thirteen, posing in a baseball uniform with one knee on a baseball field, holding the same baseball bat she saw on the floor. Lara removed the photo and looped the IV bag over the hook in the wall, then attached the other end to the man's arm.

Carly came in while she was getting the man's shoulder ready to extract the bullet. "You need a hand?"

"If you're not too busy."

"I had some shopping on tap, but what the hell, digging a bullet out of some stranger we picked up on the road should be fun, too."

"You're all heart."

As Lara worked on the man, she could hear Will and Danny moving around the house, pulling doors out of hinges and nailing them against windows in the rooms around them. She closed out the sounds of hammering and concentrated on prying the bullet out of the man's shoulder. It moved grudgingly, but after fighting with it for a couple of minutes, she pulled it free and dropped it onto a plastic plate Carly had brought up from the kitchen.

"Souvenir?" Carly smiled.

"My guess is he'll want to forget what happened as soon as possible."

"Did he ever tell you who Sandra was?"

"Girlfriend."

"Must be true love for him to hold on this long." Carly tossed the plate into a nearby trash bin. "Ah, romance. It lives, Lara, it lives."

Lara smiled back at the younger woman. Sometimes she forgot Carly was just twenty, that she had been a teenager—albeit one that was nineteen going on thirty—when they had first met.

"You and Danny are like an old married couple," Lara said.

Carly feigned hurt. "Who you calling old?"

"Danny."

"Good save, doc."

"Hey, I didn't go to three years of medical school for nothing, you know."

"Hah!" Carly said.

THEY HAD FOUR more hours before nightfall, but it always seemed like the hours went by quickly when they decided to shut down for the day. There was no basement, so they settled for reinforcing the windows and doors of the house. They had done it before, survived in a barricaded house, though Lara knew Will always preferred the constricted, one-way access of an underground basement.

"We're close to the main road, but far from any city, so it's a good chance they'll pass us right by," Will said.

"Shouldn't they be in front of us by now?" she asked. "The ghouls that were hunting us, I mean."

"They might backtrack when they realize they've passed us by."

"Would they do that?"

"Dead, not stupid, remember?"

"Dead, not stupid," was Will's motto for the ghouls. Everything Will did—or didn't do—was with that in mind. And he was right. Everything she knew about the ghouls confirmed their intelligence. More dangerously, they were organized. As far as they knew, there were two types of ghouls—the foot soldiers and the leaders. Or commanders, as Will liked to call them.

The blue-eyed ghouls…

There used to be only one blue-eyed ghoul that they knew of, and it had hunted them from Houston all the way to Starch. It was eventually joined by another blue-eyed ghoul, and although Will never saw her, Lara was certain it was Kate.

Kate.

It had been a while since Lara had thought of her. Kate was Will's former lover, the two of them having found each other at the beginning of The Purge. According to Will, Kate was a pillar of strength. That all changed when Luke, a young man Kate had looked after, died just before they reached Starch. Kate was never the same after that. She became withdrawn, and eventually disturbed, opening Harold Campbell's facility to the siege that had killed so many people and forced them to abandon what had, up to that point, been a sanctuary from the darkness.

Lara didn't like bringing up Kate. Not that she thought Will still had feelings for the other woman. Whether she had turned into a blue-eyed ghoul or not, Kate was gone now, and there was no point in lingering over her.

Out of sight, out of mind.

Lara spent the remaining four hours of sunlight tending to the wounded stranger in the room and seeing to Elise's needs. The eight-year-old girl had become self-sufficient, and she didn't need anything that Carly couldn't provide. Still, Lara felt obligated to do her part, since she was the one who had brought Elise to them in the first place.

She heard Danny pouring bottles of water on himself in one of the second-floor bathrooms as she walked past. He might have been singing, too. Badly. She smiled and jogged down the stairs to the first floor.

Will sat at a table in the foyer with one of the ammo bags opened in front of him. He was feeding shotgun shells with a white "X" marked on the outside into their four Remington 870 shotguns, having already unloaded the regular shells. The shells with "X"s were loaded with silver buckshot, their go-to ammo for nighttime. He was sweating from the heat, wiping at his drenched forehead every now and then with a paper towel. They had found a whole bundle of Brawny in the kitchen pantry.

"How's your patient?" he asked.

"I got the bullet out, and his other wounds aren't too bad. The side GSW was a through-and-through, which is the good news. The bad news is, it's the one wound that will give him the most trouble for days to come. Assuming he survives tonight."

"That's not the kind of guy who gives up easily."

She looked around her at the first floor. All the windows in the house, along with the front and back doors, were boarded up with doors pulled from closets, bathrooms, and the bedroom on the first floor. Even the second-floor windows were boarded up, because Lara knew from experience that the ghouls could climb. Will and Danny were careful to nail the barriers over the curtains so that anyone passing by on the outside wouldn't know the windows were barricaded. Of course, if they decided to come in for a closer look, that was another story.

Lara sat down across the table from Will. "He said Sandra is his girlfriend."

"Did he say what happened to her?"

"He can only nod and shake his head, so I didn't get much out of him. He should be able to talk tomorrow." She smiled at him. "Would you stay alive after getting shot three times just to rescue me?"

"One bullet, definitely. Two bullets? I'd have to think about it. But three? I don't know, that's asking an awful lot."

"My hero. I knew there was a reason I stuck around."

"It wasn't my charming disposition?"

"You're not that charming."

"Ouch." He finished loading a second shotgun and laid it down, then picked up another one. "I have a better question for you."

"What's that?"

"If we met before all this—say, in a bar—would you have ever gone out with a bum like me?"

"Maybe."

"Double ouch."

"I don't usually date military guys."

"Have you ever dated military guys?"

"No. But," she added quickly, "in my defense, no military guy has ever asked me out."

"Is that right?"

"Uh huh."

"Not even once? At a bar? A party? Or even at a good ol' fashioned bus stop?"

"Nope. Not at a bar, not at a party, and not even at a good ol' fashioned bus stop."

"Lara," Will said.

"What?"

"Will you go out with me?"

She laughed. "Let me think about it."

DUSK STARTED TO settle in at 7:30 P.M., but it got dark much faster inside the house, thanks to the closed blinds, pulled curtains, and slabs of lumber positioned over the windows. There was too much risk of exposure to hang portable LED lamps, so they made do with moving carefully around in the darkness. They were used to it, and even the girls settled into their room without complaint. It helped that they were giddy about getting their own room, which had been a rarity in the last few months.

Danny and Carly took the master bedroom (Danny had called it, after all), while Will and Lara took the room next to the stranger's. Vera and Elise's room was to their right, the man's room to their left, with the master bedroom across the hall. They had split up the four portable fans for the night.

Before settling down, Lara checked on the stranger again. His vitals had improved significantly since the last time she had checked. She made sure the boards over his window were sealed tight, with the curtains on the other side, and that the fan was angled to cover him from head to toe during the night. It was going to get very hot very soon.

She glanced down at her watch as she walked back to her room: 7:39 P.M.

It wouldn't get really dark until 8:20 P.M. or so, and then *they* would be out.

Lara found Will in their room. He had stripped down to boxers and was pouring warm water from a couple of bottles over his head, all the water pooling on the carpet around him. The fan blew in a corner, covering as much of the room as possible by oscillating back and forth, barely making any noise at all.

She smiled at Will. "Great, you've gotten water all over their carpet. The family's not going to be happy with you."

"I'll leave some money for the damages. Can't be more than a few hundred bucks, right?"

"You know contractors. Add an extra hundred to what you expect to pay."

"Hey, watch it, my dad was a contractor."

"And I'm sure he was a lovely man—who probably gouged more than a few of his customers."

He laughed. "Probably."

"Did you save any for me?"

"Four bottles," he said, indicating the extra bottles on a dresser behind them. "You want to use them in the bathroom?"

"Maybe later."

Lara walked over and slipped her arms around his waist and kissed his back. He smelled of dirt, motor oil, and sweat. She inhaled his scent and ran her hands along his chest, then slipped them down the front of his boxers. Unsurprisingly, he responded instantly.

"Don't start what you can't finish, lady," he said hoarsely.

"Is that a threat?"

He turned around and kissed her and then she was in his arms. He picked her up and carried her over to the bed. It was a girl's bed, with thick, frilly pink blankets and sheets and fluffy pillows, but it was the biggest bed they had slept on in months, even during their stay at Harold Campbell's facility. Most of the room seemed to be pink, though it was hard to tell in the semi-darkness.

She stared up at the ceiling, at phosphorescent stars that glowed in the dark, as he pulled off her shirt and kissed her neck and breasts, then kept moving southward. She let out a moan when he got to his intended destination.

She knew she smelled of the same dirt and sweat as he did, but he didn't seem to mind so much, either.

HE UNTANGLED HIMSELF from her after about thirty minutes, and she watched him, just a dark silhouette, gathering up his clothes from the floor, then slipping the gun belt around his waist and pulling on his urban assault vest.

"What brought that on?" he asked, smiling at her.

"I was just thinking about Sandra."

"Sandra?"

"The stranger's girlfriend."

"Oh."

"And I realized how happy I am."

"Happy?" he said, amused.

"Happy," she repeated. "Even now. At the end of the world. I'm happy here with you."

"In here? This house that belongs to a family that's probably dead?"

"Not here, here. But *here*. With you."

"Ah."

"This is where you say you wouldn't rather be anywhere else, either."

He leaned over and kissed her softly on the lips. "I wouldn't rather be anywhere else, either."

She smiled. "I'll go sit outside with you."

"No."

"Why not?"

"Because you're a doctor and I'm a grunt. You start sitting on watch with me, the next thing you know, I'm obsolete. So you're going to sleep and get some rest, and then later when Danny relieves me, I'll come back and we're going to do this all over again. Got it?"

She mock saluted him. "Yes, sir!"

"I'll be right back."

He kissed her again, then left the room.

NIGHT CAME A few minutes later, though the room was pitch-dark even before then.

Lara was restless and got up and dressed in the darkness. She located her shotgun leaning in a corner nearby, with the ammo pouch on the nightstand next to it.

She sat on the bed and listened.

Birds chirped from the woods on the back of the property, and crickets added their own soundtrack from the overgrown lawn around the house. The rest of the world was silent, except for her steady breathing and the soft whirring of the fan at the foot of the bed. She wondered what Will would say if she picked up the shotgun and went outside to be with him despite his protests.

But she didn't do that, because this was what Will did. She knew exactly where he was at the moment. He would be perched on the second floor, at the head of the stairs, waiting patiently in the darkness with his shotgun. There were no other ways for the ghouls to come if they made it through the doors and windows on the first floor. The staircase was what Will called a choke point—it was narrow and made it hard to push too many ghouls through at a time. The perfect spot to open fire with a shotgun loaded with silver buckshot.

The first few hours of the night were always the hardest for her. She sat still in the darkness and waited to hear banging on the front doors downstairs. Waited for the loud, tumultuous crashing of windows, signaling that the ghouls had found them. Then there would be the unmistakable boom of shotguns.

But none of those things happened.

Instead, she sat for an hour before she felt tired and lay back down, telling herself she wouldn't go to sleep, because Will was still out there, and she had to stay awake in case he needed her. She glanced over at the shotgun in the corner again. At the pouch full of shells on the nightstand.

Lara passed the time by looking around her. It was such a girl's room. Whereas the room with the stranger had sports posters, this one was covered end to end in pink, frilly things. There was a big dresser with a mirror and makeup and combs of a dozen varieties, all perfectly arranged in a row. Not a kid's room, but a teenage girl's. Maybe fourteen or fifteen. Almost a woman, but not quite. There were no pictures. Did the room's owner take them with her when the family fled?

She closed her eyes.

Just for a bit. A few minutes, then she would sit back up, in case Will needed her outside.

Just a few minutes…

SHE WOKE UP sometime after midnight. She wasn't sure if it was closer to one in the morning, because she had taken off her watch and laid it on the nightstand.

She heard movement and opened her eyes and saw a figure walking around the bed.

"It's just me," Will whispered in the darkness.

She sat up and watched him put down his shotgun, shrug off the vest, and unclasp the gun belt. There was just enough moonlight filtering in through the barricaded window behind her that she could make out his shape. He was moving much slower than normal, which was the telltale sign he was tired and sleep-deprived.

"I fell asleep," she said, rubbing at her eyes and feeling a little sheepish.

"I can see that."

"Everything's good?"

He sat down at the foot of the bed and pulled off his boots. "Everything's fine. Go back to sleep."

"Did you check on the girls?"

"I did. They're sound asleep."

"I've been meaning to check on the stranger, too."

"I already did. He's fine."

"How did he look?"

"Like he's going to see tomorrow."

"Thank you."

"It's what I do."

She smiled. "Didn't you promise me something earlier, too?"

He looked over, and she saw a brief smile crease his lips. "You need sleep more than you do sex, lady."

"I need you more."

She held out her hands. Will took them and climbed into bed with her, then immediately sought out her mouth in the darkness.

She didn't sleep again for another hour.

CHAPTER 6

JOSH

PROS AND CONS: What were they?

Pros: He was still alive. And so was Gaby.

Cons: They might not stay that way for very long. At least, not him. Gaby might last longer, but she might end up praying she were dead, too.

Conclusion: They were in deep shit.

Josh concluded that the slimy asshole with the white hair, Folger, was in charge. Or as in charge as five other guys with guns could ever allow one man to be. As Josh watched them interact throughout the day, it was obvious that while Folger considered himself the boss, the others didn't really see it that way. Folger just happened to be the guy leading them at the moment.

He had woken in Gaby's lap and known they were in trouble. It was less that he was in trouble and more that Gaby was in trouble. His life was at stake, and they could kill him at any moment, but that was just death. He was afraid to die, of course. Josh wasn't some gung-ho dumbass who though he was invincible. But he was afraid more for what they would do to Gaby once he was dead.

Like it or not, she had chosen him to protect her.

I'm the guy…

That was clear when she gave him Matt's gun. It was his job now to rise to the occasion, and Josh didn't want to let her down. More than death, he feared failure with Gaby's life at stake.

At the moment, there was a humming pain all over his face. He didn't know how bad he looked until he saw the expression on Gaby's face when he opened his eyes.

"How do I look?" he asked.

"Good," she said.

"Liar."

"Your face is a little bruised. He hit you with his gun. I think your nose is broken."

I feel like half my face is broken.

That had been an hour ago.

It took a while, but he was finally able to fight past the pain and get his bearings. They were inside a semitrailer, sitting on a thick rug, though it took him a moment to realize it was actually just carpeting, probably pulled from someone's house and repurposed. The trailer was wide and long—Josh estimated it was anywhere from fifty to sixty feet long—and about ten feet high (maybe a little higher). It was about ten feet wide from side to side. Josh had seen semitrailers being hauled around Texas all his life, but they had never looked that big to him. Now that he was sitting inside one, he realized how wrong he had been. It actually looked roomy.

His captors had transformed the interior of the semitrailer to be livable…ish. Besides the carpeting, there were small, Army-type cots along the sides, six in all, held in place by metal cables soldered to the wall. They could be folded up when not in use, like metal hammocks. There were boxes of supplies stacked all the way up to the ceiling in front and to the right of them, and a big rack with guns near the cots.

Not that Josh or Gaby could have gotten to the guns even if they wanted to. They were locked inside a cage like animals. The cage was barely three feet long and stretched all the way up to the ceiling, and from one side of the semitrailer to the other. It was padlocked, with the key hanging from a hook next to the gun rack. Josh guessed it was about ten feet away.

Too far. Way too far…

And they weren't alone in the cage.

There was a woman inside with them. She was blonde and tall and wore a Dallas Cowboys T-shirt. She kept to herself, staying to one side of the cage while Josh and Gaby sat on the other. She had a bruised right eye and her lips were cracked. She stared at Josh like a cornered animal, ready to fight them, their captors—anyone. He didn't want to think about what Folger and the others had done to her.

"Does she have a name?" Josh asked Gaby.

He said it just low enough so the woman couldn't hear, but of course they were so closely packed into the cage she probably heard anyway.

"She wouldn't say," Gaby said. "I asked her a couple of times, but she hasn't said a word."

The woman stared back across at them and said nothing.

They've hurt her. The way they'll hurt Gaby...

Over the last three hours, Josh had seen the men coming and going, their presence signaled by loud clanging of shoes against the lowered ramp at the end of the semitrailer. They left the back doors open because there was no point in closing them with Josh and the others locked in the cage. And in the day, it was probably too hot to keep them closed.

He counted six in all, including Folger. There was Del, the big guy with no neck. Then there was Betts, the one with the ugly scar who had been left behind to watch them. The other three were a medium-height guy with a dark complexion, a short man named Hiller, and finally Manley, who had cat-like eyes with slivers of yellow that made Josh shiver just a little bit whenever he caught a glimpse of the man. The others never failed to look back at Gaby, greedily drinking her in. Except for Manley. The man didn't look back at her, and for some reason that unnerved Josh even more. You didn't ignore a girl like Gaby. And if you did, you were up to no good.

They had left him his watch, a plain, ten-dollar Citizen that kept decent time. Right now it was 4:04 P.M.

At 4:30 P.M., Betts came over with three potatoes and tossed them into the cage. "Eat up. There ain't more coming."

Josh noticed that Betts had a radio clipped to his hip. The man turned and left without another word.

He was famished and grabbed the closest potato. It was baked and hot, and he almost dropped it. Gaby picked up hers while the woman just looked at the remaining potato, then watched Josh and Gaby break off chunks of theirs and feast on them. Apparently this was enough to satisfy her that the potatoes weren't poisoned, and she picked up the third and final one and devoured the potato in only a few minutes, skin and all.

Josh sat back against the cold metal wall of the semitrailer and listened to his stomach rumbling. Gaby glanced over and almost giggled. Josh smiled back at her.

"We'll be all right," he said.

She nodded, but he didn't think she believed him.

"I'll get us out of here," Josh said.

He was surprised by how certain he sounded and realized he meant it. She had put her faith in him, and letting her down, letting these men do things to her, would shatter that trust. He couldn't allow it. He *wouldn't* allow it.

He wondered how he was going to keep his promise, though.

Yeah, that's the tricky part...

HE FIGURED OUT how he was going to do it—save Gaby, and hopefully himself, too—when he saw how Betts was looking at her when he returned to the semitrailer a few minutes after bringing over the potatoes. Betts swapped out his sweat-drenched T-shirt for a fresh one from a box of clothes stacked in one of the crates. Betts didn't just show interest in Gaby, it was primal *lust.*

After Betts left, Josh said, "Do you trust me, Gaby?"

She looked at him, confused by the question. "Of course I do. What kind of question is that?"

"I can get us out of here, but I need you to trust me."

"What are you going to do?" She looked frightened and he felt bad for drawing it out, but he had to be sure.

"You just have to trust me," he said. *"Do you?"*

"Yes," she said, even though he could hear her voice trembling slightly as she said it. "I trust you, Josh. If I didn't, I wouldn't have given you Matt's gun. What are you thinking?"

The other woman was listening, though trying not to make it too obvious.

Josh looked at Gaby carefully. She was still wearing the white cotton undershirt underneath the plaid long-sleeved shirt, along with the khaki shorts and pink sneakers. He thought it was amusing that even at the end of the world, girls still went for pink if there was a choice.

Gaby saw the way he was looking at her and frowned. "Stop staring, Josh, you're freaking me out."

"When Betts comes back, can you take off the shirt?"

"What? Why?" She looked almost offended by the suggestion.

"I promise, he's not going to do anything to you. I'll make sure of that."

She stared at him, and he thought he knew what she was thinking: *"Can you actually make good on that promise, Josh?"*

He thought he could. Or maybe it was just bravado talking, a vain attempt to delude himself into thinking he could do something he had never done before in his life. It was going to be physical and tough, and he might get the shit kicked out of him. It was, essentially, something he had always avoided throughout his life.

But he couldn't avoid it now, not if he was going to get Gaby out of here.

Josh looked back at her, summoning all the confidence in the world and pushing it onto his face. "I promise. He's not going to do anything. But I think this is the only way we're going to get out of here. We have to do it now, before the others come back."

She didn't answer him right away, but after a while—twenty seconds, maybe thirty seconds, he wasn't sure—she finally nodded. "Okay. Now?"

"Not yet. When he comes back. He has to see you taking it off."

"What if he doesn't come back?"

"He will."

She gave him another long, reluctant look, but then finally nodded. "You better be right about this."

"I am."

God, I hope I am.

To make this work, he couldn't be near her, so Josh got up and moved to the other end of the cage and told her to move closer to the center, directly in front of the door. She gave him another odd look, feeling like some kind of meat being dangled in front of a lion, no doubt, but she did as he asked anyway.

The other woman continued to look on while still pretending she wasn't. Josh wondered what she would do when it went down. Would she leap to her feet to help, or stay still? His plan didn't really count on her pitching in, but he wasn't going to say no to it, either.

She was a fighter. He knew that much just from looking at her. But would she fight when the time came? Maybe…

He expected Gaby to start protesting at any moment, but she never did. Instead, she sat back against the wall and waited. It was disgusting and insulting to her, he knew, but it had to be this way. Josh knew intimately how men thought. He was one of the species, after all. Okay, maybe not a man yet, but almost a man. Man-ish. Still, he had been around enough of them to know what they said when there were no women around. He felt almost dirty knowing exactly what had been going through Betts's mind the last time he had glanced over at Gaby.

They waited, but Betts didn't show up. Josh could hear him moving around outside, so he was still there and hadn't left them. He made a lot of noise and didn't seem to care if anyone heard. But he didn't come back into the semitrailer.

Josh glanced at his watch: 6:17 P.M.

This had to happen soon. It would start getting dark around eight, and sundown would come a few minutes after that. Maybe 8:20 P.M., or close enough. The others would also be back by then. Folger didn't look like a stupid man, and he would have taken the clock into consideration during their supply raids around town. They would definitely be back before eight o'clock. Much earlier than that, probably.

Where the hell is Betts?

Just when Josh didn't think he would ever show, there was a loud clanging from the ramps and Betts appeared, covered in sweat again. He stalked forward and went straight to the box where they kept their clothes.

As Betts did that, Josh looked over at Gaby and caught her eye and nodded quickly. Gaby shrugged off the long-sleeved plaid shirt and left it lying next to her. Without his prompting this time, she sat up straighter, accentuating her chest underneath her cotton T-shirt, and stared forward as if she didn't realize what she was doing.

Josh tried to make himself as small as possible, shrinking into the corner of the cage. This was something he had mastered all his life—becoming less, even in a room filled with people. It wasn't hard to do, you just had to commit. Josh committed now, and when he peeked quickly across the cage, he saw the other woman doing the same thing.

She knows, and she's playing along. I might have some help after all...

Josh slipped his forearms over his head and looked down at the floor. There was dirt, strips of old clothes and grass, like they were sitting in a pigsty that had been re-used over and over again. Anyone who saw him would think he had drifted off into his own world; or better, had fallen asleep while curled up in a ball. Josh was using his ears to listen and his downcast eyes to catch shadows on the floor. It was a skill he had mastered over the years of middle school and high school, where eye contact with bullies was the same as challenging them to a fight he couldn't possibly win.

It didn't take long. After a few seconds, Josh heard Betts walking toward the cage. Betts didn't say a word but stood outside looking in for a moment. Josh could see Betts's shadow falling through the bars, and he could imagine the tall, scarred man staring into the cage at Gaby, raping her with his eyes.

Josh willed Gaby not to flinch, not to grab her shirt and pull it back on and run into a corner—anything to get away from what must be Betts's searing glare at the moment.

Be brave, Gaby, be brave...

Then he heard Betts walking—away from them!

For a moment, Josh was certain Betts had seen through the trap, but then a few seconds later there was the jingling of keys and then Betts's footsteps returning.

Josh prepared himself. He estimated Betts had about twenty pounds on him. Whereas Josh knew he would have no chance against Manley or Del, or even the short Hiller, Betts was another matter. Betts was all height and no width. Tall people, Josh had found, were ungainly and tended to lose their balance easily, especially those who weren't athletically gifted. Josh figured Betts was one of those people. Or at least, he hoped.

If not...

Josh heard the sound of the cage's lock turning, turning, and then *click*. Then the door opening, and Betts's footsteps getting closer, and Josh saw Betts's entire shadow moving into the cage, toward Gaby.

Be brave, Gaby, be brave...

He was sure she would scream, or get up and run away. But she didn't. He could see her body out of the corner of his right eye, the point of her pink shoes as she sat on the floor, back against the wall, her arms at her sides. *Inviting.* He couldn't imagine how much courage it was taking her to just sit there and look back at a man who had things on his mind that would horrify most people if he ever said them out loud.

That's my girl. That's my girl…

Josh waited for the right moment. He saw Betts's shadow fall over the point of Gaby's left shoe and could hear the fabric of Betts's jeans constricting as he bent down into a crouch, one foot extended in front of him. Then Josh saw another shadow—Betts's hand, reaching forward, toward Gaby.

And still Gaby didn't move. Didn't flinch. Didn't get up and try to escape.

Now.

He shot up from the corner like a rocket. Or at least, he liked to think he looked like a rocket, though in truth he probably looked more like a small bundle of clumsy hands and feet—or maybe a moderately sized boulder stumbling and fumbling its way forward. It didn't matter how he looked or how convincing, it only mattered that *he was moving.*

He was on his feet and pushing forward before he lifted his head and saw Betts, who, sensing movement, turned suddenly in his direction. Josh saw the whites of Betts's eyes as they widened in surprise, and Josh thought, *Suck it!*

He intended to barrel straight into Betts and knock the man off balance and drive him into the floor. Instead, Josh just barely clipped Betts's shoulder, because Betts was standing up, moving much faster than Josh had expected—how could someone that tall move that fast?—and twisting at the very last second. Josh did manage to get a piece of Betts, and the bigger man spun a bit and lost his balance, even as Josh flew past him and landed in a pile, grimacing with pain as his body slammed into the hard floor, the carpeting providing almost no cushion at all.

No!

Josh was still on the floor, trying to get up, when he heard Betts grunting and felt the flailing of feet and legs and God knew what else behind him, because the entire cage suddenly exploded with violence.

It was Gaby. She was fighting with Betts. Josh was still trying to come to grips with his utter failure and Gaby's attempts to save herself and him, when he saw a pair of feet rushing past him and knew the woman was joining the fray.

Oh, thank you, God.

After what seemed like minutes—though it was more like milliseconds—he finally found his footing and turned and saw Gaby, on her feet, whaling on Betts's face, while the woman was on top of him, riding his back like he was a horse. The woman had her legs wrapped tightly around Betts's waist and was raining blows down on his head. She was relentless with her attack, delivering a torrent of fists, her face twisted in unleashed fury. Not that Betts looked like he even felt them. If anything, he looked annoyed, and was trying to shake off the woman while blocking Gaby's fists as she flailed at him from the front.

Josh gathered himself, took a breath, and raced back across the small space of the cage with everything he had. He picked up speed as he went and crashed into Betts. This time he got all of Betts from the side, and they went spilling—Betts, Josh, and the woman, who was dislodged by the impact and went flying through the air. Josh didn't see where she landed, but he heard the sound of the cage's bars rattling, and he thought, *Oh, God, I hope I didn't just kill her. Please don't be dead, because I think I'm going to need you for the next few seconds.*

Josh was on the floor again and trying to get back up for the second time, but he never got the chance. Betts was suddenly on top of him and Josh felt hands—and long fingers, such damn long fingers—going around his throat. He felt stabbing, intense pain, the likes of which he had never experienced in his life—and wouldn't have thought was even possible—shooting through his entire body. Betts's face, hovering over him. Up close, the scar looked more terrifying somehow, and Josh couldn't help but wonder how he had gotten it, and if it had hurt. Maybe it had even hurt as much as Josh's neck was hurting at the moment as Betts applied pressure and tried to choke the life out of him.

Then Betts seemed to loosen his grip, and it took Josh a few seconds to realize he wasn't doing it on purpose. Gaby was standing behind Betts, hitting him repeatedly in the back of the neck, and each time Gaby pulled her hand back to strike again, it was covered with blood that got redder and darker with each stroke. Something shiny was glinting in Gaby's fingers, and Josh recognized the key to the cage. Gaby wasn't hitting Betts, she was *stabbing* him in the back of the neck repeatedly with the key.

Josh saw Betts's eyes start to roll in their sockets and felt his fingers lose strength. Finally, Josh was able to break free. He scrambled to his feet as Gaby staggered back, her right hand covered in thick gobs of blood, the key gripped between two of her fingers with the point sticking out like a weapon. She met Josh's eyes, and for a moment he wasn't sure if she was afraid or horrified or indifferent. He wanted to reach out and comfort her, but there was no time for that.

Instead, Josh turned back to Betts, who was kneeling on the floor slightly slumped over, blood gushing out of four—five—holes in the back of his neck. He was in shock and didn't seemed to be moving, but Josh could hear him moaning. Josh gathered as much strength as he could and lifted his right leg and brought it forward into the side of Betts's head. The man's entire body careened over sideways to the cage floor, where he lay shaking, staring accusingly up at Josh and Gaby.

"Come on, we have to go," Josh said as he grabbed Gaby's left hand, the one without all the blood (he wondered if he had done that on purpose?) and led her through the open cage door.

But then Josh stopped and hurried back inside, rushing over to the other woman. She was slowly pushing herself up from the floor, and he could tell she was hurt and dizzy from the blow she had taken when she flew into the cage bars.

"Come on," Josh said, holding out his hand to her.

She stared at his hand, then at him, and he could see her mind reeling, trying to decide if she could trust him, trust Gaby, trust someone other than herself right now. She finally made up her mind and grabbed his hand, and he pulled her up. She was a lot heavier than she looked.

They rushed through the cage door. Gaby was waiting outside. She had dropped the key and was clutching her arms around her chest, trembling noticeably.

"Come on," Josh said, and started through the semitrailer.

"Wait," the woman said, and Josh turned around and saw her heading for the gun rack. She grabbed a handgun off a hook—it looked like one of those black plastic guns that Folger had used to hit him—and snatched up a couple of magazines.

Good idea.

He hurried over. The rack was filled with an obscene amount of weapons, from the kind Folger carried to big rifles that looked like they probably weighed more than he did. Josh had never seen weapons like that in person, only in the movies, and they looked almost as difficult to use as they probably were to lift.

Then he saw it—Matt's silver chrome revolver. And nearby, Matt's backpack. Josh grabbed both items, shoving the gun into the backpack, then grabbed a couple more guns nearby, including as many magazines as he could scoop up with one hand. He didn't even know if they would fit the guns, but they were the same color and, well, he could find out later.

He saw Betts's radio, sitting on the box of clothes. Josh grabbed it, too, and when he looked back, he saw the woman was walking toward the cage, toward Betts, and knew what she was going to do.

"No," Josh said.

She looked back at him, bloodlust in her eyes. She wanted to kill Betts. She was *going* to kill Betts.

"No," Josh said again. "The gunshot. They'll hear it. We need all the head start we can get."

She was probably expecting a different argument, but what he said took her by surprise and, to his relief, she nodded back.

Josh picked up the key Gaby had dropped. It was still covered in blood and clumps of flesh and hair, and it made him a little queasy just to touch it. He hurried over and locked the cage. Betts was lying on his side on the floor, probably dead. It didn't look like he was moving at all, and there was a big puddle of blood underneath him.

"Let's go," Josh said, moving through the semitrailer.

The damn thing seemed to go on forever. When they finally reached the opening, Josh stopped and held back his hand toward the women. They both stopped short and waited as he stepped down the ramp, just far enough to lean around the corner. He expected to see Folger or maybe Manley standing outside. God, he hoped Manley wasn't out there—the guy scared the shit out of him. They all did, but Manley was the worst, with his reptile eyes.

But there was no one out there.

The semitrailer and the big rig that pulled it sat inside a wide and mostly empty parking lot under the baking sun. He recalled the layout of Lancing from the last two weeks he and Matt had spent looking for supplies. The parking lot was part of the city's municipal area, with a courthouse, a city hall building, and a public library behind him. The street out front led toward North Main Street, where the city's business area resided. That was probably where Folger and the rest were at the moment.

"Okay," Josh said, and the women hurried down the ramp after him.

They weren't that far from the house he, Gaby, and Matt had stayed in, and where Folger had caught them. It was about a block down to their right. The same house that a turned Matt probably still haunted. Or maybe Folger had gone down to the basement to kill Matt *(again)*. If you could even kill them once they turned.

"Where are we going?" Gaby asked, when they were all in the parking lot.

Lancing was a decent-sized city with about 12,000 people. Homes were spread out, intermingled with businesses. Across the street in front of them was a row of private homes. More, mostly older ones, were spread out to their right, and he remembered a subdivision of newer models about a mile north.

"Josh?" Gaby said, sounding anxious when he didn't answer right away. "Where are we going?"

"The business district's that way," Josh said, pointing to his left. "Folger and the others are probably there now. That's where I'd be if I was raiding for supplies. We'll go in the opposite direction. There are lots of new houses there. We can hide out in one of them."

Josh began jogging up the street and the two women followed. He glanced at his watch: 6:25 P.M.

"What about a car?" the woman said. She was keeping up with him just fine. In fact, she wasn't breathing hard at all, while Josh and Gaby were already out of breath. "We can use it to get out of here."

"It'll be dark soon," Josh said. "We're better off staying here until morning."

"But won't they find us again?" Gaby asked.

"There are hundreds of homes here. The area we're headed to has about a hundred of those in a thousand-foot square block. They're not going to search all of them, not before nightfall. We can figure out what to do in the morning."

That seemed to reassure them enough that neither Gaby nor the woman argued.

After a few minutes of walking, Josh led them across the street and through a wooded area where they couldn't be spotted from the roads. He kept them on a straight path until they emerged into an open spot with two sprawling lodges to their right. Josh remembered debating with Matt about whether to try their luck inside the buildings just a few days ago.

Sorry, Matt.

They crossed the lodges' big yards, brushing their way through its overgrown grass, and finally arrived at the subdivision. Homes were spread out from one end to the other, like identical toy buildings. He led them farther inside, passing two-story houses with dry concrete swimming pools in backyards and unmowed lawns that reminded him of jungles instead of a neighborhood.

"Look for a house with a basement," Josh said.

It took them thirty-five minutes of running from home to home, peering through windows for signs there were creatures inside, all the while keeping an eye on the sky for nightfall and their ears open for any pursuing cars. Eventually, they found a home that met their needs. It had a basement they could access through the kitchen, and Josh saw solar panels winking on the roof.

He led the women into the house through the back door, their guns out. During their long walk over, Josh had discovered that Matt did have a box of bullets in the backpack, and he had reloaded the revolver. They entered the kitchen and almost jumped for joy when they reached the basement and he discovered the door wasn't locked.

Josh pushed opened the door and peered inside. He did his best to keep his hands from shaking, though it was incredibly difficult. The lightbulbs were dead, of course, but there was enough light coming in from a window the size of a shoebox along the back wall that he could see about half of the basement.

"Stay here for a moment," Josh said.

"Be careful," Gaby said.

Josh went down the stairs slowly, the gun in front of him. Suddenly he remembered how many bullets he had shot Matt with and how Matt had just kept coming, and the gun didn't feel so good in his hand anymore. He sucked it up, though. Gaby and the woman were watching him. But especially Gaby. He had led them here; now he had to make sure it was safe, even if he had to use himself as bait.

I'm the guy, and this is my job.

I'm the guy…

He reached the bottom of the stairs, then walked to the center of the room and…waited.

He didn't speak or move, but looked around him at the dark patches where sunlight couldn't reach.

There was nothing. No movement. No sound.

God, please don't let there be anything in here…

After about two minutes, Josh breathed a sigh of relief and looked back up at the women. "Okay, I think it's safe."

Gaby hurried down first while the woman closed the basement door and locked it. They used the light from the small window to navigate around the room, looking for things they could eat. Josh found an old case of bottled water covered with a thick coat of dust near the back. He tore the plastic wrapping and handed bottles out.

"Keep hydrated," Josh said. "It's fine now, but it's going to get really hot down here when the sun comes back out tomorrow."

The woman took the proffered bottle. "Sandra," she said. "My name's Sandra."

"I'm Josh, and that's Gaby."

"Nice to meet you guys," Sandra said.

They settled down on the floor with their bottles of water. Gaby sat down next to him and struggled to lift the bottle to her dried lips. Her hand, the one still covered in Betts's dried blood, was shaking badly. After a while, she managed it, but some water splashed on her shirt, which was already peppered with specks of blood.

They couldn't find a single thing to eat, not even to nibble on, and their stomachs began growling. No one said a word as the light outside faded and the basement turned pitch black. After a while, Josh couldn't even see his own hands, much less Gaby sitting next to him. He couldn't locate Sandra across the basement from them anymore, though he heard her breathing.

Sometime in the night, Josh felt a hand touch his in the darkness. The contact came out of nowhere and momentarily alarmed him, until he remembered she was sitting right next to him. Gaby twined her fingers with his and squeezed, and Josh felt his heart skip a beat.

"Josh," she whispered.

"Yeah?" he whispered back.

"You did really good back there."

"You, too."

"You're the guy."

"Yeah?"

"Yeah."

He smiled in the darkness. Gaby's hand, in his, felt good. More than that, it felt *right.*

I'm the guy…

CHAPTER 7

BLAINE

HE OPENED HIS eyes to sunlight, with cool air blowing in his face. He was grateful he could still breathe and, more importantly, that he was somehow still alive, even after those people had found him on the road bleeding like a stuck pig. He assumed he probably looked like a stuck pig. A stuck Mexican *(half-Mexican)* pig, anyway. It was probably not the prettiest sight they had ever seen, and it was a miracle they didn't just get back in their cars and drive off. In his experience, guys like him didn't get picked up at the side of the road, especially when they were bleeding from three bullet holes.

He was lying on a bed—a soft, cushy bed that was too short—and he could feel the heels of his feet pressing against the wooden footboard. A fan rested on a dresser, blowing mercifully cool air against him, and for an instant, just an instant, Blaine thought he had woken up from a nightmare, that none of the last eight months had been real. But then he couldn't find the fan's electrical cord and realized it was a battery-powered portable fan.

Sandra would love one of those.

He heard sounds to his right and turned his head. The doctor lady was rifling through a big black bag. For some reason, she looked much younger today than when he had first seen her. She was probably in her twenties, which made him wonder if she really was a doctor. She had shoulder-length blonde hair, and from the back she could almost pass for Sandra. When she turned around, he saw crystal-blue eyes instead of green.

Sandra!

Blaine sat up quickly and regretted it right away. His entire body protested, like someone had shot him all over again. He let out an audible grunt and suddenly the woman was there, pushing him back down on the bed.

"Stop it, stop, you're going to open your stitches," she said, sounding almost annoyed with him. "If that happens, you're going to start bleeding all over again, and this time I'm not sewing you back up, do you understand?"

Blaine sighed and lay back down. He didn't have the strength to fight her. Instead, he stared up at the ceiling at a poster of Nolan Ryan in his prime, prepping for a pitch on the mound in a Texas Rangers uniform. His father used to love the Rangers, though for some reason he was never entirely sold on the Cowboys.

"I'm not dead," he said. His voice was hoarse and his mouth dry.

"No, you're not." She looked amused. "What's your name, by the way?"

"Blaine."

"Do you remember my name?"

Blaine tried to remember. "I don't know. Sorry."

"You were in and out all day, makes sense you wouldn't remember much of it. It's Lara."

"Where am I, Lara?"

"A house. We made camp here yesterday so I could take the bullet out of your shoulder. Why didn't they kill you?"

"What?"

"The men who shot you. You said there were more than five of them."

"I think so, yes."

"Why didn't they kill you? Why did they just leave you on the road like that?"

Blaine remembered the man with the white hair, Folger, telling the others, *"What's the point? Look at him. He's not going anywhere. If he makes it to tonight, then what?"*

Big mistake, asshole.

"I guess they didn't want to waste any more bullets on me," he said.

Lara looked at him for a moment, then, apparently satisfied he was telling the truth, she nodded. She walked back to her black bag and finished putting what looked like tweezers and a sewing kit back inside.

Blaine sat up again, this time slowly. There was bandaging around his shoulder, and he was almost entirely nude except for his boxers, which were stained with blood and sweat. He smelled, too. Lara had also stitched up and bandaged the bullet hole in his left thigh and the one in his right side, where most of the pain was coming from at the moment. Simply breathing hurt.

"Thank you," Blaine said.

"You should thank Will. He almost ran you over. We don't see a lot of bodies on the road, but then you probably know that."

He nodded. The creatures didn't leave bodies behind. They were efficient that way.

"I will," he said. "Thank him, I mean."

"The men who shot you. Did they take Sandra?"

"I don't know for sure."

He told her about meeting Folger and his people on the road the day before. The flat tire that had slowed them down. About Deeks dying, then Sandra taking off for the trees while he tried to distract the men.

"She's fast," he added. "She used to run track in college. But I don't know if she made it." He shook his head. "There were a lot of them…"

"We didn't find anyone out there but you and the other man, Deeks."

"Did you search the woods?"

"No. We didn't know there was anyone to search for."

"I don't think she made it," he said, shocked by how matter-of-fact he sounded. "If she had, and they left, she would have come back for me. But she didn't. And she would have come back for me…"

Lara nodded, though Blaine wondered if she really believed him. He didn't blame her for having doubts. He knew what he looked like. A big, hairy Mexican with bad teeth who didn't smile very often, and even when he tried to smile, it always seemed to come out wrong. But if she only knew what Sandra looked like, he thought amusedly, she really wouldn't believe him.

She dug out a small bottle from her black bag and handed it to him, along with a bottle of water. "Something for the pain."

"What is it?"

"Vicodin."

"I need to stay awake and alert," he said, looking at the pill bottle.

"You don't have a choice," she said. "It's either this or we're going to be carrying you around all day, and let's face it, no one's looking forward to that. Once your pain lessens, I can give you something else to get by."

He nodded reluctantly and took the bottle. He opened it and saw a dozen or so white pills inside.

"To start you off," Lara said. "Take one now. And another one in an hour if you need it. No more than three a day. Understand?"

He shook one of the pills into his palm and washed it down with warm water that tasted better than anything he had ever drunk, and he ended up drinking the entire bottle.

"Drink up," Lara said. "We have plenty more downstairs. You need to eat something so the Vicodin won't be the only thing in your stomach."

A man entered the room. It took Blaine a moment to put the face with the guy who had talked to him on the road yesterday. He was a few years younger than Blaine, with brown eyes and short black hair. Blaine only had to look at the way he was holding the assault rifle—some kind of M4 variant, though it looked heavily modified, with dents and scratches from heavy use—to realize he knew his way around guns.

"How's the patient?" the guy asked Lara.

"As long as he doesn't go running around, he should be fine," she said. Then she looked over at Blaine. "Will, this is Blaine. Blaine, this is Will."

Blaine exchanged a nod with Will. "You saved my life."

"I almost ran you over. Lara is the one who saved your life."

"Thank you, for everything. If I can do anything…"

"You wouldn't happen to know how to fix a computer, would you?"

"A computer?" Blaine shook his head. "I barely know how to turn one on."

"Yeah," Will said, disappointed. "Me, too."

HE HEARD CHILDREN laughing, which confused him.

There were two of them, and the way they talked and whispered to each other, like everything they said was their own private little secret, made him think they were actually closer than sisters. It was the kind of closeness only possible after you had seen what was lurking out there in the darkness.

Their names were Vera and Elise, and the young, pretty redhead who watched protectively over them was Carly. The other man in the group, Danny, had short blond hair and looked like a surfer, but didn't talk or act like one. One look at him and Blaine knew that, just like with Will, he was ex-military. It was easy to see the difference between men like them and Folger.

When everyone was up, Carly and Lara prepared a big breakfast, using plates and silverware from the kitchen.

"We try to eat as big a breakfast as possible every morning," Lara told him. "You never know when you might be forced to miss out on a meal later in the day."

As Blaine stood at the foot of the stairs watching them get ready to eat, all he could think about was Sandra. He was certain Folger had found her in the woods, and that certainty was like a black hole in his gut.

Will came out of the garage next door with a big crate of supplies.

"Will," Blaine said. "Can I talk to you for a moment?"

Will nodded. "Give me a sec." He walked over to the kitchen, put the crate down, then came back. "How are the stitches holding?"

"I'm not bleeding, which is a good sign, I guess."

"Good. What did you want to talk about?"

"Outside?"

Blaine headed for the door, grimacing the whole time, and was glad Will couldn't see his face. Walking was painful, but not nearly as painful as climbing down the stairs. He didn't think those damn steps would ever end. His entire right side was so heavily bandaged he felt like a walking mummy—clumsy and awkward.

Will followed him outside and they stood in the sun for a moment. Blaine looked over the tall blades of grass that covered the unmowed lawn, then at the empty and silent road beyond. The thought of Folger with his filthy hands on Sandra gnawed at him.

"I need to go," Blaine said. "I appreciate what you and Lara did for me. And I'm going to repay you guys back when I can. But I need to go. Sandra is out there, and I need to find her."

"You can barely walk," Will said.

"Doesn't matter. I still need to go. Sandra's out there."

"You even know where?"

"Up the road somewhere. I saw those trucks in the back of the house. I can take one of them if you can spare some gas."

"Gas and cars aren't the problem, Blaine. The fact that you can barely walk without grimacing in pain is. How many did you say there were? Six?"

"Maybe six, yeah."

"Let's assume for the moment you found them. And that's a big 'if.' You think you can take on all six?"

"I..." He shook his head. "It doesn't matter. I can't stay here. I can't sit down and have a big breakfast when I know she's out there. What would you do if it was Lara?"

"I'd make sure I could actually do something about it instead of just rushing off to die."

"Bullshit. You'd do what I'm doing now."

Will picked up one of the ceramic Labrador dogs squatting in front of the house and walked across the lawn. He placed the animal about twenty yards away. The dog stood one foot wide and three feet tall, and it stared back at Blaine with its tongue sticking out of its mouth like it was waiting for a treat.

Will walked back, drew his sidearm—a Glock—and handed it to Blaine. "Eighteen meters, give or take. Can you hit it?"

"What will this prove?"

"Don't you want to know you can at least shoot something once you run across Folger's gang? Or do you plan on sneaking up and whacking them from behind with a hammer? All six of them?"

Blaine automatically reached for the Glock with his right hand before wincing in pain. He took the gun with his left hand instead and turned to face the ceramic guard dog. It looked a hell of a lot farther than twenty yards. He held up the Glock and took aim.

Will stood silently next to him.

Blaine fired—and missed the damn dog by a good five feet. The gun kicked too hard. No, that wasn't true. The gun kicked the way it always did, but he wasn't used to dealing with it with his left hand.

He heard Will's radio squawk. Danny's voice: "Don't tell me, accidental discharge?"

"We're good," Will said.

"Roger that."

"Again," Will said, to Blaine.

Blaine squared up this time and took aim again, resisting the maddening urge to switch the gun over to his right hand.

He took careful aim and shot again.

"Shit," he whispered.

"Empty the magazine," Will said.

Blaine fired again, and again, and again.

After the last bullet burrowed its way into the dirt next to the dog, Blaine let the gun drop to his side. He was tired. Not from all the recoil, but from the effort, from the missing. From not even coming close.

He handed the gun back to Will and waited to be chastised. Instead, Will silently reloaded the Glock and holstered it.

"It's too far," Blaine said.

"Is it?"

"No one could hit—"

Will casually drew the Glock, turned slightly, and shot the dog's head off its shoulder with the first shot. Then he holstered the gun again.

"Shit," Blaine said.

"We'll eat a big breakfast first," Will said. "Then we'll get in our trucks, and we'll go see if we can track this Folger asshole down."

Blaine nodded back mutely.

THE BIG BREAKFAST was canned corn, sweet peas, sausages, macaroni and cheese, and slices of SPAM. They finished it off with pineapple slices and a fruit salad.

Blaine felt stuffed just looking at the food and was able to eat only a little bit. The two girls more than made up for his lack of an appetite by devouring every canned product Carly opened and put in front of them. When Danny broke out some MREs for himself and Will, Blaine tried one for Chicken Pesto Pasta and managed to swallow half of it before his stomach started actively resisting him. He flushed it down with two bottles of warm water and instantly felt guilty about using up two for himself while everyone else seemed to be making do with one.

"Plenty to go around," Danny said, seeing his reluctance. "Besides, when it rains, we just stick the bottles out and refill them."

"Don't listen to him," Carly said. "The only good thing about the end of the world is there are unopened cases of bottled water everywhere. You can't go into a store without kicking one over by accident."

Blaine felt better, because she was right. He had found the same thing while traveling with Deeks and Sandra. Food went bad, but water always stayed the same. It had never occurred to him there were so many different varieties of spring water, and most of them tasted exactly the same. Warm.

After the big breakfast, they gathered up their supplies, including the portable fans from the rooms, while Will and Danny retrieved the trucks from the attached garage.

When Lara saw Blaine trying to help out with one of the carry-ons, she shot him a quick look and snapped, "Don't even think about it. Go wait outside with the girls."

Blaine sighed and went outside, where Elise and Vera were chasing each other around a group of trees nearby. Blaine watched them in silence for a moment, not quite sure what he was feeling. There was something so out of place about the girls that it took him a moment to realize it was because he hadn't heard children's laughter in almost a year, and he was still having a hard time processing it.

"They remind us of everything we've lost," Lara said, coming out of the house behind him. "And what we stand to gain if we can find someplace where they'll be safe." She stood next to him, watching Vera and Elise, their heads barely visible in the field. "Things will never be the same, but maybe there's a little bit of hope. They seem to think so."

"Sandra thought so, too."

"What's she like?"

"Blonde. Tall. Green eyes. The most beautiful woman in the world."

She smiled. "Hopefully I'll get to meet her soon."

That made him smile, too. "I would love for that to happen."

Will and Danny pulled up in two Ford Ranger trucks, one black and one blue. Will climbed out of the black Ranger and waved him over.

Will pulled a map out of his vest pocket and spread it out on top of the Ranger's hood. "We're here," he said, indicating a point on the map along US 287/Route 69. "This is where we found you." He moved backward a little bit, then forward again. "Lancing's up here, about twenty klicks from where we are now."

"What's a click?" Blaine asked.

"Kilometer. Klick. With a 'k'."

Lara, who was tossing a carry-on into the back of the Ranger, said, "You'll get used to it. It's always klicks and meters with these guys."

"A klick is .62 miles," Will said. "Twelve miles to Lancing, give or take. If this Folger isn't a total moron, he would've looked for a place to bed down for the night—somewhere in Lancing." He glanced at his watch. "It's 8:17 A.M. You said he's traveling with three vehicles?"

"Three vehicles and a big rig."

"Big rigs are slow," Danny said, leaning on the other side of the hood. "Even if they hike out of Lancing before we get there, they'll be moving slow. The road's too dangerous to go any faster."

Blaine frowned.

It was my fault. The flat tire didn't have to happen. I was going too fast. It's all my fault Deeks is dead and Sandra is out there now.

Will folded the map and slipped it back into his vest pocket. "Let Lara take a look at your stitches one more time before we head off. In the meantime, I'll give you something you can't possibly miss with."

"You got a bazooka?" Blaine asked wryly.

"No, but I have the next best thing."

THAT "NEXT BEST thing" was a 12-gauge shotgun with the barrels sawed down to half its original length and a pistol grip that made it ideal for holding and firing with one hand.

Blaine shot at one of the big trees that Elise and Vera had been running around earlier, and found that he could hit his target—as long as the tree was only five yards away. Beyond that, he might as well be throwing pebbles. With the shorter barrel, the shotgun just didn't have the same range.

As for reloading, if he used his right arm as a wedge, he could open the shotgun, shake out the spent shells, and push in new ones. He tried it a couple of times just to make sure it was doable. Satisfied, he grabbed a pouch of shells that Danny offered and settled into the roomy back of the black Ford Ranger, where he had been lying, bleeding, just a day earlier.

"Forgive the blood," Lara said. "Some guy was bleeding all over it yesterday."

He grinned. "That dickhead, he left a real mess."

Will drove, with Lara in the front passenger seat. Danny followed in the blue Ranger with Carly and the girls. They drove down the driveway and turned south back onto US 287/Route 69.

As they headed up the road, Blaine fought the urge to tell Will to drive faster. They were cruising between thirty-five and forty, and Blaine didn't notice his right foot was pressed down hard against the floor, as if there were an imaginary gas pedal there, until it started to throb. He slowly relaxed his leg with some effort.

"What did they look like?" Will asked. "The men that attacked you."

"I only saw one of them up close," Blaine said. He conjured up Folger's face in his mind's eye. The thick white hair. The slimy smile. The low-tied gun holster. "I heard someone call him Folger. He had white hair."

"White hair?" Lara said. "So he's old?"

"No, not too old. Fifties, maybe. He just had a lot of white hair."

"Four vehicles?" Will said.

"They took our newer Jeep. The one you saw on the road was theirs. They also had two trucks. A GMC and a Ford F-150. And a big rig pulling a semitrailer."

"I don't think I've seen a big rig moving around since all of this began. You can still find gas in cars, but diesel power is a pain in the ass."

"I was surprised to see it, too."

Outside the window, Blaine saw a sign flash by, reading: "Lancing 10 Miles."

"Have you heard of Song Island?" Lara asked him.

"No," Blaine said.

Lara picked up a ham radio from the floor and put it in her lap. She turned it on and played with the dial for a moment. "The girls were playing with it one day and they found this. It's been broadcasting on the FEMA frequency every day, in a constant loop, since we found it."

She placed the radio between the front seats and turned up the volume.

Blaine heard a female voice, soft and soothing through the speakers:

"...want you to know there is hope. There are survivors on Song Island. We have food, supplies, electricity, and protection against the darkness. If you are receiving this recorded message, we encourage you to make your way to us. I repeat: we have food, supplies, electricity, and protection against the darkness. Hello. If anyone can hear me out there..."

"FEMA?" Blaine said.

"Federal Emergency Management Agency," Will said. "The people who show up when hurricanes make land or a tornado wipes out a town. The message doesn't say specifically that it's FEMA. We're guessing it could be some ex-military types or maybe an ex-Fed who managed to establish a base on Song Island after The Purge."

"Do you think it's true? That the island is secure?"

"We'll find out soon enough."

"But is that possible?" Blaine insisted. The idea sounded absurd to him somehow. "I didn't know the monsters—the ghouls—didn't like water."

"Neither did we," Lara said. "Do you know about silver?"

"What about silver?"

"Have you tried shooting them?" Will asked.

"It just pisses them off."

"Silver is their Kryptonite. It kills them on the spot. It's the second-best weapon against them other than the sun, so half of our ammo has silver in it."

"I've never heard about that. How does it work?"

"We don't know, exactly," Lara said. "But it's fatal to them."

"Look in your ammo pouch," Will said.

Blaine picked up the pouch from the floor between his feet. He opened it and saw shotgun shells inside.

"See the ones with the white 'X' on them?" Will said.

Blaine sifted through the shells. For every regular shell inside the pouch, he found one with an "X" written in white marker on the side. "I see them."

"The ones with the 'X' have silver-loaded buckshot. If we get separated, or you have to go your own way, load your weapon with the silver ammo at night. You can make your own silver bullets after that."

Make my own bullets? How the hell do I do that?

"As for this Folger," Will said, "any old shell will do."

"Once we help you find Sandra, we're continuing on to Song Island," Lara said. "You're welcome to come with us. You and Sandra both."

"It sounds too good to be true," Blaine said.

"That's what we said. But what else is there?"

"That's why there's no hurry," Will said. "If it's as safe as they claim, it should still be there regardless of how fast we get there. If not…"

He nodded, understanding. "Sandra would love a place like that."

Sandra, wait for me, baby, I'm coming as fast as I can…

Outside the window, they drove past another sign that read, "Lancing 8 Miles."

CHAPTER 8

WILL

THE SIGN READ: "Welcome to Lancing, Texas. Pop. 12,077."

Will had been hoping Lancing would be a smaller city and wasn't prepared for one with over 12,000 people in it. A city built for that kind of population meant a sprawling residential base and businesses spread out into multiple main areas.

They entered Lancing from the north end along US 287. At first there was just massive farmland to one side and sprinkles of old homes on the other. Soon, businesses appeared, then huge residential subdivisions with hundreds of newly built homes. Lancing was a growing community, and getting bigger every year.

Or it used to be, anyway.

Will's radio squawked and he heard Danny's voice: "It's not going to be easy finding someone in this place."

"Like a needle in a haystack?" Will said.

"Sure, if you wanna get cliché about it."

"Well, we wouldn't want that."

Blaine was moving around in the back seat, a bundle of energy despite his wounds. He didn't blame the big man. If it were Lara out there…

"Where's the main business district?" Will asked Lara.

She scanned the map in her lap. After a moment, she pointed up ahead. "Main Street runs parallel to the road we're on now. There should be another road coming up—West Chance Road. Turn left onto it and it should take us to Main Street."

Will slowed down, then turned left onto West Chance Road. Danny followed closely behind in the blue Ranger, his turn signal blinking. Will smiled.

"Anyone looking for supplies will make the business district their base of operations and work from there," Will said. "If these guys aren't complete idiots, that's probably where they'll be."

It was about three kilometers to Main Street. During the ride, Will could hear Blaine moving around in the back seat, peering out at every vehicle parked in the road, on the sidewalk and in driveways on both sides of the street.

Chance Road was mostly residential until they neared Main Street, so they drove past a slew of quiet homes with grass that had risen as tall as windows in some spots and gardens overgrown with weeds. Finally, small businesses began popping up around them, unmowed lawns giving way to debris-strewn concrete and sun-baked parking lots that were slowly changing color.

Will slowed down before coming to a complete stop at a big four-lane intersection, with Main Street running across West Chance Road. There was a Chevron gas station on the corner to their right, with competition in the form of a Shell to their left. The road itself was relatively clear of obstructions, with only a couple of vehicles parked haphazardly in the middle of the streets. A blue Honda had nosedived into a Wallbys Pharmacy store sign on the other side of Main Street. The sign remained standing, but the Honda no longer had much of a front end.

There was some kind of official city building across the street, with three flagpoles—one with the American flag and the other two hoisting the Texas state flag. The flags were moving with the wind, the metal latches banging loudly against steel poles. Farther up the road, he could make out more city buildings, including a courthouse and what looked like a public library.

His radio squawked and Danny's voice came through: "What's the plan, Kemosabe? We just going to sit here with our thumbs up our butts?"

"There are a couple of options," Will said. "We could drive around, make a lot of noise, and hope someone hears us. Maybe it'll even be Folger, in which case, well, we'd need to get his attention anyway."

"What's the second option?" Lara asked.

"Find a base of operations and do what we usually do. Look for supplies, survivors, and hope we find some clue to where Folger and the rest went. Chances are they came through here, but how long they stayed is the question. Or maybe they left earlier this morning, but I don't think so. Lancing looks like it could be a decent haul in terms of supplies. I don't think anyone moving between towns will be in too much of a hurry to abandon it."

"There's a Dairy Queen to our right," Danny said through the radio. "I could go for some ice cream Blizzards about now. How about you guys?"

"You're assuming anything you find will still be edible."

"As the designated Captain Optimism, it's my job to think positively."

"I assumed as much."

Will hadn't gotten "much" out when he heard the very distinctive *crack!* of a rifle splitting the air. He twisted in his seat and looked back, past Blaine and out the rear windshield at the blue Ranger parked about two meters behind him. Danny was opening his door and hopping out with his M4A1.

He heard Danny's voice, calm, through the radio: "Rifle just took out my rear windshield. Girls are on the floor."

Another shot rang out and Will saw one of the back windows on Danny's Ranger shatter. He might have also heard screams, but he couldn't be sure because at the very same moment a third shot pierced the air and Will heard the *ping!* of the bullet punching through the blue Ranger's passenger side.

Danny's voice, through the radio: "Water tower at ten o'clock. About 150 meters."

They heard the M4A1 firing back. Three shots. Will knew Danny wasn't trying to hit anything. He couldn't have hit anything over that distance, anyway. The three shots were to let the shooter know his location had been compromised. A sniper who was taking fire didn't feel quite as free to linger with his aim.

Will grabbed his M4A1 and was reaching for his door when he heard gunfire—not from behind him this time, but from *in front of him.*

He threw himself into the door and dived out just as his Ranger's windshield spiderwebbed and three bullets pierced the glass. One bullet punched through the middle of the driver's seat and the other two went astray, but by then the second shooter was firing again, more bullets ricocheting off the hood of the Ranger, one taking out a headlight.

Will was already outside and positioned behind the open door. He looked across the street, following the trajectory of the shots, and caught sunlight reflecting off metal from the rooftop of the Wallbys, about seventy meters away and slightly to his left. He instantly fired three shots in that direction, knowing he wasn't going to hit anything, but the shots served their purpose by sending the shooter scrambling for cover.

He glanced back into the Ranger at Lara, on the floor of the front passenger seat, looking back at him. She looked scared, but fine. Will looked into the back at Blaine with his sawed-off shotgun, crouched behind the front seat, looking back at him.

"You're safer in there," Will said to them.

"What if they shoot the gas tank?" Blaine asked.

"Then we'll need to find a new car."

Shooting a car's gas tank put a hole in it and the gas leaked out. That was it. The car didn't explode or catch fire like in the movies unless the bullets were incendiary rounds, which were rare—or if the shooters were using tracers, which was pointless in daylight.

He heard the sniper at the water tower fire at Danny's Ranger again. Will didn't have to look back to know Danny was in a good position not to get shot. At the same time, the shooter on the Wallbys rooftop found renewed courage and began pelting the street around Will, sometimes hitting the Ranger's open door with a lucky shot. Will hadn't fired back since those first three rounds, and neither had Danny.

Will keyed his radio: "How are the girls?"

"Girls are safe," Danny said.

"Can you get the guy in the water tower?"

"I can't even see him. What about your guy?"

"Wallbys rooftop across the street. I'll need a M79 grenade launcher to hit this guy. Maybe a nuke might work, too."

"How about a distraction?"

"You game?"

"I'll do it," Blaine said.

Will looked back at the big man, saw his eyes, the clenched teeth, and knew right away that an argument wasn't going to get them anywhere. Will said instead, "You have to be fast."

"I'll be fast."

"All right. Call it."

Blaine nodded and positioned himself against his door. He gripped the handle and waited, then counted down silently before he said, "Now!" and opened the door and lunged out, racing across the road toward the Shell on the other side.

Almost instantly, bullets started flying around Blaine, peppering the street and kicking up asphalt around him. Blaine kept his head low, arms thrown over his head, the sawed-off shotgun in one hand. He was running so fast Will didn't know if that was pure natural speed or if it was adrenaline, or maybe it was the very real fear that if he slowed down even for a split second he would die. Probably all three.

Will saw the shooter on the Wallbys make his first mistake. The man stood up on the rooftop to get a better shot at Blaine. Will peered through the red dot sight mounted on his rifle. At seventy meters, the sniper was more of a lump of black twig than an actual figure, but at least he could *see* the guy this time.

The shooter was concentrating on Blaine, firing round after round after him.

Will fired. He knew he had missed as soon as he squeezed the trigger. The bullet went low and struck the wall about a meter from the edge of the rooftop, directly below the shooter. The man reacted, taking his focus completely off Blaine and turning slightly, lifting his rifle to shoot in Will's direction.

Will pushed the red dot higher, compensated for the distance, and fired again.

His second shot hit the man in the chest and the dark silhouette seemed to stagger for a moment before dropping down to the rooftop.

"One down," Will said into the radio.

"You're my hero," Danny said.

"I never doubted it."

He glanced across the road at Blaine, peering out from behind the small white building that housed the Shell. Will gave him the "A-okay" sign and saw Blaine acknowledge with one of his own, bending over at the waist to catch his breath.

"What about the water tower?" Will said into the radio.

"Still can't see the bugger," Danny said. "Haven't heard from him in a while, though."

"You think he bugged out?"

"He's a bugger. They do tend to bug."

Will stayed behind cover, peering out occasionally across the street, expecting someone to either replace the shooter on the Wallbys rooftop or appear somewhere else to take his chances. The only positive he could see was that besides the water tower behind them and the Wallbys in front, there weren't a lot of other high places for a sniper to shoot from.

He looked back into the truck at Lara. She was still crouched on the floor in front of her seat, picking broken glass out of her hair. He smiled at the sight.

"Shut up," she said, but smiled back. Then he saw her frown. "You're bleeding."

Will hadn't realized it, but a piece of flying glass had cut his cheek. It wasn't much, just a miniscule trickle of blood. He wiped at it with the back of one hand. "Just a scratch. Are you okay?"

She nodded back. "In one piece. What about Blaine?"

Will looked over in Blaine's direction again. The big man was still behind the Shell, looking back at him before turning his attention up the street. Like Will and Danny, he was waiting for something to happen, for someone else to take a shot.

"He's alive," Will said.

"I should take a look at his wounds," Lara said. "He must have torn open some stitches running that fast."

"Later."

Will heard a faint buzzing sound, and he thought, *Dirt bike.*

The buzzing got louder just before the dirt bike appeared in the road about 120 meters behind them, coming out of a concrete parking lot. It turned left and took off in the opposite direction. There was only one rider that Will could see.

"Bugger's got a motorcycle," Danny said through the radio.

"What do you wanna do?" Will asked.

"He shot my truck. No one shoots my truck. I love this truck."

"I'll watch the girls," Will said.

He jogged toward the blue Ranger as Danny was helping Carly and the girls out of it. The vehicle looked like it had been through a war zone. There were a couple of bullet holes in the front windshield, but it was still in one piece. Carly and the girls looked as if they were in shock, but were otherwise okay. Danny climbed back into the Ranger, turned on the engine, and reversed, spinning the truck around and taking off after the motorcycle.

Will motioned Blaine over. Blaine glanced up and down the street, just to be sure, before jogging back. This time he was moving noticeably slower and holding on to his right side.

"Lara," Will said. "Blaine needs your help."

Lara hurried out of the truck, looked around to be sure no one was shooting at her, then rushed over to meet Blaine halfway. He almost fell into her arms. She grabbed him, but his weight pulled her down to the road with him. Will ran over to help, and together with Lara, he carried Blaine back to the Ranger.

"His wounds are open again," Lara said between labored breaths. "God, he's a lot heavier than he looks."

Blaine's face was covered in sweat and his eyes were rolling in their sockets.

"He's going to pass out," Will said, just before Blaine passed out.

THE SHOOTERS' BASE of operations was just past the intersection and across the street from the Wallbys. There was a group of city buildings there, including the public library, which was the big building he had glimpsed earlier. Next to it was the city's police department, which also doubled as a courthouse. Lancing's city hall was next door, though it looked remarkably small for a city of 12,000 people.

He saw the tracks of three vehicles that had recently called the parking lot home, including the multiple tire marks of a big rig pulling a semitrailer. The shooters were clearly part of Folger's contingent, the same group that had shot Blaine and taken Sandra. The pools of leaked engine oil and air coolant still gathering in the parking lot told him Folger's group hadn't left the area all that long ago. Less than an hour, give or take.

They're still here somewhere.

Up on the Wallbys rooftop, Will found a short man in military fatigues lying next to an AR-15 rifle, along with a pouch full of magazines. A cheap pair of binoculars and a Motorola radio were scattered nearby. Will collected the rifle and magazines, then searched the dead man. He found a wallet in the back pocket, which made him chuckle. Will hadn't bothered with a wallet since the morning of The Purge.

Inside the dead man's wallet, Will pulled out a Texas driver's license that identified the owner as Hiller, thirty-four, from Fort Worth. Will tossed the wallet and climbed back down the rooftop.

He kept in touch with Danny throughout the hour. The radios were still working fine, even though Danny was getting farther and farther away. After about half an hour of silence, Danny's voice finally came through the radio again: "On my way back now."

"How did it go?"

"He's alive."

"Blaine will appreciate that. What about the bike?"

"Ugh, not so much."

"One out of two ain't bad."

"What I said."

Will jogged across the street, back toward the Lancing courthouse building. Carly came out of the door with a shotgun.

"You heard?" he asked. They all carried radios, except for the girls and Blaine. It was the easiest way to keep in contact when they were on the road.

She nodded. "He's on his way back."

The others were inside the courthouse's reception area. Blaine sat on an uncomfortable-looking bench, his bloodied shirt on the seat next to him. Earlier, Will had cleared out the building by himself with a shotgun loaded with silver buckshot. There were a half-dozen empty jail cells in the back, along with offices that hadn't been used in a while. The courthouse was really one big building with a couple of offices along the sides.

They had spread out the portable fans along the floors and on the reception desk to cover as much of the room as possible. The heat was still suffocating, even with the windows and front door open. They drank every half hour just to keep dehydration at bay.

Elise and Vera had settled into some chairs in front of a fan and were drawing stick figures on the wall with markers as their long hair blew around them like confetti. They looked like they had gotten through the shoot-out just fine, which both worried and amazed him. Then again, maybe being shot at by a bunch of *men* was nothing compared to what they had seen and lived through in the last eight months. This, he thought, almost amused, probably didn't rate very high in terms of nightmare potential.

"You were pretty fast out there," he said to Blaine.

Lara had re-stitched Blaine's side and left thigh. Blaine told them he had busted both sets of stitches about halfway across the street while the sniper was shooting at him.

"It felt like I was running in quicksand," Blaine said.

Will leaned the AR-15 against the lobby desk and tossed the pouch of ammo on the floor. "Danny's coming back with the other shooter."

"He actually caught that asshole?" Blaine asked.

"It's a dirt bike. You're not going to outrun a Ford Ranger with 200 cc's."

"So he's still alive," Blaine said. It wasn't a question.

"For now," Will nodded.

Lara came out of a hallway in the back. She was wiping her hands with a white rag. Or it used to be white; it was now slightly pink from Blaine's blood. "Danny?" she asked.

"He's on his way back with a prisoner."

"Was it them? The ones that took Sandra?"

"It was them," Blaine said. He stood up and instantly grimaced with pain. "We should keep going, press them while we still can."

"We don't know if they've even left the city," Will said. "They could still be out there. There are about a dozen residential subdivisions they could be hiding in at this very moment. It wouldn't make sense for them to just leave their friends behind."

"Maybe they're not that tight…"

"We'll find out soon enough," Will said.

DANNY'S PRISONER LOOKED like he had seen better days. Any day, in fact, was probably better than today. Danny had the guy trussed up like a hog in the back of the Ford Ranger, the man's wrists and legs bound by unbreakable zip ties. He was bleeding from a nasty gash in his right cheek, and one eye was covered by a massive bruise.

He had a dark complexion, and Will guessed Mexican-American.

"Jesus, Danny," Will said, when he saw the guy lying in the back of the Ranger.

"That wasn't me," Danny said. "He sort of flew off the bike."

"How did he do that?"

"I tapped him lightly in the back with the Ranger. *Lightly*. It's not my fault he couldn't fly."

The guy was alive and alert, though he had the look of a wounded animal, dark eyes darting left and right, from face to face, as if he expected to eat a bullet any second. Maybe he wasn't very far off, Will thought, as they dragged the guy up from the truck bed and lifted him down to the parking lot to stand on his own two feet.

"He had a radio on him," Danny said. "Unfortunately, it didn't survive his flight."

"The one on the Wallbys rooftop had one, too," Will said. "Rifle?"

"Rest in pieces."

"Jesus, Danny, remind me never to send you to fetch anything that I don't want smashed to smithereens."

"Quit yer naggin'."

Blaine came out of the courthouse behind them. He had put on a new shirt and was still wincing with every step, but Will knew there was no way in hell he was going to be able to talk the guy out of this, so he didn't even bother.

"Seen him before?" Will asked Blaine, turning the prisoner slightly so Blaine could see his face.

Blaine shook his head. "Maybe, I don't know. I only saw Folger up close. The rest were a blur during the firefight."

"I wouldn't worry about it," Danny said. "This guy can't wait to tell us everything he knows." Danny pulled the prisoner closer to him and smiled. "Right?"

NOT THAT IT TOOK VERY MUCH to get the man talking.

They sat the prisoner, whose name was Miguel, on the lowered gate of the blue Ranger and handed him a bottle of water after they cut off the zip ties. He was in no shape to fight back, not that he had much fight left in him. Miguel had acquiesced to his situation, both in spirit and body. The man just wanted it to be over.

"Where are your friends?" Will asked.

"Hiding," Miguel said. "Probably, I don't know. They were supposed to help Hiller and me, but they never showed. They kept promising they would over the radio, but they never came. Then you guys killed Hiller, and I bailed."

"How did you know we killed Hiller?"

"He didn't answer his radio and he stopped shooting. I figured he was dead. I told Folger the same thing on the radio."

"Folger is the boss?"

"Hardly." Miguel took another sip of water. "He wants to be the boss, but no one respects him."

"How many of you are there?"

"Six. Well, there used to be six. You killed Hiller. So there's three of them now. Plus me, but I guess you don't count me anymore."

"I guess not. Name them."

"There's Folger, Del, and Manley."

"Six minus two is four, genius," Danny said. "Or didn't they teach you to count in bad guy school?"

"There *was* four," Miguel said. "Betts got killed last night."

"What happened?"

"We had some prisoners, but they escaped. Tricked Betts somehow, then stabbed the shit out of him in the back of the neck with a key, if you can believe it. He was dead when we found him."

Will looked over at Blaine, who had perked up. "The woman who was with me," Blaine said. "You caught her."

"Yeah," Miguel said, but he wisely shied away from looking Blaine in the eyes. "She escaped with the others."

"How many others?" Will asked.

"Two. Some kids we found in town when we first got here. There was a third kid, but he had turned, so we locked the basement door where he was hiding so he couldn't get out."

"How old are we talking about? These kids?" Danny asked.

"Teenagers," Miguel said. "I don't know how old. Sixteen or seventeen maybe." He drained the bottle of water and tossed it away, watched it bounce around the parking lot for a moment. "Got any more of that?"

"Man's going to drink us dry," Danny said, and handed Miguel another warm bottle.

Miguel opened the bottle and drank down half of it one gulp.

"The radio," Will said. "What frequency are they monitoring?"

Miguel told them.

Danny unclipped his radio from his vest and turned the frequency dial, then put the radio down on the open tail gate. They listened for a moment, but there was only static.

Miguel seemed to have expected that. He smirked. "Assholes. I knew they would leave me."

"You're saying they're gone?" Will asked.

"I figured. Or they'd be here by now, wouldn't they?"

"Maybe," Will said, unconvinced.

"Not BFFs, I take it," Danny said.

"Not in this lifetime," Miguel said, almost spitting the words out. "I only fell in with them because there was no one else. I mean, after everything happened, strength in numbers, you know? And Folger had all these guns. Who the hell knows where he got them. He was an asshole and everything, but he seemed to know some stuff that got us through the early days."

"How long ago did Sandra and these kids escape?" Blaine asked.

"Like I said, last night."

"Did you find them?"

"No. They must have been hiding. There are thousands of houses in this place. It's impossible to search every one of them. Plus you never know where those bloodsuckers could be hiding. They're fucking everywhere."

"What's with the big rig?" Danny asked.

"What?" Miguel said, as if he hadn't heard the question right.

"The big rig," Danny repeated. "Blaine says you guys had a big rig with you. It's gotta guzzle diesel like crazy, so why bother with one? For storing supplies?"

"That's partially it, but mostly it's to keep the monsters out."

"How?" Will asked.

"What, how does it keep the monsters out?" Miguel asked. "Have you seen those semitrailers? You can't tear into those things. They're like a moving safe."

Will and Danny exchanged a look. *"Why didn't we think of that?"*

"We didn't see a semitrailer when we got here," Will said.

"Folger moved it," Miguel said. "After last night, I guess he was afraid the kids would come back and try to steal it or something. Stupid, right? They're not coming back. Why the fuck would they? But Folger is paranoid like that."

"How did you know we were coming? You had that ambush set up pretty fast."

"I was on the water tower, looking for those kids. You know, to get a better lay of the land. Sound travels nowadays. I heard you coming from the highway. Called Folger on the radio and he came up with the bright idea to set up an ambush."

"What happened to Folger?"

"That dick. He took off with Del and Manley before you showed up, told me and Hiller they were going to circle around and attack you from behind. That was his master plan, anyway. I don't know what happened. Every time I radioed him, he always said he was circling around, that we should keep you occupied. Then you fucking killed Hiller and I guess they chickened out and split. Who the hell knows. He wouldn't answer the radio after I told them Hiller was probably dead." Miguel shrugged, and his shoulders seemed to droop lower than before, if that was even possible. "So, you going to shoot me now or what?"

Miguel looked at Will, then at Danny, and finally, for the first time, at Blaine.

"I'm not going to beg for my life," Miguel said. "Hell, I survived eight months when the rest of the world died. I think I got a pretty sweet deal." He managed a grin. "So go ahead. Get it over with. Just make sure I'm not the last one. That's why I'm telling you all of this, you know. So you can get Folger and Del and Manley, too, the cowardly fucks."

"You sure they left town?" Will asked.

"Wouldn't surprise me if they all split and went their own ways. Manley, in particular. He never really liked Folger and Del. Plus, he's the only one who can drive the big rig. If I was him, I'd take off with it. Get to keep all the supplies inside, too."

"All right, I guess we're done," Will said, and looked over at Blaine. "It's up to you. You decide what we should do with him."

Blaine only had eyes for Miguel. "Sandra. When you caught her last night. Did you…do anything to her?"

Miguel looked back at the big man, with an expression that Will thought was sadness, and something that almost approached (but not quite) regret. "I didn't. But I wanted to. I'll be straight with you. Man to man. I wanted to, but Del caught her, so he got her first. We were supposed to get her later last night, but like I said, she escaped with the kids first."

"Okay," Blaine said.

"Take him into the woods," Will said.

CHAPTER 9

JOSH

HE WOKE UP with Gaby's elbow in his ribs, and when that didn't work, she began pushing him back and forth until he opened his eyes and yawned. Gaby looked beautiful with the sunlight over her face, but then again, she always looked beautiful.

At the moment she also looked a little afraid. "I hear a car coming," she said in a hushed voice.

Josh sat up and listened.

He could hear a sound, but it was still too far away and he couldn't be sure if it was a car or something else. He scrambled up from some stained bedsheets. Josh moved toward the wall and stood under the small window and listened.

Gaby was right, it was a car, and it was getting closer. "I have to go upstairs," he said. "To make sure."

Gaby looked horrified at the thought. "Josh, we don't know what's up there. Anything could have come into the house last night while we were asleep down here."

"I'll be okay." He found that he could fake confidence if he tried hard enough, even if every ounce of him just wanted to stay down here in the basement with Gaby.

He picked up Matt's revolver, resting on top of the backpack where he had laid it last night. For some reason, the gun felt much heavier this morning, but maybe that was just his imagination. He stared up at the basement door and felt his heart beating loudly against his chest. It was stupid, he knew. Only an idiot would go out there. There could be bloodsuckers in the kitchen, for God's sake, that had slipped in sometime during the night and were now lying in wait for him.

He should stay down here. With Gaby. That was the smart thing.

And he was smart, wasn't he? Of course he was.

"Josh, don't go," Gaby said behind him.

"I'll be fine," he said, and before she could respond, he hurried up the stairs because if he didn't, if he let her argue, he knew he would change his mind. Josh didn't overestimate himself. Being brave wasn't something that came easily to him, especially when Gaby was there begging him to do the opposite.

He stopped at the top of the stairs and pressed his ear against the door. He listened, waiting a full thirty seconds, and didn't open the door until he was satisfied he didn't hear anything on the other side. No footsteps, no sounds of any kind at all. Of course, they could be playing possum, waiting for him. That was possible, too.

This is so stupid.

He unlocked the door, then quickly opened it and slipped out into the kitchen. He turned and closed the basement door behind him, then turned back around again, the revolver out front, holding his breath.

He was relieved to find a brightly lit kitchen, already filled with morning sun flooding through the windows above the sink as well as other windows in the living room. Everything was where it should be. He hoped.

He glanced down at his watch: 8:17 A.M.

Josh moved toward the front door, entering the foyer. More lights in the room made him breathe a little easier. He knew the bloodsuckers didn't hide in dark corners in brightly lit rooms. They hid in rooms that were dark, like that back room in the store, where Matt was bitten. The creatures weren't stupid. Far from it. They sure as hell had proven that eight months ago.

He hurried toward the window and looked out. He could hear the car getting closer. Soon, he saw the nose of a GMC turning the corner and cruising up the street in his direction. Josh lowered himself to the floor, with just his eyes peering out from behind the windowsill. The curtains fluttered above him, and he realized with slight anxiety that the window had been open all night.

How had he missed *that*? He was thankful nothing had come in during the night. God, he hoped nothing had come in during the night…

As the truck passed by on the street, Josh saw Manley behind the steering wheel, scanning the area with those cold, reptilian eyes of his. His heart began racing at the possibility of being caught by Manley. Of all their captors, the man scared him the most. There was just something so wrong about that guy.

When Manley and the GMC finally passed the house and turned right onto another street, Josh let out a big sigh and sat down on the floor to compose himself.

After a moment, he got up and headed back into the kitchen, where he opened the refrigerator and almost fainted at the overwhelming stench of rotten food. He held his breath and searched through the slabs of cheese and meat teeming with maggots. At least some life was thriving at the end of the world.

Josh grabbed a two-liter bottle of Coke and four warm bottles of water. He closed the refrigerator and finally let himself gasp for air again.

Next, he raided the cabinets and closets, looking for food. He opened one of the drawers and saw glossy silver packages of Kung Fu noodles stacked high.

Jackpot, mofos!

GABY LOOKED GLAD to see him coming back through the basement door, but she was even more glad see the bags of Kung Fu noodles in his arms. "Oh my God, I'm so hungry," she said, and quickly pulled open one of the bags and broke off a big piece of noodle and stuffed it into her mouth.

"How is it?" he asked.

"Food," she said between a mouthful of noodles.

He laughed and handed her a bottle of water. "Try not to choke on it."

"Trying," she grinned back.

Sandra gratefully took another bag of noodles from him. "Wow, Kung Fu noodles. I haven't had these since college."

"Where did you go to school?" he asked.

"Baylor. That was a lifetime ago." She wandered back to her corner, where she opened the bag and pulled out a big piece of noodle and bit into it, looking utterly satisfied.

Josh sat down next to Gaby and opened a bag. The noodles were a bit stale and didn't make that crackling sound he was used to. But they tasted okay, and that was what mattered. He happily ate his entire bag and chased them down with some warm Coke.

They sat in the basement and ate in silence. The only sounds were their chewing and drinking.

Josh found himself oddly content. Sure, his parents were probably dead, and his friends were probably all dead, too. But he had Gaby sitting here next to him, so close that every time she went to pinch noodles from her bag of Kung Fu, her shoulder rubbed up against him. She had washed and scratched away as much of Betts's blood as she could, but there were still specks of red clinging to her fingers. She seemed to not notice, though.

After a while, Gaby said, "Do you remember Peter Brolin?"

Josh had to think about it. "Peter Brolin? He went to our school, right?"

"Yeah. He graduated when we were juniors."

"Big guy? With a big nasty mole under his chin?"

Gaby giggled. He thought that was the sweetest sound he had ever heard, and it made him happy for some reason. "Yeah, him," she said.

He frowned. His memories of Peter Brolin, a.k.a. Mole Man, were not filled with happy moments. In fact, they were downright torturous, and the only reason it took him a while to recall the kid was because Josh had purposefully scrubbed the guy's existence from his mind.

"What about him?" he asked, almost afraid of the answer.

"He was the one who came to my house that night," Gaby said softly. "When everything first happened. He attacked my dad. He had changed a lot already, but I still recognized him. I don't know if he came there on his own, or…for some other reason."

"You think he came to your home on purpose?"

"I don't know. Maybe. He liked me," she said, and he could see she was reliving that night all over again.

So we share that now, too. Our mutual nightmares about Peter "Mole Man" Brolin. Fuck you, Mole Man.

"Anyways," she said, and that was it.

It was quiet again, except for the sounds of crunching. Josh was already on his second bag. Even stale, the noodles tasted damn good. Or maybe he was just really hungry. It was in those long moments of silence that Josh finally remembered the radio. Betts's radio, that he had grabbed before they left the semitrailer yesterday. He got up and went over to the backpack, opened it, and took out the radio.

"What's that?" Gaby asked.

"Betts's radio."

"Why did you bring it? There's no one out there but them."

"Exactly," he said, and sat back down and turned on the radio. He made sure not to touch the frequency dial or do anything but turn on the power.

They listened, but the only sounds they heard were static.

"Are we supposed to hear something?" Gaby asked.

Josh shrugged. "I was hoping to hear them talking over the radio."

"They might not know you took it," Sandra said from across the room.

Josh nodded. "Hopefully."

"And if they do?" Gaby asked.

"Then they'll probably try to trick us," Josh said. "Lure us into an ambush or something. I don't know. I just thought it might come in handy."

Gaby gave him an approving look. "It's quick thinking."

"Thanks."

"Can we use it to call anyone for help?"

He shook his head. "I wouldn't know where to begin. I mean, there are a lot of frequencies out there. For someone to hear me, they'd have to be tuned into the same frequency and listening at the same time, and what are the chances of that?"

"Not very good, I guess."

Suddenly the static disappeared and for a second Josh thought the radio had turned off by itself. But it hadn't. Instead, it squawked loudly, and he heard, loud and clear, Folger's voice: "Are you done?"

"I'm finishing up the subdivision now," a male voice answered through the radio.

Each time someone else talked, there was a loud squawk.

"You took your sweet time," Folger said.

"Fuck off," the other voice said.

"Does anyone recognize who Folger's talking to?" Josh asked.

"Manley," Sandra said. "I think that's Manley."

"Which one is he?" Gaby asked.

"The one with the scary eyes."

"Oh."

Josh said, "Shhh."

"They're gone," another voice was saying through the radio. *Del*, Josh thought, recognizing the voice. "We're wasting our time. Let's get out of here."

"This place is a gold mine," Folger said. "We're not going anywhere until we pick it clean."

"Who put you in charge?" Del wanted to know.

"I did," Folger said.

Josh thought he heard Del snort, but maybe that was just static.

They went back and forth like that for a while, further convincing Josh that Folger was only in command because the others didn't want the job. Or didn't care who had it. They didn't respect him in the slightest; that was obvious now.

They kept listening and discovered that Folger had the others running around town looking for them. Unless, of course, Folger had figured out that Josh had the radio and all of this was one big ruse for their benefit. Josh didn't completely ignore the possibility. Anything was possible with men like Folger. So Josh reminded himself to be careful, to take everything he heard with a grain of salt. Even so, he started to feel better about their situation the more Folger and his flunkies seemed to be getting farther and farther away from them in their search.

"They don't know where we are," Gaby said, looking as happy as he had seen her in the last few days.

"Seems that way," Josh nodded.

"You think they'll leave eventually?"

"Eventually."

"How many of these did you find?" Gaby asked, holding up her empty bag of Kung Fu noodles.

"There's a stack of them in a drawer in the kitchen. I'll go back up and get more later."

"More of this goodness?" Sandra said. "Do you think I'll suddenly know Kung Fu if I eat enough of this stuff?"

Gaby and Josh chuckled, and Sandra smiled. It was the first time they had seen the older woman smile, and Josh realized Sandra was actually very pretty. His friend Hank would say a woman like Sandra had "curves in all the right places." Not that Hank knew anything about a woman's curves other than what he saw on the Internet. Hank was a virgin when Josh knew him, and he probably died a virgin, too.

Died? He wishes. He's probably one of those bloodsuckers right now.

Morning had turned into noon, and the sun outside ceased to feel soothing against their skin. The basement was turning hot again, and without an air conditioner or any ventilation, they started to sweat. They had been lucky last night, he realized, to find the basement just as it was cooling off in the evening. And then night had come and it had cooled off even more.

"Maybe we can cover up the window," Sandra suggested.

"That might not be a good idea," Josh said. "Manley drove past earlier today. He might have glanced at the basement and seen the window. What if he comes back and sees that it's now covered, unlike before? It might make him suspicious."

"That's a big if," Sandra said.

"It's just something to consider."

Sandra seemed to think about it. "You're probably right. Those creatures might notice a covered basement window, too. They're not stupid. I used to think they were dumb animals, but they're not. They're clever."

Josh nodded. "They would have to be, to have done what they did."

"God, stop talking about them," Gaby said. She wrapped her arms around her chest reflexively. "They already scare me shitless as it is. I don't need to know they're smart, too."

"Sorry," he said.

"How old are you, anyway?" Sandra asked him.

The question caught him off guard. "Eighteen."

"You sound older."

"I do?"

"You think older, I guess is what I mean," Sandra said.

"Thanks, I guess."

"Like back there, in the semitrailer. I would never have thought of baiting Betts like that. But you did. How did you know he would fall for it?"

"I guess I know how guys think." He smiled. "We're kind of sick motherfuckers, you know."

Sandra laughed. It didn't take long for Gaby to join in.

Josh smiled. He was glad to see them both laughing. He knew they had been through a lot, especially Sandra. The end of the world was one thing, but what had happened to her afterward—and almost happened to Gaby—was beyond anything he would ever experience as a man. Josh was ashamed of his species, and even ashamed of himself whenever he thought of Gaby in an overtly sexual way, which was often.

It's the end of the world, and we're still thinking exclusively with our dicks. Way to go, mofos.

THEY HEARD GUNSHOTS around one in the afternoon.

First it was just one shot, then it was two, then three.

At first, Josh thought someone was just shooting into the air. Maybe Folger and the others were bored or trying to lure them out. He wouldn't put it past them. By now they would have gotten tired of driving all over town searching for them, and they might have decided a new tactic was in order.

But then there was a series of gunshots, and Josh knew it wasn't a trick. It was a full-on gun battle. After a while, he traced the sounds back to the municipal area, with the courthouse and the police department and the public library. Back to where they had been kept in the semitrailer. Sound tended to carry these days, Josh knew, without all the usual noises and distractions of a city filled with people.

Josh walked over to the basement window, as if he could see what was happening if he stared outside long enough. Gaby and Sandra stood next to him, and they listened for the longest time, no one saying a word.

It went on for minutes. Maybe five minutes.

"Josh," Gaby said suddenly, "try the radio."

"Oh, shit," Josh said, and ran over to the radio.

He had turned it off because no one was saying anything, but now he turned it back on and immediately heard Folger's voice: "—we're going around them."

"Hurry the fuck up, then," another male voice said. It wasn't Manley or Del. Josh would recognize them by now. How many were left? Two. Betts was dead. Or probably dead. That left the short man and the Hispanic.

"Just keep them pinned down," Folger said. "How many do you see?"

"A lot," the Hispanic said, "but only two seem to be shooting back. Dammit, they know what they're doing. They're not straying from the trucks."

"Shoot the gas tank," Folger said.

"It's not that easy," the Hispanic said irritably. "Just get over here already."

"We're on our way."

There was suddenly a burst of continued gunfire, like someone was firing on full automatic. Then one shot—and a few seconds later, a second shot—and then it was quiet.

"What happened?" Folger said.

"Fuck, I think they got Hiller," the Hispanic said.

"Hiller? Hiller, come in." It was Folger again. "Hiller! Shit. Is he dead?"

"Well, he's not shooting anymore, so probably he's dead. Are you coming?"

There wasn't a reply.

"Folger, dammit, are you coming or what?" the Hispanic asked again. He waited for a reply.

Josh and the girls waited anxiously, too.

"Folger? Folger!"

There was no reply.

They waited, but they didn't hear anything else. The radio had gone dead.

"It's over," Josh said.

"What do you think happened?" Gaby asked.

"Sounded like a gun fight. Maybe Folger and his buddies met their match."

"Maybe the new people shot and killed the fuckers," Sandra said.

"They killed one, at least," Josh said. "Hiller. The short guy."

"How many does that leave?" Gaby asked.

"Four. I didn't hear Betts on the radio once. Either he's dead or he's not running around."

"Serves him right," Sandra said, and Josh saw her exchange a look with Gaby, as if to say, *"You did nothing wrong."*

Gaby nodded back at the other woman, but said nothing.

Josh glanced around the basement, then at Gaby and Sandra. It was such a small room, and it was so hot. They weren't going to be able to stay in here forever, he knew that now. Hell, they might not even be able to last the day.

So what other options were there?

"Stay here," Josh said. "I'm going to find out what happened."

"What?" Gaby said. "Are you crazy? You can't go out there. Even if there's only four of them left, there's still *four* of them left, Josh."

"Or maybe they're running," he said, trying to convince himself. "You heard Folger on the radio. He was supposed to go around and get into the gun battle, but he didn't. I think he's running. So that leaves the people they were shooting at."

"We don't know who those people are, either. They could be just as dangerous as Folger. Or worse."

"She's right," Sandra said. "We don't know who they are."

Josh nodded. They were both right.

Not that it mattered. Whatever happened, they still couldn't stay down here. Not forever.

"I won't let them see me," he said. "I'll hide, sneak around, keep a low profile."

"This is crazy, Josh," Gaby said.

He could see how worried she looked, but instead of making him relent, it only steeled his resolve. Seeing her like this made him more courageous, because he had to protect her. He couldn't do that down here.

I'm the guy…

"We have to find out," Josh said. "We can't stay down here forever."

Sandra and Gaby exchanged a look, and he knew he had gotten to them.

"Be careful," Gaby said.

"I'll be back. I promise."

He headed for the stairs. He had Matt's gun tucked into his front waistband. He touched the handle now, just to make sure it was still there.

You and me, Matt ol' buddy, all the way.

PROS AND CONS: What were they?

Pros: He was still in one piece, and so was Gaby. They were in a place Folger and his people couldn't find. He liked their chances of staying hidden for a while, living off food in the house. Eventually, they could probably do something about the heat.

Cons: They couldn't stay down there forever. Eventually they would have to come out. The food would eventually run out. The basement would eventually get too hot as summertime churned on. And cabin fever would eventually get to them. It was why they had never stayed in one town for too long, back when it was just him and Gaby and Matt, and why they had kept moving ever since the end of the world. *Eventually*, everything ran its course.

Conclusion: He had no choice. He had to find out what had happened along Main Street. He had to find out if Folger and the others were still out there, and who the people they were trading gunfire with were. God knew he didn't want to leave the basement, leave Gaby, but there was no choice. Sooner or later, they would have to venture back out into the real world.

Or what was left of it, anyway.

The good news? He had Gaby.

Well, he didn't *have* her, but he was *with* her, and that was a pretty good start.

Josh moved through the subdivision slowly, taking his time. The heat was already becoming insufferable, and he didn't want to think about how much hotter it was going to get in another few hours. He darted between houses, heading south, which would take him back to Chance Road, and from there he could pick his way toward the municipal area. It made sense that the new arrivals would stumble across Folger's people there, and a shoot-out would erupt. It must have been like stumbling across a nest of snakes. He just hoped the new arrivals weren't snakes, too, or it was back to the basement.

He peeked into houses as he passed, filing them away for future reference in case they did have to stay in the basement a little longer. He saw empty homes, some with fading brown stains along the windowsills. Blood splatters. Josh was surprised that so many of the houses looked undisturbed, as if their owners had simply decided to abandon them. He liked to think most of them got away, but of course that was bullshit.

He moved at a brisk pace, staying behind houses whenever he could, though there were long spots where he had to run across open spaces because there was no shelter or places to hide behind. He walked through the tall, overgrown grass of the lodges and was relieved when he finally reached the more wooded areas again.

Josh trudged through someone's farm and skirted around a barn that looked just a bit too creepy. There was no telling what was hiding in there, watching him through holes along the rotted wall. Just the thought made him shiver involuntarily. Eight months later, and he still couldn't get used to the idea of *things* hiding behind every window, in every building, waiting for the first hint of darkness to come out. How he managed to keep going, without going crazy, was a mystery, but he figured it probably had something to do with Gaby.

He slowed down when he finally reached one of the half-dozen or so houses along Chance Road that sat directly across the street from the municipal area. Hiding behind a house with brown and white bricks, he could see the three buildings across the street, sitting side by side. It was quiet, and the silence unnerved Josh more than he wanted to admit.

The first thing he noticed was that the semitrailer where he, Gaby, and Sandra had been held last night was gone. There were no signs of it, and he wondered if Folger and the others had in fact taken off after the shoot-out. In its place, there were two trucks he hadn't seen before—one blue and the other black. They both looked shot up, with broken windows.

Suddenly there was a loud explosion *from behind him* and Josh almost pissed his pants. He fell to the ground so fast he smacked his face into the dirt and stunned himself, but he quickly got over it because someone wasn't just behind him, they were *close to him*. He felt sick to his stomach. How had he managed to walk all the way from the woods to the house without seeing them? Better yet, how had they managed not to see *him?*

Josh kept very still, pressed flat against the warm dirt. The wall of the house was to his left, but there was only overgrown grass to his right. He prayed it was high and thick enough to conceal him when he heard footsteps approaching. He closed his eyes and willed his entire body not to move. He might have forgotten to breathe, though he couldn't really be sure at the moment.

Then the sounds of footsteps mercifully faded, and Josh finally managed to summon enough courage to force his eyes open again.

He could see a figure moving in front of him. *Away* from him.

Oh, thank you, God.

He lifted his head slightly, watching as the man—a big man, though he looked like he was in pain and was leaning a bit on one leg as he walked—crossed the street, holding something in his left hand. Josh looked for a long time before he decided it was a gun. A shotgun. One of those sawed-offs that Mel Gibson carried in *The Road Warrior*. That shotgun was responsible for the big boom he had heard moments ago.

The man was walking back toward the courthouse.

Josh pushed himself up into a crouch. He looked over his shoulder, in the direction he thought the man had come from. What was back there? What had the man shot? He considered backtracking to find out. Maybe an animal…or a person.

The gun battle was over a long time ago, even before he had started off from the house. Folger and the others seemed to have left, or maybe they were hiding in another part of town, waiting to strike. Folger struck him as that kind of conniving asshole. If Folger was still around, the man with the shotgun hadn't seemed particularly concerned about it. And Josh was sure he hadn't seen the man before—he would remember someone that big—so he wasn't part of Folger's crew.

Josh remained still and went over his options. The way he saw it, he didn't really have a whole lot of choices. It was either stay here or go back.

He decided to stay put for a while, to see who else came out of the buildings across the street. He remembered what the Hispanic had said over the radio. There were a "lot" of people in the two trucks, but only two men were shooting back at them.

He reminded himself that Gaby and Sandra were waiting for him back at the subdivision. By now, they would be worried, especially

Gaby. How long had he been gone? Josh checked his watch.

A little over fifty minutes.

He decided to give it thirty more minutes before heading back.

INSTEAD, HE STAYED for forty minutes.

Then forty became an hour.

He couldn't leave. Not yet. Gaby was probably hysterical by now, but he reasoned he had to stick it out. He had to make sure he saw them first, this new group of people. The fact that they had fought it out with Folger was a good sign. What was that old saying?

"The enemy of my enemy is my friend."

He just hoped his enemy's enemy didn't turn out to be his enemy, too. That was a very real possibility. But he didn't have many choices at the moment. This was the world he lived in now. And here, he had to take chances, like back in the semitrailer with Gaby and Betts. He had put her in harm's way by playing a hunch. The old Josh would never have done something so reckless, so risky. But the old Josh was dead, replaced by Josh 2.0. Time would tell which version of him was better.

Finally, Josh's patience was rewarded when the police station/courthouse doors opened and he saw two men emerge. Neither one was the same big man with the shotgun Josh had seen earlier. He could tell because they were thinner (not skinny, just leaner) and carried assault rifles, sidearms, and looked like they had some kind of assault vests on, though Josh was still too far away to make out details.

Josh got off his butt and went into a crouch. He watched one of the men close the tailgate of the blue truck before they started talking about something. Strategy, maybe. He couldn't quite tell who was in charge. Maybe they both were. Maybe neither.

A moment later, the big man with the sawed-off shotgun came out, still walking gingerly on one good leg. Josh wondered if the man's limp was from this afternoon's gun battle with Folger. The big man joined the first two at the truck, and they looked at a map spread out across the black truck's hood.

The three men were talking, pointing at the map and up and

down the street, when the courthouse doors opened again and two women came out. Then behind them, two little girls. They ran around the trucks, chasing each other. They looked to be seven or eight, and they were *laughing*.

Josh waited and listened and watched.

He considered all the new evidence and weighed his options again.

Pros and cons: What were they?

Pros: These could be potential allies. People who took care of kids who were obviously not afraid of them were the exact opposite of people like Folger and Manley and the others. Maybe these new people were even married and those were their children. Even better. That meant family, loyalty, and bonding. People like that might welcome additions to their group.

Cons: Or they might not. Just because the people in front of him looked decent, it didn't mean they were. Maybe instead of a semi-trailer, they were keeping their victims locked way inside the courthouse. And these people were obviously violent. They were good at it, too, to have fought off Folger's people. Even killed one of them. Could he really trust his life, and by extension, Gaby's, to people who were so good with guns?

Conclusion: *Fuck it.*

Josh pulled Matt's gun out of his waistband and laid it down on the dirt and stood up and began walking across the street. He did it quickly, trying to think as little as possible, because he knew if he thought about it too much, he would change his mind.

Have to risk it. Have to risk everything…

One of the kids saw him first. She said something and pointed, and the men turned. The first two men unslung their rifles. The two women were staring. The big man with the shotgun seemed to be making sure he had shells in his weapon.

This is a mistake. I'm going to die.

Oh God, I'm going to die.

"Don't shoot!" he shouted across the street, raising his hands as far above his head as they would go. "I'm not armed! Don't shoot!"

They watched him for a moment, then one of the men jogged forward. "Stop!" the man shouted.

Josh stopped in his tracks and didn't move. He was in the middle of the street, and instinctively glanced left and right before realizing, *Oh, right, no traffic.*

The man moving toward Josh looked young and had slightly brown-ish blond hair. He moved smoothly toward Josh, then circled him, the point of his rifle aimed low. Not threatening, but ready.

Please, don't shoot me, he thought, but was too afraid to say the words out loud.

The man continued circling him, looking him over, probably checking him for weapons. "What's your name, kid?"

"Josh."

"What are you doing here, Josh? You alone?"

"Yes," he lied, his heart racing. "Josh. My name's Josh. Please don't shoot me."

"You already said that," the man said, looking slightly amused.

"I did?"

"Yep."

"Oh. Please don't shoot me."

"Only if you tell me your name."

"But I—" Josh realized the guy was messing with him and stopped. "Oh."

The man chuckled, then motioned for Josh to move forward. Josh did, but it took a few seconds before his feet would start behaving normally enough that he didn't almost fall on his face with every step.

Josh heard the man moving behind him, but he decided to concentrate on the group waiting for them instead. The other man with the rifle was scanning the roads and the area, while the women had gathered up the kids and put them into one of the trucks. The girls peered curiously out at him through one of the few windows that was still intact.

"Hey, kid," the man behind him said.

"Yes?" Josh said.

Please don't shoot me.

"You know anything about computers?" the man asked.

"What?"

"Computers," the man said, as if that was the most normal topic in the world to be talking about at the moment. "You know anything about computers? You look like you do."

I do?

"A little," he said.

"You know how to fix them?"

"A little," he said again. This conversation was going in a very odd direction. "Why?"

"Just wondering. You can put your hands down now."

"Oh, thanks."

"No sweat. Hey, you wanna hear a joke?"

"Um, okay."

Just as long as you don't shoot me.

"So these two subway conductors are out to lunch one day, and one of them says to the other, 'You know what, I think my sex life is getting too boring.' The other guy asks, 'Why do you say that?' The first train conductor groans, then says, 'Well, it's always the same thing. In and out, in and out, and I never get anywhere!'"

Josh didn't know whether to laugh, or cry, or beg the guy not to shoot him again.

"You're all right, kid," the guy said.

Oh, thank you, God.

CHAPTER 10

LARA

THE KID SAID his name was Josh, and they put two and two together and deduced he was one of the two teenagers that escaped the man named Folger's captivity last night. Which meant he knew where Sandra was, a fact that instantly got Blaine to move toward him, so fast that the poor kid stumbled back and almost fell down in surprise—or fear.

Will quickly grabbed Josh by the shirt collar and kept him upright. "Relax. This is Blaine. He's been looking for Sandra since yesterday. Where is she?"

"You know Sandra?" Josh asked, looking at Blaine.

"Yes," Blaine said, and Lara could almost see him restraining himself from shouting questions at the kid. "Where is she? Is she okay?"

"She's fine," Josh said, though looking at him, Lara thought he knew something else that he wasn't saying. It was probably about Sandra, after she had been captured by Folger and his men yesterday, while Blaine lay bleeding and dying in the road.

She thought about the Sundays…

No. Don't think about them.

It had been months since she had remembered the Sundays ever existed. She had scrubbed them so thoroughly from her mind that it took a lot to trigger her memory of those days with them. But now, listening to Josh and Blaine, and thinking about what Sandra had gone through since yesterday, all those tainted memories came rushing back.

"I'm going inside to see if Carly needs help," she said, and hurried back into the courthouse before Will could catch her eyes.

Carly was near the cells in the back, pulling blankets and bedrolls out of the moving crates they had transferred inside earlier. Despite the attempted ambush by Folger and his men, they had decided Lancing was too big a city to just abandon. Which meant they were going to need a place to stay, and the courthouse was as good a place as any unless they found a better location. They could easily barricade the two front windows and door, as well as the two extra doors in the back. If push came to shove, there were the cells in the back. Lara didn't look forward to being literally locked inside those, but she reminded herself that she had been in worse situations.

Lara walked over and helped Carly unpack their belongings—just the essentials they would need to sleep through the night. It wouldn't be a very comfortable temporary base, but it would do for now.

Until we get to Song Island.

God, please, let it be real…

"Was that one of the kids who escaped last night?" Carly asked.

"Yeah," Lara said. "And Sandra's alive, too."

"Wow, that's good news. I bet Blaine was happy to hear that."

"He was."

The girls raced around the front reception area and wound their way through the courthouse. They seemed to have boundless energy, and Lara could only look after them and smile. For a while, she hadn't been sure if Elise could adapt. But she had. They all had.

Adapt or perish.

"So what's this make, three more people?" Carly asked.

"If they decide to come with us."

"Of course they will. After what they went through? Trust me, they'll come with us. Until last year, I was a teenager, too. I still know how teenagers think."

"God, I forget how young you are sometimes."

"Good, because I feel fifty years old," Carly said, and made a face.

Lara laughed. She really did sometimes forget just how young Carly was. Heck, she sometimes forgot how young most of them were. She wouldn't be twenty-six for another month, but she already felt so much older than that.

Twenty-six going on forty…

She heard the front doors opening and looked back to see Will coming in. He walked over to them, dodging Vera and Elise as they darted across the room. He smiled after them, and seeing that brought a smile to Lara's lips, too.

"Are we going after Sandra?" Lara asked.

"Josh is taking Blaine and Danny to her now." He glanced at his watch. "Once they get back, Danny and I will go looking for supplies. If we're lucky, we'll find a better place to spend the night. Josh said they were staying in a basement in one of the subdivisions. That might work out better for us than out here in the open."

"Great," Carly said. "So I'm doing all this unpacking for no reason?"

"Probably."

"Then I'm going to fix the girls something to eat. I could use a snack, too."

Carly headed off, leaving them alone at the holding cells.

When Carly was gone, Will asked, "You okay?"

"Don't I look okay?"

Lara pulled some new shirts out of a crate. The one she was wearing was already damp from the heat. She went through at least two shirts on a good day, and more when it was really hot, which it usually was. For the life of her, she couldn't understand how Will and Danny managed to wear the same odor-drenched clothes throughout most of the day, and sometimes for days at a time until, inevitably, either she or Carly complained.

"Not really," he said.

"I'm okay. Why wouldn't I be?"

"You know you can talk to me."

"I know. I just don't have anything to talk about right now, that's all. But if I do, you're the first person I'll come to. Promise."

He slipped one hand around her waist and kissed her neck. She sighed and inhaled his usual mix of sweat and dirt.

"Blaine must be excited," she said.

"Yeah, I guess."

"You guess?"

"I don't really know the guy."

"You saved his life."

"I wouldn't say I saved his life. I gave him a ride. You did more for him than I did."

"Well, he thinks you saved his life."

"It's his right to. This is still America, after all."

"I can't figure out if you're just being humble or if you're being a jerk."

"That depends. Which one turns you on more?"

She turned around in his arm and sought out his mouth. His hands were already tugging her shirt out of her waistline and were searching for more when the radio clipped to his vest squawked and they heard Danny's voice:

"We just arrived at the house the kid was staying in."

Will grunted, pulling away from her briefly to key his radio. "Roger that."

"Nice neighborhood," Danny said. "We should get a couple of places here. Ones with really big lawns. The girls can raise the kids and we can have barbeques on the weekends."

"Why just the weekends?" Will asked, playing along as usual.

"Because if I had to see your face seven days a week, I'd probably shoot myself. That, or turn on the car engine in my garage and end it peacefully. I haven't decided yet."

"You guys sound like married old ladies," Lara said, rolling her eyes at Will as she pulled herself free and walked off, tucking her shirt back into her pants. "I'll go help Carly make dinner. A woman's work is never done."

BLAINE RETURNED LATER with Danny and Josh and a pretty teenage girl Josh introduced as Gaby. But there was no Sandra, which explained why Blaine looked like someone had punched him in the ribs, then shot him three more times. Lara thought about going over to comfort him, but realized she didn't really know him all that well, and she wasn't sure how he would take it. Maybe he didn't want some stranger to comfort him at that moment.

The positive news was that Sandra was still alive.

"She left about an hour after Josh did," Gaby told them.

They were gathered back inside the courthouse, eating canned fruit. Gaby seemed to relish every drop of the same syrupy flavor that Lara had grown tired of, and she envied the teenager's appetite.

"She found a car in the garage of the house we were hiding in," Gaby said. "There were keys, and she packed up as much stuff as she could carry. The last I saw of her, she was driving off."

"Did she say where she was going?" Will asked.

Blaine had apparently heard all this before, either on the ride over or at the house, and he left the courthouse without a word. Lara considered going after him again but thought better of it. He didn't look like he wanted company.

"She went looking for him," Gaby said, looking back at the door after Blaine. "She thought he was dead. She said he had been shot, and he looked like he was dead when they dragged her out of the woods and threw her into the semitrailer and brought her here."

"Why did she go back looking for him if she thought he was dead?" Carly asked.

Lara thought she knew the answer. She looked over at Will, but he didn't catch her glance. She would go back for him, too, even if she knew he was dead. She knew without a doubt Will would do the same for her.

"She wanted to bury him," Gaby said. "He wasn't bitten, so he wouldn't have turned, right? Isn't that how it works?"

"We're not sure," Lara said. "I don't think anyone is."

"Sandra didn't think he had turned, anyway, which was why she went back. Or maybe she just wanted to be sure he wasn't still lying out there on the road." Gaby shrugged. She turned her attention back to the can, tilting it up to her lips, and drank down the sugary liquid. "God, these are good."

Carly handed her another Del Monte can, this one with peaches.

"Are you sure?" Gaby said, looking almost embarrassed by her appetite.

"We have more than enough to spare," Carly said. "Take it."

She took it gratefully and pulled open the top lid and dug in. "God, these are so good," she said again, between mouthfuls of peaches dripping with syrup.

Gaby was young and painfully pretty. Even though Gaby's hair was dirty and her face hadn't seen makeup in months, Lara couldn't help feeling a little bit jealous looking at the teenager. She didn't have to guess why Josh stood so close to Gaby at all times. Josh was a decent-looking kid, with disheveled brown hair that she guessed someone had cut for him recently (probably Gaby) and mellow brown eyes that weren't quite as striking as Will's. There was really nothing extraordinary about Josh physically, and she couldn't picture the two of them together in high school. They were about the same height, which made the poor kid stand out even less.

But she had to admit, Josh had done a remarkable job keeping the two of them alive, especially after they were captured by Folger's men yesterday. It had been his idea to escape, Gaby said, and Lara saw the way Gaby responded to him. She might not have given him the time of day eight months ago, but things had changed since.

Lara saw Will looking down at his watch. "Three fourteen," he announced. "That gives us two hours to find a better place to bed down for the night. If we don't find anything by then, we'll come back and fortify the courthouse."

"Be careful," Lara said.

He nodded and went outside, where Danny was already waiting.

That left Lara and Carly with Josh and Gaby. She watched the blonde teenager devour the can of peaches until there was nothing left.

Wish I had that appetite...

"Danny said you guys were going to some island," Josh said. "Is that true? He said it might be safe. Like a sanctuary."

"Song Island," Lara nodded. "And that's what we're hoping—that it's safe. It's somewhere on Beaufont Lake in Louisiana. It's better if you hear it for yourself."

Lara went into the back to grab the ham radio. She turned it on as she walked back, and the recorded female voice was already in mid-message:

"...broadcasting on the FEMA frequency to any survivors out there. We want you to know there is hope. There are survivors on Song Island. We have food, supplies, electricity, and protection against the darkness. If you are receiving this recorded message, we encourage you to make your way to us. I repeat: we have food, supplies, electricity, and protection against the darkness. Hello. If anyone can hear me out there. This is Song Island on Beaufont Lake in Louisiana. We are broadcasting on the FEMA frequency..."

"It's a recorded message," Lara said, turning the sound down a bit. "It repeats the same message over and over."

"Who's broadcasting it?" Josh asked.

"We don't know. Will thinks it's possibly some ex-military types, or maybe ex-government officials. Someone who knows about the FEMA frequency."

"Why wouldn't they just say who they were?"

"I don't know, maybe they just wanted to keep the message short."

"That means they have power, right?" Josh said, brightening up. "You'd need power to send that kind of message."

"It could be hydro power," Lara said. "The facility where we were staying before this used a water turbine to generate electricity. These people are on an island, so it makes sense if that's how they're getting their electricity, too."

"Song Island?" Gaby said. "I've never heard of it. Then again, I've never been outside of Texas." She glanced over at Josh. "What do you think? Is it possible?"

"Maybe," Josh said, though Lara didn't think he was sold on the idea. "It's definitely possible. Why not? It's an island, surrounded by water. If the bloodsuckers have a thing about water… *Do* they have a thing about water?" he asked, looking over at Lara and Carly.

"I guess we'll find out, because we're going there," Lara said. "The two of you are welcome to join us."

"God, yes," Gaby said quickly. "Right, Josh?"

"Count us in," Josh said without hesitation.

Josh would run through a wall for her.

Ah, teenage love. Or possibly lust.

Close enough.

LARA AND CARLY got Josh and Gaby settled into the courthouse, even though they fully expected Will and Danny to tell them they were moving. That was usually how it happened. After that disastrous night at a bank outside the city of Cleveland, Texas, that had nearly cost them their lives, Will was determined to not let it happen again. The ghouls had proved too intelligent and too creative for him to risk being hunkered down inside a building that could be breached. The best way to avoid them, Lara had learned, was to actually *avoid* them.

Dead, not stupid.

That meant hiding. She wasn't ashamed of it. In fact, she preferred it. Hiding was always a better option than fighting, especially when your enemy had an endless number of (*undead*) bodies to throw at you.

Lara found Blaine outside the courthouse, under the hood of a beat-up white Toyota truck with the letters "TRD" on the side. It was covered in dust and looked like it had been abandoned some time back, but must still be working because it hadn't been in the parking lot the last time she was out here. Lara saw a key in the ignition.

Blaine pulled his head out from behind the hood of the truck. "Hey."

"Going somewhere?"

"After Sandra."

"Did you talk to Will?"

"He understands."

"So you're going by yourself?"

"It's my thing," he said. She thought he was going to elaborate, explain his "thing" to her, but he didn't.

"I can't talk you out of it?"

"Why would you want to?"

She thought about it and realized he was right. "I wouldn't."

He slammed the hood back down and wiped blackened hands on a rag, then walked around the truck and leaned into the driver's seat and turned the key. The truck jumped to life.

"Sounds good," she said.

"It'll do," Blaine nodded. He turned the engine off and sat behind the steering wheel for a moment. Then he seemed to make up his mind about something and looked at her. "I don't have any right to ask, but can you spare any food and supplies? I already talked to Will about weapons, and he's going to let me have one of the AR-15s to replace the shotgun."

"I'll put a care package together for you. When are you leaving?"

"Whenever you're done."

"Give me ten minutes," she said.

"SHOULD WE TRY to talk him out of it?" Carly asked. "I feel like we should."

Lara was putting Blaine's care package together using one of the smaller crates. She packed blankets, bedrolls, pillows, canned food, and toiletries, utilizing the space to its maximum, a trick she had picked up over the months. She packed the box with the intention of it being used by two people. Maybe it was a fantasy, but she thought Blaine would want that, and the optimist in her wanted that happy ending for him.

"Will didn't," Lara said.

"That's Will and Danny. I mean we, as in us."

"I don't think I can. I tried, but I just didn't have my heart in it. Wouldn't you want Danny to come after you, if that was you out there?"

"Of course I would. But only if I knew Danny wasn't limping around with three bullet holes in him. How long do you think he's going to last out there? He can barely walk, Lara."

"Danny wouldn't care."

"Danny can be an idiot, too," she said.

Lara smiled. "Love makes you do crazy things."

"I guess so. God knows I love that guy. Bad jokes and all." She looked back at Gaby, playing clapping hand games with Elise and Vera, while Josh watched with a big grin on his face. "She looks like you."

"Who?"

"The girl. Gaby. A younger version of you. Did you look like that ten years ago?"

"God, ten years ago," Lara said, looking over at Gaby. She did see a slight resemblance. Had it really been that long since she was an eighteen-year-old teenager? It felt like another incarnation. "Maybe," she said.

"You guys could pass for sisters."

"I already have a sister."

"Really? You never told me that. What's her name?"

Lara gave her a look and rolled her eyes.

Carly laughed. "God, I'm so dense." She smiled at Lara before suddenly grabbing her in a big bear hug. "It's nice to be the little sister for a change. I'm tired of always being the big sister. It's too...much...*work.*"

Lara laughed. "Okay, okay. Only if you promise to do what I say and clean your room so I don't have to."

"No promises."

The radio clipped to Lara's hip squawked, and she heard Danny's voice: "Ladies, when was the last time you went to church and repented your sins to our Lord and Savior Jesus Christ?"

"Stupid Danny, always ruining a great moment," Carly said, wiping away tears.

That almost made Lara cry, too, but she somehow managed to fight through it, if just barely.

LARA WENT OUTSIDE with the crate and put it into the back seat of the Toyota. She opened the lid and took out a small white bag.

Blaine was slipping on a gun belt. A Remington 870 and an AR-15 rifle lay across the hood of the truck next to him.

"You sure you won't change your mind?" she asked. "Song Island isn't going anywhere. We'll go back with you to find Sandra tomorrow."

"I can't wait that long. She's out there now, Lara. She went back for me. I need to find her." He tossed the weapons into the front seats. "Thanks for the care package."

"Oh, and this." She handed him the white bag. It was leather and at one point someone had used it to carry makeup.

"I don't need makeup, Lara," Blaine said, grinning at her.

She smiled back at him. "It's an impromptu aid kit." She unzipped the bag and pulled out a plain white bottle. "I restocked your painkillers, for when the pain kicks in. And trust me, it will, sooner or later."

"More Vicodin?"

"Tramadol. Not quite as strong as Vicodin or Percocet. At this point, I'm supposed to tell you not to take more than three a day, but I doubt you'll listen anyway." She put the bottle back into the bag and pulled out a roll of gray duct tape. "This is for your wounds, if and when they open again. Let's hope they don't, but if they do, this will do in a pinch. Clean the wound as thoroughly as you can, then use this to keep it closed so it can heal up. It'll hurt, but it'll also keep you from bleeding out."

He took the duct tape hesitantly. "Isn't this something MacGyver would do?"

"I don't know who that is."

"He's a guy on TV. He did crazy things with household items." Blaine shook his head. "Never mind. Does this actually work?"

"I would have given you superglue, but we don't have any."

He gave her another doubtful look, probably wondering if she was just messing with him now.

"Superglue works wonders to close up a wound," she said. "But since I don't have any on hand, duct tape will have to do. Just make sure to clean the wound first." She reached into the bag and took out a small bottle of rubbing alcohol. "This will do the trick. Then squeeze the wound together and apply as much duct tape as you need to cover it up. That'll give it time to heal and keep it from opening again."

"Why don't I just do that now?"

"Because I spent a lot of time stitching you back together and properly dressing the wounds. This is worst-case scenario. If you ever need to reach for this white bag, you're already in trouble."

"You're the doctor, doctor." He took the bag from her and put it on the seat next to the AR-15.

"Third-year medical student, actually."

"I sold car parts for a living and did part-time work in my uncle's garage in Dallas. Trust me, third-year medical student is a better doctor than I could have afforded even before the world went to shit."

He climbed into the truck and looked back out at Lara, and for a moment she thought he was going to announce he had changed his mind, that he was going to stay with them after all.

Instead, he said, "Thank you. Not just for the supplies. But for everything. For saving my life. You didn't have to do it, especially now with everything the way it is, but you did, and that means a lot to me. One of these days, I'm going to pay both you and Will back. I just don't know how I'm going to do it yet."

"You'll have to stay alive to do that."

He grinned at her again. "That's the plan. But I have to find Sandra first. She means everything to me. If she's not here beside me, I might as well just lie down and let those monsters drain me dry."

He closed the door and turned on the engine.

"Blaine," she said, leaning closer to the door so he could hear her over the engine. "We may still be here in a day, or a week, or we might be gone by tomorrow morning. It all depends on what's out there and how safe we can be by remaining here. But if you can't find us, remember Song Island across the border."

"We'll find you again, Sandra and me. You can count on it."

She was convinced that he believed every word. She nodded and stepped back. "Be safe."

He put the truck in gear and pulled out of the parking lot.

She watched him drive off, going up Chance Street in the direction they had come, speeding up with urgency a second later and then, just like that, he was gone, the sound of his truck engine fading with him.

Good luck. God knows we all need some these days.

CHAPTER 11

WILL

THE FIRST ASSEMBLY of the Lord building was a big, squat structure on the right of South Main Street, about four kilometers from the courthouse. Lancing had a surprisingly large number of houses of worship, most of them more elaborate and bigger than the First Assembly of the Lord. Will was sure they all had basements, but the others were too large and in the busier parts of town. That would draw attention, something they didn't need at the moment.

Right now, he was purely in SERE mode—Survival, Evasion, Resistance, and Escape. The grunt in him wanted to stop and fight, to take the ghouls head-on and see what would happen. If it were just him and Danny, he might have done just that. But it wasn't just them. There was Lara, Carly, and the girls to think about.

Sometimes it still amazed him what he had gotten himself into. Taking care of civilians was one thing, but Lara…she complicated matters. She made him think differently. Act differently. Take fewer risks. She was a game changer, and for the first time in his life, Will cared about living to be an old man.

So he knew exactly what Blaine was thinking when the big man had told them he was leaving. Danny knew, too, because Danny had Carly. Before they left the courthouse, they gave Blaine everything he would need to find a car and get it running. They also gave him as much ammo as he could carry. Will figured Blaine would probably end up needing it sooner or later, especially if he had the bad luck to get caught up in the wave of ghouls hunting them. Considering

Blaine's run of luck lately, that was highly likely.

The First Assembly of the Lord had a parking lot that was mostly gravel. Danny, behind the wheel of the Ranger, pulled into it now, and they heard the crunch of loose pebbles under the truck's tires. They spotted a couple of cars in the parking lot, but apparently the end of the world hadn't convinced any of the church's followers to rush over for salvation. Or if it had, they hadn't made it.

They climbed out of the Ranger and grabbed the Remington 870s from the back. The shotguns were always preferable in close-quarters situations, whereas the M4A1s, slung over their backs, were more for long-range work. They wore their stripped-down urban assault vest over T-shirts and cargo pants, and carried just enough equipment for emergencies, with the rest piled up back in the courthouse.

They entered the church through a side door and were relieved to find that the layout was very simple. It was essentially one big room up front, with a reception area/baptistery that stretched about three meters from the front door, seventy percent of the church made up of the nave and pews; and finally, the lectern. An empty choir section looked back at them from one side of the church as they moved quickly across the communion area. All of it looked bright and sunny under large stained glass windows.

There were two rooms in the back. One led into a big office that apparently doubled as a sort of guest room, or possibly a consultation room, with couches, comfortable armchairs, and fold-out beds. The second room led into a big closet with janitorial supplies stacked on shelves and a large black piano covered by heavy tarp. Dust swarmed Will like thousands of floating termites when he pulled at the covers to see what was underneath.

He was surprised they had gone through almost the entire length of the church without encountering one ghoul. That was the case with most of Lancing. The city seemed to have very few of the creatures around, which was both a relief and eerie. Every city, regardless of size, had its share of ghouls. Lancing, on the other hand, was unnervingly lacking.

They went back into the nave and looked around, and it didn't take Danny long to find it. He went up the sanctuary, past a dust-covered communion table, and saw the big double doors on the floor, with metal rings for handles.

"Someone said they wanted a basement?" Danny announced.

"Big?" Will asked.

"Big enough."

"What about the doors?"

"Might have to reinforce them on both sides. Everything looks doable."

"Let's open 'er up."

Will stood next to Danny and they exchanged a brief nod, then grabbed a ringed handle each and pulled the doors free. Dust and time erupted into the air like a smoke grenade. They fought through the haze and took a quick step back, unslinging their shotguns in the same motion.

They stared down at complete darkness. There were no windows, so that was a plus.

Will grabbed three glow sticks from his pouch, snapped them, and tossed them into the basement, spreading the sticks around. Danny did the same with four more. Soon, they could see the basement's interior—or most of it, anyway, from their angle—against the green neon light. What the glow sticks didn't reveal, they swept with the tactical flashlights underneath their shotguns.

"Tornado basement," Will said.

"Tornado taketh, God builds a basement to preventeth," Danny said.

"That makes absolutely no sense."

"Of course it does. Open your mind."

It was a good-sized basement, essentially one big room about twenty meters across and just as wide. He saw a row of shelves to one side and more bulky, tarp-covered items along the walls. It was clear the church had been using the basement as a secondary storage area. A flight of metal stairs with big, wide steps led down.

"After you," Will said.

"No, after *you*," Danny said. "I insist. Besides, I'm the one with kids."

"Point taken, grandpa."

"Get off my lawn," Danny said.

THEY CLEARED THE basement in less than five minutes, finding nothing down there but old shelves and older boxes and more old stuff hidden under faded tarps. A door at the back opened up into a small bathroom, which, like the rest of the basement, hadn't been used in a while. There was a toilet and a sink, and little else.

Danny gave the bathroom a once-over. "A little backup water for flushing, some Drano to clear out the pipes, and maybe four or five weeks of intense cleaning with the strongest disinfectant known to man, and I wouldn't mind spending a few reading hours in here."

"Good luck with that," Will said.

"I'm serious. It could work."

"Captain Optimism."

Danny grinned at him. "You got any magazines?"

"I'll settle for some LED lamps."

Danny went back to the truck to retrieve those LED lamps. When he returned, they hung the lights from dangling hooks along the ceiling and walls, lighting up the basement like it was day. Or brighter than day, actually, since the LED lamps were notoriously hard on the eyes.

The basement, with its high ceiling, looked cavernous against the light, and Will thought it would work, even if they had to stay down here for more than a few days. Maybe a week, depending on how much Lancing had to offer in terms of supplies and, more importantly, danger. He was certain they had lost the ghouls back at Grime, but with so much at stake, he couldn't rely on gut instincts alone.

Not anymore…

THEY DROVE BACK to the courthouse, and Will saw Lara in the parking lot waiting for them. She had a shotgun slung over her shoulder, a sight that always made him smile.

"Blaine's gone," Lara said, as soon as he climbed out of the truck.

Will nodded. He had known Blaine would be gone by the time they came back.

"Should we go after him?" she asked.

"No," Will said.

"Why not?"

"Man's gotta do what a man's gotta do," Danny said, climbing out the other side of the truck. "Besides, he's probably halfway back to Grime by now."

"We don't have any right to stop him," Will said. "I'd go back for you, too, bullet holes or not."

She smiled, pleased, and walked over and kissed him. "My hero."

"Get a fucking room," Danny grunted.

"What else did you guys find besides the church?" Lara asked, ignoring Danny.

Will glanced down at his watch: 4:13 P.M. "There wasn't much time for anything else. But Lancing's a good-sized city; we should be able to stock up on the necessities before moving on to Beaufont Lake. For now, we need to do some work on the church before nightfall, so we should get over there as soon as we can."

"I'll get the others," Lara said, and hurried back into the courthouse.

Will looked around them at the city. It was quiet. He hated when it was this quiet. Even the birds seemed to sense something was coming. A murder of crows circled the roof of the Wallbys, dark wings flapping wildly. Will wondered how much of Hiller was still up there.

"What?" Danny asked behind him.

"Hmm?"

"You got that look."

"What look?"

"That 'I smell shit in the air' look."

Will frowned. "Where are they?"

"Yeah, you noticed that, too, huh?"

"Hard not to."

"Yup," Danny said. "Where the hell are they?"

They looked around at the city in silence, mulling the same question over.

Where the hell are they?

THEY PACKED EVERYTHING back into the trucks, including the two new kids, and drove over to the First Assembly of the Lord. Both Rangers looked worse than they really were. The bullet holes and shattered windows could be patched up and replaced, the engines ran perfectly fine, and the bad guys hadn't managed to shoot holes in the gas tank.

Thank God for amateurs.

The two new kids seemed to fit right in, but he wasn't too surprised by that. They had been surviving on their own for the last eight months. You had to be tough to do that, possess the kind of mettle most adults didn't have. The teenagers didn't really have weapons, except the revolver Josh had gone back across the street to retrieve. The gun was silver, but the bullets weren't.

"Silver bullets?" Josh said, when they told him about it. "I wish we had known about that. How did you guys know?"

Will told the story about being caught inside a derelict apartment building in Houston. It was the night of The Purge, and Will and Danny, along with their Harris County Sheriff's Department SWAT brothers, were supposed to be clearing out a drug den. Instead, they had found a nest of ghouls, and Will and Danny had ended up fighting for their lives for most of the night, moving from floor to floor, room to room. Until, finally, they had stumbled across two silver-edged crosses, either abandoned or forgotten by their owners. They had been using silver ever since.

"That's amazing," Gaby said. "It's like some kind of sign from God, isn't it? Who just leaves two crosses behind when they move? And those specific crosses, with silver? When you needed them the most, there they were."

"Will doesn't believe in God," Lara said. "I didn't use to, either, but now, I'm not so sure. Maybe not God, but some kind of divine being, watching out for us. I don't know. It's hard to just dismiss it. The silver, the crosses, these things that come out at night…" She shook her head. "I was raised in an atheist family. My mother would be horrified if she heard me waffling on this now," she added with a smile.

"I don't believe in God, either," Josh said.

Gaby looked surprised. "But your family goes to church every Sunday."

"Yeah, but that doesn't mean I believe in it. It's just that, I don't know, I haven't seen anything that tells me God exists."

"Josh, there are bloodsucking creatures that come out at night. If those things can exist, why not God?"

"I don't know," Josh said. The kid was struggling to express himself. "I just don't think the existence of one necessarily proves the other. Okay, I believe in bloodsucking monsters, or ghouls, or whatever you want to call them, but that's because I've *seen* them. Show me something God has done, and I'll believe in him, too."

Gaby looked exasperated. "Whatever. You're all crazy. You can't see what's right in front of you. I know there's a God, and he's looking out for us. He gave Will and Danny those silver crosses."

"You're just going on faith."

"Of course I am. That's what religion is, Josh. It's *faith*."

Josh was about to reply, but he stopped himself and reconsidered. He said instead, "Where do you even get silver bullets, anyway?"

Smart kid.

"You don't," Will said. "You make them. One of our main priorities when we go out on supply runs is to look for silver. When we get the chance, we melt the stuff down and cast it into bullets. That's why we only carry three types of weapons. Nine-millimeter for the Glocks, 5.56 for the rifles, and buckshot for the shotguns. That means you'll have to dump the fancy six-shooter."

Josh nodded. "It's not mine, anyway."

Josh and Gaby exchanged a brief, private look. There were some bad memories associated with the gun, apparently.

"How have you guys been avoiding the ghouls?" Lara asked.

"By hiding, mostly," Gaby said.

Josh added, "If we find a good hiding place in a town with enough food and supplies, we'll stay for a while. It's only until those things run out that we move on. It's worked for us so far. Until a few days ago, anyway."

"You're both from Dallas?" Lara asked.

"Ridley, Texas," Gaby said. "It's close to Dallas."

"Close enough that we get most of their TV," Josh said. "That's how I learned about what was happening. Reports coming out of Dallas, even before it hit Ridley."

"What about your parents?" Lara asked them.

"I don't know about mine," Josh said. "They went out on one of their date nights and never came back."

"My family didn't make it," Gaby said.

"I'm sorry," Lara said.

The teenage girl nodded, then turned to look out the window. Josh reached over and put his hand over Gaby's.

Lara sat back in her seat, clearly regretting having ever brought up the topic.

"Where were you when it happened?"

"How did you survive?"

Those were the questions on everyone's mind when they met someone new. As if knowing how someone else had survived added to the information wall about the how, why, and when of the current world.

It was human nature. The need to *know.*

IT WAS 5:16 P.M. by the time they got everything transferred from the trucks and into the First Assembly of the Lord's basement. There were no nearby garages and no real good choices to hide the trucks but the parking lot, so they decided to bring everything in rather than risk losing anything during the night. Thankfully, they had two additional pairs of hands in Josh and Gaby, so the transfer went much faster than usual.

While the others adjusted the supply crates along the walls and made room for eight people, Will and Danny left to visit a local hardware store a few blocks away. There, they loaded the Ranger with lumber—more than they needed, but Will didn't feel like making a return trip if they fell short.

They didn't bother with the stained glass windows or doors in the church. If the ghouls found them, they were coming in regardless. Instead, they reinforced the twin basement doors on the outside, then barricaded the interior side with two layers of lumber before sticking support beams under them in case of a prolonged assault. Through trial and error, they had found that basements were always the easiest to defend. Once you reinforced the doors, they were essentially impregnable.

When they were done, Danny turned to the others. "Bathroom's through that door in the back. It's a little icky—okay, I wouldn't want to use it with a twenty-foot pole—but if you gotta go, you gotta go."

They had crates full of the small 16.9-ounce water bottles, along with a couple of the five-gallon variety, the kind used for water coolers. The rest of the supplies were spread out, occupying nearly half the basement space. Bedrolls had been laid out, and Vera and Elise were already working on coloring books Danny had found for them during their stay in Grime a week earlier. Will wasn't surprised to see Josh and Gaby sticking close together.

Kids in love in the apocalypse, he thought with a slight smile. That would make a great title for a book. Or maybe a TV show. Something on the CW, of course.

He glanced at his watch: 7:41 P.M.

NIGHTFALL, AND HE waited for them to attack.

But they didn't.

An hour after nightfall, he was still waiting.

And they still didn't attack.

Around ten at night, Will sat very still at the foot of the metal stairs, his back to the basement doors, and listened. He heard snoring around him, but the four oscillating fans, all set on low, dominated the room with their quiet, soothing whirring. They had turned off most of the LED lamps except for the one that sat next to his feet. The lamp was on its lowest setting, providing just enough light for Will to make out the sleeping forms in the basement.

Eleven o'clock came and went, and still no attack.

After midnight, Danny untangled himself from Carly, slipped on his assault vest and picked up his weapons, then walked over soundlessly. He sat down on the steps with a can of fruit. He pulled the tab and tossed the aluminum lid into a nearby heavy-duty trash bag hanging off the stairs, then poked at a pair of pineapple slices with a plastic spork.

"Anything?" Danny asked, keeping his voice low.

"Not a squeak."

"Nothing at all?"

"Nope."

"That doesn't sound right. We lost them in Grime, but they must have picked up our scent by now."

"Must have."

"Maybe we're just really, really that good."

"Yeah, that's the ticket."

"Spooky."

"Yeah." Will picked up the Remington and stood. "Wake me when you get scared of the dark."

"Sure thing, pa."

Will walked over to Lara, asleep on top of her bedroll, rather than inside, because of the heat. She lay on her left side, slightly curled up with her back to him. He watched the fan nearby playing with her hair and smiled. She looked beautiful asleep.

He laid down the Remington and stripped off his vest and gun belt, then lowered himself next to her. Even asleep, she seemed to sense his presence and rolled over to her other side, her head coming to rest against his shoulder, while her right hand somehow ended up on his chest.

Will closed his eyes and thought about staying awake for a few more minutes. He couldn't chase away the nagging feeling that the ghouls were planning an attack very soon. It didn't make a damn lick of sense that there were no ghouls in Lancing, Texas. What the hell was going on out there? What were they *waiting* for?

But the attack never came, and soon Will drifted off to sleep.

And for the first time in a long time, he saw Kate.

CHAPTER 12

BLAINE

HE LEFT LANCING with plenty of sunlight to spare. The Toyota was in good working shape, with plenty of gas in the tank when its owner had abandoned it eight months ago. The car battery hadn't worked when he had found it, but Will and Danny carried spares in the back of their trucks, along with solar-powered chargers that delivered trickle charges to keep them filled until they were needed.

It was a pretty smart setup, and it didn't surprise Blaine that a pair of Army Rangers would think of something like that. Back when Blaine was traveling with Deeks and Sandra, they had simply swapped car batteries. Not exactly Boy Scout always-be-prepared, but then again, he was just some guy from the bad part of Dallas, so what the hell did he know about preparedness?

Blaine had the map spread out in the front passenger seat, not that he really needed it. From Lancing, it was a straight shot up US 287/Route 69 back to Grime. If Sandra was headed back there—back to where he was shot—she might end up in Grime again after not finding him on the road.

He drove as fast as he could, which was about forty miles per hour. When he didn't see anything looming on the road up ahead, he gunned it up to fifty, but even that was pushing it. Going fast was the reason he was separated from Sandra in the first place, a fact that weighed him down like a devil on his shoulder.

For some reason, he hadn't been shocked when the girl had told him Sandra was gone. That was his Sandra—spirited, full of passion and independence and fire. Suddenly free of the clutches of Folger, the first thing she would do was go back for him. Even if she thought he was dead. It made perfect sense only if you knew Sandra the way he did.

After a while he drove past the familiar two-story house from last night. It looked bigger, more isolated than he remembered. Blaine made a mental note of the house's location. You never knew when you would need a house for the night…

He glanced at his watch: 3:26 P.M.

Blaine began to slow down as he approached the old Jeep sitting in the middle of the road. Folger's Jeep. Exactly where Folger had left it. There were no other vehicles and no signs of Sandra.

He felt deflated and shot all over again. For some reason he had been almost certain she would be here, waiting for him, as if she knew he would be coming for her.

God, what was he *thinking*?

HE DROVE SLOWLY through Grime. He had no idea what kind of car she was driving. The girl had been too afraid to come out of the basement when Sandra had driven off. And the kid, Josh, had never bothered to check the garage, so he didn't know what car was in there, either.

Grime wasn't a particularly big town, but it did cover about four square miles, according to the map. That meant too many stores, buildings, and houses that weren't connected to Pine Street, the main road through town.

Blaine drove as slowly as he could, honking his horn as he went. If she was here, she would hear him. Probably. Or maybe she would think it was some crazy person and stay exactly where she was—hidden. After Folger, he wouldn't blame her.

It all added up to the same thing—finding her was going to be next to impossible.

But what choice did he have? Sandra was out here, somewhere, and he had to find her. Losing her to Folger and his men was like a knife through his gut, more painful than the bullet that had gone through his side or in his shoulder or thigh. No painkiller was going to dull that sensation. And to have been so close earlier today, only to lose her again…

It was *maddening.*

It took a while, but eventually he reached the end of Grime and stopped in the middle of the road. Blaine sat still for a moment, looking at the rearview mirror, back at the town behind him.

Would Sandra keep driving? No, that didn't make any sense. Why would she go backward, in the direction they had come? There was nothing back there. Dallas, maybe, farther back. But why would she go back to Dallas? The city, with its massive population, was more dangerous than out here, where the people were spread out and the buildings weren't thick with the monsters—or *ghouls,* as Will called them.

No, Sandra wouldn't go all the way back to Dallas. So where would she go next? He didn't think she would leave Grime just yet. The closest big city farther down US 287 was Woodville, which was too far away to make in the daylight left. Sandra wasn't stupid, so she would stay in Grime at least until tomorrow. He was almost certain of it.

Blaine put the truck in reverse and headed back into town. Except this time, instead of sticking to Pine Street, he started taking smaller roads, still honking his horn, looking for signs of survivors. Any damn sign at all.

He drove along dirt roads, passing homes that had been here for decades, possibly longer. A church that looked more like someone's house and a long building with a bright red roof. A Family Dollar store advertising a sale, a Chevron gas station at the corner of a busy four-way intersection.

Blaine slowed down and glanced at the truck's gas gauge. He was almost down to a quarter tank. Jesus, how long had he been driving?

He glanced down at his watch: 5:16 P.M.

He was pushing it now. Pretty soon, he would need to find shelter for the night, and that meant stopping his search. If he didn't find her today, she might be gone by tomorrow morning, and that knowledge hung over him like a black cloud. Sandra would be looking for a place, too, if she hadn't found one already.

Blaine stepped on the brake.

He had been looking at this all wrong. Sandra would know night was coming, too, so she would be looking for a place to spend the night.

A safe place.

BLAINE DROVE BACK up north along Pine Street with renewed purpose. This time he was looking for a building that looked safe, that could last the night. Sandra would be looking for the same thing, and from the main road, just like him.

He passed two, three churches, surprised that a town this small had more than one. He kept driving, until he realized he was almost out of Grime completely—again—and began to slow down. He saw a Shell truck stop to his right, with a parking lot dotted with two, maybe three dozen semitrailers and big rigs. The stop was in a somewhat deserted part of town, surrounded by undeveloped land and woods in the back.

But it was the semitrailers that got his attention.

He remembered what Miguel had said, about why Folger and the others were dragging a semitrailer around with them: *"Have you seen those semitrailers? You can't tear into those things. They're like a moving safe."*

Blaine remembered seeing the look on Will's and Danny's faces. They hadn't thought of it, but were wishing they had. And Sandra was kept in a semitrailer before she escaped. She would have known about their potential as a safety net.

There were cars in the Shell parking lot, sprinkled among the hulking semitrailers, as he pulled inside. The pumps served mostly diesel, which was probably why he didn't see very many cars frozen in line waiting for service. There were a couple of trucks, one with a pump dangling from its open tank.

He parked next to a big rig with hot rod flames shooting along the sides—it looked new, like it had been in service for only a few years—and a black big rig dragging one of those trailers with cars in the back, though this one was only half-full.

He got out with the AR-15 and began walking along the row of vehicles, banging on the sides as he went. He also started screaming, hoping that if he made enough noise, she would hear him.

"Sandra! Sandraaaaaaaaaaaaaa!"

His voice bounced off the metallic sides of the semitrailers, and he stopped to listen for a reaction. There was nothing, so he continued, rounding the back end of a trailer and banging on the next one, opening the back doors of the ones that weren't locked, though most of them were.

"Sandraaaaaaaaaaaa!"

He kept at it, banging on every trailer, shouting out her name each time he turned the corner and started on a new row. He felt like a madman and wondered if he was in fact mad.

Maybe. Probably.

Not that it mattered. He had to find her.

He had to find her.

The sun was still oppressive, and he was already sweating after only a few minutes of walking. Soon, he had other things to worry about, like the throbbing in his side. Blaine paused every now and then to catch his breath and let the pain subside.

Then he continued, starting over, calling out her name, banging on steel.

He lost track of how many big rigs he passed, how many rows he walked through, and how many times he shouted out Sandra's name. His throat started to hurt about the same time his legs started to feel a little wobbly.

After a while, Blaine stopped to gather himself, pressing one hand against the heated side of a semitrailer just to keep himself upright. Breathing became difficult again, and Blaine realized he had left the bottle of painkillers in the truck.

Way to go, asshole.

He was still leaning against the semitrailer when he heard the sound.

He wouldn't have heard it if he weren't standing perfectly still, trying to somehow will the misery coursing through his body into submission. It wasn't working, but it did keep him quiet as a mouse, enough to hear one of the doors of the semitrailer behind him slowly, carefully opening. Blaine looked over his shoulder and saw a man's head leaning out. The man was tall, with short blond hair, and as he turned his head, scanning the area, he had specks of yellow slivers in his eyes that reminded Blaine of cats' eyes.

The man had apparently expected Blaine to keep moving and

wasn't prepared to find him leaning against one of the trailers right next to him.

They locked eyes for a moment, and Blaine thought, *I know you, don't I?*, as the man pulled out his right hand and Blaine saw the steel barrel of an automatic handgun.

Blaine twisted around—too fast, and he almost heard the stitches in his side popping—and ducked just as the man lifted his gun and fired. The bullet slammed into the side of the semitrailer behind Blaine and ricocheted. Blaine swore he could hear the *zing-zing!* of the bullet over his head—not once, but twice, the first time when it came at him, and again when it ricocheted, nearly clipping him even as he was going down.

Blaine was unslinging the AR-15 as he slid down, willing every ounce of his body to *move move move*, even though it seemed like he was stuck in quicksand. He managed to get the strap of the rifle free, and he was still sliding down when he squeezed the trigger. The AR-15 leaped uncontrollably in his hands. Unlike the AR-15s he and Deeks had, someone had converted this one to fully automatic, and one heavy squeeze of the trigger unleashed nearly half of the magazine.

The guy was taking aim again when Blaine's bullets stitched the side of the open trailer door and kept going and going until one of them hit the guy in the neck, and he careened out of the trailer and landed on the hard concrete ground in a pile.

Blaine stopped firing about the same time his butt hit the ground. He stared forward at the blond guy as he lay at an odd, twisted angle, blood gushing out of a surprisingly small hole in his neck. The man's eyes were open, and he stared blankly back at Blaine, mouth opening and closing, like a fish trying to catch its breath on land. A thick pool of blood spread underneath the man, much faster than Blaine thought was possible.

He stared back into the cat-like eyes.

I know you, don't I?

The man closed his eyes, and his body seemed to sag, and then it stopped moving completely. His bleeding started to slow to a trickle, and the pool of blood stopped getting larger and settled, looking amazingly bright red underneath the scorching hot sun. Blaine and the dead man were squeezed into the confined space between two semitrailers, which was much hotter thanks to the two vehicles absorbing and coughing the heat back and forth between their steel bulks.

Blaine didn't know how long he sat there and watched the guy bleeding onto the warm concrete. The AR-15 rested in his lap, but it felt much heavier than before, and he had to push it aside in order to slowly rise, one hand holding the rifle as a crutch, the other searching along the side of the semitrailer behind him for extra support.

He was finally able to struggle to his feet and stumble off. He didn't have to look down to see he was bleeding again, that blood was seeping through his T-shirt. After some painful shuffling, he finally gave in and glanced down briefly. There was a nice, palm-sized patch of blood at his waist.

By the time he made it back to the Toyota, he was certain someone had moved it. That was the only explanation for why it took him so long to reach the damn thing. He was sure of it, though the screaming from deep in his gut became so loud and insistent he had to push the thought out of his mind and reach into the passenger side and grab the white, girly makeup bag.

He fished out the bottle of pills, shook out two, and downed them in one gulp. He climbed into the truck and sat in the passenger seat and waited, but nothing seemed to be happening. Why wasn't anything happening?

He shook out two more pills and dropped them into his mouth, crunching them first this time, hoping that would make some kind of difference. It must have, because he began to feel better almost instantly.

Blaine closed his eyes. The sun was too bright. It shouldn't be that bright. Why the hell was it so bright? What he wouldn't give for a little shade. Or a little nightfall.

That's crazy talk.

He chuckled to himself.

Or he thought he did. The noise might have been something else. He swore it even sounded like a car engine, approaching…

IN HIS PAIN-ADDLED dream, he was back with Sandra, and she was leaning over him, poking and prodding at his wound. Well, one of his wounds. When she lifted her hand, her fingers were covered in blood, but she still looked gorgeous with long blonde hair falling over half of her face. He was reminded all over again of what he wouldn't do for her. Which was nothing.

Sandra.

But if it was just a dream, why did it hurt so much?

She smiled at him, dried tears staining her cheeks. "Hey, there."

"I'm dead," he said, his voice hoarse (from all the screaming, probably).

"Not yet." She stroked his face, her fingers warm against his skin. "I got blood all over your face."

She picked up a rag from somewhere and swiped at his cheeks and jaw.

"This isn't a dream?" he asked.

"God, I hope not," she said, and laughed, except it came out as a half-laugh and half-sob.

"How did you find me?"

"I heard gunshots."

"This guy tried to kill me. He's probably still there…"

"Is he dead?"

"Pretty sure."

"Screw him, then." Her bloodied hands were busy just beyond his peripheral vision. "I went back for you, you know."

"I know. That's why I'm here. I came back for you."

She smiled. "Funny how it all worked out."

"Yeah," he said, and smiled back at her.

She kissed his forehead gingerly, then lingered with her face next to him, and he marveled at the green of her eyes. "The wound in your side's opened up. I'm not sure what to do."

"There's a white bag."

"I see it."

"Inside is some duct tape."

"Duct tape?"

"Apparently it's the next best thing to superglue."

"Superglue?"

"A doctor told me. Well, third-year medical student. Close enough."

She gave him a doubtful look, then picked up the small white bag, opened it, and pulled out the roll of gray duct tape. She looked at the duct tape, then over at him. "Are you sure?"

"No, but use it anyway. Pull a strip that's big enough to cover the wound. Then pinch it as tightly closed as you can with your fingers and cover it up."

"I don't know, Blaine..."

"It's okay. I'm all hopped up on painkillers anyway. I won't feel a thing."

"Okay," she said, still unconvinced.

He couldn't see her working, but he heard her tearing a strip off the duct tape. She picked up a bloodied bandage and tossed it out the open door. Then, giving him a brief but still very doubtful look, she put the duct tape over his side. He felt the cotton mesh against his skin, but didn't really feel much of anything else. There was just a lot of numbness.

She sat back and took in her handiwork. "Are you sure this was a good idea?"

"Am I still bleeding?"

"Well, no."

"Then it was a good idea."

She gave him a wry look. "Smart-ass."

"Where's your car?" he asked.

"Nearby. Why?"

"How did you get it to work?"

"What do you mean?"

"I mean, the battery still worked after all this time?"

"Oh." She shrugged. "The family whose house we stayed in had solar panels on the roof. They had the car battery charging the whole time. Why?"

"I dunno. Just curious, I guess."

She gave him an odd look. "You're close to dying and that's all you can think about? How I got an eight-month-old car to run?"

He somehow managed to grin, though he couldn't really vouch for how it came out. "I used to work on cars in my uncle's garage back in Dallas. I guess I was just curious."

"So now you know."

"Yeah."

She frowned at him. "You almost died."

"But I didn't."

"But you almost did."

"But I *didn't*." He reached up and stroked her cheek. "Face it, lady, you're not getting rid of me that easily. I don't care how many times you call the cops."

She smiled and leaned against his hand, and he felt her tears falling over his fingers.

IT WAS 6:17 P.M. when he was able to sit up, and Sandra transferred a box with bottled water, canned fruits, and a half-dozen bags of Kung Fu brand noodles from her car to his truck. Her white Ford Neon had barely any gas left, and she had been looking for supplies a mile away when she had heard the gunshots, arriving to find him lying unconscious and bleeding all over the seat of his truck.

She helped him into a new shirt from the care package Lara had packed for him. He hadn't even known there were clothes in there until Sandra rifled through it. "Boxers, too," she said.

"Lara's very thorough, I guess."

"What kind of people are they?"

"Good people. They found me on the road and picked me up and put me back together. They didn't have to, but they did."

She nodded. "I want to meet them so I can thank them."

"That's the plan."

She settled behind the steering wheel before glancing down at the gas gauge. "I think we need more gas."

"There's enough to make it back to Lancing."

"Let's hope so."

She slammed the door shut and turned on the engine.

"You didn't hear me screaming your name?" he asked.

"You were screaming my name?" She flashed him an amused look.

"Yeah."

"I'm sorry I missed it."

"I'm not. It was kind of pathetic."

"Now I'm *really* sorry I missed it."

Sandra drove them out of the truck stop, turning left and heading back along Pine Street/US 287. "Are you sure they'll still be in Lancing? What if we get there and they're gone?"

"The only reason they'd leave early is if something happened that put the group in jeopardy."

"How will we find them when we get there?"

"They were staying at a courthouse. The same place where Folger was keeping you in the semitrailer."

"Did you get them? Folger?" she asked.

"I got one of them, and Will got another one."

"What did they look like?"

"Why?"

"I just need to know…"

She kept driving, both hands on the steering wheel, and wouldn't look at him.

"It doesn't matter, Sandra," he said.

"Of course it matters," she said quickly.

"Not to me."

"Bullshit. It matters." Her voice was cold and matter-of-fact.

"No, you're wrong. It doesn't matter."

"You say that now. But it matters. Maybe not now, but later. It'll come up and it'll *matter*."

She drove in silence for a while, her fingers tightening around the steering wheel. They hadn't gone more than a minute before tears spilled down her cheeks and she stepped on the brake. He had to grab the door handle to keep from getting thrown into the dashboard.

She put the truck in park and looked over at him. She was crying freely now. "You're lying to me," she said through the tears.

He leaned over the seat. It took a lot of effort and a sharp jolt raced through his body, but he did his best to ignore it. He cupped her face in his hands, then kissed her softly on the lips.

She blinked back at him, and she looked as vulnerable as he had ever seen her.

"The day I found you was the best day of my miserable life." He smiled. "This changes nothing. Not a goddamn thing. Look at me, and tell me I'm lying to you."

She looked at him. Closely. Reading. Trying to decide if he was lying to her…

"Do you believe me?" he asked.

She nodded, and the tears rolled down in waves and she lunged forward and grabbed him in a tight hug. Blaine grimaced, the pain exploding through his body, but he said nothing and didn't make a sound, and held her back as tightly as he could.

CHAPTER 13

WILL

IT WAS SOMEWHERE between being awake and being asleep—a netherworld of sorts. That was the only explanation for why he was walking in a park, through a large baseball field with short, recently cut grass.

No one cuts grass anymore.

Slowly, the sights became familiar, and he pieced together the evidence.

There, a gazebo surrounded by hurricane fencing, with a sign across the entrance gate reading: "Gazebo Reservations Available." Long piers extending out into a still lake, and men and women in shorts and hats casting fishing lines with night crawlers attached to hooks. Behind him, kids playing baseball on a big, well-manicured diamond as parents cheered them on from the stands. The sound of aluminum bats striking cowhide-covered baseballs.

He was in Deussen Park, back in Houston.

A hot day, and he was wearing cargo pants and a T-shirt. He left the baseball diamond behind and walked across a large parking lot dotted with cars and trucks with empty boat trailers, though he couldn't spot any boats on the lake at the moment. The water was unsettling in its stillness, except for the occasional ripple caused by a soft wind. Lake Houston never had much shelter from the winds, so this was another oddity his mind couldn't quite explain.

"You're over-thinking it," a soft, familiar voice said.

Female. Very familiar.

"Oh, come on, you've forgotten about me already, Will?"

She stood in the distance along a two-meter-wide wooden walkway where the park ended and the water began. She wore a plain Sunday dress, but it looked radiant on her. He had forgotten how beautiful she was, how physically different from Lara. Taller, with a fuller chest, curves, and long, toned legs. She was at least thirty meters away, but for some reason he could make out every detail, which really shouldn't have been possible.

Kate.

She smiled across the parking lot at him. "Come on, Will, you know this isn't real, don't you?"

"What is this, then? A dream?"

"In a way. Come closer."

Suddenly he was standing next to her on the wooden walkway, and when she walked, he walked alongside her. They crossed the park casually, passing elderly men in tan hats perched on overturned pails with fishing poles, but no one seemed to have caught anything.

"This is Deussen Park," he said.

"Yes," she nodded. "You like this place. So do I. We have that in common, though I don't think we ever talked about it, did we?"

"No."

"I used to come here with my father," Kate said, "when I was younger. I had some of the best times of my life here. I was free then. But then again, what girls aren't at that age?"

"I can't picture you as a little girl, Kate."

"We were all little once, Will. Then we grow up, and we accept the reality of being an adult. Making decisions. Life-and-death struggles."

Deussen Park was clean, wide open, and free to use. He remembered making a point to come here at least once a month, if just to toss some bait into the water. Not that he ever went home with a lot of fish. That was never the point, anyway.

There wasn't much of a wind today, and yet it wasn't terribly hot.

"Don't take it so seriously," Kate said. "It's just a dream."

He looked closely at her. She hadn't changed much since the last time he had seen her, over five months ago. He remembered shooting her, back at Harold Campbell's underground facility, on the night the ghouls had laid siege to the place.

"No," she said.

"No?" he repeated.

"I didn't die that night. Not really."

"I didn't say anything."

"You don't have to."

"You can read my thoughts..."

She laughed. It was a beautiful laugh, full of life and energy and spirit. It was so unlike her. The Kate he knew was solemn and serious. He wondered if this Kate, the one he was walking with in this very strange dream that seemed at once real and so artificial, was in fact the real Kate, the one he never got to know.

"Yes," she said. "In a way. I'm sorry you never got to know me before...everything."

"You couldn't have been that different."

"Oh, I was. Very different. Driven. Ambitious. Frankly, the type of girl who never would have given you the time of day if you had asked me out in a bar. I guess you could say I was even a little stuck-up."

He smiled, and she laughed again.

"But that's the past," she said. "We're both beyond that now, aren't we? There's no use in clinging to the past. It's time to move on. Don't you want to move on, Will?"

"Do I?"

"Of course you do. And you should. I'm talking about the future, Will. And where we fit into that future."

"We?"

"We. The ones you call ghouls."

"You're one of them now. Lara said she saw you that night in the facility..."

"She was right. I was there."

"But you're...still you."

She gave him a pitying look, like a mother regarding an uncomprehending child. "This is just a dream, Will. Don't take it too seriously. How many times do I have to tell you that?"

"Then I don't have to take you seriously if this is all just a dream."

"You can ignore me if you want. But I'm real in the sense that this is me. Talking to you right now."

"I don't believe in psychic powers. You should know that."

"Funny, coming from a guy who deduced ghouls had a hive-like mind that allowed them to communicate. Remember?"

Will smirked. "So I was right."

"You've been amazingly prescient about a lot of things. The honest truth is, even he's impressed with you."

"He?"

"The one you call the blue-eyed ghoul. The first one you saw, outside the bank in Cleveland."

"Lara said you had blue eyes, too, when she saw you that night at Harold Campbell's facility."

"I did."

"Why?"

"I don't know. It just is. I haven't asked him, and he's never told me."

"You don't care?"

She shrugged. "Eventually, maybe."

"But you're like him now."

"To a lesser extent, yes."

"You control them. The ghouls."

"I have control *over* them, yes."

"So what are you exactly?"

"I don't know how to put it into words." She seemed to think about it, then smiled. "Maybe the assistant supervisor. I'm not the top dog, but when the boss is away, I get to play."

He smiled despite himself.

"It's the best analogy I could come up with," she added.

"You don't sound like a bloodthirsty ghoul right now. You sound …"

"Human?"

"Human."

She laughed that same lyrical, poetic laugh that didn't seem entirely real. "Because it's easier if I come to you this way."

"How are you doing this? How did you get into my dream?"

"Your mind is tired, Will. You're exhausted. When was the last time you had a good night's sleep that lasted more than a few hours? Hard to remember? That's because it's been a while. You're tired, Will. Very, very tired. And you should be, because you're right. We are hunting you."

"*You're* hunting me."

"Yes. He put me in charge. He thought I would be able to track you better, because of our past relationship."

"Because we slept together that one time."

She laughed again. "I like to think it went beyond that."

"Maybe it did."

"But it was good, that one night, wasn't it?"

He ignored the question, and said instead, "So you know where I am right now."

"Of course."

"Then why haven't you attacked?"

"What's the point? I don't have enough ghouls with me for a full frontal assault. 500 or 600 ghouls aren't going to take the basement. Like you always do, you chose too well. Even if we could break through the doors, I would lose too many."

"You care about them?"

"They're like my children."

He looked at her again, trying to see if he could pierce through the artificial veil that was Kate and see into the real Kate, this *new* "Kate" that had taken over the woman he had once known and, for one night, had loved.

But he couldn't see anything beyond an attractive brunette smiling back at him.

"What do you want from me?" he asked. "What's the point of all this?"

"I want you to give up, Will."

"Give up? That's your big sell? Just give up?"

"Giving up doesn't mean the end. Giving up means to stop fighting, stop running, and accept. You have to know, in your heart of hearts, that you can't win this. There are billions of us and there are thousands of you left. *Barely* thousands. You're not a stupid man, Will. Crunch the numbers. You know full well you're just delaying the inevitable."

Will smiled. "Then why are you so desperate to snuff us out if we're so insignificant to you?"

She sighed, sounding almost exasperated. "Because we have other things to do that don't involve you. But your continued existence—well, let's just say it bothers him. He would like to nip it in the bud."

"He sounds human."

"We were all humans, once. Like me. Like all the other children."

"Ghouls."

"That's such a nasty word."

"It's appropriate."

"Perhaps to you."

"If you're really Kate, then you know I don't give up easily. Even when the odds are against me."

"Of course I know, but I had to try anyway. I have to ask, though. Do you really think you can win this?"

"Maybe."

"Be practical, Will," she said, again with that air of motherly annoyance. "You're not just fighting us, you're fighting each other. Humans as a species are unworthy of survival. You're dying, being hunted like dogs, and yet you still find time to indulge in petty violence against one another. Humanity is not worthy of this planet."

"So I should just give up?"

"They depend on you. Danny. Lara. The others. If you let go, they'll let go, too. There's no point in fighting this. You know there's no point in fighting this, Will."

"And if I don't just...quit?"

She stopped and looked at him, and Will felt a breeze and shivered slightly, only to realize it wasn't from the air around him, but from the hard, piercing stare of her eyes.

"Then we'll keep hunting you. Wherever you go, wherever you think you're safe, you won't be. Never truly safe. We'll always be there at your door. Every hour that ticks down to nightfall will feel like the end of the world. Give up and save yourself all the misery, all the sleepless nights, all the pain of seeing your friends and lovers be lost to you one by one. Because it will happen. You know it, deep down. You're a soldier, Will, you've fought in wars. You know this is a war you can't win."

Will looked around him, at the short grass, the still lake, the fishermen perched on their overturned pails. It all looked so real, but he knew it was all a lie. There was nothing real here, just a construct of his mind. Even Kate, standing next to him, beautiful in her dress, was not real.

"You still don't think I'm really here, do you?" she asked, slightly amused.

He didn't answer.

"Oh, ye of little faith. It's a miracle you've survived this long, Will." She stepped closer to him, and he could feel her breath against his face, and it was cold and lifeless. "Give up, Will."

"No."

"You can't win."

"That's never stopped me before."

She looked like she was going to laugh, but instead she stepped away and turned around until her back was to him. "Have it your way. But don't say I didn't warn you when it starts going bad. Because it will. This world belongs to us now, Will. You're the anomaly. The cockroach in the light."

"These cockroaches have silver bullets."

"You think you have enough silver bullets for a few billion foes?"

"Attack, and find out."

She looked back and smiled. "Not tonight, dear, I have a headache. Besides, I'm a little busy at the moment. Can you hear it?"

"Hear what?"

"Listen closer. Can you hear it now?"

Will listened, but he didn't hear anything except the water lapping softly behind him, a child squealing with delight as she reeled in a catfish, and an old man grumbling as he packed up for the day.

Then he heard a slight, but very distinctive sound. Drifting to him from afar.

Pop-pop-pop.

It was the sound of gunfire. So light, so far away, that the noise was surreal, like faint echoes from history. He looked around him but couldn't trace the origins.

"I found him, Will," Kate said. "I found Blaine."

CHAPTER 14

BLAINE

"HERE?" SANDRA SAID, stopping the Toyota in the middle of the road.

Blaine leaned forward a bit to look past her at the two-story house, like some ancient relic from the past towering behind a sea of tall grass that hadn't been mowed in eight months. It looked the same as the first time he had passed it a few hours ago.

"That's it," Blaine said. He glanced at his watch: 6:57 P.M.

They could have easily reached Lancing before nightfall, but the more Blaine had thought about it, the more he wasn't sure he could find Will and the others if they had moved away from the courthouse, which they had already been planning to do when he left them. If they went all the way to Lancing and couldn't find the others, then what? They would have to find someplace to stay the night. That would take time and effort, neither of which he had very much of at the moment.

"You guys stayed here for the whole night?" Sandra asked.

"The windows and back doors are already reinforced. We can do the same to the front door."

"No basement?"

"None that I saw."

"Risky," she said, clearly not sold on the idea.

"It's probably the least risky choice."

She turned the truck into the driveway. With the grass grown on both sides of them, it felt like driving through a forest, albeit one with a smoothly paved road. The Labrador statue with its missing head still sat in the front lawn, while its companion guarded the front door.

Sandra put the truck in park and reached for the lever when he stopped her. "Wait."

"What?"

"Just in case." He reached into the ammo bag on the floor and grabbed a handful of shotgun shells with a white "X" marked across them.

"What's the 'X' for?" Sandra asked.

"They're filled with silver buckshot. You know how when we shoot the ghouls, they just keep coming?"

"They're impossible to kill."

"Not with silver."

"Silver?" She gave him another doubtful look. "Where did you learn that?"

"Will and the others have been using it since day one."

"And it works?"

"I don't know. I haven't used it before. They say it works, and I believe them. Why bullshit about this?"

She nodded. "They wouldn't."

Blaine ejected shells from the Remington shotgun and shoved in new ones with silver loads. "What are you carrying?"

She took a Glock out from behind her back. "I grabbed it last night."

"I have some ammo for that." He dug into the bag and came out with a magazine with an "X" across the side. "This should fit the Glock."

She reloaded the Glock, then gave him an amused look. "First duct tape and now silver bullets. Who are these people, the Lone Ranger and Tonto?"

THE INSIDE OF the house looked the same as it had this morning, with a repurposed door leaning against the wall next to the front door. The door still had long nails driven through it, ready to be re-used. Blaine wondered if Will and Danny did that on purpose, leaving a convenient way for someone else to seal the place later.

"We'll need a hammer or something to nail them back in place," Blaine said.

"I'll check the kitchen." Sandra walked off with her Glock at her side.

Blaine took the opportunity to struggle over to the foyer, where he sat down on a comfortable wooden chair. He made sure he could hear Sandra in the kitchen behind him, sifting through the drawers, before he took out the bottle of Tramadol and shook out two more.

As Blaine swallowed down the pills, he remembered Lara telling him jokingly, *"At this point I'm supposed to tell you not to take more than three a day or you'll run the risk of addiction, but I doubt you'll listen anyway."*

Smart girl, he thought, squirreling the bottle away.

Sandra came back with a rubber mallet. "Will this do?"

"Probably."

"You all right?" she asked, looking at him with one hand on her hip.

He smiled. That pose never failed to get his blood pumping. "I'm fine. Why?"

"You look pale."

"It's hot in here."

"I'll open a window." She smiled. "Just kidding."

He waited a few more seconds until he was sure the pills were kicking in. When he stood up and didn't feel any pain—or at least, not as much pain—he knew they were (mostly) working.

He and Sandra didn't have any trouble putting the door back in place. The nails were straight enough, and he banged the ones that were slightly crooked back into the correct angles. While Sandra held the door at a slight angle—so the length covered as much of the doorway as possible—he hammered the nails into the walls on both sides.

That done, they stepped back and gave it an appraising look.

"It looks decent," Sandra said. "We'll have to thank your friends for making it so easy."

"At this rate, I'll spend the rest of my life thanking them," Blaine said.

WITH AN HOUR until nightfall, they ended up in one of the rooms upstairs. It was clearly a girl's room, decorated with pink dressers, pink bedsheets and, of course, pink blankets. The idea of staying in the same room from this morning, where he lay half-dead, didn't appeal to him at all. They considered the master bedroom, but it was too far away from the stairs.

They had some time, so they lay down on the bed and he held her in the semidarkness of the room. They didn't say a word, neither one of them wanting to ruin the moment. The feel of her body against him was more than he could bear, but doing anything else was out of the question in his current condition.

Eventually, they got up and left the bedroom and walked the short distance to the top of the stairs, where they sat down next to the supplies crates they had brought in with them. Blaine put down the ammo bag with the shotgun shells and spare magazines for the AR-15 and Glock.

There were a couple of windows behind them, and tiny remnants of sunlight filtered inside through doors fastened over the frame. The stairwell was exactly in the middle of the house, with a perfect view of the kitchen and its island counter below. The second floor was a bit of an oddity—it was split up into two sections, which were joined in the middle by a walkway, like a bridge, with the stairs to one side and additional bedrooms on the other.

"It'll be dark soon," Blaine said. "If they find us and start up the stairs, I want you to go back into the bedroom and close the door."

"Not without you."

"Sandra…"

"No." Her voice was calm but firm. "Not without you. Not again."

He didn't think there was any point in arguing, so he said, "All right."

They sat and waited.

At 8:30 P.M., it got pitch-dark outside, and the less light he had to see by, the more tense he became. Slowly, the pain around his stomach came back. He shook out another pill from the bottle and saw Sandra look over. She sat in the darkness with him but was close enough that he could see the concern on her face.

"How many of those have you taken already?" she asked.

"Not nearly enough," he said glibly, hoping that would prevent what he knew would come next.

It didn't.

"You should rest," she said. "You can't keep going on pills alone."

"I'm not. I have you."

Her face remained grave. "I'm serious, Blaine. You need to rest. You were shot three times yesterday. That's not going to heal any time soon."

"There'll be plenty of time for rest later."

She sighed, but didn't pursue it, even though he could tell she wanted to. Instead, she laid her head against his left shoulder.

He was sure the ghouls would have found them by nine o'clock, but they hadn't. Or if they had, they didn't attack right away. He sat in the silent blackness with Sandra next to the stairs and listened.

For anything. For *something.*

He heard nothing, just the wind outside, sometimes pushing up against the wall or windows. He tried to imagine what ghouls moving through the lawn, with its forest of grass, would sound like. Barefoot movements were hard to detect, but dozens, maybe hundreds, might be easier to pick up.

Ten o'clock came and went.

Sandra started to relax next to him and wasn't clutching the Glock quite as tightly anymore. "Maybe we got lucky," she whispered.

"Maybe," he whispered back.

They were both wrong.

About ten minutes later, there was a loud crashing noise from the front of the house. Before the sound had even finished its echo, another loud crash erupted from the back. He recognized the sharp noises instantly. God knew he had heard them often enough—they were the very real clamor of shattering glass.

They're coming through the windows.

Blaine looked back at Sandra, her face awash in growing terror. He couldn't remember the last time she had looked this afraid, and he wondered if his own face mirrored hers. He hoped not. He wanted at least to give a reassuring look, as impossible as that seemed at the moment.

The sound of crumbling glass was soon followed by a cacophony of tumultuous, battering noises—flesh against wood. The ghouls had broken through the windows, only to find thick wooden boards in their path, and they were now beating on the barricades with their bodies. They hadn't even bothered with the front door, he realized. Was that because they knew it was pointless, or did experience tell them windows were easier targets?

"Stay here," Blaine said, and got up and rushed over to the bridge.

He looked down to his right, past the living room and at the four windows at the back of the house. The doors nailed over the windows were holding, though they trembled slightly each time the creatures struck them again and again and *again.*

He had forgotten how terrifying these moments could be. They had been so lucky the last few months, hiding at night and moving in the day. He remembered distinctly the first few days, the horror and terror of what was happening. The end of the world, playing out before his eyes. All those memories came flooding back now.

He hurried back to Sandra.

"Can they climb?" she asked when he reached her.

"I don't think so," he said. Could they? He had never seen them climb before…

"Are you sure?"

"I don't know. Why do you ask?"

"I hear something on the roof."

Blaine looked up at the ceiling. Not that he could see anything but a fan and pieces of peeling white paint above him. Earlier in the day, he had seen plenty of cobwebs and insects up there, too. He couldn't see anything now in the pitch-darkness.

"What did you hear?" he asked.

"I don't know. But it sounded like footsteps. You said they can't climb?"

"I don't think so. I've never seen them climb before, but I guess…"

Why wouldn't they be able to climb?

It wasn't like climbing took a lot of skill. All you needed were hands and feet, and the ghouls had both of those. So why couldn't they climb?

"It wasn't noise from downstairs?" he asked, hopeful.

"No," she said, shaking her head. "Something else, moving on the roof."

"I don't hear anything," he said, just before a large rectangular section of the ceiling on the other side of the bridge opened up with a loud creak.

The attic door!

A ghoul, its skin blackened and wrinkled, gaunt features mostly skin and bones, fell out of the freshly opened rectangular hole and landed on the second floor in a crouch that reminded him of a praying mantis. The figure was so emaciated Blaine thought he could almost hear bones clacking against joints as it moved.

The creature, resting on its haunches, searched the darkness and found them. Then it was running across the bridge in their direction. Blaine lifted the AR-15 and fired a shot and hit the ghoul in the chest. It was so close that he couldn't have missed even if he had tried. The ghoul seemed to stumble on something and flopped to the floor a couple of feet from Blaine, where it lay still.

"Holy shit," Blaine whispered.

Silver bullets. I can't fucking believe it.

He was rejoicing over that fact when something else—three—no, four—no, *ten*—bony shapes fell out of the attic opening. They were already rushing across the bridge at Blaine, moving silently, atrophied faces contorted in rabid poses.

Blaine switched the AR-15's fire selector to full-auto and squeezed the trigger. The room lit up with a strangely hypnotic staccato effect and one ghoul, then two, then three fell, but each time one ghoul splashed to the floor, another leaped over it and continued coming straight at him. All the way in the back, under the attic door, Blaine saw even more ghouls falling through the opening.

Blaine kept firing, backpedaling, and watching with horror and fascination as the ghouls fell like bowling pins. Even as he squeezed the trigger and kept it pressed, his mind was telling him he was using up the magazine, that he was going to be empty soon and there were still going to be *too many ghouls.*

By the time he fired his last shot, there were still five ghouls climbing over their dead. Others were leaping over the pile of bodies and using the four-foot-tall walls flanking the bridge as a catapult, launching themselves into the air. One of them came straight at Blaine and he managed to get the AR-15 up in time, smashing the stock of the rifle into its face and knocking it sideways, the blow carrying the creature across the room.

Then Sandra was there, firing her Glock into the remaining four creatures. She caught one as it was trying to leap up the bridge wall. The creature tumbled down through the opening. She kept firing, missing some but hitting others, until all three ghouls went down and didn't move.

Blaine didn't bother reloading the AR-15. Instead, he snatched up the Remington shotgun and turned to face the ghoul he had knocked out of the air. It was back on its feet and glowering at him when he shot it from ten feet away, obliterating the upper half of its body with silver buckshot. What remained of the creature keeled over to the floor, thick black blood oozing out onto the carpet.

"Blaine!" Sandra screamed.

Blaine turned back in time to see ten ghouls—no, fifteen—no, *too many to count*—falling down through the attic opening across the floor, like drops of rain, a never-ending flow of *click-clack*ing bones and pruned skin and hollowed faces.

"Room!" he shouted. "Get back into the room!"

Sandra backed up, struggling to reload her Glock. She gave up and turned and fled toward the room with the pink dresser and pink bedsheets.

Blaine began firing. Racking and firing, racking and firing, buckshot vaporizing the creatures, tearing flesh from bone—or what little flesh they had left over their bones—with brilliant efficiency. Their bodies were so thin, the flesh so weak, that each shotgun spray took out two, sometimes three ghouls at the same time.

But more of them were falling through the attic door every second.

Too many. Too many!

"Blaine!" Sandra shouted behind him. "Come on!"

He fired his final shot and snatched up the ammo bag and the AR-15 and ran to her. She was holding the door open and waiting, face contorted in mortal terror, when he rushed inside, ignoring the pain rippling through seemingly every inch of his body.

Merciful God it *hurt!*

She slammed the door behind him and locked it.

"Help me!" Blaine shouted.

He dropped his weapons and grabbed the pink dresser and pushed it toward the door. Sandra ran over to help as the ghouls began crashing into the door on the other side, the wall shaking from the impact. The wall hadn't even stopped trembling from the first assault when they crashed into it again, and again, and *again.* What looked like green neon stickers on the ceiling fell down and peppered the carpet in little glowing stars.

They pushed the big wooden furniture across the room. The only sounds were the ungodly loud crashing noise from the other side of door and the dresser's legs grinding away against the carpeted floor, tearing off chunks of fabric as it moved grudgingly.

Finally, they got the heavy dresser into position, just as a big chunk of the door tore free and Blaine saw dark black eyes peering in through a jagged hole. He drew his Glock, shoved it into the hole, and fired. He heard what he thought was a shriek and the eye was gone.

They stepped back from the door and listened to the pounding continue, the door and the wall and the dresser shuddering and threatening to fall apart with every loud crash.

The door won't hold. God help us, it won't hold.

Blaine snatched up the shotgun and handed it to Sandra. She took it without a word. He gave her the bag of ammo, then reloaded the AR-15 with the remaining magazine.

"Do we have enough?" she asked.

"I don't know. I hope so."

She began feeding shells into the shotgun, careful to choose only the ones with the white "X" written on the side.

Blaine hurried to the window. He peered out through a small sliver along the top that the door nailed across the window didn't quite cover. He saw darkness and a thin trickle of moonlight over the front lawn. There was so much grass between the house and US 287 he had difficulty making out the long stretch of highway in the distance.

Then, slowly, he began to make out shapes and forms moving along the tall blades of grass.

Ghouls.

There were a lot of them, so many he felt something in the pit of his stomach give, and suddenly the pain in his side and thigh and shoulder didn't seem to matter anymore. There were so goddamn many of them. Hundreds.

Thousands.

And among the unending tide, Blaine swore he saw something

he had never seen before. A pair of eyes. *Glassy blue eyes* in the middle of an obsidian ocean, staring back up at him, as if they could actually see him.

But that was impossible. Wasn't it?

A blue-eyed ghoul. Now I've seen everything.

He looked over at Sandra and found her staring back.

The door trembled violently in front of her, the room around them shaking every few seconds from the onslaught. How many were outside that door right now? A dozen? Maybe a hundred? How many could they possibly squeeze into the second floor before there was no more room? A few hundred?

"A lot?" she asked.

"A lot," he said.

He considered telling her about the blue-eyed ghoul, but realized it didn't matter. Blaine walked over and sat down on the bed with the pink covers and pink fluffy blankets. Sandra sat down next to him.

Another big chunk of the door, high above the reinforced dresser, splintered and flew across the room, but they didn't pay any attention to it.

Instead, Blaine reached over and took her hand and squeezed. "I'm glad I found you."

"You didn't find me, I found you," she said, smiling back at him.

Blaine put the AR-15 down on the bed and drew his Glock, held it in his lap. She leaned over and cupped his face in her hands and kissed him gently. She tasted of the road and the Texas heat, and he couldn't get enough.

He saw the hole in the door behind her crack a little wider, and a ghoul tried to shove itself inside. It succeeded in getting one side of its body almost all the way through before Blaine shot it through the chest and watched it go limp, the top half of its body looking as if it had merged with the door in some kind of strange experiment gone awry. But then something on the other side grabbed the dead ghoul by the legs and pulled it free, and almost immediately a second ghoul was there, trying to squeeze in through the same hole.

Blaine shot it, too.

Soon the small splintered hole in the door grew wider, and now two of the creatures tried to push their way in at the same time. They couldn't move the dresser, so they were trying to go over it. Blaine shot both of them, and their slack bodies were quickly pulled free and two more took their place.

He lowered the gun to his lap, then wrapped both arms around Sandra and looked away from the door, willing the sounds into the background, and concentrated just on her. Her smell, the feel of her body pressed against his, the contact of her hair in his face.

"What now?" she whispered.

"I don't know," he whispered back.

"There's always the closet. It looks pretty big. Stretching room and everything."

He smiled. "Yeah?"

"Yeah."

It wasn't such a bad life. He had gotten what most people never had—a second chance. And he had her. Sure, it took the end of the world for it to happen, but what the hell, eight months wasn't so bad.

He heard the door break, splitting into pieces, and the dresser tumbled backward under a massive assault.

Blaine emptied his Glock into the door, into the mass of black squirming skin, while Sandra began blasting with the shotgun next to him.

He was reaching for another magazine when the first ghoul made it inside.

Blaine shot it in the face from four feet away and watched it flop to the floor, but then two more—five more—no, a few hundred more were already taking its place…

BOOK TWO

THE HUNTED

CHAPTER 15

JOSH

PROS AND CONS: What were they?

Pros: They had fallen in with a group of pretty decent people, including two ex-Army Rangers. That was a major pro right there. Matt had been a good friend and a good partner, but Matt wasn't an ex-Army Ranger. Or an ex-SWAT commando. Will and Danny were both.

Cons: He couldn't think of any at the moment.

Conclusion: Things were looking up. *Hell yeah.*

It was the first time in a long time that Josh remembered sleeping all the way through the night. Usually his sleep was filled with nightmares and memories and fear, and he would oftentimes wake up in the middle of the night wondering if this was the day, if this was the moment he was going to die.

That wasn't the case this morning as he opened his eyes and stared up at the LED lamps hanging from the ceiling, set to low so they didn't blaze a hole through his eyeballs like they usually did. The basement was closed off from the rest of the universe, the better to keep it beyond the reach of the bloodsuckers. Or ghouls, as the others called them.

Josh sat up on his bedroll and looked over to his right, expecting to see Gaby, but she wasn't there. Instead, he heard voices and saw the doors at the top of the stairs were open, the thick slabs of wood used to reinforce them leaning nearby. He was the only one still in the basement, a realization that made Josh panic momentarily until he remembered the voices from above him.

He wiped sleep from his eyes and glanced down at his watch: 8:16 A.M.

Jesus, he had slept for more than twelve hours? Was that even possible? He didn't remember the last time he had slept for more than four or five hours at a time. All that waking up in the middle of the night, the nightmares, the fear, was not conducive to naps.

Josh stumbled up from his bedroll and looked for his tennis shoes. He found them nearby and pulled them on. He heard the voices traveling down from beyond the stairs again. Just the women.

Nice going, chump. Way to make a first impression.

He climbed up the stairs and slipped out through the basement doors and looked sheepishly around. Gaby sat on one of the pews playing some kind of clapping game with Elise and Vera. Carly was nearby watching them, one of those pump-action shotguns hanging off her shoulder from a strap. Lara walked back from the front of the church, also with a shotgun hanging off her shoulder. *They looked like road-weary warriors*, he thought, feeling a touch unmanly with just the Glock handgun stuffed in his front waistband.

Gaby looked over at him and smiled. "Look who's finally awake. We thought you were going to sleep forever."

"Why didn't anyone wake me?" he asked, slightly indignant.

"You looked like you needed all the sleep you could get," Carly said. "Besides, there's nothing pressing to do. Breakfast is over there," she added, pointing at some food laid out on a long bench nearby.

Josh was about to tell them he wasn't hungry when his stomach growled involuntarily, just low enough that only he could hear. Which was good, because he didn't really need the added embarrassment of a rumbling, empty stomach, too.

He walked over to the table and grabbed some Vienna sausages and was surprised to see fresh bread on a plate. Well, half a loaf, anyway. He nibbled on it and was shocked by how good it tasted. Of course, that could just have been the fact that it was the first piece of fresh bread he had eaten in months.

"Enjoy it," Carly said, "it's pretty much the last loaf we'll be making for a while."

"How did you make this?"

"It's bread, Josh, not gold from wine," Carly said, amused. "All you need is dough and fire. We have both. Well, we had both. Kind of short on the dough part at the moment."

"Eat up," Lara said. "We already ate most of it—it's only fair you get the final piece."

He discovered he was actually starving. Josh grabbed some bottled water, and even warm as always, it tasted almost as good as the bread going down.

"Where's Will and Danny?" he asked.

"They went out to do some scouting," Lara said. "They'll be back soon."

"Any word on Blaine or Sandra?"

"No, unfortunately." Lara looked at him for a moment, then asked, "Is that comfortable?"

She was looking at the gun in his waistband.

"Not really," he said, slightly embarrassed again.

"Come with me."

He grabbed the remaining piece of Vienna sausage and followed her back down to the basement. "These sausages are really good," he said, taking the final bite and wiping his fingers on his cargo pants.

"Those are the last ones, too. We're reaching lots of 'last ones' these days."

"Maybe Song Island has more."

"Hope springs eternal."

"And fish. They'd have fish, don't you think? Being on an island? I could go for some fish."

"What about lobsters while we're at it?"

"Yeah, those too. Why not?"

Lara led him to their stack of plastic moving crates. She opened one and pulled out a gun belt with a holster, which she handed to him. "It beats walking around with a gun stuffed down your front waistband."

Josh put it on. It was one size fits all. He cinched it, then tried holstering the Glock. The belt fit just fine, and it even had a flap to flick over the gun so it didn't fall out of the holster. There were also small pouches in the back and sides.

"Ammo," Lara said, and handed him four magazines. "The ones with 'X' on the side are silver bullets. The ones without are plain bullets."

"The silver bullets actually work?"

She nodded. "They really, really work."

He slipped the magazines into the pouches and instantly noticed the difference in weight.

Lara smiled at him. "Look at you. Bad-ass Josh."

He grinned back at her. "If only I had this in high school."

"If you did, I'd be reading about you in the news, Josh."

He laughed. "Oh, right."

HE WENT OUT into the parking lot with Lara when Will and Danny were half a mile from the church. Josh blinked in the sun, the heat already doing its job making his pants and shirt stick to him, and it was just morning. It would get much, much hotter in a few more hours.

They watched the black Ford Ranger, with its missing windows and duct-tape-covered windshield, turn into the parking lot and stop in front of them. Danny was driving, Will in the passenger seat.

Lara walked over to Will as he climbed out with his rifle.

Danny walked around the hood of the truck, grinning at Josh. "Look at you, all grown up and holstered. I definitely don't want to mess with you now."

Josh felt his cheeks flushing a bit. "Thanks, I guess."

"We're doing some shopping later. You should tag along."

"I will," Josh nodded.

"Good," Danny said, and smacked him on the shoulder, so hard that Josh flinched a little.

THEY GATHERED BACK in the parking lot an hour later, after Will and Danny had eaten. Josh felt a little underdressed next to the two men, who were both wearing some kind of slimmed-down version of an assault vest. They had radios connected to throat mics, and they carried rifles and shotguns. He only had the Glock in a hip holster.

Danny, as if reading his mind, grinned. "Don't worry, kid, one of these days you'll get a cool assault vest just like us. And a shotgun, too, if you're a really good boy."

"Gee thanks, Dad," Josh said, playing along.

Danny laughed and said to Will, "I like the kid, he's got spunk."

"Is that what he has? Spunk?" Will asked.

"Either that, or Cheetos." Danny glanced back at Josh. "You got spunk or Cheetos, kid?"

"I'll go with spunk," Josh said.

"Spunk it is."

Danny climbed in behind the wheel and Will took the front passenger seat. Josh slipped into the back, feeling like he was about to travel somewhere with mom and dad all over again. Except his new mom and dad were heavily armed and had probably killed a lot of people before the end of the world, which made their *"Don't make me stop this car"* a hell of a lot more menacing.

Josh saw Will press a Push-to-Talk switch connected to his radio and say into the throat mic, "We're good to go." He listened, then responded, "See you in a few."

"Got any more of those?" Josh asked.

"What's that?" Will said, looking over his shoulder.

"Throat mics. They look cool."

"That's because they *are* cool," Danny said.

"Sorry, kid," Will said. "We had two other pairs but lost them a while back. If we pick up some more, we'll let you know."

"Besides," Danny said, "they wouldn't look nearly as cool if everyone had one."

"Yeah, that, too." Will nodded.

"You guys are messing with me, aren't you?" Josh asked.

"Not at all," Will said.

"Of course we are," Danny said, backing them out of the parking lot and turning onto the empty road.

DANNY DROVE SOUTH, back in the direction they had come last night. Josh caught sight of an RV park to their right, then a chicken fast food joint to their left with two cars forever frozen in the drive-through lane. He wondered how that had gone down, with the car's occupants pulling up to the drive-through speaker box only to get something they weren't expecting.

Must have been one hell of a surprise. I went out for chicken and all I got was dead.

They drove for another couple of minutes, passing a McDonald's, a Burger King, and a pair of Valero gas stations on opposite ends of the same block, which had to be a first. There was a hardware store with a truck buried in the side wall and a battered motorcycle along the shoulder, missing its front tire.

Finally, Danny slowed down, passing a car wash to their left. He maneuvered around an overturned white Volkswagen Josh hadn't seen yesterday. Danny kept going for about twenty more yards, then turned into a parking lot. Josh glanced up at the big sign as they drove under it: "Lancing Veterinary Clinic."

"Someone has a sick dog?" he asked.

"Vets keep a lot of drugs inside," Will said. "Small clinics like this one are always preferable to the hospitals. They're too big, too many dark rooms. A place like this carries less risk."

"Yeah, but animal drugs?"

"It's just labels, and what can and can't be sold to humans without a prescription. Antibiotics, for instance. Think about it this way: what do they test most drugs on first, before they sell them to you and me?"

"Animals," Josh said.

"Exactly."

"With just mild chances of barking side effects," Danny said. "*Woof.* Excuse me, ahem."

There were two vehicles in front of the brownstone building, a blue Honda with its front windows rolled down and a slightly beat-up moped with the key still in the ignition. Danny parked next to the moped and they climbed out, Will and Danny slipping their rifles behind them and unslinging the shotguns. Danny grabbed one of the portable LED lamps and clipped it behind his gun belt, which looked much heavier than the one Josh was wearing.

"Close-quarter action calls for shotguns," Danny said. "Better maneuverability and spreading power."

"Josh," Will said, handing him an empty gym bag. "Stick with us for now."

Josh took the gym bag and nodded. He opened it and saw a second bag inside.

Will tugged open the glass door of the clinic. It pulled free without a fight for a brief second before the spring pulled it close again. They looked through the glass and the layer of dirt smeared on it at the empty front lobby. There was enough sunlight to make out chairs against the front wall, a receptionist desk across from them, and a hallway on the left side.

Will took hold of the door handle again and waited for a beat while Danny got into position. When Will pulled the door open this time, Danny slipped smoothly inside, raising his shotgun. Will nodded at Josh, who darted in after Danny. Will was right behind him as a brief wind twisted inside the room just before the door softly slid shut after them.

A large swath of brownish color *(dried blood)* covered one side of the wall, parts of it hidden in dark shadows. Josh heard clicking sounds and saw lights appearing from underneath the barrels of Will's and Danny's shotguns.

Gotta get me one of those, too.

Danny moved toward the reception desk, then peeked over it, his shotgun always moving in front of him. He pulled his head back and headed toward the hallway to their left. Josh followed, Will bringing up the rear. Sunlight illuminated most of the hallway, and what they couldn't see at first, Will's and Danny's flashlights illuminated.

It was a small clinic, with four doors along the hallway, including a restroom at the very back. They passed a door marked "Office" to their right, then came up to one marked "Exam Room."

Danny put his hand on the door of the exam room and leaned against the wood to listen. After a while, he pulled his head back. "Did I tell you I used to have a dog?"

"No," Will said.

Danny threw the door open and Will slipped inside, disappearing for a brief moment before there was a loud boom that made Josh flinch. Then he heard what sounded like something landing on a table. He peered into the room and saw a ghoul lying half-on and half-off the end of an exam table, half of its body sheared by buckshot. It looked dead, thick black blood dripping onto the polished tile floor under it.

Silver buckshot. It actually works.

Suck on that, mofos!

Danny went into the exam room and unclipped the LED lamp from his belt. He turned it on to full power and the room instantly swelled with light. Danny set the lamp on a counter as they began rummaging through drawers and shelves.

"What are we looking for?" Josh asked.

"Syringes, gauze, gloves, small vials of medicine," Will said. "Anything that looks useful goes into the bag. Lara will pick through it later."

Josh carefully stepped around the dripping ghoul blood and opened the closest drawer. He looked in at boxes of gloves and gauze tape stacked in neat rolls. He tossed them into the bag. Will and Danny put everything they found on the counters, and Josh scooped them up, careful with unopened boxes containing small vials. They quickly filled the bag, and Josh had to open the second gym bag. He began filling that one up, too.

"His name was Rocky," Danny was saying. "Cutest dog you'll ever see. He had this long tail he loved to wag. And he wagged and wagged and wagged. I thought about calling him Waggler, but you know, that would have been weird."

"Cause Rocky isn't weird for a dog," Will said.

"It's not weirder than Waggler. I mean, can you imagine? 'Come here, Waggler! Come here, Waggler!' That's just weird, man."

"So what happened to Waggler?"

"You mean Rocky."

"Right, Rocky."

"Well, everything was just fine and dandy, until one day my uncle accidentally ran him over. Or at least, he said it was an accident. Personally I thought the old-timer had it in for Rocky."

"Ouch."

"That's what it said."

Josh chuckled.

"I like this kid," Danny said.

"Don't encourage him," Will said.

THE THIRD AND last door in the hallway was a janitor's closet that doubled as a garbage room of sorts, with old, used items in cinched garbage bags along a metal shelf. They opened one of the bags and found used rags. Another yielded used sponges.

With two gym bags full of syringes, pill bottles, and other medical supplies, they headed back to the front lobby. Josh carried one bag while Will carried the other. They were in the parking lot and under the bright, hot sun again, and Josh was feeling good. He had done his part and had even learned that silver actually worked on the ghouls, just as promised. The idea that he could finally kill these things made him strangely giddy.

Suddenly both Will and Danny froze in front of him, and as Josh tried to figure out why, he heard the distant echoes of gunfire in the air. It didn't take long to realize where it was coming from.

The church.

"It's Lara," Will said. He was holding one hand over his right ear—over the earbud. "Someone's attacking the church."

They ran to the truck. Josh hadn't even gotten all the way inside when Danny turned on the engine and put the car in reverse and stepped on the gas. Josh careened across his seat, the gym bag falling to the floor. He picked himself back up as the truck sped out of the parking lot and onto the road, swerving around the same overturned Volkswagen.

"We're coming," Will said calmly into his throat mic.

Jesus, he's calm.

"ETA ten minutes," Will said.

"Five minutes," Danny said, gunning the gas. Josh heard the truck roar loudly under them.

"Five minutes," Will repeated into the radio. "Hold on, we're coming."

The truck shot forward and Josh toppled in his seat a second time.

Danny maneuvered around cars in the road, swiping other vehicles that he couldn't get around fast enough. Soon he was driving almost entirely on the shoulder, the buildings around them flashing by in a blur.

Will had put down his shotgun and was unslinging his rifle. His voice, still unfathomably calm: "Josh, when we get to the church, you need to stay in the truck."

"Gaby's in there," Josh said.

"Have you ever shot someone before?"

I shot my friend Matt, he thought, but said instead, "No."

"Stay in the truck," Will said, and the hard, unmistakable, *"Don't argue with me"* tone in his voice reminded Josh so much of his father.

Josh nodded. He wondered if he was secretly relieved and just didn't have the courage to admit it. After all, they were running *toward* gunfire. It wasn't something he had ever pictured himself doing. Ever.

More gunshots. Louder somehow, more persistent.

"Danny, faster," Will said.

Danny didn't answer, but he somehow coerced the truck into going even faster. Josh didn't think that was possible, but he was wrong. The truck started to shake violently as they tore down the street.

CHAPTER 16

LARA

HER BOYFRIEND, WHO could very well end up being the love of her life, had told her about his dream last night. More importantly, he had told her about *who* was in that dream with him.

"It felt real," Will said. "But unreal at the same time. It's difficult to explain. Like being caught between sleeping and waking. It's hard to tell what it is while you're in it. It's still hard to tell now."

"But Kate was there?" she asked.

"Yeah."

"And she specifically mentioned Blaine."

"Yes."

"What else did she say?"

"That was it."

"Is he alive?"

"I don't know."

Dreams.

It wasn't bad enough the ghouls were hunting them—now they were invading their dreams, too. Lara might have even felt indifferent about it if it had been someone else who had showed up in Will's dream.

But no, it had to be Kate.

Kate, who Lara had seen that night when the ghouls laid siege to Harold Campbell's facility. Not the Kate she knew, however briefly, but the ghoul version of Kate. The new Kate.

Of course it had to be the ex-girlfriend.

She believed Will when he said he didn't think it was a dream. Not entirely a dream, anyway. Even the third-year medical student in her had come to believe a lot of things lately. Things she would have scoffed at just eight months earlier. Lara was always a practical person, a direct result of her upbringing. She went where the evidence took her, not where her imagination led. But she had seen too many things to start ignoring the possibility of something as metaphysical as psychic dreams now.

Of course, just thinking those words (*psychic dreams*) made it sound absurd.

After Will and Danny came back from their early scouting run, they left again with Josh in tow. That left Lara with Carly, Gaby, and the girls. The time away from the men always gave her other things to do, like keep up with hygiene. She and Carly had amassed an impressive crate with nothing but feminine products over the months, something Gaby gleefully attacked, having gone without most of them for so long.

Gaby was brushing her teeth with a battery-powered electric toothbrush in the basement bathroom when Lara found her. They had cleaned as much of the bathroom as they could—or as much as humanly possible. Even if they left the church tomorrow, at least they could enjoy the bathroom now. Lara and Carly had learned to carve out as much of the old world as they could, even if it was just for a few days—or in some cases, a few hours. You had to make do with the simple pleasures, or else the long days and nights wouldn't be worth it.

"Are you and Josh having sex?" Lara asked Gaby.

The teenager almost choked on the toothbrush, eliciting a smile from Lara.

Gaby quickly washed and rinsed out the toothpaste into the sink with bottled water. Lara thought her cheeks were flushed red. "God, no."

"Oh, I thought… Sorry, I shouldn't have assumed." Something else occurred to her, and she asked, hesitantly, "You're not…?"

Gaby giggled. "No, I'm not that, either."

"Josh?"

"I don't know. You think?"

"Well, if you're not having sex with him, then I'm guessing probably."

Gaby leaned against the sink and seemed to think about it. "We never talked about it. It never occurred to me to even think of him in that way. I always just thought of him as more of a little brother."

"He's not that little, Gaby."

"I know." She smiled. "I know he likes me. That's obvious. I just don't know how I feel about him, you know, in that way."

"You wanna know what he thinks?"

She laughed. "He's a guy, Lara. I know what he thinks."

Lara smiled, too. She could imagine how popular Gaby had been back in high school. The tall and athletic frame, the better-than-average breasts, and the long blonde hair. She must have driven the boys crazy and made the girls nuts.

"Just in case," Lara said. She took out a small white-and-blue box from her back pocket and handed it to Gaby.

"The patch?" Gaby said, taking the box.

"Just in case. It's easier to use than the Pill, and stopping everything to pull out a condom might not be very romantic."

The Ortho Evra Patch, otherwise known to women everywhere as "the patch," was a contraceptive device placed on the body that released estrogen and progestin. It did one thing and did it well—it prevented unwanted pregnancies. Lara and Carly had been using it for a while now, because the patch was more efficient than the Pill, which required daily dosage and didn't last quite as long. One patch was good for an entire week, and you didn't need it for the fourth week during your period. They usually found them by the packs in drug stores, probably because, Lara guessed, contraceptives weren't in high demand at the end of the world.

"Were you sexually active before?" she asked the teenager.

"A few guys," Gaby said. "I wasn't a slut or anything."

"I didn't mean it that way. God, I hope you didn't think I meant it that way."

"It's cool," Gaby said. She opened the box and pulled out the two-inch, peach-pink squares. "My mom got me the Pill when I was sixteen."

"So, you haven't had sex since…?"

"Just once. With Matt, and it was only the one time when I was on my period."

Lara knew about Matt, a young man who had traveled with Gaby and Josh after The Purge. He was gone—turned, according to

Josh, when one of the ghouls bit him.

"That was smart," Lara said. "Waiting for your period."

"I'm not as airheaded as people think."

"You never struck me as being an airhead, Gaby."

"No?"

"You've survived eight months in...*this*. I think you're anything but an airhead."

"Thanks." She shrugged. "Sometimes it's easier to let people think that about me. When people think you're not very bright, they don't expect a lot from you." She grinned. "And I can get away with more."

"Smart girl."

"Shhh," Gaby said, putting a finger to her lips. "Don't tell anyone."

"Scout's honor."

Gaby tucked the box into her back pocket. "You think I should? With Josh?"

"I don't know the two of you well enough to say either way. What do you think? Do you like him?"

"I do. I just never thought of him in that way. How did it work out for you and Will?"

"It took a while."

"How long?"

"About three months. Things were a little hazy back then."

"Josh and I have been hiding together for eight months. He's a really good guy." She smiled, and Lara could tell she genuinely liked Josh. "And he hasn't tried anything. Ever. Which is really cool of him."

"He does look like a good guy."

"He is."

"Besides, it's slim pickings out there."

"Yeah, getting slimmer every day." Gaby made a face. "Then again, it's easy for you and Carly to say. Your men are hot."

Lara laughed. "They are, aren't they?"

"What about Will?" Gaby said, grinning mischievously. "Wanna share him?"

"I bet I know what his answer would be if I asked him."

"Men."

"Yeah, men," Lara smiled back.

Gaby was about to respond when they both heard a loud *bang* from above them—from the church.

"Stay here!" Lara shouted.

Gaby stared back at her, frozen in place.

Lara was already running. She snatched up the Remington leaning against the bottom of the stairs without ever breaking stride. She climbed the stairs, taking the steps two—then somehow, three—at a time, when she heard screaming *(Elise!)* and what sounded like male voices, shouting. She couldn't make out the words, but as she took the last step and burst out onto the chancel, she braced herself for the worst case scenario.

She saw, in the blink of an eye, the girls and Carly, hiding behind one of the pews in the center of the nave. The girls were stricken with terror, an image that seared itself into Lara's soul. Carly didn't have her shotgun, her Remington leaning against a pew well beyond her reach. Hearing Lara coming up from the basement, Carly looked up, and the other woman pointed desperately to her left, at the hallway that led to the side door and connected to the parking lot.

Lara turned just as a man emerged out of the connecting hallway, his head appearing from behind a post with a round knob at the top. He was tall and thin, with a large shock of white hair, and he was aiming an AK-47 assault rifle in Carly's direction.

The man with white hair shouted, "Stay down! Don't do anything stupid!"

Lara racked the shotgun, the loud sound drawing the man's attention. He turned and saw her and dived back into the hallway just as Lara fired, obliterating the post and cratering the wall in the spot where the man had stood just a second ago.

She heard but didn't see the man shout, "Fuck!"

Lara quickly grabbed the doors to the basement and looked down and saw Gaby at the bottom of the steps. "Stay inside!" Lara shouted, and slammed both doors shut. Without the extra lumber Will and Danny had put on the doors last night, the doors were easy to swing.

She looked up as a second man—tall, with a thick neck and bald head—ran out of the hallway. He also had an AK-47, and he spun and saw her and opened fire, and Lara leaped to the floor as the podium in front of her splintered into a thousand pieces. She scrambled up and ran for cover, thin slivers of wood whipping around her like bullets.

I'll never make it. I'll never make it!

She threw herself forward, diving headfirst into the choir section, landing on the back of her neck. Lara swore she had snapped her spine, but when she could still scramble back up to a sitting position behind the thick wooded wall that separated the choir from the chancel, she realized she was still in one piece. Barely.

She had two seconds to rejoice before the man began firing again, bullets chopping through the panel. Lara lunged flat against the floor, her face pressed into the dust-covered carpet as the man kept firing and firing, stitching the barrier above her in a ragged line, probably hoping to hit her if she had begun crawling away. She hadn't, but he didn't know that.

Lara grabbed the radio from her hip and shouted into it, hoping someone could hear her over the vicious sound of assault rifle fire and shearing wood: "Will! We're under attack! Two men with assault rifles!"

"We're coming," Will said through the radio, in that calm voice of his that both soothed and annoyed her. "ETA ten minutes."

Then she heard, in the background of the radio, Danny's voice: "Five minutes."

"Five minutes," Will repeated. "Hold on, we're coming."

"Hurry!"

Lara dropped the radio as the last bullet punched through the wooden panel behind her. She heard clacking sounds and knew they were reloading.

Five minutes?

Then she heard gunshots, and to her amazement, knew they were from a Glock handgun, coming from the other side of the church. The old Lara would never have known something like that. But the new Lara, who had spent hours and days and weeks learning to shoot with Carly and Will and Danny, knew what a Glock sounded like.

Carly!

She heard the AK-47s firing back, and suddenly the Glock stopped shooting. Lara thought she could even hear the sound of wood crumbling under the unrelenting assault, and even through that, screaming.

The girls!

Lara took a breath and stood up and saw, in a heartbeat, the two men: the man with white hair and with the one with the bald head—standing near the base of the chancel, calmly firing into the nave, their bullets smashing into the pews Carly and the girls were hiding behind. Lara saw flashes of clothes and hair—Elise and Vera, on the floor, hands thrown over their heads, screaming at the top of their lungs as wood splintered around them.

Stay brave, girls, stay brave.

The man closest to her, the bald one, must have sensed her, and he began turning around. Lara shot him from ten yards away and watched the top portion of his body, including his face, turn into a bloody red pulp.

The man with the white hair spun around and opened fire. Lara had to drop back behind the choir section, what was left of the wooden panel barrier exploding into chunks around her, pelting her hair and clothes and arms with sharp, stinging wooden spikes. Lara clutched the shotgun, refusing to let go, sliding the fore end back and forward to load another shell into the chamber.

Five minutes, Will? You've got to be kidding me!

She heard the Glock shooting again, interrupting the seemingly never-ending volley of AK-47 fire. Then the man with white hair shouted, "God, shit!" and he stopped firing, but the Glock kept shooting.

Lara peered through a big hole blasted in the wooden paneling and saw the man with white hair running away, dragging one leg behind him. He was bleeding, blood gushing out of his right leg from a gunshot wound. It looked bad.

Must have hit an artery.

The man was dodging bullets and moving and trying to reload his AK-47 at the same time. Sections of the hallway around him were being chipped away by nonstop gunfire from the nave. He looked as if he was in shock, and she almost felt sorry for him. He finally gave up on the rifle and tossed it away, then lunged into the hallway, leaving a thick trail of blood behind him.

Lara pushed herself up from the floor, shaking loose pieces of wood from her hair, and stood up slowly, cautiously. She saw Carly across the nave, shooting after the man with white hair. Carly had stepped out from behind the pew and was unloading shot after shot after shot, looking as calm as Lara had ever seen her.

You go, girl.

Elise and Vera were still hiding behind the pew—or what was left of it—their bodies pressed against the floor. They had stopped screaming. A dozen or more of the pews around them were shredded with bullets. It was a miracle all three were still alive.

Carly finally stopped shooting, but only because her magazine was empty. She slapped in a fresh one and jerked back the slide. She glanced down the hall, but there must not have been any targets, because she finally looked over as Lara climbed out of the choir section, shotgun aimed at the hallway.

"Are you okay?" Carly shouted across at her.

"I'm okay," Lara shouted back.

There was debris all over the floor, and she felt pieces of the altar and podium crunching under her boots.

"Lara, you're bleeding!" Carly shouted.

"What?"

Lara looked down at herself, but couldn't find any blood. She looked higher, at her chest, shoulders—until she felt small drips of wetness against her left arm. There were thin rivulets of blood washing down her arm, all the way to her fingertips. She was surprised she was bleeding, because she didn't feel any pain at all.

When did that happen?

She had apparently been bleeding for a while, leaving behind a thin trail of blood all the way from the choir section. She sat down heavily on the carpeted floor and laid the shotgun down next to her, within easy reach in case the man with white hair came back. Her vision blurred a bit, but she managed to look away from her bloodied fingers and over to the man lying awkwardly on the steps in front of her. She remembered he was bald and had a large, meaty neck, but she wouldn't have known all those things now because there was just a big splotchy red mess where his head used to be.

So that's what a shotgun blast at close range does to the human body.

She became aware of Carly crouching next to her, holding her up because she had lain down at some point. "Oh shit, you're such a bleeder, Lara," Carly said, her voice somewhere between panic and laughter.

"It's okay," Lara heard herself say. "Bullet went clean through, I think. You just have to clean the wound and wrap it up and I'll be fine. It's okay," she said again, unable to take her eyes away from the dead man in front of her.

Two. That's two people I've killed now.

There was loud popping gunfire from outside the building, and she instinctively reached for the shotgun. But she couldn't find it. Someone must have taken it. Or had she left it somewhere else?

She opened her mouth to tell Carly that she couldn't find her weapon, that the man with white hair was coming back and Carly had to be ready to fight him off again, but nothing came out. Instead, she felt extremely tired, and despite her best efforts, Lara closed her eyes and lost consciousness.

WILL WAS SMILING down at her when she opened her eyes. There was a throbbing in her left arm, a mixture of pain and an itch she desperately longed to scratch.

I thought getting shot would hurt a bit more.

"Five minutes," Will said. "You couldn't have waited five minutes?"

She smiled up at him. "What happened to the other guy? The one with the white hair?"

"He met us in the parking lot."

"And…?"

"And that was it."

"Oh."

"How does it feel?" he asked.

"How does what feel?"

"To get shot."

"You don't know?"

"I've never been shot before."

"But you've been to war."

"I have."

"And you've never been shot?"

"Never. I guess I've just been really lucky."

"Good for you." She tried to sit up, and her entire body exploded with sensations she didn't think were possible and never ever wanted to feel again.

Oh, so there's the pain.

Will helped her lean back against the basement wall. Someone had cut away her shirt's left sleeve and wrapped the wound with gauze tape, and she was wearing a makeshift sling using materials from two different-colored shirts.

"You did this?" she asked.

"I cleaned it, sutured the wound, and wrapped you back up," he smiled. "I'm no third-year medical student, but I think I did all right."

"You did fine as long as I'm not bleeding to death."

"You're too kind."

"But did you have to mutilate my shirt, too? Do you know how hard it is to find good shirts in the post-apocalypse?"

"Sorry." He sat on the floor next to her, hands over his knees, watching her closely.

He wants to make sure I'm fine.

"I want a new shirt," she said.

"I'll take you shopping once we get to Beaumont."

"When are we going to Beaumont?"

"As soon as you can stand up."

"I thought we were staying here for a while."

"Lancing's run its course. Too much bad mojo here."

"'Bad mojo?'" She flashed him an amused grin. "First it's cavorting at a park in psychic dreams with your ex-girlfriend, now it's bad mojo? My, have we changed."

He laughed. "I can be pretty open-minded when given the chance. Besides, we all took a vote, and we decided to skedaddle, as Danny would say."

"I didn't get a vote."

"I voted for you."

"How kind of you. Should I ask what I-slash-we voted for?"

"You could, but it's my constitutional right as an American not to tell you."

He was still watching her very closely, with that very serious look that told her he wasn't going to be deterred.

"I'm fine," she said.

"I know. The bullet went clean through. You'll be tap-dancing in a few days."

"I don't know how to tap dance."

"You'll be learning how to tap dance in a few days."

"Sounds good." She sighed, then looked back at him, matching his serious gaze. "What is it?"

"I'm afraid."

That caught her by surprise.

Will wasn't afraid of anything. Even in the midst of life and death, he was always calm. She had come to see him as the Plymouth Rock in her life, keeping her anchored in the moment, but longing for the future, a reminder that everything would be fine and all she had to do was believe in him.

To hear him admit he was afraid made her shiver a bit.

"Why?" she asked.

"It's Kate. What she said in the dream."

"It was just a dream…"

"It was more than that. It was really Kate."

"What else did she say?" Lara asked, almost afraid to hear the answer.

"She told me it wasn't going to end until this was over. Until *we* were over. They're going to keep coming after us, Lara. That scares me, because it means whatever I do, wherever we go, it might not be enough to protect you."

"I'm fine," she said, and leaned over and kissed him lightly on the lips. "And I'll stay fine as long as you're with me. As long as we're together."

She smiled at him, hoping some of that got through. Maybe it did, because he smiled back and suddenly he looked like his usual Will self again.

Strong and assured and calm. Always calm.

"What else did Kate say in the dream?" she asked.

"She knows we're here. In this basement."

"So that's the real reason we're leaving."

He nodded.

"The others?" she asked.

"Outside, getting ready."

"Is it still morning?"

"A few minutes past noon."

"You should have woken me up earlier."

"You needed the rest. And besides, we still have plenty of time. We can be in Beaumont in a few hours, barring any troubles along the road."

"That's the tricky part, isn't it?"

"That's always the tricky part, yeah."

"We'll be fine," she said, hoping that he understood she didn't mean just about Beaumont, but about everything.

He did. "We'll be fine," he nodded, and smiled at her again.

"Okay, then. Now, about getting me a new shirt..."

THE OTHERS HAD packed most of their things back into crates and carried them out to the parking lot while she had slept. There were only a few crates still left in the church when she emerged from the basement.

The girls were helping out with the smaller items, though Vera actually managed to carry one of the ammo bags by herself. Elise made do with their backpacks, filled with clothes, shoes, and socks. Little things they had come to rely on, that they could still call their own. Lara felt guilty watching them do all the work while she could only manage her shotgun and her personal backpack. She didn't like having only one arm.

She walked across the chancel and stopped when she saw the thick patch of dark red on the brown carpeted stairs. The body was gone, and she wondered briefly where the others took it before deciding she would rather not know.

She went outside, where Danny was stacking crates into the back of a Honda Ridgeline truck. Will and Danny had switched the damaged Ford Rangers for the Ridgeline and a white Nissan Frontier. Both trucks looked new, with four doors apiece. The trade-off was the truck beds, which were smaller and couldn't carry everything they were used to taking with them. To make up for that, Will and Danny had hitched a five-by-ten U-Haul cargo trailer behind the Frontier. It looked more than spacious for all their crates.

She stepped around a dried blood trail leading out of the church's side door that ended in a big puddle of blood ten feet into the parking lot. There were bullet casings, but no body. She didn't bother asking where the man with white hair was, either.

"Look at you," Danny said. "Walking wounded. You know Will and I have never actually been shot? And we've been to Afghanistan."

She touched the butt of her sidearm. "I can change that."

He laughed, throwing his hands up. "Don't shoot! I surrender!"

"Just keep it up." She looked around the parking lot. "Where's Will?"

Danny pointed across the street. "We found where they were hiding. Sonsofbitches were just waiting for us to skedaddle before coming over. Marauding assholes just aren't as honorable as they used to be."

Will was jogging back toward them now, crossing the street, then the parking lot.

"Find anything?" she asked.

"A Jeep," Will said. "Could have been the one Blaine lost."

"What about the semitrailer?" Danny asked.

"No signs of it. They either dumped it or parked it somewhere else."

"Weren't there supposed to be three of them?" Lara asked.

"I didn't see anyone else," Will said.

"Maybe the third one left earlier with the big rig," Danny said. "Wouldn't surprise me. A gang that marauds together don't necessarily stay together. Too bad, too. That semitrailer might be worth finding. They must have collected a lot of things over the last eight months."

"I'd rather we don't find it," Lara said. "I don't want to use what they took. God knows how they got it, if this is how they've been surviving since The Purge."

"Yeah, but they could have had some *really* cool stuff," Danny insisted.

The others came out and piled what they were carrying into the back of the two trucks, but those quickly filled up and they started loading the cargo trailer. The guns and ammo stayed with them inside the vehicles, like always.

Lara walked over to the Ridgeline and climbed into the front passenger side, while Josh and Gaby took the back seats. It was harder to climb in and out of vehicles with one arm in a sling.

Carly boarded the Frontier with Danny and the girls.

Lara watched Will and Danny talking outside the truck, but she couldn't hear anything over the roar of the air conditioner blasting in her face. Carly and the girls were enjoying the air conditioner of the

Frontier almost as much, the girls sticking their faces toward the cool air between the two front seats.

"Oh my God, air conditioning," Gaby said in the back seat. "I think we should live out of trucks from now on."

"I'm all for that," Josh said.

"How did you guys get from place to place?" Lara asked.

"Matt had a truck."

"Whenever we found a place that was safe, we tried to stay as long as possible," Gaby added. "As long as the supplies lasted, anyway, which was never that long. It always got too dangerous after a while, so we kept moving."

"The only good thing about the rest of the world turning into bloodsucking monsters was all the stuff lying around," Josh said. "It'd be nice if some of it tasted better."

"Just give me canned peaches any day," Gaby said.

Will and Danny finally walked over to their respective vehicles. Will climbed into the Ridgeline and unclipped his radio, sticking it on the dashboard where it was held in place by freshly installed Velcro.

"We good?" he asked them.

"Good to go," Josh said.

Gaby nodded.

"Let's get out of here," Lara said.

The radio squawked and they heard Danny's voice: "Let's blow this joint."

They headed out of the parking lot, the Ridgeline up front, with the Frontier dragging the cargo trailer behind them. They turned back onto the road and headed south.

Lara glanced at her side mirror as the First Assembly of the Lord receded into the background, until it was finally gone completely. People went to church for forgiveness, didn't they? And she was fleeing one. So what did that say about her?

She looked forward, surprised to find herself wallowing in moody thoughts. She didn't want the others to see, especially Will.

I've killed two men now.

It wasn't just the deaths that stuck with her, it was the fact that she was supposed to feel guilty…except she didn't. Not a bit. And that, more than anything, kept pricking at the back of her mind. Had she really changed that much?

"We good?" Will's voice, bringing her back. He reached over

and squeezed her hand.

She smiled back at him, putting as much conviction into it as she could muster. "Shoulder aside, we're good."

"We'll be fine."

"I know." To her surprise, she believed it.

As long as you're here with me…

"Have you ever been to Beaumont before?" she asked.

"No."

"What about you guys?" she asked Gaby and Josh in the backseat.

"I never left Ridley until eight months ago," Josh said.

"I've been to Dallas a few times," Gaby said, "but that's about it."

"I've never been to Dallas," Josh said. "Which is sad, considering it's just next door. What's it like?"

"Loud," Gaby said.

"That's it?"

She thought about it a little bit more. "Pretty much."

"Blaine's from Dallas, too, right?" Josh said. "Sandra said they left Dallas together after everything happened. I wonder what happened to him?"

Lara looked over at Will. She could tell he was wondering the same thing.

Are you still alive out there, Blaine?

CHAPTER 17

BLAINE

WE SHOULD BE dead.

But they weren't, and the only proof he needed was Sandra sleeping against him, the soft beating of her heart telling him they were still very much alive.

They were inside a room. It was small, designed for less than two people, though you might have been able to squeeze in one more if you didn't mind the lack of leg room. It was hidden in the back of the pink bedroom's closet, a six-by-five stainless steel space. It had a lock and a vault-style door handle, and Blaine had felt a rush of disappointment when he thought he might need a key to get in. But Sandra had tried turning the handle and it had spun invitingly, without hesitation.

There was a set of keys inside, resting on a small shelf along one side of the wall. Two wrenches, a small portable LED lamp, and a cordless phone still docked in its station were lined up next to the keys. It was crowded at first, but they had managed to cram inside and swing the door shut, the handle spinning automatically as soon as the latch caught, and Blaine heard at least three locks snapping into place, one after another. The walls were so thick the room barely shook when the ghouls crashed pointlessly against it. The noises from outside came through two air vents—oval-shaped holes with mesh wiring about two inches wide—along the sides.

It was a safe room.

And it was well-hidden, too. It was only after retreating all the way into the back of the closet that they had even stumbled across it. At first he had been perplexed, but that had changed quickly when he realized what he was looking at.

Blaine had never actually seen a safe room in person, but he had seen schematics. This one wasn't the most expensive or elaborate, but it clearly served its purpose well enough—it kept things *out.* The wrenches, he concluded, were for the bolts connecting the pieces of the room together.

Blaine turned off the LED lamp sometime during the night. He didn't need it to hear the ghouls outside, thumping against the door a few feet from him. They couldn't get to the air vents because the back part of the safe room was embedded within the wall itself. Blaine guessed the homeowners had assembled it piece by piece, another major draw of the simple design.

There was nothing about the pink bedroom to suggest its owner needed a safe room. He wondered if there were other rooms like this installed in the other bedrooms. Will and the others hadn't seen it when they were here yesterday, but they hadn't really searched. Blaine had seen their crates—they had enough clothes for a few lifetimes.

The ghouls kept pounding on the door for what seemed like hours, long after Blaine and Sandra had retreated inside. Blaine listened, feeling the slight (very slight) vibrations from every impact. They attacked for hours on end, well into the night and early morning hours.

Then, finally, they just stopped.

By then, Blaine had been forcing himself to stay awake, but his side had begun hurting again, and he felt sore all over. His pills were outside, along with everything else. He closed his eyes, intending to only take a brief nap, but ended up falling asleep with Sandra's head in his lap.

HE OPENED HIS eyes to find Sandra standing in front of him, looking through a peephole in the door. Though he had no way of knowing for sure, he was certain it was daylight outside. It was one of those things his body just knew without actually seeing, an evolution of living in a world where darkness brought death.

The LED lamp was on and Blaine could make out Sandra's tall frame, which put her just under the vault ceiling.

She looked over her shoulder and smiled, radiant even against the unnaturally bright light. "We made it."

"We did," he smiled back.

Jesus, my body feels like it's on fire.

He managed to suppress the grimace so she wouldn't see. "See anything out there?"

"Not much. There are clothes over the peephole."

"Can you open it?"

"I don't know." Sandra looked around the polished steel interior of their surroundings. "What is this place, anyway?"

"It's a safe room."

"How do you know?"

"I've seen one before. Duncan, this guy I used to work with, had catalogs of the stuff. He was going to get into the business of installing safe rooms for rich people across town. Said they all wanted one after 9/11."

"You think the other rooms have one, too?"

"Probably. Unless the daughter is just a special case."

"How do you drag something this heavy up here?"

"You don't have to. You can install them section-by-section. You can even expand it out the back just by buying more sections."

"I guess that's convenient." She walked back and sat down next to him. "Are you okay?"

"Sore."

"Where?"

"All over."

"That bad?"

"I forgot my painkillers outside."

"Oops."

"Yeah," he said.

She leaned against him for a moment. "Did Duncan ever get around to starting that business?"

"Nah. He decided to rob rich people instead. Thinking back, maybe he never really planned to install safe rooms for them."

"Would Duncan know how we get out of here?"

"Turn the lever."

"That's it?"

"Pretty much. It's designed to keep people out, not to keep you in once you're inside."

She stood up and walked back to the door. She put her hands tentatively around two of the three handles that jutted out from the center, like a boat's steering wheel. Sandra looked back at him. "Just turn it?"

"Counter clockwise," he said, miming it for her.

Sandra took a breath, then turned the handles counter clockwise. They spun and kept spinning.

"Keep going," he said.

She kept spinning until the lever stopped and they heard the three locks disengaging one by one.

"Push it," he said.

She did, but the door didn't budge. She stopped pushing and looked back at him, hands on her hips. "It pushes open? Are you sure?"

"I'm sure. You can't pull it, there isn't enough room."

"Good point." She turned back to the door and put her weight on it this time, and the door slowly began sliding outward an inch at a time. She grunted. "There is definitely something blocking the door."

"Probably shelves. Or lots and lots of clothes."

"I'm going with the former," she said between gasps. "Clothes aren't this heavy."

Sandra was finally able to open the door wide enough to slip outside. Blaine didn't remember the door being that heavy, but then again, he was probably filled with adrenaline last night and everything seemed easier.

He heard heavy grunting and what sounded like metal and furniture being dragged around the room.

"It's most of the shelves," Sandra shouted. "And a shoe rack, I think. They brought most of the clothes down, too. Too bad everything's for a teenage girl. It looks pretty expensive. I wonder where you buy brand-name stuff like this out here in the boondocks?"

Blaine smiled. Women and clothes…

Sandra removed enough of the closet's obstruction that she was able to push the safe door all the way open, letting just a small sliver of sunlight inside. Immediately, Blaine knew they had overslept.

He glanced down at his watch: 12:25 P.M.

They had slept through the entire morning.

It was the vault. Being inside something that impenetrable was like being in a cocoon. Their bodies had taken full advantage of it, allowing them to catch up on sleep they had missed out on in the last few days.

Sandra stuck her head back into the opening and said, "I'll be back," in her best impression of Arnold Schwarzenegger from *The Terminator.*

He grinned, and got a smile back from her.

Sandra reached into the vault and picked up the shotgun. She turned left and disappeared from his field of vision. With nothing to do, Blaine sat back and waited. He heard her walking along the second floor, then going down the steps.

It might have been a few minutes later, or possibly a few seconds later, when she finally came back and crouched in front of him. He wasn't even sure how she had gotten from the first floor all the way up here and back into the vault again without him hearing or seeing her coming until she was suddenly just there.

She held a water bottle in one hand and his pill bottle in the other. She shook out a couple of pills and he opened his mouth like a drowning man and swallowed. She tilted his head back to help him drink. He hadn't realized how weak he was, how racked with pain, until he found the simple act of slurping down water such a monumental task he wanted to give up on it about halfway through. Thankfully, Sandra was persistent, and he chased the pills down with warm water and sighed with relief.

"You should see the other side of the safe door," Sandra said. "There's black blood and slabs of flesh and…other things all over it. They must have been smashing into it long after I dozed off."

"They were."

"I wonder why they stopped."

"Losing battle. They're not stupid."

"I guess not. There are bones everywhere outside."

"A lot?"

She nodded. "How's the pain?" she asked, watching his face closely.

"Managing. The pills help."

"Don't take too many of them. You'll get addicted."

"It's either addiction or death, babe."

"Not while I'm around." She took the painkillers from him before he could protest and put them away in her pocket. "From now on, you'll only take what you need, not what you think you need."

"You're no fun."

She grunted. "I already lost you once. I'll be damned if I'm going to lose you again to some damn pills."

SANDRA DROVE THE Toyota while Blaine rested in the passenger seat. They had a quarter tank of gas left, more than enough to get to Lancing and either find a new vehicle or siphon gas from another car. Blaine knew from experience that eventually the gasoline left behind in vehicles and stored underneath the gas stations would either evaporate or become unusable, but that was still a few years off. If they were still driving around Texas looking for sanctuary in a few years, gas was probably going to be the least of their worries.

Sandra turned left off the driveway and put them back onto US 287 heading south toward Lancing. "You still think they'll still be there?" she asked.

"Unless they left for some reason," he said.

Blaine glanced at his watch: 1:17 P.M.

"What time is it?" she asked.

He told her, adding, "We slept through half the day."

"God, no wonder I feel so good. I haven't slept that well since all of this began. Did you guys ever find out whose house that was?"

"I don't think we ever looked, no."

"Too bad. It would have been nice to know who to thank. I saw some of the pictures. They looked like a nice family."

He nodded. All the family portraits he had seen in the past eight months had looked like nice families. But wasn't that the point of a family portrait? Everyone dresses up in their best clothes and makes believe for the camera?

Blaine found that if he thought about other things besides the rippling pain coursing through his body, he was able to endure it. Or at least, that's what he told himself as he turned toward the window, pretending to look out at the passing scenery, when he was really hiding his grimace from Sandra.

BY THE TIME they reached Lancing, there were no signs of Will and the others. They went to the municipal area and checked the courthouse first. He couldn't find signs anyone had spent the night, which meant they had either left the city yesterday—which was unlikely, given how cautious Will was with the others' lives—or they had found another place.

It was either one or the other, but it wasn't like Blaine could track them. Lancing was a town of 12,000 people, with enough businesses and residential subdivisions that it would take weeks to search every house and building. He was also well aware they had, at most, five hours before it was time to look for shelter.

They spent the first hour driving around town, sticking mostly to the main roads, because that's what they guessed the others would have done. Sandra drove slowly, taking her time. After a while, they had to stop for gas, but instead of siphoning from another vehicle, they traded up to a four-door Chevrolet Silverado instead. The fact that the key was sticking out of the driver's side floor and the tank was still three-quarters full made picking the Silverado a no-brainer.

Blaine swapped the car batteries, and they were rolling down the windows and continuing along Main Street a few minutes later. The Silverado had a dozen country music CDs stuffed into the driver's sun visor, and Blaine slipped George Strait's *Greatest Hits* into the CD player, then cranked up the volume in hopes of attracting attention.

After a while, Sandra slowed down and stopped the Silverado in the middle of the street.

Blaine reached over and turned the volume down on George. "What are you thinking?"

"I'm thinking we're not going to find them," she said with a slight frown. "At least, not like this. Not just driving around."

"How did you find me?"

"I told you, I heard gunshots."

"Maybe we should try that."

"Gunshots?"

He shrugged. "What do we have to lose?"

"What if there are other people in the city besides them?"

He thought about that for a moment, then lifted the AR-15 from the floor. "It's either that or keep driving around aimlessly until we reach the highway. Then what, drive back again?"

"Yeah, okay."

Sandra turned off the Silverado's engine and they climbed outside. Blaine blinked under the sun and wasn't sure if the heat or the pain was more annoying. He called it a tie and fought the urge to beg Sandra for his bottle of pills.

Sandra had the shotgun, and she climbed up into the back of the Silverado's flat bed and fired off three rounds into the air. She waited, then fired the remaining four shells. As the final thunderous blast echoed across the cloudless sky, she was already—urgently, he saw—reloading.

She climbed down the Silverado and stood in the street next to him. They didn't hear anything in response to the shotgun blasts except the sound of the wind and the fluttering of birds' wings in the air. Blaine thought he might have heard a car engine in the distance, but after listening, realized it was just one of the metallic flagpole latches banging away.

Blaine drew his Glock and fired three shots into the air. He stopped, waited ten seconds, then fired three more shots. This time he waited a full minute before firing the rest of the magazine, spacing each shot off at ten-second intervals.

He quickly reloaded. "If they're still here, they would have heard those shots from the other side of town. Sound travels these days."

"Let's give it some time," she said. "It's not like we have any other place to be."

Sandra leaned against the Silverado. Her hair was already sweaty and matted to her face. He reached over and flicked the strands away, and she smiled at him. He smiled back.

They drank warm water and waited five minutes. Then five became ten, then twenty.

"No one's coming," he said, after thirty minutes.

"Let's wait a little longer," she said.

Thirty minutes became an hour.

"No one's coming," she said. "What now? If they've left the city, where would they go?"

"South," Blaine said, looking down Main Street. "They're headed to Beaufont Lake in Louisiana. The easiest path there would be along US 287, then switch over to the I-10 and Highway 90 in Beaumont. From there, they'd probably take one of the smaller roads farther south to Beaufont Lake."

"They told you that?"

"Will showed me a map, and that's the quickest way to Song Island. If we keep going south on US 287 to Beaumont and they're still on the I-10, we should be able to catch up to them before they take one of the smaller roads off the interstate."

"All that from a map you saw?"

"You sound impressed."

"I thought guys were bad with directions."

"That's a filthy stereotype."

She laughed. "Okay."

"One more thing," he said.

"Yeah?"

"I need my pills."

"In an hour."

He groaned. "I don't think I'm going to make it to an hour."

"Don't be such a baby," she said, and walked around the Silverado's hood back to the driver's side.

"I'm really hurting here, babe," he said after her.

"You'll live."

"Babe, please," he said, trying his best not to beg, though it was pretty damn close. "I need more pills."

She rolled her eyes. "God, if I knew getting shot would turn you into such a drama queen, I'd never have gone back for you."

"Wow," he said, feigning hurt. "Just wow, babe. That's harsh."

She laughed. "Get in, Meryl Streep."

THEY DROVE DOWN Lancing's Main Street for a few more minutes before the road became Highway 96 and, about a mile later, joined up with US 287/Route 69. Eventually, the businesses began to thin out and they were back in the countryside, passing thick patches of overgrown grass swaying in the hot sun on both sides of a series of never-ending rickety fences.

"No cows," Blaine said quietly, almost to himself.

"What?" Sandra said.

"No cows," he repeated. "What happened to all the cows?"

Sandra peered at the land around them. "You're right. When did the cows start disappearing?"

Blaine remembered seeing cows as recently as a few weeks ago, when they were entering Grime. There had been cows and horses grazing on the abundant grass. Once, he had seen a couple of riderless horses roaming the streets, the *clack-clack* of their hooves like loud gunshots moving up and down the roads. He had wondered where they were going. Were they looking for their owners?

There were no cows or horses anymore. At least, none that he could see. There were no carcasses of the animals, either, which was even more disturbing.

Where the hell are the animals?

He hadn't seen a dog or a cat in months, now that he really thought about it.

Where have all the animals gone?

They drove past a sign along the side of the road: "Beaumont, Texas 15 Miles."

Maybe Beaumont has the answers…

CHAPTER 18

WILL

THEY REACHED THE outskirts of Beaumont, Texas, by two o'clock in the afternoon, which was better time than Will had expected, given they were stuck at thirty-five miles per hour on the road. There were a couple of reasons for that. The roads got more dangerous the closer they got to a major city—and Beaumont definitely qualified, with its 118,000 population within an eighty-five-square-mile radius. There was also more debris, leftovers from the days even before The Purge. The leftovers piled up, and wind and time added to the growing menace. There was also the cargo trailer to worry about, and losing that would have been calamitous.

It was easy to tell when you were nearing a big city. The roads started to clog up with abandoned cars and personal items left behind, twisting and turning in the wind, bleached dry in the sun.

During the trip, Lara would pick up the ham radio and turn it on, and they would listen to the same recorded message from Song Island. Will wondered if Lara was afraid the message would stop, and if it did, what that would mean. He wasn't entirely sold on Song Island, but it seemed to give her and the others hope, and who was he to take that away from them?

Hope was good. Hope kept you fighting. No one knew that more intimately than a soldier who had been in a war zone.

As they neared Beaumont, Will began looking for possible safe harbors along the feeder roads. There were plenty of buildings, stores, homes, and brand-new subdivisions. But he couldn't settle, not with the knowledge of what was chasing them.

Kate, of all people…

They were alongside Willowstone Mall, the city's main shopping center, when the highway suddenly became impassable, and Will pulled over to the shoulder and stopped. There were simply too many vehicles in front of them now, and the big trucks weren't going to be able to maneuver around the wall of metal, cast iron, aluminum, chrome, and rubber.

Will grabbed the radio off the dashboard: "Danny, I think we're stuck."

"We haven't tried going over them yet," Danny said through the radio.

"I don't think that's going to work."

"Oh come on, we won't know until we try. The girls will love it."

"Maybe next time."

Gaby was leaning against her window, smiling at the familiar gathering of department stores that made up the Willowstone Mall to their right. "Wow, I'd kill to do some shopping right about now."

"You'd definitely have to kill a lot to do any shopping," Josh said. "There are probably a gazillion of those bloodsuckers in there."

"Josh is right," Lara said. "The ghouls are everywhere. They use the department stores as nests."

"Figures," Gaby sighed.

Lara looked over at Will. "If we can't go around this traffic, where does that leave us?"

"I'm not sure," he said. "Let's get a better look outside."

Will climbed out of the Ridgeline while Danny walked over from the Frontier.

"Monster trucks," Danny said. "We need monster trucks. Then we could just go right over these suckers. I even came up with a name. The Danny-ator."

"The Danny-ator?"

"Yeah, you know, like the Terminator. But with my name. Don't steal it."

"Try and stop me."

Will climbed onto the hood of his Ridgeline and took a pair of binoculars from one of his pouches. The sea of cars stretched endlessly across all four lanes—two northbound and two southbound. The only positive was that the highway wasn't elevated, so they would be able to break off and take the feeder roads whenever they needed to. But even the feeders were congested with vehicles.

Lara climbed out behind them. "What do you see?"

"Cars. Lots of cars," Will said.

"The man has a flair for understatement," Danny said. "Monster trucks," he said to Lara. "That's the ticket."

"God help us," Lara said.

"That's what Carly said when I told her. What's the deal with you girls? No love for the monster trucks?"

"No, just the thought of you behind the wheel of one, Danny."

"Hey, I'm an excellent driver."

"Whatever, Rain Man," Lara said.

Will climbed down from the hood of the Ridgeline as the others climbed out of the trucks and formed a mini-circle around him. They hadn't been outside for more than a few minutes, and everyone was already sweating in the heat.

"How are we going to get around that?" Carly asked, looking at the traffic.

Will had to admit, it was an imposing sight, as if all of Beaumont had decided to leave at the same time. And maybe they had. Beaumont was a smaller city compared to Houston or Dallas, and the ghouls might have saved them for the second wave of attacks. That would have given the residents time to digest what was happening elsewhere—on TV, the radio, or the Net—before eventually deciding to converge on the highways in a mass exodus. He had seen it happen during hurricanes.

Will glanced down at his watch: 2:26 P.M.

"How are we for time?" Lara asked.

"Six hours and counting before nightfall," Will said. *Thank God for Texas summers.* "We have time."

"We're not getting around that in six hours," Danny said.

Will shook his head. He would have preferred to pass Beaumont in a day and be well beyond the city limits by nightfall. He remembered how many threats they'd had to deal with in Houston. Beaumont had a fraction of Houston's population, but 118,000 was still an impressive number of potential ghouls hiding in darkness, waiting for night. And that wasn't counting how many Kate would bring with her.

Kate. It had to be Kate, too.

"We'll use the feeders and look for a place to hole up for the night," Will said.

"What kind of places are we looking for?" Josh asked.

"Small, defensible, and preferably not close to places like a mall. Keep an eye out."

They nodded and anxiously climbed back into the trucks, thankful to return to the air conditioners. Danny lingered behind until it was just the two of them on the highway.

"Kate?" Danny asked.

"Yeah," Will nodded.

"Psychic dreams. Jesus. What's next? Undead creatures from the pits of Hell?"

"That'll be the day," Will said.

HE GOT LUCKY and found what he was looking for a few miles up the highway. It was along the feeder road, inside a strip mall with an Exxon gas station up front and three other buildings flanking it. The place was surrounded by giant car lots selling new and used vehicles.

"See it?" Will said into the radio.

"I see it," Danny said through the radio. "God bless Miguel. He was a piece of shit human being who insisted on shooting other people in the back, but at least he gave away valuable information freely."

Will led them off the feeder road and into the strip mall, passing the Exxon. They drove by a Discount Tire Shop and then an Auto Zone before turning a corner with a Budget Rent-a-Car. It was behind a small furniture store called Elmo's, in an open parking lot with contents visible all the way from the elevated highway.

"Are you kidding?" Lara said. "We're spending the night in those things?"

"Whoa," Josh said, leaning between the front seats. "I never once thought about using those."

"What?" Gaby said. Then, "Oh no, not those again."

Will stopped the Ridgeline in front of the first semitrailer, one of many lining a truck stop in the back of the plaza. The area took up nearly half of the concrete space, with one big building in a corner surrounded by at least fifty, possibly sixty, trailers resting on back tires and propped up by their landing gear. Their solid steel sides gleamed in the sun.

They climbed out of the trucks.

Will glanced over at Gaby. She looked pained. "You good?"

She looked over and nodded. "If we have to, then we have to."

"Just this once."

She nodded again, trying to convince herself. "Okay."

Tough girl.

"Spread out," Will said, "and look for one that doesn't have a lock on the doors. We'll need two, preferably side by side. If you find one unlocked, be careful. You don't know what might be hiding inside."

Will drew his Glock and replaced the magazine with one marked with an "X." Danny and the others did the same thing.

"You're with me, kid," Danny said to Josh.

Gaby stayed behind with Carly and the girls. "We'll just wait here and soak up the sun," Carly said. "Whistle if you need anything."

"Lara," Will said, "you should stay behind, too."

"I'm fine," she said.

"Your arm..."

"It's a lot better. Besides, I'm a righty, anyway."

He thought about arguing but saw the look on her face and decided against it.

She walked next to him as they moved through a row of about twenty trailers, testing the back doors as they went. Most of the trailers had simple locks that could be opened with a key, though some had more expensive-looking security devices on them. They went along the row, pulling at doors but finding none that would yield.

Danny said through the radio: "Locked, locked, and locked. Any luck on your end?"

"Not a one," Will said into the radio.

"We might have to break into one of these things."

"Looks like."

"Good thing I packed that bolt cutter..."

Danny was probably right. The owners of the trailers hadn't been sloppy enough to leave their property unlocked, even if there was nothing inside to steal. He guessed it was because no one liked the idea of someone playing around with their things.

"Semitrailers?" Lara said after a while.

"It's not an entirely bad idea, and I wish I had thought of it."

"Wouldn't it get claustrophobic in there?"

"Maybe after a while, but we're not going to be spending that much time in them. We should be able to cross into Louisiana by tomorrow, then Beaufont Lake later the same day." He noticed she was looking at him closely. "What?"

"I've never seen you this anxious to get to Song Island."

"I'm not."

"So what is it? This thing with Kate? The dream?"

"That's part of it."

"That's most of it, you mean."

He wrinkled his nose at her. "One person invading my thoughts is more than enough, thank you very much. I don't need you in there, too."

She looked like she was warming to the idea. "Can you imagine? Your ex-girlfriend and your current girlfriend knowing everything you're thinking?"

"Heaven forbid," he said, and faked shivering.

She laughed. "But I'm a lot nicer than Kate. At least, my skin is probably softer."

"Only in real life."

"What does that mean?"

"When I dreamt about her, she was the old Kate."

"Oh."

He smiled. "It was just a dream, Lara."

"Still, I don't know how I feel about you spending quality time with your ex-girlfriend in a park. Dream or not, a girl can get a little nervous."

He grabbed her by the waist. She let out a surprised yelp as he pulled her to him, very careful not to touch her left arm in the sling. He kissed her deeply, passionately, and she moaned against him. They were still lip-locked and sweating under the sun when Will's radio squawked and they heard Danny's voice.

"I think it's time for that bolt cutter," Danny said. He waited for a response, and when he didn't get one: "Guys? You still there? Ghouls get ya? Oh, man, you're doing something bad to one another, aren't you? Gross. She's wearing bandages, too. Double gross."

"WHAT CAN'T BOLT cutters do?" Danny said as he clamped the sharp metal teeth down over a lock and snapped it in two with a solid crunch. "Not a whole lot, that's what. Anyone got a sandwich they want split in half?"

"Danny and sharp objects," Carly said, shaking her head.

Lara laughed, and so did Gaby and the girls.

"What?" Danny said, and stepped away from the truck.

Will grabbed the doors and threw them open. He didn't worry about the possibility of ghouls waiting for him on the other side. Ghouls didn't do locks, and they certainly didn't bother locking a room back up after they left.

The musty odor of time and dust swarmed them in a thick fine mist. Everyone coughed and backed away from the trailer. The vehicle itself was empty, its floor, sides, and ceiling heavily scratched by past cargos. The trailer sat in the middle of the lot, where it had been wallowing in the heat for months now, and there was nothing to make it stand out from the others. Which was what Will wanted.

He grabbed the ramp and lowered it to the ground, then climbed up with an LED lamp, hanging it on a hook along the ceiling. He pegged the trailer's length at twenty-two meters long and four meters high, more than enough room to move around comfortably.

He walked back to the opening. "All right, let's start moving what we need in here while Danny cracks open the second trailer."

Everyone moved with purpose, including the girls. They transported the ammo, guns, food, and personal items from the trucks over to the trailers. They had done it so many times now it was second nature, and Will found he didn't have to tell anyone what to bring. They just knew. Even Josh and Gaby got with the program in no time.

Will climbed down the ramp and walked over a meter and threw open the second trailer once Danny broke the lock. The others were piling boxes and moving crates into the first trailer behind him, their boots and sneakers clanging loudly back and forth.

Too loud. It's too loud.

Danny saw the look on his face. "What now?"

"Footsteps," Will said.

"Where?"

"In the trailer. It's too loud."

"So?"

"Noises, Danny."

Danny listened to the others moving noisily around in the trailer behind them. "Yeah. Way too loud."

"Let's go shopping."

"Awesome. You going to buy me something pretty this time?"

"We'll see," Will said.

ELMO'S NEXT DOOR had what they were looking for—mattresses. They carried what they needed over to the semitrailers until they had enough to cover most of the floors.

"Really? Mattresses?" Lara asked.

"To keep the noises down," Will said.

"And sleep like a baby," Danny added. "These things are expensive. Who can afford these things?"

"Rich people," Josh said, helping Will carry one of the mattresses up the first trailer's ramp.

"God, I love being rich," Danny said.

Once the mattresses were in place, Will had them move around inside while he listened, and he was pleased with the result.

"We're good to go," he announced. "Drill 'em."

Danny brought out a battery-powered drill and went up and down the trailers, creating holes in the floor and along the sides, far enough apart to not be readily obvious if someone went searching under the vehicles. It was going to be claustrophobic enough inside without trying to fight for air. The holes, as small as they were, would fix that problem without giving their positions away.

Dead, not stupid.

Will and Danny drove the trucks over to the Discount Tire store and parked inside the garage. They slammed the doors shut and locked them from the inside, then slipped out through a side entrance. Even if other survivors stumbled across the trucks and raided the supplies in the cargo trailer, the loss wasn't anything that couldn't be replaced by raiding nearby stores and buildings. They had become, much to his surprise (but very much to his approval), brutally efficient in the last few months.

It was almost five in the evening by the time Will and Danny began walking back to the others. He took a moment to glance over his shoulder at the highway behind them. Quiet and congested, with cars frozen in place, it made for an eerie sight.

"You think your girlfriend's going to find us?" Danny asked. "Kate struck me as the persistent type."

"Ex-girlfriend."

"Same difference. What's with you and the crazy ones, anyway?"

"Lara's not crazy."

"Not yet."

"I'm going to tell her you said that."

"Hey, hey, let's not start throwing each other under the bus now," Danny said.

THEY WAITED UNTIL an hour before sundown before entering their respective trailers. Will and Lara, with Josh and Gaby, in one, and Danny with Carly and the girls in the other. They pulled the doors closed, and with the LED lamps hanging from the ceiling, the interior of the trailer looked like some otherworldly cave with blindingly white lights.

The semitrailer doors didn't have locks on the inside, but Will had made sure to choose trailers with simple door designs that could be chained in place from the inside. They slid steel bars across the latches as a secondary measure. The chains were taut enough that they could probably withstand most assaults, but it never hurt to have a backup plan.

Hope for the best, prepare for the worst.

Will heard Danny doing the same with his trailer's lock next door. He said into the radio, "We good?"

"We're spiffy and dandy," Danny said through the radio.

"All right, let's go silent. I'll see you tomorrow morning."

"Try not to wake me up unless it's absolutely necessary. A man needs his beauty rest, you know. The ladies, too, I guess."

Will glanced briefly his watch: 7:56 P.M. "Thirty minutes, give or take."

Josh and Gaby settled into the back. Will watched Gaby closely. He didn't blame her for her reluctance to climb back into a semitrailer. It was more than that, though. Gaby had killed a man during their escape. And yet, she hadn't made a scene about his plan.

She has no idea how tough she really is, or what she's capable of.

He glanced over at Lara, trying to stave off sleep next to him. "With any luck, we'll be in Beaufont Lake by tomorrow evening."

She nodded and leaned tiredly against him. He slipped his arm around her waist, careful to avoid putting any pressure on her left arm.

"Go to sleep," he whispered.

"I will if you promise not to dream about your ex-girlfriend again," she whispered back.

He smiled. "I'll do my best."

DARKNESS CAME AT 8:29 P.M. on the dot.

The temperature dropped noticeably, even inside their steel confines. He turned off the LED lamps, and his world would have been pitch-black if he weren't wearing the night-vision goggles. He used them to navigate back to Lara.

He sat down next to her, the Remington shotgun in his left hand. The M4A1 rested on another mattress nearby, along with a second Remington and half the ammo they carried with them. Danny had the other half.

Will felt Lara slide against him as he took the night-vision goggles off. It wasn't nearly as hot inside as he had feared, and with nightfall coming, the temperature would be just north of bearable. At least, bearable enough to sleep through, though Will didn't think he would be getting a lot of sleep anyway.

What was that Kate had said? "*Your mind is tired, Will. You're exhausted.*"

She was right. He was exhausted down to his bones, and had been for the last few months, ever since they were forced to abandon Harold Campbell's facility. He was moving on fumes, warm bottles of Red Bull, pure black coffee that tasted more like sludge, and energy bars. Not to mention fear. Not for himself, but for Lara. For Carly. For Danny and the girls. He stayed awake because he had to.

He thought about Song Island. Maybe things would change once they got there.

Hope for the best, prepare for the worst.

He couldn't really make out Josh and Gaby behind him without the night-vision goggles, though he could hear their slight movements against the mattress. They weren't asleep, not yet, and maybe they were purposely trying to stay awake. He didn't really need them awake, but he wasn't going to tell them what to do. They had survived out here for eight months on their own, and Will figured they had earned the right to be as paranoid as he was.

It took thirty minutes before he heard the first one moving outside, bare feet slapping against concrete as it went down the row of semitrailers. Lara heard it, too, because her body stiffened next to him, and he felt her hand reaching for her Glock.

Will slipped his hand around her waist to let her know he was there. She relaxed a bit, but not much. He kept his other hand on the Remington, lying on the mattress next to him.

He felt safe in here, surrounded by the preparations they had put in place. Even if they were discovered, getting in was another matter entirely.

What had Miguel said? "*Have you seen those semitrailers? You can't tear into those things. They're like a moving safe.*"

Thanks for the idea, Folger, you dead piece of shit.

The noises outside became more obvious as a single ghoul became two, then two became a dozen. Then he heard them moving on the roof above him. They were hopping from trailer to trailer, and each time one of them landed and leaped off, the steel container trembled slightly in their wake.

On cue, his right ear clicked, and he heard Danny's voice, soft and calm, but clearly whispering on his end: "I'll huff, and I'll puff, and I'll blow your semitrailer down."

"You felt that, huh?" Will whispered.

"Felt it, heard it, and smelt it. How many do you think? A dozen?"

"At least."

"They can't sniff us, right? Cause I haven't taken a shower in a while."

"I don't think so, no."

"Good. Carly says I reek. Maximum BO."

"Go to sleep. Nothing's going to happen tonight."

"Sleep. Right. That's going to happen." Danny paused, then added, "A clown wakes up one morning and decides to visit his doctor. His doctor takes one look at him and asks, 'So what's the problem? Why are you here?' To which the clown replies, 'I dunno, doc, I woke up this morning and I just felt funny.'"

"Go to sleep," Will said.

Lara was looking at him in the darkness.

He shook his head and whispered, "Just Danny being Danny."

She laid her cheek against his chest, and Will tightened his arm around her. His hand accidentally brushed against her breasts. "Not tonight, dear, we have company," she whispered, her words slurred by the Percocet she had taken for the pain earlier.

He smiled and wondered how the kids were doing back there. He couldn't tell if they were moving, or even breathing.

Will caught a flicker of movement from the corner of his left eye. He looked over at the breathing hole about a meter from the end of his mattress and saw something flitting across the other side of the opening.

Black eyes stared up through the hole, searching, searching…

Dead, not stupid.

Will lifted the Remington to his lap and slipped his finger into the trigger guard, but he didn't thumb off the safety yet. From his angle, he could see the tiny drilled hole, but the ghoul wouldn't be able to see much of anything except for the ceiling directly above it. And there was nothing up there to give away their position or indicate there was anything inside. The closest LED lamp was three meters away, but the creature wouldn't be able to pick it up with the naked eye given its limited angle.

Hopefully.

Ten seconds later, and the damn thing was still there, under the trailer, looking through the hole.

Had it smelled something? Seen something? *Sensed* something?

They weren't stupid. Turning hadn't robbed them of their intelligence, even if it had reverted them to an almost primal, animalistic state of being.

And animals could sometimes sense their prey…

Will inched his forefinger toward the safety switch of the Remington and was about to slide it into firing position when the black eyes on the other side of the breathing hole disappeared.

He had started to relax when he heard footsteps on the roof above him again, and this time they didn't disappear right away like before. These new sounds were lingering.

Will flicked the safety off the Remington, mindful of the soft *click* it made, such a minor noise sounding like an explosion in the stillness.

They were still up there, moving around lazily. What the hell were they doing up there? He fought back the urge to start firing with the Remington. He could probably pick them all off with a few choice blasts from down here.

Tempting...

When he looked back down at the breathing hole, the black eyes were back.

Will didn't move, didn't make a sound.

Go away, you sonofabitch. Shoo.

After about thirty seconds, the searching eyes obeyed and disappeared again, replaced by dark asphalt in the background.

A moment later, the footsteps above him also vanished.

Will waited, wondering if this was some kind of feint.

Dead, not stupid.

Ten seconds.

Twenty.

Thirty...

And still just asphalt below him through the hole, and no hints of a tremor above him on the roof.

Will allowed himself to breathe again and lessened his grip on the shotgun after flicking the safety back on. He slowly lowered the weapon down to the mattress next to him, still within easy reach.

After a while, the ghouls must have been convinced the semi-trailer lot was clear, because there was a loud flurry of movement, fading away from them...

...and then silence.

He relaxed a bit.

Lara had gone to sleep next to him. He could also hear the teenagers snoring lightly in the back. Or maybe it was just one of them. It was hard to tell.

He sat awake and waited, listening, trying to feel the slightest vibrations from outside. Soft wind against the steel walls of the containers, debris blowing across the concrete parking lot. What may or may not have been a car horn in the distance, or possibly just his imagination playing tricks on him.

He lost the battle to stay awake around three in the morning, and was surprised he didn't dream of Kate again.

CHAPTER 19

BLAINE

THEY HADN'T BEEN in a city as big as Beaumont since they had abandoned Dallas, so it felt a little odd to be driving up a highway that was suddenly stuffed with cars, giving him flashbacks of afternoon rush-hour traffic. Except there were no horns, no fumes, and none of the grinding sounds of machinery inching forward every few seconds.

There were vehicles in their path when they approached the outskirts of the city, but it only got worse as they continued on. Whenever the highway seemed to thin out and become passable, another huge block of cars appeared to prove him wrong.

After a while, Sandra began stopping more than she was moving. Finally, she simply stopped and parked next to an overturned Ford truck and a red Camaro buried in its exposed belly.

She sat back, then let out a frustrated sigh. "It's not going to get any better, is it?"

"Doesn't look like it," Blaine said. "Want me to drive?"

"You can't even walk."

"I can walk fine."

"Oh yeah? Get out and show me."

"Not now, it's too hot outside."

"Right." Then she smiled at him. "Besides, I like this. Driving you around. It's liberating. I just wish the damn road would cooperate."

Blaine wondered if Will and the others had encountered the

same thing and how they got around it. You could go around the city, but that would add a lot of time to the schedule. Maybe even a day. No. Sticking to the highway, or near it, was the shortest route.

"What time is it?" Sandra asked.

He glanced down at his watch. "Three fourteen."

They had made pretty good time since Lancing. The highways between towns and cities were always easy to travel, and it wasn't until you hit the towns that things got complicated.

"Look," Sandra said, pointing.

Blaine looked at where she was pointing, saw a Burger King to their right, in front of a big sprawling group of buildings. A mall, with a Sortys department store taking up most of the space on this side of the structure. The parking lot was almost entirely empty.

He searched out a sign and found one near the street that read: "Willowstone Mall."

"Is this really the time to go shopping?" Blaine said.

She rolled her eyes. "No, not the mall. In front of it."

She pointed again, and following her a second time, he saw a Cavender's Boot City store near the feeder road. It was in front of the mall and squeezed between a Best Buy and a Petsmart. Cavender's sold cowboy boots and hats and general Western wear. It wasn't exactly the kind of place he visited regularly.

"I need new boots," Sandra said. "This pair's getting a little worn around the heels."

He looked down at his own sneakers. They were dirty and worn around the edges. They were blue once, but were mostly white now, the colors faded from heavy use.

"Let's go shopping," he said.

THEY PULLED INTO the Cavender's and parked between a beat-up brown Toyota truck and a white Ford F-150. The storefront windows were intact, and there was enough sunlight that he could see racks of jeans, boots, hats, and belt buckles. There were a lot of belt buckles.

Yee haw.

The second he climbed out of the Silverado, Blaine flinched with pain. He stopped for a second and looked down, expecting to see blood on his shirt, and was relieved when he didn't. Still, there was no mistaking where the pain was coming from. He felt like sitting down to catch his breath, but Sandra might be watching, so he forced himself forward, toward the front door of the Cavender's instead.

"You think any of those jeans will fit me?" he asked.

He was at the doors, reaching for the handle, when he stopped. He saw Sandra's reflection in the store's glass door, and she wasn't alone.

Sandra stood frozen next to the truck, with some kind of alien standing behind her. No, not an alien. It was a *man* wearing some type of black gas mask, with a large, elongated clear lens and two small breathing filters jutting out from the sides like shorn tusks. He was wearing some kind of gray hazmat suit. Not the big, bulky kind, but the thin, tactical types he had seen soldiers wearing on the news. The suit was light enough for the man to wear a gun belt with a holster. The Browning automatic that should have been in the holster was instead pressed up against Sandra's temple.

Blaine spun, drawing his Glock. The sudden, quick movement made him grimace as pain shot through him like some pissed-off demon from Hell. He pushed away the pain and concentrated on taking aim at the man standing behind Sandra instead. He couldn't see the face clearly through the gas mask, but he could see dark, small black eyes. The man was at least half a foot shorter than Sandra, and the sight of him holding her at gunpoint struck Blaine as absurd.

"Put the gun down or I put a bullet through her brain," the man said. His voice sounded hollow behind the gas mask, but there was no mistaking the menace.

Blaine didn't lower his gun. He wasn't stupid enough to think doing so would magically free Sandra. And maybe Sandra knew it, too, because she looked right back at him. He saw fear in her eyes, but also grim determination. The guy had snuck up on Sandra before she had even had the chance to slam the truck's driver-side door shut.

"That's not going to happen," Blaine said.

"You wanna get her killed? Is that it?" the man asked.

"It's not going to happen," Blaine said again.

"Tough guy, huh?"

"You expect me to believe you'll let her go if I put this gun down?"

The guy might have grinned. It was hard to tell, because Blaine couldn't see the man's mouth. His eyes did seem to narrow, in the way eyes did when people were grinning.

"I guess you're smarter than you look," the guy said.

"No one's ever accused me of that before."

The guy chuckled. "Not like you have a choice, though."

"I got a gun, I got a choice."

"You think so?"

"You hurt her and I hurt you. Simple as that."

"You're right. It is as simple as that. The problem with that is, though?"

"What's that?"

"I got friends and you don't."

This time Blaine heard them, except it didn't matter, because he couldn't take his gun away from the guy standing behind Sandra anyway. If he had, he knew the guy would end it right there and shoot him dead. Instead, Blaine let two more men come up on both sides of him, fighting every instinct to turn around to confront at least one of them.

He risked a quick glance left, then right—less than a second each time, but just long enough to see they were both wearing the same hazmat suits and holding M4 rifles pointing at him. They had come from around the corners of the Cavender's, moving surprisingly cat-like for guys in chemical suits.

Had they been waiting there this whole time? Probably. Just like the guy behind Sandra had been waiting to sneak up on them. Hell, they probably saw the Silverado coming from a mile away. God knew they were the only car still running in the city for miles all around. He couldn't imagine the noises they must have made moving along the highway.

"Here's the plan," the guy behind Sandra said. "I'm going to count to five. If you don't drop your gun, they're going to start shooting. Oh, and just in case you're thinking of taking that shot anyway?"

The guy moved until he was completely hidden behind Sandra's bigger frame. And because he was shorter than her, he didn't have to bend at the knees. Blaine thought that was kind of absurd, too.

"Go ahead," the guy said, like a ventriloquist speaking through Sandra. "Shoot back and you'll hit her. I'm guessing you don't want to do that. Not to this fine piece of ass, am I right?"

Blaine saw Sandra's reaction, and this time it was all fear. The moment had passed, they both realized. They were royally fucked.

"One," the guy said.

He didn't get "two" out before Blaine lowered himself to the ground in a crouch, then laid the gun down carefully, feeling the barrels of the two M4 rifles tracking him every step of the way.

"All right," Blaine said. "Let's talk about this."

"Good boy," the guy said, coming back out from behind Sandra.

The man to Blaine's right hurried forward and kicked Blaine's gun away, while the one to his left grabbed him by the shirt collar and pulled him up, then threw him into the Cavender's glass door. Blaine felt balls of flame raining down on him, but did his best to stamp out any sounds before they could leave his lips.

"Be careful!" Sandra shouted behind him. "He's already hurt!"

The man who had thrown Blaine into the glass door looked back at Sandra. "Where?" he asked. Blaine heard a thick country accent.

"He was shot in the side," Sandra said.

"Which side?"

"The right side."

"Good to know," the guy said, then he turned back around and punched Blaine in the right side, directly over the duct tape.

Blaine felt blinding pain and lost control of his feet and went down like a sack of meat and bones, quivering in a pile on the scorching hot concrete walkway.

THEY WERE IN the Sortys department store employee lounge, sitting on a plastic couch. Mason, the guy who had threatened to shoot Sandra in the head, straddled a chair in front of them, his chin resting on the backrest.

Mason tore at a big stick of jalapeno-flavored beef jerky and devoured it in a few bites. He looked even shorter outside of the hazmat suit, with uncombed black hair just this side of greasy. He wore cargo pants, Army boots, a white T-shirt, and the same gun belt he had worn over the hazmat suit. When he grinned, Blaine saw a big gap where he was missing a front tooth. The guy was five-four, tops.

The room they were in was bright, with an open window near the ceiling. Dust and paper were scattered along the floor, and an overflowing wastebasket sat in one corner.

There was another guy in the small room with them. It was the same cowboy who had given Blaine a nice "hello" to the side with his fist. Blaine was still smarting from that, and he gave the cowboy a once-over with cold, hard eyes. The man was dressed almost identical to Mason, but instead of a white T-shirt, he had on a black one. Other than that, he looked like a taller, skinnier version of Mason, and Blaine thought he could probably break the guy over his knees.

"Keep dreaming," the cowboy said, smirking back at him.

Mason snapped his fingers, directing Blaine's eyes away from the cowboy and back over to him. "So, one more time. You don't know the guys that came through earlier today?"

"No," Sandra said, her voice calm.

That's my girl.

Mason looked over at Blaine. "And I don't suppose you know them, either?"

"No idea," Blaine lied.

"They were packing some pretty impressive firepower," Mason said. "We thought about doing to them what we did to you, but there was something about those two guys, the way they held their weapons…" Mason shrugged and bit off another big piece of beef jerky. "Not worth the hassle. We're just caretakers here, after all."

"Here" was the Willowstone Mall, the big, sprawling complex behind the Cavender's Boot store. Mason and the cowboy had brought them over with the third man, whose name Blaine didn't catch, and who had disappeared as soon as they were inside the dark, dank confines of the mall. They had walked through the Sortys department store, passing racks of unused clothes. *At least they'll never run out of things to wear*, he remembered thinking.

He had noticed right away there were no barricades against the windows or doors, and there were shadows everywhere—at least a good half of the store was untouched by sunlight. Mason and the others didn't look disturbed by this shortcoming, though. At first

Blaine thought it might have been the hazmat suits, giving them some kind of false confidence, but he quickly realized it was more than that. It wasn't that Mason and the others thought they were safe in here. Blaine somehow felt that these men *knew* they were safe. How, he couldn't fathom.

"So," Mason said, eyeballing Blaine again. "What are we going to do with the two of you? That's the question."

"Why aren't you scared?" Blaine asked.

"Of what?"

"*Them.*"

Mason smiled. "We don't have to be. We're…partners."

"Partners?" Sandra said. "With *them?*"

"They're not as mindless as you think."

Blaine remembered what Will had told him about the ghouls: *"Dead, not stupid."*

His mind raced back to that night at the house, looking down from the pink bedroom window and seeing the blue-eyed ghoul below. A lone figure staring back up at him, eyes brimming with intelligence.

"In fact, they're pretty fucking smart," Mason said. "How did you think they managed to pull this off? One night, that's all it took." He snapped his fingers. "That takes planning. Intelligence. Discipline. They have it in spades."

"I don't understand," Sandra said. "You're 'partners' with them? How?"

"Survivors might be a better word. We do something for them, and they let us live. It's not a bad trade-off if you really think about it. What's better—running around like you two, always trying to beat the night, or being able to live your life without worrying all the time that it's about to get dark? I'll take that trade-off any day."

"It's not like you can kill the fuckers," the cowboy said.

They don't know about silver.

"Well, you can kill them with sunlight," Mason said. "But that's only half the day, and it's not like you can holster or fire the sun whenever you want. Have you ever tried shooting these things?"

"Yeah," Blaine nodded.

"I've shotgunned one in the face and the fucker just kept coming."

"I put a machete through the forehead of one and it didn't even feel it," the cowboy said. "You can't fight that."

"That's how they beat us, you know," Mason said. "They're unkillable. Well, maybe if you used a nuke, but who the hell knows even then?"

It occurred to Blaine that Mason didn't have to do this, sit here talking to them, trying to justify what he was doing. But he was.

Why?

"So what now?" Blaine asked.

"Now, you decide what you want to do with the rest of your life," Mason said.

"Meaning?"

"You have a choice. You can keep doing what you've been doing. Running from city to city, hiding in basements, praying they don't find you tonight, or the night after that, or the week after that. Or you could do the smart thing and join the club. I got plenty of hazmat suits for two more."

"That simple, huh?"

"It's that simple."

"Bullshit," Sandra said.

Blaine could tell Mason was surprised to hear that coming from her. Maybe they had expected him to say it, to be the dissenting voice, and not Sandra. He detected a slight tweak along the corner of Mason's eyebrow that might have been amusement.

"There's more to it than you just 'partnering' with them," Sandra continued. "What is it that you're *really* doing for them?"

Mason grinned. "Well, that's a little hard to explain."

HE DIDN'T EXPLAIN it. Instead, he showed them.

Mason led them out of the Sortys employee lounge. The cowboy walked behind them with the M4. Blaine noticed the guy kept at least ten yards between them. Not that Blaine had any ideas about wrestling that rifle away. Even if he wasn't hurt, even if each step didn't make him wince just a little bit more, he couldn't risk a fight now, with Sandra so close and Mason right in front of them.

No, this wasn't the time. Not yet. He had to wait for the right moment, the right circumstances. It would come. It always came, sooner or later.

As they passed the jewelry section of Sortys, Blaine noticed some of the glass counters had been smashed. Jewelry was scattered everywhere, some on the floor, crunching under his shoes. He imagined someone excitedly bashing the cases open, grabbing the expensive merchandise, and then having second thoughts. What the hell were you going to do with jewelry now?

But then he saw it—silver. The pieces were under one of the still-intact glass displays. A fancy pen, a folded label under it boasting that it was 100% silver. A whole set of silverware—forks, spoons, and butter knives. Things no one looked at twice, but invaluable in the new world. Blaine made mental notes.

They continued through the shoe area before exiting the opened gates where the department store connected to the rest of the mall. Their shoes squeaked against the dirty ceramic tile floor, the only noise in the entire place. The stores were open around them, basking in sunlight pouring down from the skylights.

"There isn't a single creature inside the mall during the day," Mason said, up-front. "That's the compromise. This place is all ours. It's not a bad way to live, if you think about it. The mall has everything we need to survive. Food, shelter, entertainment."

"Entertainment?" Blaine said.

"There are two gyms in the place. Basketball court, track, everything to keep busy. Plenty of non-perishable food to last years. Bottled water, soft drinks. Endless boxes of the stuff from around the world, just lying around. You can die an old man eating this stuff." He chuckled. "I'm not saying you'd be a very healthy old man, but hey, you'd get to be old."

Mason led them up an escalator frozen in place.

As he took the first step, Blaine thought, *Steps. Awesome.*

He did his best to hide his discomfort as he took the steps one at a time, but he thought the cowboy might have picked up on it. When Mason and Sandra started to outpace him, Blaine forced himself to move faster.

Two figures looked down at them from the second-floor railing. They were both wearing hazmat suits and carrying M4 rifles, and he could tell by their shapes that one of them was a woman. The hips were a dead giveaway. Their weapons looked new. In comparison, he remembered the scratches and dents on Will's and Danny's rifles.

By the time they reached the second floor, Blaine was winded but fought through it and kept moving anyway. Sandra had stopped and was waiting for him, and she reached out a hand and he took it. She squeezed and smiled at him. *"Our secret,"* that smile said.

"Beaumont's a big city," Mason was saying, his voice echoing off the second-floor storefront windows and the big glass skylight above them.

A thick pool of sunlight poured down on top of them like an ocean, illuminating almost all of the second floor.

Including the bodies.

Dozens. Hundreds.

Thousands.

At first Blaine thought he was staring at a cemetery covered in dead bodies, but then he realized they were still alive when he saw their chests moving slightly underneath their clothes. They looked like coma patients, stuck somewhere between sleep and death, with grotesquely thin frames, gaunt faces, and cheeks hollowed from malnutrition. Some looked frailer than others, and some were no more than just skin and bones, reminding him, in so many ways, of ghouls.

A woman lay less than six feet from the tips of his dirty sneakers. He couldn't tell her age; all he could see was a skull underneath loose flesh that fell over her face like a flimsy, thin piece of see-through film. They all looked like that, and it was impossible for him to tell adults from children, old men from boys. Their hair looked like dried-up leaves exposed to the sun too long, and he was reminded again of freshly buried corpses.

The sight of them—and the sheer *number* of them—took his breath away. They were spread out across the entire second-floor structure, and he could spend all day counting without ever getting to the end.

He looked behind them, and there were more spread out on that side of the floor.

There were so many there was absolutely no space to walk once they stepped off the escalator. Even the two people in hazmat suits watching them couldn't move very far without stepping on an arm or a leg.

"Beaumont has over 100,000 people squeezed into an eighty-five square mile radius," Mason said. "They turned most of the population, but not all of them. The rest are here."

"What...is this?" Sandra asked, her voice almost a whisper.

"It's a farm," Mason said. "A blood farm. Don't ask me how they do it, but they put these people in some kind of coma. They don't wake up. Ever. Then they...well, you know what they do."

"They feed on them?"

"Ding ding, give the lady a cookie."

It wasn't until Sandra said the word "feed" that Blaine noticed the teeth marks along the arms of the woman in front of him. Not just her arms, but along the sides of her neck as well. He imagined there must have been more, but her clothes covered up the rest. He turned slightly to look at an old man wearing shorts next to the woman and saw similar markings along his arms and legs.

We're their food. This is what happens to food. You store it, then you feed on it when you're hungry.

I think I'm going to throw up.

Next to him, Blaine could almost feel Sandra's entire body trembling slightly.

"They're alive?" Blaine asked.

"They're breathing, yeah," Mason said. "As to whether they're really still alive?" Mason shrugged. "Hell if I know."

"No one's ever woken up," the cowboy said behind them.

"So they just feed on these people...over and over?" Sandra asked. "And you let them?"

"Let them?" Mason almost laughed. "I guess you could put it that way. We just do the grunt work. Keep the place secured during the day while they sleep. At night, well, we try to stay out of their way."

"And what happens then?" Blaine asked.

"What happens to what?"

"To the rest of you when night falls?"

"Nothing. They leave us alone. That's the deal."

Sandra looked over at Mason, then back at the cowboy, then over at the other two in the hazmat suits. "And you're fine with this? All of you? Leaving these people to be...victimized over and over every night?"

They stared back at her with blank faces, though Blaine detected a slight movement in the woman's face behind the gas mask just before she looked away.

Sandra focused her stare on Mason. "How could you do this? To your own kind?"

If she had expected Mason to retreat, Sandra would have been disappointed.

Instead, Mason glared back at her. "It's a new world, honey. We're doing what we have to in order to stay alive." Mason drew his Browning automatic and held it at his side, then looked at Sandra before shifting his dark black eyes over at Blaine. "The question is: what are the two of you willing to do in order to survive?"

"HE'S DESPERATE FOR us to join him," Blaine said, later, when they were back in the Sortys employee lounge.

Sandra nodded. She sat on the sofa, rubbing her hands together as if she were cold. "Why, do you think?"

"Maybe he's running out of people. There's only five of them. Mason, the cowboy, the third guy, and the two on the second floor. It explains why they didn't risk attacking Will and the others. Not enough people to start a fight they don't know they can win."

There was a window above them, too small to escape through. Not that Blaine thought they could have gotten far anyway, without weapons or a car. There was a reason Mason had put them back in here. They weren't going anywhere except through the door, and there was a guard outside named Lenny. He was the third man from Cavender's.

They had two options that Blaine could see: join up or be killed. Mason had shown surprisingly little interest in harming Sandra, which both comforted and disturbed him. Sandra was not the kind of woman you ignored. At least, not after the first few minutes of being in the same room with her. But Mason revealed zero inclinations toward her, and neither had the cowboy, though Blaine had noticed Lenny stealing a glance at her when he had taken up position outside the door earlier.

Blaine's mind returned, as it had every other second of the last thirty minutes, to the people on the second floor.

Thousands. There has to be thousands up there...

"We can't, Blaine," Sandra said after a while. "I won't do it."

"We don't have any choice."

"There's always a choice."

"They're probably not going to kill us, Sandra. They're going to give us to the ghouls. They're going to add us to those people up there. I don't want to see that happen to you."

She looked down at her hands. "I can't, Blaine. I'd rather die than be a part of this. I don't ever want to become like Mason, taking the easy road out. But I also don't want to become like those people on the second floor. Do you understand?"

He nodded. "I understand."

Blaine took the bottle of Tramadol from his pocket and shook out two, gulping them down without bothering to swallow. Mason had given him back his pills, though Blaine didn't for a second believe the man was being altruistic. Mason wanted to turn them to his side, and letting him die didn't figure into those plans.

"How long does it usually take for those things to work?" Sandra asked.

"A few minutes."

"How many do you have left?"

He looked into the bottle at the dozen or so pills. "Not many…"

"There should be some over-the-counter painkillers around the mall. They won't be the same, but …"

"Yeah," he said, saving her the trouble of lying to him.

They looked over at the door as the doorknob turned. The door opened and a woman entered. They both instantly went quiet, and the woman stopped for a moment, like she had just barged into a room with two conspirators. Which wasn't far from the truth.

She had short brown hair and brown eyes, and she looked much smaller without the hazmat suit. She wore cargo pants and a T-shirt like the others and had a gun belt around her waist, though it looked too big for her frame. She closed the door behind her, then pulled out bags of Doritos from a brown plastic bag and tossed them over.

"They're a bit stale, but they're edible," the woman said. "It's as good as you're going to get around here, despite whatever Mason told you."

Blaine remembered how the woman had looked away from Sandra's accusing stare back on the second floor. She was the only one.

"Thanks," he said. "Do you have a name?"

"Maddie."

"I'm Blaine, this is Sandra."

Maddie nodded and turned to go.

"Is it worth it, Maddie?" Sandra asked.

The question stopped Maddie, and she turned to look back at Sandra. Blaine realized she was much younger than he had thought. Late twenties, though she wasn't wearing any makeup and that made her look slightly older. She was pretty, but in the same room with Sandra, you could get away with calling her homely.

"Is what worth it?" Maddie asked.

"Selling out the human race," Sandra said. "Is it worth it?"

"It's either this or become one of the people on the second floor. Or one of *them*. Honestly, I don't know which is worse, and I hope to never find out."

"Can we trust him?" Blaine asked. "Mason. Can we trust what he says?"

"Mason's an asshole," Maddie said. "But yeah, you can trust him on this. We lost a couple of guys a few months ago, so we're short-handed. More and more people with guns are rolling through this place every week. Most of them are smart enough not to risk searching a mall, but you get the occasional idiots, and we have to deal with that."

"What happened to those guys that came into town before us?" Blaine asked, hoping to sound just uninterested enough to not make her suspicious.

Maddie shrugged. "They're up the road somewhere. Mason sent someone to keep an eye on them until they leave."

"So he's not going to attack?"

"With what? These yahoos?"

Blaine smiled. He decided he liked her.

"If you're smart," Maddie continued, "you'll sign up. It's either that or keep running and constantly looking over your shoulder. I know what that's like. It gets old pretty fast."

"So you're saying it's worth it," Sandra said.

There was an overtly accusing tone to Sandra's voice that made Blaine flinch, and he saw it affect Maddie the same way. Sandra wasn't trying to make friends, and he wondered what she hoped to gain here. Didn't she know they were at the mercy of these people, that antagonizing them wasn't going to help the two of them one bit?

"It depends on what you want out of this life," Maddie said matter-of-factly. "You'll have to decide for yourself."

Maddie opened the door and left. Blaine caught a glimpse of the tall, broad-shouldered Lenny outside, turning as the door opened, but before he could look in, Maddie closed the door in his face.

Sandra looked quickly over at Blaine and said in a low voice, "Gaby and Josh and the others. They're still in the city."

"Sounds that way."

"Maybe we can get them to help us."

"I don't see how."

"Gunshots, maybe. Draw their attention. The way you drew my attention back at Grime. The way we tried to call them in Lancing. Sound travels these days."

"We'd need guns…"

"We can get guns," she said, looking at the door.

"Too risky. Let's wait."

"For what?" she asked, looking unhappy.

"Maddie."

"What about her?"

"I think she's the key," he said, though he didn't quite know how yet.

BEFORE NIGHT FELL, Maddie returned with another plastic bag containing more food and warm bottles of Gatorade that she handed to Sandra. She was already wearing her hazmat suit but had her gas mask clipped to her hip. Lenny wasn't at the door anymore, but they still kept it locked from the other side.

Blaine was standing under the window, watching the sun descend outside, and with it, the very familiar sense of dread. Mason wasn't entirely wrong. Constantly having to outrun the darkness was a pain in the ass. The knowledge that each night you survived only meant another day where you had to do it all over again was tiring, and sometimes he just wanted to stop.

"What now?" Sandra asked Maddie.

"You'll need to stay in here during the night," Maddie said. "They usually leave this part of the mall alone. Mostly it's straight up to the second floor to do what they have to do."

"Why the suit?" Blaine asked. It had been on his mind all day.

"It's how they tell us apart from, well, you," Maddie said. "One of them told Mason to wear it, so we wear it. I don't know where they got the suits, to be honest with you. After a while, you become used to it. It's actually pretty comfortable, even out in the sun, which is a nice bonus, I guess."

"You said 'one of them' told Mason to wear the suits? You mean one of the creatures?"

"Yeah. There's one of them that talks to him from time to time." She watched them closely, as if trying to gauge if they believed her. "It has blue eyes," she said after a while.

Blue-eyed ghoul!

"Blue eyes?" Sandra said. He could hear the disbelief in her voice.

"Yeah," Maddie nodded. "Damnedest thing I ever saw. Blue eyes, and it stood tall. You know, like a human. Well, I guess it used to be human, but it still carried itself like one."

"What does it say to Mason?" Sandra asked.

"It tells him what they need us to do, that sort of stuff."

"Was it a woman?" Blaine asked.

"What?" Maddie said, her eyes darting to him.

"The blue-eyed ghoul," he said. "Was it a woman?"

"I don't know," Maddie said, and seemed to think about it for a moment. "It's hard to tell with them. Why?"

"I was just curious."

She stared at him, disbelieving his answer.

"After tonight, then what?" Sandra asked.

Maddie looked back to her. "Mason will want an answer by morning."

"And if we say no?"

"Then he'll probably shoot you. Or hand you over to the creatures. I don't know. I do know that it's in your best interest to say yes."

"We're thinking about it," Blaine said.

He said it quickly, before Sandra could answer. He needed Maddie on their side, and the more she considered them potential allies, the better. Blaine didn't think he had a chance in hell of convincing Mason, the cowboy, or Lenny.

Maddie is the key…

"Think fast," Maddie said. "Mason will kill you. I hope that isn't something you're doubting. He will, and he won't lose sleep over it for a single night."

"He had a gun to my temple," Sandra said. "I don't doubt that at all."

Maddie nodded and opened her mouth as if to say something else, but stopped. She turned and left instead. Blaine heard a key turning in the lock, then footsteps fading down the hallway.

Sandra looked over at him. "It would be nice, wouldn't it?"

"What's that?"

"To not have to keep looking over our shoulders. Not have to keep trying to outrun the day."

He nodded. "It would be nice, yeah. But it hasn't come to that yet. Give me until tomorrow."

"Then what?"

"I don't know yet."

He could see how tired she looked, how beaten down and exhausted by the last few days. She opened the bag and pulled out a box of animal crackers and two Gatorade bottles, one lemon-lime and the other Hawaiian punch.

She tossed him the crackers. "Your favorite."

Blaine caught them and sat down next to her. He opened the box and fished out an elephant and took a bite. It wasn't bad. Sandra opened one of the Gatorade bottles and drank from it. For a moment, they sat quietly and drank warm artificial drinks and snacked on slightly stale animal-shaped cookies. From time to time they glanced up at the fading light coming from the other side of the window.

"Gatorade," Sandra said. "I used to hate this stuff. Hated it even more when it was warm like this. Now? It's not so bad."

Blaine felt bloated after a half-dozen crackers and handed her the box. He didn't have to look up at the window or glance at his watch to know that night was closer. The room had started to get dark around them, inch by inch, until he couldn't see half of the employee lounge anymore.

"That thing about the blue-eyed ghoul," Sandra said. "Do you believe her?"

"Yes. Because I saw one, that night at the house."

She looked at him, shocked. "Why didn't you tell me?"

"I thought we were going to die. And when we didn't... I guess I just forgot."

"Did it...say anything to you?"

He shook his head. "I saw it from the second-floor window. It was in front of the house while the rest of them were attacking. Like it was coordinating the attack, I guess."

"You think it was a woman? You asked Maddie if it was a woman."

"It could have been. It looked like a woman. But like Maddie said, it's hard to tell with them."

Sandra looked back toward the door. "Blue-eyed ghoul or not, I don't want to think about what's going to be happening outside that door tonight."

"Then don't."

"How can I not?"

She leaned her head against his shoulder, like she was finally lying down for the first time after centuries of being awake. Blaine wrapped his arm around her body and pulled her tight.

"We have to get out of here," she whispered softly. "We can't be a part of this."

"I have a plan. But we'll need Maddie's help."

"You think she'll help?"

"God, I hope so, otherwise there's no plan."

"Are you going to tell me?"

"Not yet."

"Why not?"

"Because I haven't been able to convince myself it has a chance in hell of actually working yet."

"Oh. That good, huh?" she said, smiling a bit.

"Yeah."

Soon, they were swallowed up by darkness along with the rest of the employee lounge.

"Blaine?" she whispered in the darkness.

"Hmm?"

"When I went back to find your body and you weren't there?"

"Yeah?"

"I wasn't going to leave Grime."

"What do you mean?"

"I mean, that was it. I was going to find a place and lie down, and that would have been it."

"Oh." He didn't know how to respond. After a while, he said, "I'm glad you didn't."

"Me, too," she whispered.

Blaine tightened his arm around her and heard her sigh in the darkness.

Outside the mall, beyond the window, he thought he heard what sounded like rats scurrying. But of course he knew it wasn't rats.

It was a much more dangerous infestation…

CHAPTER 20

JOSH

PROS AND CONS: What were they?

Pros: He was with Gaby. Not just with Gaby, he was lying on his bedroll with Gaby in his arms.

Cons: None.

Conclusion: *Gaby was sleeping in his arms.*

Small rays of sunlight penetrated the semitrailer through one of the breathing holes a few inches to his left, where the floor met the side wall. There was just enough light for Josh to see Will moving around. Lara was still asleep, and Will moved around her. He slipped on his assault vest and began filling up the pouches, then wrapped his gun belt around his waist and holstered his Glock.

"Lara said you and Danny were Army Rangers," Josh said.

"That's right."

"You guys were in Afghanistan."

"We were."

"What's the difference between this war zone and that one?"

Will smiled, as if he found the question amusing, and Josh once again felt like a kid asking his dad questions that, to his old man, were obvious.

"There's a lot more of them here," Will said. "Other than that? Not a whole lot. It's still hard to tell friend from foe when the sun is up, and the roads are still deceptively dangerous."

"I would have never made it through boot camp. Much less Ranger training."

"You'd be surprised."

"You think?"

"You never know what you're capable of until you don't have a choice. Everyone thinks they have a certain limit, a threshold, things they are able and willing to do in order to survive. That only lasts until they're actually confronted with it. When there's no turning back, when there's just one path and one path only, you'd be surprised how hard you can fight. Take you for instance."

"Me?"

"I'm guessing you weren't a two-sports athlete in school."

Josh grinned. "Lucky guess."

"But look at you now. You're alive. With a pretty blonde sleeping in your arms. Where do you think all those two-sport jocks in your school are right now?"

"Running around outside at night in their birthday suits would be my guess."

"But not you. Did you think you would survive the end of the world?"

"Not in a million years."

"And yet you did. Eight months later, and you're still going strong. That whole thing in Folger's semitrailer was impressive. You came up with that."

"It was survival instinct," Josh said, feeling a bit embarrassed by the praise. "I didn't know what else to do."

"Exactly. You were confronted with a situation that would have resulted in something unacceptable. Maybe they would have killed you, maybe not, but they would have definitely done something to Gaby. Faced with that, you fought and you survived."

"I didn't even know it was going to work."

"Like I said, you never know what you're fully capable of until you have no choice."

"Thanks," he said, feeling himself swelling with pride.

"It wasn't a compliment," Will grinned at him. "It was an assessment. Don't doubt yourself. You're capable of more than you think you are. You already proved that when you survived, while the vast majority of the world didn't. They failed—but you didn't. That girl is depending on you. Don't let her down."

"I won't," Josh said, and he realized he meant it. Every word of it.

Will glanced down at his watch. "Sunup is in five minutes. I have a mission for you, if you're up to it."

"I am," he said quickly.

"We're going to be moving out as soon as we can, but it's going to take about an hour to fill up the gas tanks and get everything moved back to the trucks and cargo trailer. Take Gaby and see what else is out there, including on the other side of the freeway."

"Just recon?"

Will smiled. "Yeah, just recon. Don't go inside. Make a mental list of places we can hit for supplies if we have the time, then come back here. Understand?"

"Gotcha."

"Do *not* go inside, Josh."

"Don't go inside," Josh repeated.

GABY WAS ALL for doing a little reconnaissance. She had usually stayed behind whenever Josh and Matt went out for supplies when it had been just the three of them, but he could tell by the way she quickly answered that she had been waiting for this moment. He was glad because it meant spending more time alone with her.

Josh was anxious to get out there again, but it wasn't until he started walking through the plaza's big lot that it occurred to him this was his first supply run without Matt. It felt strange to be walking outside with Gaby, but she looked to be in good spirits. He figured it was because she was free of the claustrophobic constraints of the semitrailer.

For the third time in as many minutes, Josh touched his Glock to make sure it was in his hip holster. The Glock was still loaded with silver bullets, and he had a second magazine loaded with regular ammo in a pouch. Gaby was also wearing a gun belt, but she didn't look like she was used to it yet.

"What are we looking for?" Gaby asked, when they reached the Exxon gas station.

"Anything we can use."

"Supplies?"

"More like medicine, weapons, and silver."

"I can't believe we survived this long without knowing about silver."

"Better lucky than good, I guess."

They peered into the Exxon. It was a combo gas station and Taco Bell. He smelled rotting meat from inside and immediately shut off his smelling faculties when he got the first whiff. Gaby made a face and they quickly jogged across the street to another strip mall, this one full of electronic stores, a GameStop, a Payless shoe store, and a Verizon outlet.

"You need a new phone?" Josh asked.

"God, I used to text so much. I miss texting. Don't you?"

"Not really. I miss the Internet."

She smirked. "You miss Internet porn, you mean."

"Wait, there are other things on the Internet besides porn?"

"I miss shopping," Gaby said wistfully.

It was amazing the things they used to do before the end of the world. Getting a car, finding a girlfriend, worrying about exams late into the night. All of those things had seemed so important, once upon a time. Now they were like bad jokes that weren't quite as funny as he had once thought. He wondered if this was what it was like to grow up.

What was that saying his mom liked to use on him whenever he acted like a brat? "*When I was a child, I spake as a child, I understood as a child, I thought as a child: but when I became a man, I put away childish things.*"

Something like that.

They walked past a Radio Shack and looked in through the smashed windows at thick dark patches in the back.

"I miss Matt," Gaby said quietly.

"Me too," Josh said.

They walked silently for a while, weaving their way through the parking lot. Josh peered in at parked cars, hoping to spot something valuable. They found a lot of old, dried blood on car seats, doors, windows, and floors. Empty cans of soda. Water bottles. A Chrysler yielded an iPod that wouldn't light up when he tried to turn it on.

After a while, Josh stopped, and Gaby stopped with him.

"What is it?" she asked.

Josh looked around them. "Will said not to wander off too far."

"But we haven't found anything yet. I don't want to go back

empty-handed."

Josh considered their options. If they kept going straight, it would just take them farther away from the others. So what else was there? He glanced over at the street to their left, and the elevated highway behind that.

"We can try the other side of the highway," he said.

"Race ya!" she shouted and dashed off.

Josh ran after her, but she was much faster, even with the gun on her hip. Gaby had always been a natural athlete, and she had bounded across the parking lot before he had even managed the halfway point. Soon she was on the feeder road and running up the sloping side of the highway. By the time he reached the feeder road, she was already hurdling the guardrail and was waiting for him on the other side.

"Come on, slowpoke!" she shouted down.

Josh grunted. He might have been a survivor while everyone bit the dust, but that hadn't improved his athletic ability. He chugged his way up the hill, which was a lot harder than it looked, until he finally reached Gaby. She laughed and pulled him over the railing. He slumped down on the other side, next to a big red Ford truck with gaudy stripes along the sides.

"God, you're out of shape," Gaby said.

"Hard to believe, but this is the best shape I've ever been in," he said between gasps.

"That is hard to believe."

"Oh, that hurts," he said, and slowly pushed himself back up to his feet. Then he grinned at her, shouted, "First person across wins!" and raced off across the highway lanes.

He heard Gaby laughing as she raced after him, shouting, "Cheater!"

He laughed and reached the other side of the highway first, sliding to a stop in front of the railing just as she caught up to him. He doubled over and gasped for breath again as she put her hands on her waist and gave him a disapproving look. She was breathing hard, but it was nothing compared to what he was going through at the moment.

She's right. I am out of shape. Jesus H. Christ.

"You cheated," she said.

"You cheated in the parking lot."

"Okay, fair enough."

Then she grabbed him by the shoulders and pulled him toward her and kissed him hard on the mouth. Josh was still gasping for breath when she did it, and he ended up breathing a big lungful of air down her throat. He recovered quickly enough to kiss her back, but he knew he was clumsy and out of practice—which was funny, because he had never had any practice to begin with.

Gaby finally pulled away and smiled at him. "Wow. Did you just blow a big gust of air down my throat?"

He laughed, doing his best to hide his embarrassment. "You sort of caught me unprepared. Sorry about that."

"I didn't say it was bad. It was just…new. Have you ever kissed anyone before?"

"Does my mom count?"

"You kissed your mom on the mouth? Gross!"

He grinned. "Don't you?"

She rolled her eyes. "There's no shame in admitting you've never kissed a girl before. Lots of guys have never kissed a girl."

"I'm eighteen, Gaby, of course there's shame in that."

She laughed. "You're probably right. What else haven't you done yet?"

"If I've never kissed a girl, what else do you think I haven't done yet?"

She pretended to think about it. "Let me see…"

He grabbed her and pulled her to him. He kissed her hard and deep, putting everything he had into it. It was a sloppy and wet kiss, and amateur hour for sure, but she didn't seem to mind. She leaned into the kiss, and Josh lost count of how long they stood there at the side of the highway just kissing under the scathingly hot morning sun.

After what seemed like the best eternity of his life, he finally had to let her go so they could both catch their breath.

She took a step back and smiled at him. "Not bad. I'm going to put this up on my blog so all my readers will know about it."

He blushed a bit and decided to power through it with a big, awkward grin. "Make sure you disguise my name. I don't want girls knocking down my door demanding free samples."

"I'll call you Bosh. How about that?"

"Eh, it's better than Dosh."

They exchanged another smile, and Josh thought he saw her cheeks redden just a little bit.

Whoa. I think just made Gaby, the hottest girl in school, blush.

Suck on that, mofos!

HE SAW IT initially from the elevated vantage point of the highway while he was waiting for Gaby to catch up. It was a small plaza with two buildings in it, and the sign read: "Medical Budget Care." Josh took that to mean it was some kind of clinic, or maybe a business that catered to clinics. Which meant medical supplies, either way.

He led Gaby down the highway and toward the plaza, holding her hand the entire time. He felt giddy, like a kid on the first day of school.

"Is this a good idea?" Gaby asked when they crossed the feeder road and reached the concrete parking lot, stepping around decorative shrubbery.

"We'll take a quick look. If there's nothing, we head back."

"Let's just hurry."

He let go of her hand as they approached the buildings. The first and closest structure only had one floor, with "Beaumont Health Resources" written in big, blocky white letters on its side. The red brick building next door had two floors, but he couldn't spot any signs.

"I don't think we have time to search both buildings," Josh said. "So we'll have to choose. The big red building or this one?"

"Why me?"

"You're prettier."

"Can't argue with that." She seemed to think about it. "Okay, this one looks promising," she said, indicating the building in front of them.

"Are you just saying that because it's the closer of the two buildings?"

"That's entirely possible," she smiled.

"Good enough for me."

They approached the front entrance—two glass doors under an arching black plastic canopy. They passed two silver four-door sedans, almost identical, except they were slightly different models. Josh glanced briefly into the closest car and saw blood on the seats and what looked like an old cup of Starbucks on the driver's side floor.

He turned his attention back to the building. It had two big windows on opposite sides of the door, one with closed blinds, the other unblocked, and Josh saw an empty reception area on the other side. It looked exactly like the veterinary clinic that he, Danny, and Will had gone into back in Lancing.

And there was a nice surprise in that place, too.

Josh drew his Glock and took hold of the glass door. When he tried pulling it, the door opened without resistance.

"Are you sure this is a good idea?" Gaby asked behind him. "I know we don't want to go back empty-handed, but this seems like an awfully bad idea, Josh."

"It'll be okay," Josh said, trying to convince himself, too. "We have the right ammo this time."

This is so stupid. Stop right now and go back.

"But just to be safe," he said, "stay behind me, okay?"

"My hero."

Maybe she's right. Maybe we should turn back now.

God, this is so stupid.

But he had come this far, and he hated to turn back now. Will was right about one thing—no one would have put money on him surviving the end of the world. He had proved them all wrong. Even Matt, who was bigger and taller and stronger, eventually went, too. And yet, here he stood, persevering, with Gaby next to him. Who would have seen any of this coming?

Josh pulled the door open to reveal the lobby. It was just as empty as it had looked through the window, with enough natural light to illuminate every corner and nook. The lack of dark shadows made him feel better, and Josh relaxed a bit and stepped inside.

"Stay here," he said, and hurried over to the window with the closed blinds. He grabbed the long stick dangling from the top of the window and twirled it and the blinds opened up, throwing more sunlight into the room.

As with the pet clinic, there was a reception counter directly ahead of the front doors, and cheap, flimsy-looking chairs lined the lobby walls. The counter had a sliding opaque glass door left partially open, and Josh glimpsed a messy desk with papers everywhere and a splash of brown that he took for long-ago dried blood. There was a single hallway leading into the back and doors into rooms on both sides. The sunlight didn't reach farther than five yards into the hallway, so everything else after that was a mystery.

Josh looked back at Gaby, standing nervously at the door. "You didn't, uh, bring a flashlight, did you?"

She shook her head. "You didn't say anything about a flashlight."

"Yeah, my bad."

She smiled. "Your bad?"

He smiled back. "My bad. People still say that, right?"

"You mean the dozen or so people we've met since the world came to an end? Then no, I don't think people say that anymore."

"I—" he started to say, but he never finished because he heard it, the *sound of movement*, and he turned his head back toward the hallway, just as a dark shape rushed out.

Before Josh had time to fully process what he was seeing, something big and heavy and monstrous crashed into him, knocking every ounce of breath out of his lungs. Josh flew backward and fell to the floor on his back with a solid *crunch*ing sound, and the figure was already on top of him, looming large.

Stupid. You should have stayed outside. God, you're so stupid!

The Glock was gone. It had flown out of his hand even before he hit the floor. He didn't know where it was now. He might have heard Gaby screaming, but that could just be the ringing in his ears. That, and the immense pain from his back, where he had slammed into the hard floor, and from his chest, where the figure had smashed into him.

It wasn't a ghoul. It was a man. And he was wearing a dark gray hazmat suit—the thin kind worn by soldiers. The man inside was much bigger than Josh, and a hell of a lot heavier, too. Josh felt as if he had been broadsided by a speeding car, not by a man whose face was blurred behind some kind of gas mask.

Josh processed the information in the three or four seconds it took the guy to scramble up and sit on Josh's chest and punch him in the face. He hit Josh once, then again, and again. Josh knew he was bleeding before he felt the blood trickling down his face. His nose was definitely broken, and maybe one lip was cut. Or both.

He tasted blood.

Just for good measure, the guy punched him a fourth time before slowly climbing off him. From his vantage point, the guy looked like a giant, stretching, stretching, almost touching the ceiling with his height. The man reached down and started pulling out his holstered sidearm. It looked like a Glock. Josh saw dark brown eyes behind the wide gas mask lens looking down at him, and he wanted to ask the man what the hell he was doing, why he was wearing that stupid suit to begin with.

Josh couldn't get the words out. His chest and back were racked with involuntary spasms, his face throbbed, and it felt like every bone in his body was broken. He ached all over.

He thought about looking for his gun, but he didn't know where to start. He wasn't sure he was even still lying on the floor looking up at some stranger in a hazmat suit about to shoot him. Maybe he was just imagining all of this. Or dreaming it. Maybe he was actually still in the semitrailer, trying not to make too much noise, or even breathe at all, so afraid the ghouls might hear him.

Maybe—

He heard a gunshot. It was booming, massive, and it added to the chaotic ringing in his ears. First there was just one gunshot, then there was a second one, and Josh thought, *Well, that's it. I'm dying now.*

But he didn't die.

He didn't feel the new set of pains from his chest, where he expected them. The guy was aiming for his chest, so that's where the bullets would have gone. Only there were no bullets, because the guy hadn't fired.

Josh watched, unable to really comprehend, as the man in the hazmat suit fell to the floor next to him in a crumpled heap of dark gray, shiny fabric. There was no blood at all, though Josh did see two holes in the man's back, spaced about two inches apart. When Josh raised his head a little bit, he saw the blood inside the man's suit.

He looked over at Gaby standing nearby, holding her Glock in both hands. She was staring down at the dead man on the floor, before pulling her eyes away and looking at him.

He remembered Gaby from a few days ago, with the bloody key gripped between her fingers like a weapon, stabbing Betts's neck. That Gaby had been on the verge of tears, and had shaken for hours afterward.

This Gaby, looking back at him, was strangely calm. "Are you okay?" she asked.

He managed to nod, but when he opened his mouth to answer, pain shot through him. He laid his head back down on the floor instead and stared up at the ceiling.

Idiot, you should have stayed outside.

You're such an idiot…

CHAPTER 21

LARA

SHE HADN'T THOUGHT she would see another one, or maybe she had just been hoping she wouldn't see another one. But there it was, lying on the floor of the clinic with two bullet holes in its back.

A man in a hazmat suit.

Another man in a hazmat suit.

This suit looked different from the ones she had encountered with Will and Danny in Dansby, Texas, all those months ago, but Will said it was the same type of suit. Level B, he called it. Not the big, bulky Level A with its own breathing apparatus. Back in Dansby, they had encountered ten men in Level B hazmat suits, determined to keep their loyalties to their ghoul masters. Here, there was just one. Or at least, just one they could see. Lara couldn't decide if that was a good thing or a bad thing.

"It must be nearby," Will said.

"Do we even wanna find it?" Danny asked.

"Yes," Lara said. "If we know it's around here somewhere, we have to look for it."

They were talking about a blood farm, the same kind they had found in Dansby. Men, women, and children harvested by the ghouls to supply them with a never-ending flow of fresh blood. Because the ghouls couldn't watch over the "farms" in the daytime, they needed human collaborators to do the job. That was where these men in hazmat suits came in. They wore the suits to distinguish themselves from other humans, to let the ghouls know they were part of the team. Lara had learned all this from a young collaborator named Kevin.

"And then what?" Will asked her.

"What does that mean?"

He was looking at her carefully, in that calm, non-argumentative way that was, nonetheless, argumentative. It sometimes annoyed the hell out of her.

"We can't take them with us, Lara," he said. "You know that. What happened the last time we stumbled across one of these farms?"

"We freed one of them."

"No, we got lucky. We still don't know how they put those people in a coma. Or if it's even a coma. Even you didn't know, and you're the doctor."

Third-year medical student, she thought, but didn't say it out loud.

"We need to stay on course, keep going," Will continued.

"They could be around here," she insisted. "Hundreds. Maybe thousands. This city is thousands of times bigger than Dansby."

"Even more reason not to try to find them."

"See no evil, hear no evil, is that it?"

"In this case, yes."

She was flustered. It had been a while since she had thought of Will as someone who wasn't always and completely on her side. She felt that now, and it was a terrible, hollow feeling. The worst part was, he was so damn cold and detached about it.

"Danny?" she said. "What do you think?"

"I think he's right," Danny said, almost apologetically. "Carly, the girls, you, and those teenagers. We don't have the ability to save any more people. Hell, we don't even have the space. Once we get everyone to Song Island, and it turns out to be the safe haven we hope it is, then we can come back here. It's not like they'll be going anywhere, right?"

She was suddenly annoyed with both of them, but especially with Will. But most of all, she hated knowing they were both right. They had the others to look after. The girls. Josh and Gaby. One of these men had almost killed Josh.

But knowing and accepting were different animals. She felt guilty and angry at the same time, and the feeling made her skin crawl.

"Lara," Will said, putting a hand on her shoulder. She wanted to shake it off, but she willed herself not to. "This is my call. Okay?"

She looked at him. His call. He was doing it again, taking the burden of the hard decisions, putting it on himself. Because he could handle it. Because he was Will, ex-Army Ranger, ex-SWAT commando, and there was nothing he couldn't handle.

But she knew better. She saw him at night, when he wasn't so sure, so steely-eyed, when they made love and he sighed against her like any other man, not the Superman everyone else had come to rely on. She remembered when he had confessed that he was afraid, back in Lancing.

"That scares me," he had said, *"because it means whatever happens, wherever we go, it might not be enough to protect you."*

Protect me. He does everything to protect me.

"What about him?" she asked, looking down at the dead man on the floor.

"I think it's a bit too late for him, Doc," Danny said.

"Let's go," Will said, "before more of them show up. A city this size has got to have a pretty big blood farm, and it must take more than one asshole to watch over it."

The others were waiting outside. The trucks were gassed up, and their supplies were back where they belonged. Carly was outside the truck, the girls peering out of a window over her shoulder, the air conditioner blasting away at their hair.

"How many?" Carly asked.

"Just the one," Danny said.

"That's a good thing, right?"

"Where there's one, there're usually more. And they must have heard the gunshots, but they didn't show up, so…" He shrugged. "Maybe they're scared and know we're bad men with guns."

"Either way, we're not sticking around to find out," Will said.

"I like that idea," Carly nodded.

Danny climbed back into the Frontier with Carly, while Lara followed Will to the Ridgeline.

"I'm sorry," he said, when it was just the two of them outside.

"Don't be," she said. "You're looking out for us, doing what's best. And you're right. We can't do anything for them anyway."

She thought about Megan, a girl they had saved from the Dansby blood farm, only to lose track of her during the siege at the facility that very same night. Lara didn't even know what happened to

Megan, and in the months since, she had always wondered if bringing Megan back with them had been the right thing to do. It had felt like the right thing at the time, but Megan might think otherwise now. She would still be at the farm, yes, but she would still be alive.

Or some kind of "alive"...

"Still, I'm sorry," Will said.

She gave him a pursed smile, her own way of apologizing. He brushed hair out of her eyes, a simple move that always made her feel like a teenager. "What about Gaby?"

"What about her?"

"I think one of us should talk to her. About what happened."

"She's a tough kid. She'll be fine."

"That's it? She's a tough kid so she'll be fine?"

"I've seen people like Gaby before, Lara. She'll be fine."

Lara wasn't convinced as they climbed back into the Ridgeline. Josh and Gaby were in the back, and Lara fought the urge to flinch at the sight of Josh's face. His eyes were bruised and swollen, his left eye in particular puffed up to twice the size of his right. His nose was broken, with a small Band-Aid over the bridge. His lips were cut, but they had stopped bleeding. Although Lara was sure the teenager was in some pain, he looked more embarrassed than hurt.

Gaby, on the other hand, looked fine sitting next to Josh, handing him a bottle of water every other minute and fussing over him. Lara wondered if it was all a front. Maybe Gaby was going through some things inside her head that she couldn't express in words. Lara remembered the first time she had killed someone. It still lingered with her, something she didn't think would ever go away.

And this wasn't even Gaby's first time. They knew about Betts and how Gaby killed him so they could escape. Both times, Gaby was justified in what she did. Lara would have done the same in her place. Carly, Will, and Danny, too. But they were older, and they had seen more. Gaby was eighteen, but looking at her now, fussing over Josh, Lara couldn't tell if that calmness was an act, a brave front, or the real thing.

Either way, that's a tough girl. Maybe Will's right.

"You guys ready?" Lara asked.

"Good to go," Gaby said.

Josh gave her a thumbs-up. When he tried to talk, his words

slurred, a combination of the pain medication she had given him and his bruises, so he had stopped trying.

Will started the Ridgeline and eased them back onto the feeder road, where they continued parallel to the highway. There was just enough space along the small roads that they could use them instead of braving the congestion, even though every other half mile meant driving up onto the sidewalks, sometimes even the lawns, before moving back to the streets.

It was slow going, but they were making steady progress. Lara was worried about the Frontier behind them. It was pulling the cargo trailer and had more trouble going up and down the sidewalks, so she kept in touch with Carly as much as possible.

"How's it going back there?" she said into the radio.

"It's going," Carly answered. "I wish Danny was a better driver, though. It's like being stuck in a car with an eighty-year-old man with arthritis who refuses to admit he has arthritis. It's annoying."

"I drive fine," they heard Danny say through the radio. "In fact, I drive great. They used to call me Danny the Driver because I drove so well."

Lara smiled. She could picture Carly rolling her eyes. "Let us know if you need to stop or if something happens."

"Will do," Carly said.

Will leaned over and said into the radio, "Stay frosty."

"Oh, I'm frosty," Danny said. "I'm so frosty, they used to call me Danny the Frosty Snowman."

This time Lara actually rolled her eyes.

USING THE MAP, they were able to abandon the feeder road system and start using smaller streets, eventually returning to the main highway when US 287 became I-10 and they began moving east instead of south. It was still slow going on the interstate until they broke through near the edge of town.

By 11:11 A.M., they left the city of Beaumont behind.

Not long after, they were driving through a thickly forested area, with towering trees on both sides of the highway. Will estimated they would cross the Texas-Louisiana border in about forty-five kilometers, or klicks as he put it.

"What's that in miles?" Gaby asked.

Lara smiled. She was glad she wasn't the only one having trouble with Will's kilometers.

"Twenty-eight miles," Will said. "Give or take."

"You could have just said that in the first place," Lara teased.

He gave her a mildly annoyed look, which made her grin. She liked needling him whenever the opportunity presented itself, because there were so few opportunities with Will.

"Road looks pretty clear," he said, already moving past the topic. "It gets tricky once we're across the state line. Beaufont Lake isn't exactly easy to get to, and we'll have to leave the interstate, take a small road farther down south. And from there, find a spot to launch to Song Island. Hopefully there will be a marina or two nearby that we can use."

"Hopefully?" Gaby asked worriedly.

"There has to be," Lara said. "How else did the people already on Song Island get to the island in the first place?"

"Makes sense," Gaby said.

I hope so.

WHEN THEY FINALLY drove across the Texas-Louisiana border, Lara felt great relief. It occurred to her that she hadn't thought they would ever actually get out of Texas alive, and the simple act of crossing an imaginary line on a map was like a great big weight lifting from her chest.

There was no celebration or fanfare in the truck as she watched Texas recede in her side mirror. Not that you could really tell where the Lone Star State ended and the Bayou State began. The sun-drenched stretch of interstate concrete looked the same here as it had for the last thirty miles.

The road ahead of them thinned out noticeably, and it became a rare thing to see cars on the road. Which made sense, since they were now moving through flat farming country. Sometimes they went for whole chunks of minutes without seeing another sign of civilization, though she caught sight of the occasional farmhouse or barn in the distance, swamped by overgrown grass, or a garden overcome by weeds.

After a while, the monotonous sight of vast farmland got the better of her, and, lulled by the cold air conditioner blasting away against the bright sun outside, her eyelids started getting heavy.

She didn't remember when she closed her eyes, but when she opened them again, it was almost two hours later and the Ridgeline was exiting I-10, having slowed down almost to a crawl in order to maneuver around a big pile-up between a couple of trucks and a big rig in front of them.

She sat up in her seat, rubbing at her eyes. She saw buildings, stores, and gas stations around her again. "Where are we?"

"A town called Salvani in Beaufont Parish," Will said.

She glanced up at the review mirror and saw Josh and Gaby sleeping in the back, Gaby's head resting on Josh's shoulder. They looked comfortable, like a couple.

"Will, you should have woken me up," she said, slightly annoyed with him.

"Maybe next time."

Lara heard stirring behind her as Josh and Gaby were woken by their voices. Josh stretched and yawned, while Gaby rubbed her eyes and looked out the window.

"Wow, civilization," Gaby said. "I didn't think I'd ever see it again."

Lara caught sight of the reddish-tinted rooftops of a La Quinta to their right as Will took the feeder loop. He turned into the right exit, passing a Shell gas station, before turning onto Ruth Street. She glanced at her side mirror and saw Danny in the Frontier following closely behind.

"Waffles," Gaby said longingly in the back seat. "It's been ages since I've had waffles. I would absolutely kill for waffles right about now."

Josh nodded in agreement, but apparently still didn't trust himself to speak. He had become even more bruised and purple in the hours since his encounter with the man in the hazmat suit back in Beaumont. The swelling was worse, and it would probably take a day for everything to start going down.

They passed the Waffle House sign, letters spelling out the restaurant's name in yellow square blocks hoisted high in the air. Passed a Conoco gas station, a Sonic fast food restaurant, and an Archer Sports and Outdoors warehouse. Lara glanced at a big billboard ad for teeth cleaning along the side of the road, and suddenly the stores and buildings gave way to homes and open, undeveloped land.

"Are we close?" Lara asked.

"We're almost there," Will said. "Ruth Street becomes Route 27 and keeps going until we're alongside Beaufont Lake. Sixty klicks, give or take." He added quickly, "About forty miles."

She smiled. "Thanks."

"Sure."

"People actually live out here?" Gaby asked. "What do they do for fun?"

"People can get used to a lot of things when there aren't any other options," Lara said. "Adapt or perish."

They were up to forty miles per hour now, traveling down a two-lane road with nothing but farmland and sun-bleached acres to one side—occasionally broken up with more dying, brown foliage—and a string of ancient-looking telephone poles on the other. She thought the poles made for a strangely poetic sight, stretching into what seemed like infinity in an almost perfect line.

She looked up at the wide-open sky. "How are we for time?"

"Three-fifteen," Will said. "We're doing good."

After a while, Route 27 curved slightly left before straightening back out again. They drove in silence for another thirty minutes, and Lara started to see bayous below them whenever they drove over a bridge.

We're getting closer…

She saw a big body of water to their left, on Will's side of the truck. Josh and Gaby saw it, too, and they moved anxiously toward the driver's side to look out their window.

Beaufont Lake was big and visible from Route 27, and it looked like it went on endlessly. The water had a nice blue tint to it, not the brown of the Texas lakes she was used to. Lara felt her heart quickening in her chest, the anticipation and exhilaration returning after lying dormant for so long.

"Beaufont Lake," Gaby said, almost as if she couldn't quite believe it.

They drove past a massive power station with huge, domed towers sparkling under the hot sun. Maybe a hydro power station, like the kind Harold Campbell built into his underground facility. It was right next to the lake, so that was a possibility. There were no signs of people, but the fencing and entrance gate looked intact. Lara wondered if there were people hiding in there. It was certainly big enough. She decided there probably weren't. Sanctuary was only as good as the supplies you had, and she didn't think anyone could survive with the supplies scattered around this mostly deserted area of the world.

They kept going, and for a while they didn't see anything of note again. That was, until a small town rose out of the nothingness. There was a sign for a marina on the other side of a bridge they were crossing, reading, "Jackson-Miller Marina" in faded letters next to a turn. Will drove across the bridge, and Lara saw boats in the marina.

"We need boats, right?" Lara said.

"We're still too far from Song Island to launch here," Will said. "We need to get closer."

"What if we don't find another marina farther down?"

"There has to be one. If not, we'll come back."

Lara never caught a sign that introduced the small town they were driving through, and soon they were making a huge left turn before turning right a little bit later. They were going south again, still traveling on Route 27. The town disappeared behind them, and Jackson-Miller Marina along with it.

They drove for another thirty minutes, passing marshlands and swamps on both sides of them. Nothingness became the order of the day once more. Trees became rare sights, shade from the harsh glare of the sun even rarer still. She wondered how long she would last out here, on the road without a car.

Probably ten minutes...best-case scenario.

After a while, the road started to curve right, and Will slowed down to twenty miles per hour.

He picked up the radio from the dashboard. "Danny."

Danny answered from the other end: "What's the word?"

"We're almost there. Slow down."

"Roger that."

Will put the radio back on the dashboard. "Start looking for a marina."

"Which side?" Lara asked.

"It'll be on my side. Look for buildings, warehouses, parked trucks. Any signs of civilization."

"I haven't seen signs of civilization for the last hour, Will."

"There should be something here."

"What if—" She didn't finish, because she saw the sun glinting off metal rooftops up ahead on Will's side of the road. "Buildings," she said, somehow managing to keep herself from shouting it out.

"I see it," Will nodded.

There were two buildings—a big garage and what looked like a gazebo in the middle of nowhere. As they got closer, Lara saw a wooden sign pointing into an asphalt parking lot. She tried to read the sign, but it was so badly scarred by time that she could only make out the word "Marina." There were numbers, which she guessed was a phone number, or possibly hours of operation.

Will turned left into the parking lot.

There were two white trucks parked next to the gazebo, and the garage was bigger up close, and longer. At least a four-car garage. There were a half-dozen vehicles, mostly trucks, parked near the shores in orderly fashion. She expected to see trailer hitches with boats in the back, but there weren't any. She did see boat ramps to their right.

Where are all the boats?

They parked and Lara climbed out, stretching her legs, grateful to finally be moving again. The pain in her left shoulder had mostly disappeared overnight, and what remained had continued to fade during the long drive, thanks to a combination of rest, water, and painkillers. She could move the arm easily enough without the sling, though she still felt some throbbing every now and then and did her best to keep as much pressure off it as possible.

Walking closer to the edge of the parking lot, she could see where the launches fed boats into a small, man-made inlet that continued south, connecting to the main body of Beaufont Lake. Directly across from the inlet, farther up the road, was the first livable spread she had seen for miles. It was a white, two-story house surrounded by hurricane fencing. A green boathouse stood out to its left, and she could just barely make out two boats hanging from the rafters. The house had a big, wide-open parking lot, though no garages; and farther back, a big gray, plain-looking building that was too long to be another house. Storage, she assumed.

"I wouldn't mind a place like that," Gaby said, shielding her eyes from the sun as she looked across the inlet at the house.

"I guess we know where we're staying if Song Island doesn't pan out," Lara said. "Speaking of which... Where is it?"

"Where's what?"

"Song Island."

"Oh. I guess it'd be out there...?" Gaby pointed toward the large expanse of calm water, blinking against the sun. "Shouldn't it be out there somewhere? It is an island, right?"

"Should be..."

Gaby drifted back to where Josh was standing, gazing off into the distance, probably looking for the mythical Song Island, too.

So where the hell is it?

The suddenly very real possibility that they might have come all this way for nothing made her chest tighten a bit. It took the sight of Carly, walking toward her with a big grin on her face, to get Lara to push those downbeat thoughts away.

"We made it," Carly said. "I can't believe we actually made it."

Lara smiled back at her. "Never doubted it."

"Never?"

"Okay, maybe once or twice."

"I knew it."

Carly laughed and wrapped Lara up in a big hug, slipping her arms around Lara's waist instead of over her arms. Lara laughed, too, because she knew exactly what Carly was feeling. The road from Harold Campbell's facility had felt, at times, never ending, with one roadblock after another. Doubts had begun to creep into her thoughts even if she had refused to acknowledge them until now.

Lara heard a fake *clicking* sound next to them and looked over at Danny, miming taking a picture of them with his fingers. "This is going into the Rolodex for tonight."

"Way to ruin a great moment, babe," Carly said.

Lara saw Will nearby, peering through a pair of binoculars at something in the distance. She walked over to him, trying to see what he was looking at. The sun was in her eyes, and she couldn't see much except calm, glistening water under an empty sky.

"Do you see it?" she asked, unable to keep back the anxiousness in her voice.

He lowered the binoculars and handed them over to her. "Have a look."

"Is it out there, Will? Song Island?"

"Just look."

She took the binoculars from him, her hand shaking a bit. Will stood next to her as she held them up to her eyes and looked across the lake. "Where am I looking?" she asked, frustrated. "I don't see anything."

"Here," Will said. He stood behind her and guided her slightly to the left. "There. See it?"

She saw it—a big structure rising out from the lake itself. It was tall and looked a bit like a pencil, getting smaller the higher it went, though it was barely discernible in the distance and was surrounded by water. There was something else, like a ring of children's glitter sparkling under the sun, encircling the structure.

"It's a lighthouse," Will said behind her. "Doesn't look completely finished, but I'm pretty sure that's a radio antenna sticking out of it. That's where the FEMA broadcasts are coming from."

Lara realized, breathlessly, that the lighthouse wasn't rising out of the water on its own. It was jutting up from a patch of land in the middle of the lake, previously obscured by the rippling heat against the surface of the water. Now that she was staring at it, the land seemed to sprout before her eyes, rising and rising until it presented itself to her in all its glory.

She caught her breath, afraid it would disappear like a mirage if she lowered the binoculars or looked away for even a second.

Song Island...

CHAPTER 22

BLAINE

THEY APPEARED AS soon as the sun abandoned the world for another day. They weren't just on the rooftop of the Sortys department store, they were all around them. He couldn't see them, so he didn't know how many there actually were, but he could hear and *feel* them along the walls, the floor, and every inch of the building, and that told him everything he needed to know.

Sandra lay on the couch in his arms, as quiet as he had ever seen her. With the painkillers still kicking around in his system, Blaine didn't feel a whole lot of pain, but the drugs also kept him wide awake for most of the night, listening to the ghouls as they traveled back and forth, through, above, around, and, he swore, *underneath* him, too.

He tried not to think about what was happening on the second floor of the mall. He tried not to picture those poor souls up there. Did his best to shut out the images of teeth marks along arms and legs and necks of prone victims, hanging somewhere between life and death.

Did they know what was happening to them? Were they crying out right now, tormented by the fact that no one could hear them?

His skin rippled with a sensation Blaine hadn't felt in a long time. A combination of fear and shame and hopelessness.

"Is it the pain?" Sandra asked.

"No," he whispered back.

"Oh."

It stayed with him until he finally fell asleep around three in the morning. He closed his eyes, and when he woke up, the feeling was still with him, in his mouth, like a lingering bad meal regurgitated over and over.

He also felt the renewed, unwanted sensation in his side. He quietly pulled his pill bottle from his pocket and shook two pills out, then popped them into his mouth.

"Go easy on them," Sandra said, lying against him, her eyes still closed.

"Just two."

"How many do you have left?"

"Not a lot."

"Go easy," she said again.

They heard footsteps approaching, and Sandra untangled herself from him and stood up just as the door opened and Mason came in. He was wearing his hazmat suit, but not the gas mask, looking absurd with his head sticking out of the shiny gray uniform. Maddie was behind him, but Lenny, who sometimes watched the door, wasn't outside this morning. Blaine had learned last night that the yahoo with the country accent was Gerry. He wasn't there, either.

"Rise and shine," Mason said. "Decision time. Are you with us or are you against us?"

He smiled at them, but Blaine didn't believe there was anything remotely heartfelt about the smile. Just to prove Blaine's thoughts correct, Mason casually laid his right palm over the butt of his holstered Browning.

Blaine looked past Mason at Maddie. The two of them were almost the same height and looked like teenagers playing at being soldiers. Maddie was clearly uncomfortable with what was happening, but she looked committed nevertheless. If not to Mason, then to survival, and that meant standing behind the man with the gun.

Blaine wondered if he could get to Mason and end this, but the man was too far enough away. Even on his best days—and he was far from that at the moment—there was no way he could take that distance before Mason shot him dead.

"I don't think we have much of a choice," Blaine said.

"You speak for her, too?" Mason asked, eyes going to Sandra.

"Yes," Sandra said quietly.

"Are you sure?" Mason smiled. "You don't sound like you're

very sure."

He sounds like a fucking game show host. All of this is just fun and games to him.

"Yes," Sandra said again, louder, though not necessarily with any more conviction than the first time.

"All right, then." Mason clapped his hands. "First order of business is breakfast. Then we'll get the two of you fitted for suits. You look like the kind of gal who could make the color gray work. You certainly got the tits and hips for it."

Sandra glanced over briefly at Blaine and frowned.

He tried to smile reassuringly back at her.

God, I hope this works…

IT DIDN'T TAKE much to convince Blaine that Mason didn't really trust them. For one, the man wouldn't give them their guns back. Or let them carry any kind of weapons at all. The only thing he issued them, other than their ugly gray hazmat suits and gas masks, were radios.

"What about our guns?" Blaine asked.

"You won't need them," Mason said. "You see anything, you hop on the radio and we come running."

"You get guns when you prove you deserve them," Gerry added.

Mason left them with the cowboy, who sat by himself at a table across the food court from them. Gerry ate greedily from a can of SPAM. Blaine wondered how long it would take before the cowboy accidentally stuffed too much of the canned meat into his mouth and choked on it.

With my luck, never sounds about right.

"When would that be?" Blaine asked instead.

"*When you deserve them,*" Gerry said. "Which part of that don't you understand? You want I should speak slower so you can *habla*?"

Blaine grinned back at him. He wasn't sure which part of Gerry he disliked more—his face or his country twang.

"What exactly will we be doing?" Sandra asked Maddie, who was sitting at another table nearby.

Sandra sat next to Blaine, both of them in their hazmat suits, the gas masks on the round metal table in front of them. The seat was uncomfortable and dug into Blaine's ass even through the suit. He picked at the can of tuna with a flimsy plastic spork while Sandra ate a can of chicken. There was plenty of canned food to go around, Maddie told them, showing them boxes and boxes of the stuff in a storage room next to the Sortys employee lounge.

"Guard duty, mostly," Maddie said.

"Without weapons?" Blaine asked.

"Guard watch," Maddie corrected herself. "You don't need weapons for that."

The food court was next to the non-working escalator they had previously taken up to the second floor, and Blaine could see the guy Maddie had been standing guard with yesterday still up there. His name was Bobby, and he had yet to take the gas mask off, so Blaine still didn't know what he looked like underneath it.

"It's not that bad," Maddie said. For a second, Blaine thought she was trying to convince herself more than them. "After a while, you get used to it. It's boring work. When it's your turn, you stand on the second floor and watch the sleepers. That's what we call them."

"Food" is more like it.

"What happens if one of them wakes up?" Sandra asked.

"They don't," Maddie said.

"But what happens if they do?"

"They don't," Maddie repeated. "At least, none of them have woken up before in all the time I've been here."

"You don't know what the ghouls did to them?" Blaine asked.

"Not a clue," she said. Then, "'Ghouls'?"

"That's what they look like to me," he lied. "Ghouls."

Maddie smiled a bit. "Yeah, you're kind of right. They are ghoulish looking, aren't they?"

Everything about this is ghoulish.

"What now?" Blaine asked.

"I'll show you the rest of the mall first," Maddie said.

"Bullshit," Gerry said, his voice coming out of nowhere. For a moment Blaine had forgotten he was even there. "Why the fuck are you showing them where everything is?"

Maddie flashed him an annoyed glance. "They already joined us, dickhead. What's the point of hiding things from them now?"

"Just because they say they're 'with us' doesn't mean they're actually *with us*, you idiot."

"Go fuck yourself," Maddie spat back.

Gerry shot up from his seat, so fast he almost knocked the can of SPAM from his hands. Blaine instinctively reached for his hip, for the gun that wasn't there. Not that Maddie needed his help. She sprang up from the table and glared back at Gerry.

Blaine was wondering how badly this was going to go when all of their radios squawked at the same time, and he heard a male voice that was new to him: "They're moving."

"Where?" Mason's voice responded through the radio.

"Leaving, I think," the man said.

"Who's that?" Sandra asked.

"Dirk," Maddie said. "He's the one Mason sent to watch over the people who came through here yesterday, before you guys showed up."

Will and the others.

"He's watching them now?" Blaine asked, trying to sound as neutral as possible. He could see Gerry, still standing and wound up, watching him closely from across the food court.

"He's been watching them since yesterday," Maddie said.

"Yeah, they're definitely moving," the man named Dirk said through the radio. "If you want to do something, this is going to be it. We're going to lose our chance in a few hours."

"No," Mason said. "Stay out of sight."

"Are you sure?"

"Did I stutter?"

"Come on, we can take them," Dirk insisted.

"Stay the fuck out of sight," Mason said.

"Okay, okay," Dirk said, and the radio went quiet.

Maddie picked up her can of tuna and tossed it into a trash can that was almost topped off. "Dirk's an okay guy. He can be a bit of an idiot sometimes, but he's a guy, so that comes with the territory."

"Tell me about it," Sandra said.

The two women exchanged a brief knowing look.

"Come on, I'll show you where everything else is," Maddie said.

Blaine and Sandra got up and followed Maddie away from the food court. He could feel Gerry's eyes, like lasers, burrowing deep into his back the entire way.

"SPAM CAN LAST for over five years if you store it right," Maddie said. "Of course, whether you want to still be eating SPAM five years from now is another matter entirely."

"You sound like you know this from experience," Blaine said.

She laughed. "Yeah, we weren't exactly the richest people in our county."

"Where you from originally?"

"Travis County. Around the Austin area."

"I thought Austin was a rich city," Sandra said.

"I said around the area, not actually in it. We didn't have a lot, so we made do. I also grew up hunting. I killed my first deer when I was thirteen. I'm pretty handy with a hunting rifle, but this assault rifle stuff is all new to me. It kicks like a bastard."

"What about the country boy?" Blaine asked. "Gerry."

Maddie snorted. "He's mostly talk. Don't let him get to you."

"He got me pretty good yesterday," Blaine said, feeling the soreness in his side all over again.

"Yeah, he's good with the cheap shots, too, you have to watch out for that."

Maddie led them back through the Sortys department store, where the group made their base camp. They passed racks of clothing and shoes and towels sitting undisturbed on the same hangers from eight months ago. There was just enough sunlight from the windows up front to navigate by.

"Why Sortys?" Sandra asked.

"Mason decided," Maddie said. "It's close to the food court and it faces the highway. Other than that, I don't know."

"Does he decide everything?" Blaine asked.

"Pretty much, yeah."

"Who put him in charge?"

"He was the guy who made the deal with the creatures. The ghouls."

"How did that happen?"

"I don't know. Bobby and me met up with him about two months after everything went tits up. He already had it set up pretty good here, with Gerry and Dirk, and a few other guys."

"Lenny?"

"No, Lenny came later. I don't even remember those other guys' names. Dan or Phil or something." She shrugged. "Out of sight, out of mind, as the saying goes. They're dead now, anyway."

"What happened?"

"People driving by, like you two. That's why Mason pulled up on you like he did. He doesn't want to take any more chances. The last time he did, his guys got killed."

"Is that why he didn't attack the other people who rolled in before us?"

"Pretty much. He's an asshole, but he's a smart asshole. He doesn't fight battles he knows he can't win."

"I guess that's why he decided to betray his own kind," Sandra said.

Blaine saw Maddie physically flinch next to them.

Oh, Sandra, you gotta learn to stay quiet, baby. This is no time to be riling up the only person who may be our friend in this entire place.

He said quickly, "He was trying to survive. Hard to blame him for that. We all do what we have to do."

"That's right," Maddie said.

Sandra looked over at him, half angry and half questioning. He shook his head back at her, thankful Maddie had moved farther in front of them and couldn't see.

They eventually reached a back hallway in the department store Blaine guessed used to house the Sortys staff.

"This is where we stay," Maddie said. She led them past a half-dozen rooms, all offices that now held sleeping bags and sofas and boxes of food and supplies. "I guess eventually you'll be able to grab one of these rooms."

"When Mason's sure we're fully onboard," Blaine said.

"Yeah, something like that."

Maddie led them to the very back and pushed open the door into a room about the same size as the employee lounge. There was a bank of security monitors along one side of the wall, and a half-circle desk and a small jail on the other side. Half of the jail cell contained boxes, the other half housing five, maybe six plastic moving crates filled with weapons. He saw shotguns, handguns, and hunting rifles. Everything was just far enough away from the bars that he wouldn't be able to reach in and grab a gun.

"Store security," Maddie said. "Cameras don't work anymore, of course, but there's nothing wrong with the jail. All the weapons and ammo we could find from the mall and from the buildings around the city we've been able to search so far. People out here really like their guns."

Blaine spotted his Remington 870 leaning against a crate.

"Yeah, that's yours," Maddie said. "You'll get it when Mason says you can have it back. Before then, I can't help you."

"Who has the key to the jail cell?" he asked.

She smiled at him. "Wouldn't you like to know."

"Is that an invitation to search you?"

She laughed. "You wish."

Mason has the key. Of course he does.

"Come on," Maddie said, and headed back to the door.

Blaine and Sandra followed her out, and when Maddie had gotten far enough ahead of them, Sandra said in a low voice, "Are you trying to piss me off on purpose?"

"What?" he said, matching her quiet pitch.

"First that bullshit with Mason out in the hallway, and now the flirting?"

"Flirting? I wasn't flirting."

She rolled her eyes at him and walked ahead. "Whatever."

Blaine followed her, wondering if she was right. *Was* he flirting with Maddie? He didn't think he was. He was being friendly, trying to win her over. That was the point, wasn't it? She was the only person here who was a potential ally, and he was doing his best to bring her over to their side. If he was flirting at all, it wasn't on purpose.

Or at least, he didn't think it was.

Blaine was still trying to justify himself in his own mind when he heard two soft, faded *pop-pop* sounds in the distance.

He stopped and listened and heard the echoes.

Maddie and Sandra heard them, too, and also stopped in the hallway.

"Was that...?" Sandra said.

"I think so," Maddie said. She pulled her radio free and keyed it: "Did anyone else hear that? Were those gunshots?"

"It's Dirk," Mason said through the radio. He sounded more annoyed than angry. "That son of a whore. I told him to stay the hell away from those people."

"STUPID DIRK," MADDIE said, looking at the dead man lying face-down on the floor, still wearing his hazmat suit. The man would look like he was sleeping if not for the two holes in his back and the blood pooled inside his suit.

They were inside some kind of clinic along the highway, across from where Will and the others had spent the night before. That was according to Mason, who had been tracking Dirk's movements since he had sent the man out here to watch them. As for Dirk, he did something Mason told him not to—he showed himself to Will's group—and ended up dead for his efforts.

The lobby showed signs of a struggle, with a couple of overturned chairs and blood that wasn't Dirk's, because all of Dirk's blood was in his suit. There were two shell casings, so Dirk had never even gotten off a shot, though his killers had taken his gun.

Gerry came out of the hallway behind them, holding a radio in one hand. "The moron turned off his radio and left it in one of the rooms."

"Dumb bastard," Mason said. He looked up at them. "See what happens when people don't do what I tell them? I told Dirk those people were too dangerous, but he didn't listen. This is what happens when you don't listen to me."

They were all wearing gas masks, and it was odd seeing the world through the clear lens. He could tell from the way Sandra fidgeted in her suit next to him that she felt the same way. The suit was surprisingly comfortable in the sun, which he supposed was the point of the special fabric. The gas mask was another story. Besides the fact that it made his voice sound strange, he didn't like the feel of the plastic pressed against his face. Maddie and the others didn't seem to even realize they were wearing masks anymore.

"You sure you don't know who they were?" Mason asked Blaine.

"Yeah," Blaine said. From his experience, people who couldn't lie tended to over-explain things, so Blaine kept his answer as short as possible.

"Doesn't matter. They're gone anyway."

"We should go after them," Gerry said.

Mason glanced over at him. "Why the hell would we want to do a fool thing like that?"

"They killed one of us. We can't just let them get away with it."

"He was an idiot who didn't follow orders. You want to disobey orders, too?"

"That's not what I said," Gerry said, and Blaine could hear his voice getting softer, less confrontational. "I'm just saying, this sets a bad precedent."

Mason laughed. "Precedent? You're out of your mind. Just do what I say. Shit, I've kept you people alive for this long, haven't I?" He looked over at Blaine and Sandra. "The noobs get manual labor duty. Bring him back to the mall."

Mason turned and left, with Gerry following silently.

"Were the two of you friends?" Blaine asked Maddie.

Maddie looked down at Dirk. "I wouldn't go that far, although he wasn't really that bad a guy. Probably a bit too high-strung and thought too much of himself, but that doesn't make him much different than the rest of these bozos. But friends? I wouldn't say that, no."

She followed the others out of the clinic.

Blaine and Sandra exchanged a look, then glanced down at the dead body. They had seen plenty of dead bodies, but never one in a hazmat suit before.

"Maybe we can find a wheelbarrel to move him," Sandra said.

"Or a shopping cart," Blaine said.

Sandra sighed. "You take the arms and I'll take the legs…"

THEY DIDN'T HAVE to go far with Dirk. The others were waiting outside in a red Ford truck. Sandra and Blaine grunted their way from the clinic to the parking lot and tossed Dirk into the back, where Gerry was sitting. He moved away as the body landed near his legs and shot Blaine a look. Sandra and Blaine climbed into the truck and sat across from Gerry while Mason drove them back to Willowstone Mall.

Back at the mall, Sandra and Blaine followed Maddie to the second floor, where she introduced them to Bobby. He was a young kid with long blond hair and dark brown eyes, and he looked much older than his twenty-two years. But then again, they all looked older.

Bobby had shown up in Beaumont with Maddie, the two having met on the road. He was also mute, which explained why he was always so quiet. He nodded to them when Maddie introduced him, then drifted off, turning back to the sleepers scattered about the second floor.

"That's just how he is," Maddie said. "But if you need someone to watch your back, you won't find a better partner. Plus, he won't talk your ears off."

Blaine glanced over, wondering if Bobby had heard, but the young man didn't react if he had.

"How many of them are up here?" Sandra asked.

"Thousands," Maddie said. "I tried counting a few months ago, but I stopped around 2,000."

"Over 2,000?"

"Yeah."

"Where do they come from?"

"I don't know. Most of them were already here when I arrived with Bobby. The rest were brought here by the ghouls. Sometimes they'd show up with just one, sometimes dozens at a time. You never know." She shook her head, and he thought she looked almost sad. "Try not to think too much about it. After a while, you get used to it."

Maddie turned and walked back down the escalator.

Looking after her, Blaine wondered if Maddie really had gotten used to it, or if she was putting on a front for them. He hadn't heard a whole lot of conviction in her voice and thought it was probably more of the latter.

Maddie is the key.

They spent most of the afternoon on the rooftop, wearing their hazmat suits and occasionally taking off their gas masks to drink warm water or eat canned fruits. Guard duty meant watching the empty highway and the wind picking up debris and tossing it around the empty city. Blaine had never felt so alone as he did sitting up there with Sandra and Maddie, guarding a city that had housed over 100,000 souls at one point.

Every now and then, Mason, Lenny, or Gerry (sometimes a

combination of the three) would leave the mall, but they were always back less than an hour later. Each time they left, Blaine found himself wondering if he could hurt Maddie, take her gun, and escape with Sandra. He probably could, even in his condition.

But how far could he and Sandra go on foot? Their Silverado was parked in front of Sortys, but there was no sign of the key. Without the Silverado, they would have to take one of the other cars in the parking lot. And if they couldn't find one with the keys nearby and a working battery under the hood, they would have to look farther out. Blaine wondered if Mason would let them go if they did make a run for it, the way he had refused to confront Will's group. That was the best-case scenario. The worst case had Mason taking it personally and committing to chasing them down.

No, not yet.

If things went sideways, he could consider that option. There was still another way, one that didn't involve hurting Maddie. One that involved *convincing* her.

"You and Bobby came straight to Beaumont?" Blaine asked Maddie.

"We spent a few weeks in Austin, gathering supplies," she said, between spoonfuls of pineapple dripping with syrup. "Then there were smaller towns between here and there. We thought about trying Houston, but it was too big. You know what big means, right?"

"A lot of them."

"Right. So we mostly avoided Houston. I know this guy with a cabin near Sabine Lake. It has good hunting grounds, and there aren't a lot of people there. We were headed there when we stumbled across Mason in Beaumont."

"He introduced himself with those rifles, too?"

She snorted. "Yeah. He made us the same offer he gave you. It looked like he had a good thing going here. Plus, you know how it is on the road. It's sleep with one eye open, always looking over your shoulder at the sky." She put down the spoon and looked off at the highway in the distance. "If I'm really, really lucky, I'll make it another year. Meanwhile, I don't want to spend every second of it wondering when they're going to get me. You know? That's no way to live."

Sandra watching Maddie closely, and maybe he saw her soften a bit toward the other woman. It was hard not to. Maddie wasn't a monster—not even close.

"You did what you had to," Blaine said.

"Yeah, I know," Maddie nodded. "But like you said, it's a hell of a way to survive."

They sat on the hard roof and said nothing for a while. Blaine thought he heard car engines in the distance, but noticed he was the only one who turned his head. He waited, but nothing appeared, and he chalked it up to his imagination running overtime.

Maddie saw his face and smiled. "It's the quiet. It plays with your mind. Makes you think you're hearing something that isn't there. Pretty soon you'll start to see things, too." She handed him a pair of binoculars. "Use them before you grab the radio. It'll usually turn out to be nothing."

"How many people come through here a day?" Sandra asked.

"Once or twice a week is more like it. Yesterday was the first time we saw two groups of people in the same day." She narrowed her eyes amusedly at Blaine. "You sure you don't know those people?"

"What did they look like?" he asked.

"Doesn't matter. They're gone. Probably in Louisiana by now if they keep on the I-10."

"What about this cabin at Sabine Lake?"

"What about it?"

"You don't want to find out if it's still there?"

"Oh, it's still there. Where's it going to go? It's a cabin."

Blaine caught Sandra's eyes, and knew she understood where he was going.

"You don't think it's worth getting to anymore?" Sandra asked. "The cabin?"

"Compared to this?" Maddie said. "You know how many of them are out there. It's going to take a fortress to keep them out of a cabin, even one that remote. Sooner or later, they'll find it."

"What about an island," Blaine said.

"Island?" Maddie looked over at him. "What about an island?"

"I bet an island could keep the ghouls out. Even better than a cabin or a mall could."

"Yeah, sure, but where would you find an island?"

"Let me show you something," Blaine said.

HE FOUND A ham radio in a Best Buy next to the Sortys, then grabbed a handful of new batteries from a rack near the cash registers. He made sure Gerry, Mason, and Lenny were nowhere to be found before he powered the ham radio up and hunted down the FEMA frequency.

"What am I listening for?" Maddie asked.

"Give it a minute," Blaine said.

He stopped fiddling with the dial when he heard the familiar female voice:

"...Song Island on Beaufont Lake in Louisiana. We are broadcasting on the FEMA frequency to any survivors out there. We want you to know there is hope. There are survivors on Song Island. We have food, supplies, electricity, and protection against the darkness. If you are receiving this recorded message, we encourage you to make your way to us. I repeat: we have food, supplies, electricity, and protection against the darkness. Hello. If anyone can hear me out there. This is Song Island on Beaufont Lake in Louisiana. We are broadcasting on the FEMA frequency ..."

Blaine was watching Maddie's expression the entire time, trying to gauge her reaction to the message. At first she looked confused by what she was hearing, but that quickly gave way to shock, followed by...hope?

Or maybe he was reading her wrong. He was never particularly good at reading women. Sandra knew that firsthand.

"Is it true?" Maddie asked, once the message started repeating itself.

"To be honest, I don't know," Blaine said. "But if it *is* true...?"

"What about the water? The ghouls can't cross water?"

"I don't know that, either. But they've been on that island for months now, and they're still out there."

"But you don't know for sure," Maddie insisted.

"I don't know anything for sure, no," Blaine said. "I just know that this message has been repeating for months now. Every day, without fail."

"It could be on some kind of a loop."

"I'm sure it is. But the fact it's running in a loop at all..."

"Power," Maddie said, the realization dawning on her. "They have power."

He could see it. He had her. Or he was *close*. "Exactly. They have a power source. You can't run a radio tower without electricity."

"It could just be an emergency generator. We have them here, too."

"Sure, but to broadcast continuously, twenty-four hours a day, seven days a week, for months now?"

She nodded. "That's a good point." She went quiet for a moment, lost in thought. Then, "It would be nice to have power again. Plumbing. Running water…"

"You could come with us," he said.

She looked up at him with genuine surprise. "Where? Song Island?"

"Why not?" Sandra said. "You and Bobby. You wouldn't have to do this anymore. I know this isn't something you want to be doing for the rest of your life."

They didn't have to be mind readers to know how Maddie felt about doing this forever. They could read it on her face.

"Come with us," Sandra said.

Blaine was glad to let Sandra make the invitation. It wouldn't have sounded nearly as believable or sincere coming from him, even if he did mean every word of it. He was never particularly good at playing the softy, either.

"Bobby, too?" Maddie asked.

"Yes, of course, Bobby, too," Sandra said.

Maddie nodded. But she didn't answer right away.

Blaine exchanged a quick look with Sandra. *"We're almost there."*

"I need to talk to Bobby about this," Maddie said.

IT TOOK HER less than thirty minutes to talk to Bobby.

Blaine took that as a good sign, though he could have been very, very wrong. Fatally wrong. But Blaine didn't think he was. Still, the idea of putting his and Sandra's fate in another person's hands made him skittish. In those thirty minutes of waiting, he went through every possible scenario, most of them ending with him realizing, too late, that he had read Maddie wrong from the very beginning.

By the time Maddie climbed back up to the rooftop of the Willowstone Mall where he was sitting with Sandra, it was two in the afternoon, and the sun was at its full force, blasting away at everything under it. Even inside the protective hazmat suits, Blaine could feel sweat dripping along his armpits and back.

He heard sneakers crunching gravel and looked over as Maddie walked toward them. Despite his best efforts, he couldn't read the expression on her face. He wondered if she had gone to Mason and sold them out, or if he had cemented a new ally.

God, don't let me be wrong about her.

"Did you talk to Bobby?" Blaine asked.

"Yeah," Maddie nodded.

She paused and seemed to look off at the highway in the distance. He imagined she was trying to work her way up to something.

Blaine exchanged a worried look with Sandra.

Finally, Maddie said, "We're going to have to kill Mason and the others, you know that, right?"

Blaine nodded. He fully expected that. "Yeah, we know."

This time Maddie looked over at Sandra when she said, "Because he's not going to let us go. Not without a fight. And if we leave him alive, he'll come after us. Sooner or later, we'll have to deal with him, and it might as well be now."

"We understand," Sandra said. "How are we going to do this?"

"Depending on when we leave, I've got a few ideas."

Blaine grinned at her. "You've been thinking about this for a while, haven't you? How to take out Mason and the rest?"

She grinned back at him. "Maybe."

He listened to her lay it out. It was a pretty good plan. He was right; it was obvious she had given it some thought even before they had shown up. The more he thought about it, turning it over in his head as they stood up there on the roof discussing it, the more Blaine was convinced it could work. All they really needed was a little bit of luck and some timing. And if push came to shove, it was four against three, so the odds were in their favor.

It was a good plan.

That is, it *was* a good plan, until Lenny decided to fuck everything up.

CHAPTER 23

WILL

MARCUS, THE MAN who had showed up in the pontoon to pick them up, stood next to Debra, who drove the boat across Beaufont Lake and toward Song Island, still just a shimmering patch of land in the distance.

The pontoon was seven and a half meters long and looked like a floating raft with four recliners someone had decided to tack on. Then, just for good measure, they had added an admiral's high-back reclining chair in front of a steering wheel in the middle. Faded slick vinyl covered the chairs, and the floor matting made walking surprisingly unadventurous, even in boots.

A three-inch heavy-duty deck rub rail with impact bumpers surrounded the boat, and there was just enough space to squeeze everyone inside, though it was a tight fit. Of course, it didn't help that they brought two crates of supplies with them. On the plus side, the crates became impromptu seats. They also carried their personal items in backpacks, along with two heavy duffel bags—one for weapons and the other for ammo. It wasn't everything they had, but it was all they could fit and still bring everyone on the first trip. Will was wary about leaving anyone behind.

The pontoon moved along at a steady clip, powered by a V8 battery that was amazingly quiet. Will remembered going fishing with Marker, his former Harris County SWAT commander, and how Marker's aging boat's motor sputtered plumes of smoke and leaked gasoline before it even made it out onto the water. Compared to that trip, the pontoon ran like a dream.

As they neared their destination, Will eyeballed Song Island at about one kilometer long. He had no idea about its width, given that they were approaching it from just one direction. The lighthouse/radio tower sprouted from the eastern side—possibly northeast—and not from the center as he had thought when he had first seen it through the binoculars. He guessed the eastern section was also where the survivors congregated, and probably where the main buildings were located. Thick jungle foliage covered nearly the entire western half.

Tall, glinting objects encircled the slightly jagged, oval-shaped outline of the island. Using his binoculars, he picked up an impressive array of solar panels, held in place by long, thin steel poles reaching almost as high as the trees. From a distance, they looked like flagpoles with shiny metal boards on top, soaking up the sun's rays in crystalline cells. He could only see one side of the island, but it was clear the fence of panels extended entirely around. He did quick calculations in his head, using his guess of the island's width and length, and came up with…a hell of a lot of solar panels.

Will lowered the binoculars. He stood at the front with Lara and Carly, and the girls sat on opposite sides of the reclining seats. His M4A1 was slung over his shoulder, something that neither Marcus nor Debra had objected to before they had boarded the pontoon boat.

Marcus and Debra had shown up at the marina less than an hour after they had arrived. Their vehicles had been spotted coming down the road by a watcher in what Marcus called the Tower—the combination radio tower and lighthouse. From the Tower, you could apparently see the shoreline along the western cove of Beaufont Lake.

"How many people are on the island?" Will asked.

"Eleven," Marcus said. "Well, nineteen now, counting you folks."

The six-foot-tall Marcus, in his khaki shorts, Hawaiian shirt, and sandals, looked like a yuppie who had wandered too far from his natural habitat, the big city. His blond hair and blue eyes were incongruous against overly tanned skin. Marcus was in his thirties, and Will had thought *stockbroker* the first time he had seen the man riding up to the marina in the pontoon.

Debra had similarly tanned features, though she looked like she actually belonged out here on the water. Shorter than Marcus by about half a foot, she was also wearing sandals and shorts, along with a loose-fitting T-shirt. Debra had a lean face, not exactly unattractive, but she was far from either Carly or Lara or the girl, Gaby. Rough hands that clearly spent a lot of time working outdoors guided the boat's steering wheel with confidence. Frankly, she looked like the type of person a guy like Marcus would hire for a few days to take him fishing on her boat.

Neither Marcus nor Debra were armed, though Will glimpsed the barrel of a revolver in the slot under the boat's steering wheel, within easy reach for Debra. Marcus had been all smiles as the two of them had drifted up the inlet. It occurred to Will that smiling was something Marcus did well. Like breathing.

"Eight more people is a lot," Will said. "Is adding that many to the island in such a short time going to cause problems?"

"I don't see why it would," Marcus said. "There's plenty of room and plenty of food. Plenty of fish in the lake around us, too. You guys like fish?"

"I like fish," Danny said.

Danny stood in the back of the boat with Josh and Gaby. His M4A1 was slung over his shoulder. The fact that he was back there and Will was up front was no accident. If either Marcus or Debra noticed, they hadn't said a word.

"Can you fish?" Marcus asked Danny.

"You didn't say I actually had to catch my own fish," Danny said.

Marcus laughed. "Don't worry, there are plenty of people who don't mind reeling in your share. Debra here's one. It's not like there's a lot to do on the island. You can only explore it so many times before you run out of room."

"Free food without having to work for it? This sounds like my dream job."

"Why aren't you armed?" Will asked Marcus.

Marcus smiled at him. Apparently he had been anticipating the question. "We have guns on the island, of course, but we don't carry them around. There's no need."

"What about the creatures?"

"We don't have to worry about them, either."

"Is it the water?" Lara asked.

"Something in the water, yeah," Marcus nodded. "I can't tell you what exactly, not my department. But it's like the sun to them. For some reason, they don't go anywhere near it."

"Do you see them at night?" Carly asked.

"Along the shores, yeah," Marcus said. "But you'd need binoculars. We're too far from land to see anything with the naked eye, especially in the dead of night. You can see most everything that happens on this side of the lake from the Tower, including anyone approaching the marina."

"That's where the radio signal is coming from?" Lara asked.

"I think they were planning to run their own radio station. I have no idea."

"Whose idea was it to use the FEMA frequency?" Will asked.

"Karen's. Most of this is Karen's idea. I guess you could say she's our fearless leader."

"Welcome to Song Island," Debra announced, pulling back slightly on the throttle until they were drifting, carried forward by their momentum.

Up close, the island looked much bigger. It was still around one kilometer long, give or take, but there was enough foliage, vegetation, trees, and sandy beaches to give it the impression of being a much more expansive place. The solar panels also looked more prominent, each collection tray raised at least ten meters high. And he was right the first time—the solar panels wrapped completely around the island, like a string necklace.

"What's the story behind the solar panels?" Will asked.

"A company called Kilbrew Resorts bought Song Island about six years ago," Marcus said. "They were going to turn it into a private island for rich people, powered exclusively by solar and wind power. It was supposed to be a paradise for the environmentally-conscious. You know, get the hippie rich people from the cities someplace to play and let them leave with a clear conscience, all that good stuff. Unfortunately, they never got around to installing the wind component, but they did finish most of the solar installations."

"Is that how you're powering the radio tower?" Lara asked.

"It uses very little energy to broadcast," Marcus said. "The rest of the power goes to the rooms in the main resort buildings. We have more than enough left over for other things like TV, DVD players. The little things that make life worth living."

"You guys get cable, too?" Danny asked.

"They're installing it next week," Marcus said, playing along.

"NFL network?"

"That's extra, so no."

"Bummer."

"You mean there are finished rooms on the island?" Carly asked.

"Finished-ish, I guess you'd say," Marcus said.

"But roofs and walls and the like?" Carly pressed.

"Most of them, yeah. I think you'll like it here."

"Docking," Debra announced.

Debra had slowed the pontoon down almost to a crawl as they approached one of three piers sticking out of the island like wooden fingers. The piers were along one end of a clear, sandy white beach. There were already five other boats tied up, including two more pontoons and three fishing boats of different sizes and varieties.

A young man in his early twenties jogged along one of the piers in cargo pants and an LSU Tigers football jersey. He waved them over, and Debra slowly sidled the pontoon alongside him.

"That's Berg," Marcus said. "He was already at the marina when everything went to hell. Came to the island with us and hasn't stepped foot off the place since. I don't think he wants to, either."

"Smart kid," Danny said. "Why go out and fight monsters when you can sit here on the sandy beaches and fight crabs? Though I hear those can be pretty dangerous, too."

"You're thinking of the wrong kind of crabs, babe," Carly smiled.

"Never mind, then."

Berg, like Marcus and Debra, had dark, tanned skin from too much exposure to the sun. He grabbed a rope Marcus tossed over, the other end already tied around a metal cleat on top of the pontoon's gunwale. Berg pulled the boat over the last few meters, then tied it into place around a metal anchor.

"You're good," Berg said. Then he looked over at Lara and Carly and grinned, flashing crooked and slightly yellowing teeth. "Hey, ladies, welcome to Song Island."

Watch it, kid, I'm armed and you're not.

THEY PILED OUT of the pontoon and walked up the middle pier, Will using the time it took to travel from one end to the other to familiarize himself with his new surroundings.

The beach went on for quite a long stretch, taking up a good section of the southern side of the island, until it was abruptly cut off by encroaching trees and grass on both ends. There was enough sand and beach here to make for a very decent resort, which was probably why someone had spent a lot of money to do just that. The trees grew tall, providing plenty of shade, and the bushes were thick. The lake was invitingly blue, and he saw fish breaking the surface around them.

Behind the woods, he saw the looming structure Marcus called the Tower. It looked very much like a lighthouse, with a fat, cylindrical bottom that extended upwards, getting smaller as it neared the top. Will guessed it had to be about forty meters high, which made it taller than your average lighthouse. The height also made it a brilliant perch to see in every direction. Will saw two sets of windows, one near the top and a second set near the middle, which told him the Tower had at least three floors, not counting the unfinished section at the very top. There was supposed to be a glass housing up there, along with a revolving beacon that was never installed.

Marcus led the way up the pier, while Debra and Berg busied themselves with the pontoon behind them. Danny was all the way in the back, as planned. Will carried the heavy duffel bag holding half of their weapons and ammo. Danny carried the other half. He was surprised by how little interest Marcus and Debra had paid to what they were bringing on board the pontoon with them, almost as if they expected a level of paranoia from their visitors.

"You said eleven people?" Will asked Marcus. "How many of those came because of your broadcast?"

"Three so far, not counting you folks," Marcus said.

"I thought there would be more," Lara said. She walked beside Will, carrying her backpack over her good shoulder. While minus the sling, she still favored her right side whenever possible.

"I guess not everyone has a radio," Marcus said. "Or listens to the old FEMA frequency. I think more will show up in time."

A large, nondescript concrete building, aesthetically incomplete and the size of a four-door garage—and just as squat—sat at the end of the piers, the four windows facing them propped open. Will glimpsed boat supplies, machinery, and shelves with cartons of gasoline, oil, and thick, three-strand twisted ropes inside. The shape and construction of the boat shack reminded him of Harold Campbell's facility.

They finally reached the end of the pier, where Vera and Elise instantly broke off from the group and hopped onto the beach and began racing around, laughing and kicking gobs of sand around them. The entire group found themselves stopping as one and staring after the girls, and for a moment, no one said a word.

Will exchanged a look with Lara. She gave him the kind of smile he hadn't seen in a long time—happy and utterly content. She reached over and took his hand and squeezed. He smiled back at her.

"Haven't heard that in a while," Marcus said.

"There are no children on the island?" Lara asked.

"Two, but they're not exactly the outdoorsy type."

"We're definitely coming back here and going for a swim later," Carly said with a big grin.

"Oh hell yeah," Gaby laughed.

"It's not bad," Marcus said. "But you'll really love the hotel."

"Girls!" Lara called.

Elise and Vera reluctantly ran back, but not before grabbing handfuls of sand and flinging them into the air and running through them. They were still picking sand out of each other's hair as the group continued along a man-made cobblestone pathway connecting the end of the piers with the boat shack and leading across the beach. The pathway was about five meters wide, the same width as the piers. It was big enough for vehicles and a gaggle of civilians to come and go without getting sand in their shoes.

"You don't have any guards?" Will asked.

"Don't need any," Marcus said. "Why? You plan on giving us trouble?"

Will smiled back, though he could imagine his smile wasn't nearly as winning as Marcus's.

The cobblestone pathway led them off the beach and through the woods. Will instantly became alarmed by the darkness within the trees to both sides of him and had to force himself to temper his instincts. Instead, he listened to birds chirping, the rustling of animals scurrying around branches and foliage. It was quiet, almost peaceful, and for a moment he was able to let himself go, become lost in the natural beauty of his surroundings. The only intrusions were the loud *clack-clack*s of their shoes on the hard stones.

He noticed black lampposts positioned every two meters along the pathway. There had been similar ones posted along the piers and beach. Each lamppost housed a lightbulb inside a glass container at the top.

"Solar-powered lampposts?" Will asked.

"Good guess," Marcus said. "LED lights. You can't beat it."

"We carry portable LED lights with us."

"Then you know how bright they can be. Wait till sundown. This island will be lit up like a Christmas tree, and none of it costs anything except the sun rays in the day."

"That's efficient."

"There are lampposts like this all around the island," Marcus added. "They store power by day, light up at night. We never have to worry about them as long as the power cells have the sun to draw from. So basically, it's all good unless the sun blows up, which, hopefully, won't be for a while yet."

The leisurely welcoming walk through Mother Nature lasted for about fifty meters before they emerged onto the hotel grounds. It was quite a sight, even (as Marcus had put it) in its "finished-ish" state.

The resort hotel and its surrounding area were designed to take up nearly two football fields' worth of space. He imagined the resort would have looked pretty spectacular when completed, but at the moment he saw a pair of unfinished swimming pools out front, each shaped into a giant peach and separated by the cobblestone pathway. On an island surrounded by water, swimming pools were the type of thing only rich people could come up with.

Likewise with the ornate water fountains scattered around the yard, in the shape of various fishes—catfish, bass, and what looked like bigmouth buffalo. The ceramic sea life was dried and cracked, the fountains devoid of water, the mouths homes to birds and their nests. Someone had attempted to turn a big section of the front yard into a garden before giving up.

Will expected to see a thick jungle where the yard used to be, but instead he smelled freshly cut grass. "You guys mow the lawn?"

"Tom and Jake take turns every other week," Marcus said.

"Where do you get the gas?"

"There was a lot stored in the supply shacks, and we make supply runs on land every few weeks or so, whenever we run low on something. Things are spread out around here, but we can usually get what we need in less than a day's drive."

"Using the vehicles in the marina?"

"We have keys for every one of them," Marcus said.

"Aren't you afraid someone will steal them?"

"Not a chance. We stripped the batteries and there's barely any gas in the tanks. We bring the keys, including the batteries and gas, when we need to use them. No one would bother stealing those cars. Too much hassle."

The cobblestone pathway serpentined its way from the beach, through the trees, and all the way to the hotel's large twin front doors sitting on a raised patio. Before it reached the doors, it branched off in a half-dozen separate directions around the hotel grounds, circling the water fountains, swimming pools, and building foundations laid out but never built upon. A small army of palm trees stood at attention around the hotel to give the resort a faux tropical theme.

The hotel wasn't even close to being done, with much of the exterior aesthetics still missing. In its current state, the huge, sprawling building looked almost generic, and its second floor was missing. Will saw work equipment on the rooftop and wondered what else was up there that they could use. The developers had managed to erect a sign, held in place by scaffolding and metal mounts, over the front doors of the hotel. It read, "Kilbrew Hotel and Resorts" in big white letters.

The Tower loomed in the background and slightly to the right, near the northeast cliff of the island. The building was entirely white, without the colored stripes or design patterns usually used to distinguish lighthouses. He guessed the developers had never gotten around to painting the conical structure. Closer now, he could see four windows from his limited angle, two on the second and two more on the third floor. With the four other windows he couldn't see, the Tower gave its inhabitants a maximum 360 view of the surrounding lake and island.

Using the Tower's distance from them and adding in the walk from the beach, Will pegged the island's width at under a quarter of a kilometer, or 250 meters, give or take. The island was definitely longer than it was wide, which made the Tower's view all the more important.

A sniper's dream.

"The radio that's broadcasting the message," Lara said. "You said it's coming from the Tower?"

"That's right," Marcus said. "There's a computer set up on the third floor."

"Who's up there now?" Will asked.

"Tom's usually up there," Marcus said. "He comes and goes, but that's his usual haunt."

"How much power is needed to keep the broadcast going twenty-four-seven?"

"Surprisingly, not a lot. We monitored the heck out of it the first week, but it's incredibly efficient. This entire island is. I think that was the whole point."

They approached the raised patio.

"But never mind all that," Marcus said. "Let's get you folks out of the sun. I'm sure you're sick and tired of it by now."

"Hallelujah," Gaby said.

"The others are all waiting in the hotel. You can't blame them, it's probably 105 degrees out here." He wiped a bead of sweat on his forehead for effect. "Welcome to Louisiana in the summer, folks."

"It's got nothing on Texas," Lara said.

"Are we comparing heat indexes for state pride now?" Will smiled over at her.

She smiled back. "Texas proud, baby."

They walked up a half-dozen marble steps, covered slightly in dust and dirt and bird excrement, to the two big doors of the hotel. The patio was constructed of the same shiny black marble and surrounded by a meter-tall wooden railing. A pair of solar-powered LED floodlights hung above them.

A woman in her late thirties stood at the top of the steps waiting to greet them. For a moment, she reminded him a bit of Kate. She was tall and attractive, with dark hair and piercing brown eyes, and something about the way she stood told him she used to be someone important before The Purge and she was reluctant to give that up.

Marcus introduced the woman, saying, "This is Karen, our fearless leader. She's the reason we're all here in the first place."

"Welcome to Song Island," Karen smiled. "We're glad to finally get some new faces around here. If you need anything, just let me know. Anything at all."

Politician, Will thought right away.

"I could use a bath," Carly said.

"We have that, too."

"What is that humming in the background?" Lara asked.

"That," Karen said, "is air conditioning."

Marcus grabbed one of the doors and pulled it open, and Will was instantly swamped with cold air seeking escape from the building. He was pretty sure Lara involuntarily sighed with pleasure next to him.

TWO OF THE people calling Song Island home were in the lobby, including a man named Tom, who Marcus had mentioned earlier. Tom was wearing khaki shorts and a gun belt, making him the first person Will had seen on the island who carried a weapon out in the open.

Tom was eating an apple and reading a book while sitting in an armchair behind the reception desk. He came over and shook their hands. The man had a strong grip, which fit his huge six-two frame. Will pegged Tom at 250, most of that muscle, which was quite a feat given the quality of food available these days.

Will thought right away, *Ex-cop.*

"*Mi casa es su casa,*" Tom said. "Or whatever the Spanish word for island is."

"*Isla,*" Lara said.

"*Me isla es su isla,* then," he smiled. It wasn't quite as winning a smile as Marcus's, of course.

The other person they met was a young kid playing some kind of space game on a fifty-inch LED TV in one corner of the lobby. He looked all of twelve. Marcus introduced him as Kyle, and the kid, hearing his name, glanced over and gave them a cursory look, though Will noticed he gave Gaby a little bit more time than the rest of them.

Kyle raised a lazy hand and said, "Hey."

"What is that, an Xbox?" Josh asked.

"Yeah," Kyle said. "You play?"

"A little."

"I got *Halo* and *Call of Duty* and a bunch of other games here."

"Cool."

And just like that, Kyle looked back at his game, the rest of the lobby instantly forgotten. He was moving some kind of soldier through a futuristic battlefield.

Marcus chuckled. "Kid plays that thing day and night. I'd say he's doing it to escape reality, but frankly, his mom says he was like that before this mess."

"Kyle is Debra's kid," Karen explained. "You can't blame the boy. Everyone has to cope in their own way."

"There's enough electricity from the solar panels to waste on games?" Will asked.

"We have more than we need here," Karen said proudly. "Marcus, why don't you show them to the rooms. I have a feeling the ladies are dying to see them."

"Follow me," Marcus said.

He led them past Tom, who had gone back to the reception desk and his book. Will glanced at the cover as they passed, catching the name of the author, Ludlum something, but not the title. Tom looked up and caught his eye, and they exchanged a brief, perfunctory nod.

Marcus continued into a hallway, leaving the lobby behind. "Basically, pick whichever room you want—there are plenty to go around. Obviously you should try to stick to the completed sections of the hotel. There're a lot of nails and construction leftovers scattered throughout the unfinished portions. So if you're feeling adventurous and end up stepping on a rusted nail, we might have to cut off a limb, and no one wants that."

The hallway curved slightly to the right the farther they went. Most of the flooring was completed with more of the shiny black marble tiles, but the walls were plain white, and there was still uncovered Sheetrock lined with dried caulk in certain sections and heavy doses of spackling over drywall. Some light fixtures above them didn't have covers or lightbulbs, and wires dangled from drilled holes. And these, he reminded himself, were the *finished* sections of the hotel.

Marcus told them about the hotel's construction as they went.

The hotel's floor plan consisted of a long hallway marked "Hallway A" (the one they were in now), with rooms to the left and right, the door numbers starting with A100 and counting upward. Hallway A was designed for fifty rooms, twenty-five on each side, and it was the only completed section of the entire building. There was supposed to be a complementing hallway running parallel to their left ("Hallway B"), connected by a series of hallways and hotel event rooms, but the developers had never gotten around to laying foundations. It was now impossible to tell where the other planned half of the hotel was supposed to go, thanks to the overgrowth of weeds.

As they moved through Hallway A, people began coming out of rooms to greet them. He wondered what they had been doing before now. Didn't they already know newcomers were arriving on the island?

A young woman named Sarah came out of her room first. She was in her late twenties and had a daughter, Jenny, who was blonde and the spitting image of her mother. Sarah was friendly, while her daughter shyly introduced herself to Elise and Vera. The two girls enthusiastically introduced themselves back, but that didn't seem to win the girl over, and Jenny slowly wandered behind her mother before disappearing into their room without a word.

"Don't mind her, she's a little shy," Sarah said.

Will thought her voice sounded familiar, and Lara picked up on it, too. "You're the voice on the recorded message," Lara said.

"Guilty."

"You don't know how often we listened to that recording on the way over here."

"Oh, God, I don't know how to respond to that," Sarah said, looking both pleased and a little embarrassed. "You guys should get settled in. Al and I are cooking up something good for tonight. I hope you like fish. That's Al's specialty."

"As long as it doesn't come in a can," Lara smiled.

"Would fresh from the lake work?"

"God, yes."

They continued up the hallway, where they met a man in his fifties—the Al that Sarah had mentioned. Al had a bit of a gut, and for some reason was trying to hide his bald spot with a comb-over. Will found that both odd and amusing.

"Finally, new blood!" Al bellowed at the sight of them.

Al's belly shook a bit as he said it, from either too much food or too much beer, or maybe both. If it was the latter, Will wondered where Al was hiding the good stuff. In his room, maybe. He and Danny had lost their taste for beer over the last eight months. Beers were simply not meant to be drunk warm.

"Just got here myself," Al said. "You guys play poker?"

"I only gamble with my life," Danny said.

Al laughed. "When you guys get settled, look me up. I can't get anyone here to give me a decent game."

"We hear you're a good cook," Lara said.

"Good is subjective," Al said. "But since I'm the only cook on this island, I guess that makes me technically the only good cook."

Al chewed their ears off about fish and cooking for another five minutes until Marcus butted in and dragged them away.

Farther up the hallway, they met a young man named Jake, who came out of his room to meet them, along with his girlfriend Sienna. They were both in their early twenties, though Sienna, with her round, cherubic face, could have passed for a teenager. Both looked friendly enough.

"You cut the grass," Will said to Jake.

The young man nodded. "Just the front grounds, mostly. We don't mess with the back areas too much—no point since there's nothing back there."

"Welcome to Song Island. You'll love it here," Sienna said.

Carly sniffed Sienna. "I smell shampoo."

"The hotel stocked up on shampoo and soap before all of this happened," Marcus said, "so there's plenty to go around. There are stacks and stacks of the stuff in the storage closets, and some in your rooms, I'm sure."

"Oh, I think I'm going to love it here," Carly said, smiling brightly at them.

Marcus led them farther up the hallway. "Let's get you guys settled in. I know you're all worn out just getting here."

"How long ago did the others get here?" Lara asked.

"Al got here just two weeks ago, and Jake and Sienna were the first people who actually made it here because of the broadcast. That was about three months ago."

Marcus finally stopped and turned around. "This is it. As far as we go. Feel free to choose any rooms you want. Most of them already have everything you'll need—towels, blankets, et cetera—and everything else can be found in the supply closets that we passed earlier. Any questions?"

"Just one," Danny said, way in the back.

"Yes, Danny?"

"You got hot showers here? My BO is even getting on *my* nerves."

Carly sighed. "He's not kidding."

"Thanks, babe."

"I got your back," Carly smiled.

THERE WERE TWO nightstands, one on each side of the bed, and a big dresser across the room. Metal brackets jutted out of the wall where a flat-screen LED TV was supposed to go. A big oval mirror hung from the wall next to the bathroom.

He had to admit, even a half-finished room at the Kilbrew Hotel and Resorts looked better than anything Harold Campbell had put together in his finished facility in Starch. It was certainly a step up from the basements they had been sheltering in during the trip here.

The floor had lush carpeting and a fan dangled from the ceiling. Not that they were going to need a working fan any time soon. The room was already cold, even though he had just turned on the air conditioner a few minutes ago. The bed was a queen, with fluffy pillows and a large blanket waiting for them. There was just a bit of dust, which meant everything had been prepared days—possibly weeks—ago.

Lara made a beeline for the bathroom, rubbing slightly at her left shoulder.

"How's the shoulder?" he asked.

"It's itchy," she said, making a face. "I'm doing my best not to scratch it, but it's really hard. But you wouldn't know anything about that, Mister I've-never-been-shot."

She disappeared into the bathroom, where he heard the sink faucet turning on and the squeak of plumbing not put to use until now coming alive. Then a second later, Lara shouting, "Yes!" followed by water pouring into the sink bowl.

"Found working plumbing?" he called over.

"What was that Gaby said?" she called from the bathroom. "Hallelujah!"

Will leaned the M4A1 and Remington against a comfortable-looking armchair in a corner next to a mini-fridge. He opened the fridge out of curiosity and found it empty. The fridge wasn't plugged in, so he plugged it in and heard the small engine start up instantly. Satisfied that the outlets were working, he pulled the plug free.

Will walked across the room to the patio window and slid it open. He stepped out into the unfinished patio—really, just a half-circular concrete shape—and the heat immediately tried to reclaim him. He squinted in the sunlight and looked to his left, where he heard another window sliding open before Danny stepped out onto his own unfinished patio.

"Nice, a room with a view," Danny said.

They looked across at about thirty meters of empty, undeveloped land and the wall of trees sprouting up on the other side. The grass in the middle was already up to five inches in some spots.

"Too much green, though," Danny said. "I like my view a little more blue-ish."

"How's the mini-fridge in your room?"

"Wanting. I did find an uneaten mint in a corner. You?"

"Someone must have stolen our mint."

"Bummer for you."

"So what do you think?"

"About all this paradise?"

"Yeah."

"It's paradise." Danny paused, then added, "It's damn perfect. Sandy beaches, blue water, air conditioning, and working plumbing. What's not to like?"

"Yeah," Will said.

They didn't have to say anything else, because it wasn't necessary. He knew Danny was thinking the same thing.

It's too perfect.

"Stay frosty," Will said.

"I'm so frosty I can barely feel my fingers," Danny said.

Will went back into the room, sliding the patio door shut behind him and feeling the cool breeze right away, thanks to a pair of vents along the ceiling. Will stood under one of them for a moment.

Lara came out of the bathroom with a big smile, her freshly washed face still glistening. She toweled down her wet hair, and he was surprised to see her just wearing panties and a lacy white bra, gauze tape covering up part of her left arm. "Bathroom definitely works. Haven't used the shower yet, but it looks like it works, too. Won't that be something? Two showers a day? How long has it been since we had working plumbing?"

"Since we left the facility."

"It feels longer." She walked over to the bed and sat down. "I'm going to need to change my bandages. You're going to have to help."

"Sure."

"This place…" She ran the towel over her wet hair. "It's safe, right? They've been here for eight months, and the ghouls haven't attacked. They were right. It really is the sanctuary they promised."

"It sounds that way."

"But you don't really believe it yet. Hope for the best, prepare for the worst?"

"Yeah."

"Eight months, Will," she said. "*Eight months.* And you saw how everyone is. They're not afraid. I've seen fear, and these people…they don't look afraid. At all."

He nodded. Will didn't take his eyes off her. The way her hair fell over her shoulders and the soft blue flicker of her eyes when she moved her head. He had never seen her happier, and he wanted desperately to keep her this way.

"What?" she said, finally looking over at him.

"Hmm?"

"You're staring."

"Am I?"

"Yes."

"I'm just reminded of how beautiful you are."

"I'm already out of my pants, mister. You don't have to work that hard."

He smiled, and she returned it.

Lara put the towel down and leaned back suggestively on the

bed. "Come here," she said, patting the bed next to her. "Come to momma."

"Sexy."

She laughed. "Oh, shut up and get over here."

"What about your arm?"

"I only need one good arm. Now come *here* before I change my mind and go take a nice, hot shower instead."

He went.

CHAPTER 24

BLAINE

IT WAS AROUND five o'clock, with nightfall about three hours away, when they finished eating in the food court. Mason and Gerry were gone, checking on noises they had heard coming from the south side of the city. They kept in radio contact, but it would be a while before the two returned, even using a couple of ATVs. Lenny, the only one left at the mall who they had to worry about, was doing his rounds outside, something he did every day before nightfall, according to Maddie.

That left Blaine and Sandra time to talk to Maddie and Bobby in the Sortys employee lounge. Or just Maddie, since Bobby couldn't say a word and stood guard at the door, looking over at them occasionally.

"Tomorrow, I'll wake up early and come get you like I'm supposed to," Maddie said. "I'll give you my handgun, and Sandra can use Bobby's. We'll stick with the rifles."

"How many magazines do you have for the handguns?" Blaine asked.

"Two. Counting the one already in the gun. So that gives you a total of thirty rounds each."

"You can't get more weapons?" Sandra asked. "I know there are four of us against three of them, but still, I'd feel better if we had more firepower on our side."

"It's not gonna happen. Believe me, I've tried. Mason keeps everything inside the jail in the security room, and he has the only key."

"What happens if you use up your ammo?" Blaine asked.

"We don't," Maddie said. "I swear, the guy used to be a tight-ass CPA or something before all of this. He counts every bullet we have. He won't even let us do target practice—that's why most of these assholes can't shoot the broad side of a barn."

"That doesn't sound very smart," Sandra said.

"He says it's also to keep us from exposing ourselves in case someone's coming through the city. Which I guess makes sense. He likes to say that surprise is his friend."

Blaine thought about how Mason snuck up on them outside Cavender's.

He's got a point there.

"Except for Gerry," Maddie said.

"What about Gerry?" Blaine asked.

"Gerry is Mason's little bitch. They argue like a married couple, but at the end of the day, Gerry is the only person Mason trusts. So Gerry gets all the ammo he can carry."

"How many magazines do you think they have on them now?" Sandra asked. "Can't be many. How much do those belts of theirs hold?"

"A half dozen, maybe. They get pretty heavy once you start loading them up."

"Maybe we'll get lucky and they'll decide not to burden themselves with too many magazines tomorrow," Blaine said.

Maddie grinned wryly at him. "Sure, there's always that."

"You wouldn't know it to look at him, but he's the optimist in this relationship," Sandra smiled.

Blaine glanced at Bobby. "Can he shoot?"

"A little," Maddie said.

"What about Mason and Gerry?"

"Honestly, I don't know. Whenever we've gotten into scraps with people, I was always at the mall and they were out there."

"Because he trusts Gerry and not you," Sandra said.

"Pretty much, yeah."

"How well can you shoot?"

"I've been hunting with my dad since I was a kid, like I said, but that's with hunting rifles. Assault rifles aren't the same thing. Plus, it's different when someone's shooting back at you, you know? I don't know how I'd be in an actual gunfight, to tell you the truth.

Too bad you two aren't ex-Special Forces or something—then we'd give you our rifles."

Blaine smiled. "We're not, but those guys that came through earlier? The ones that killed Dirk?"

"What about them?"

"Two of them were Special Forces. Army Rangers."

Maddie smirked at him. "So you do know them."

"They saved my life. Too bad Mason didn't try to take them on, because he'd have gotten his ass handed to him and saved us the trouble."

"They're headed to Song Island, too," Sandra said. "We're going to be joining up with them."

That seemed to alarm Maddie.

She's afraid of what they'll think when they learn she used to wear a hazmat suit.

"They don't have to know," Blaine said.

Maddie looked at him, then over at Sandra, who nodded, too. "They don't have to know," Sandra said.

Maddie relaxed, then glanced at her watch. "It's going to get dark in a few hours." She looked over at Sandra. "Mason would shit a brick if he found out, but I stashed away some boxes of bottled water to take showers with every now and then. If you want..."

"God, yes," Sandra said, before Maddie even finished.

Blaine discreetly sniffed the air around him and couldn't disagree. He wondered if there were enough bottles for him, too, but decided to save the question for later, possibly after all the killing was done.

HE WALKED THROUGH the mall with Maddie, the gas mask tapping against his hip. Bobby walked slowly behind them, quiet as a mouse. The mall didn't just look cavernous, it felt it too, the sounds of their footsteps against the floor tiles echoing up and down the building.

"What happens at night?" he asked.

"You mean when the ghouls come out?"

"Yeah."

"We stay out of their way. In our rooms. Sometimes Mason

comes out to talk to them."

"To the blue-eyed ghoul."

"Yeah. You think I'm crazy, don't you?"

"No."

She looked quickly over at him. "So you believe me?"

"Yes."

"Why?"

"Because I saw one, too."

"Is this you trying to be funny? Because if it is, I'm not laughing."

"No, this is me being serious. I saw one myself a few days ago before we came here."

Maddie looked relieved. "At first I thought I might have just imagined it. Mason says it comes and talks to him often, but I only saw it the one time with my own eyes, and that was months ago."

"What was it doing the time you saw it?"

"It was just standing there, talking to Mason."

"You heard it talk?"

"I think so."

"You're not sure."

She shook her head. "It wasn't like I was right next to them. But I could hear Mason talking to her. It. Whatever."

"It's hard to tell with them, but I think the one I saw used to be a woman, too."

"For a moment, I thought it was a human woman, but then I realized it was a ghoul. I'd never seen one like that before, and I never saw it again after that."

She shrugged, and Blaine let it go.

"So you just stay out of their way," he said.

"Yeah. We're just the day crew, is how Mason puts it. We stay out of their way, and they ignore us even if we're caught outside. As long as we're wearing these suits and gas masks. I don't know how they know, but I guess they recognize the suit or something."

"Maybe they're told."

"What do you mean?"

"By the blue-eyed ghoul."

"Maybe. I don't know. I try not to think too much about it. Knowing those things are out there is bad enough. I don't want to start thinking about what *else* is out there." She shivered. "God, just thinking about—"

She was interrupted by a loud gunshot that seemed to explode across the silent mall.

They both turned back toward the Sortys department store.

Sandra.

HE FOUND SANDRA in the women's section of Sortys, sitting on the floor with her back against one of the clothing racks, holding a Glock in her hand and staring at a dead body crumpled on the floor in front of her.

Sandra looked up at him, her face plastered with shock. "He tried to…" she said, but didn't finish. She didn't have to. He knew what had happened as soon as he saw the look in her eyes.

Blaine kneeled down next to her and she fell into his arms. He held her, taking the gun away just to be safe.

He glanced at the body, which was lying on its stomach. Without having to see the man's face, he knew it was Lenny, with blood pooling underneath him. Lenny's hip holster was empty.

Maddie and Bobby arrived a few seconds later, both out of breath.

Maddie looked at Sandra, then at Blaine, before taking in Lenny. "Shit. This is going to complicate things."

"We'll deal with it," Blaine said. He looked around the area. "Where's his rifle? Wasn't he carrying a rifle?"

"Yeah, an M4. All military stuff. Mason took about a dozen of them from a surplus shop nearby."

"So where is it now?"

"It has to be around here somewhere. Bobby, spread out, look for Lenny's rifle."

They searched around the clothing racks, and when they couldn't find it, spread out farther.

Blaine turned his attention back to Sandra. Her eyes drifted over to Lenny's body. She looked calm, but there was an alertness, a barely controlled energy about her that he recognized as adrenaline.

"Where did he put his rifle, Sandra?"

"I didn't see it." He couldn't detect any quivering in her voice.

"Just the gun." Her eyes went to the Glock in his hand. "I just saw the handgun."

"How did you get it?"

"While he was on top of me…"

"Okay… Okay."

He heard Maddie and Bobby walking back behind him. He looked over and caught Maddie's eyes.

She shook her head. "I can't find it. He must have put it somewhere else before he…" She stopped and said instead, "I can't find it."

"At least we have another gun now," Blaine said.

"This changes everything. We can't wait until morning now. You realize that, right?"

"Yeah. How long before they come back?"

"I don't know—" Maddie began to say, when their radios squawked, cutting her off.

They heard Mason's voice: "We're on our way back. ETA thirty minutes."

Everyone stood still, including Bobby, who didn't look like he was breathing at all.

Seconds went by before they heard Mason's voice through the radio again: "Anyone there?"

Maddie unclipped her radio and pressed the transmit lever: "Roger that. Thirty minutes."

"What's going on over there? What took you so long to answer?"

"Sorry, I had my hands full," Maddie said, exchanging a look with Blaine.

He nodded, letting her know she was doing a good job. That seemed to help.

"Where's Lenny?" Mason asked through the radio.

"He's in the bathroom," Maddie said. "You want me to fish him out?"

"Tell him we're coming back in thirty minutes. Mason out."

"Roger that." Maddie ran her hand over her face and gave Blaine a look that barely concealed her nervousness. "Thirty minutes. They must be on the other side of town. If he didn't hear the gunshot, they were probably on their ATVs at the time. Otherwise, he would be hauling ass over here."

Maddie crouched next to Lenny's body. She turned it over with some effort. He was skinny, but a lot heavier than he looked. Blaine saw a bullet hole in his chest. Maddie grabbed a spare magazine clipped to Lenny's belt and tossed it over to Blaine.

"How are we going to do this?" Blaine asked.

"I don't know," Maddie said. "This kind of throws my plan out of whack. We don't have the element of surprise anymore."

"Maybe we still do."

"How you figure?"

"They don't know Lenny's dead, and they still don't know what we're planning. They're going to walk through that door blind, expecting everything to be just the way they left it."

"Yeah. So?"

"What if everything is?"

"I'm listening..."

THEY HEARD THE ATVs coming from a distance, the loud motors making a ruckus against the stillness of the city. Two Yamahas, yellow and black, appeared out of the parking lot and rode up the sidewalk, stopping in front of the doors into Sortys. The men climbed off and pushed their way inside, their rifles slung over their backs.

He was hiding behind a clothing rack lined with Nike sportswear, just close enough to the front doors to see both men as they entered, but far enough away not to be noticed. Or at least, he hoped he couldn't be noticed.

Somewhere else in the department store, Bobby was hiding behind a counter, waiting to pop up with his M4. Even if the kid couldn't shoot—or hit the broad side of a barn, according to Maddie—Blaine only needed him to aim in the right direction. The M4s had semi-automatic and three-shot burst capabilities.

As soon as Mason and Gerry entered the store, they stopped at the sight of Maddie, waiting in the aisle in front of them. She was too far away for Blaine to see her, but he knew where she would be and heard her just fine.

"We have a problem," Maddie said.

"What kind of problem?" Mason asked.

"It's Lenny."

"What about Lenny?"

"He's dead."

"What?"

As Mason and Gerry started to process that bit of news, Blaine popped up from behind the clothing rack, took aim, and fired.

He realized he was still too far from his targets as soon as he shot and watched the bullet obliterate the head of a mannequin two feet behind Gerry's head.

Shit!

Before he could get off a second shot, Mason and Gerry were moving, reacting amazingly fast to the ambush. One second they were standing in front of the doors, exchanging words with Maddie, and the next the glass doors behind them shattered as Maddie opened fire with her M4, letting the bullets fly in a loud, thunderous three-round burst.

Pieces of mannequins exploded and flew everywhere, and the ear-splitting sound of three assault rifles firing at the same time erupted like rolling thunder. Even though he had been anticipating it, the loud and continuous hammering of gunfire inside a confined building still managed to startle him.

Gerry turned slightly to his right, tracking where Blaine's shot came from. Blaine didn't know if the yokel actually saw him, but that didn't stop the man from opening fire in his direction anyway. A pair of plastic mannequins exploded in front of Blaine, forcing him to crouch as he ran for cover.

Blaine got off a second and third shot—both going wild like the first one—even as he lunged to the floor in a desperate act of self-preservation. The Nike clothing rack above him was ripped apart by Gerry's bullets, and pieces of clothing fell on top of him and bits of shredded fabric scattered into the air. He marveled at how much damage a thirty-bullet magazine could do in a series of nonstop three-round bursts.

He crawled away as quickly as he could, seeking shelter behind a shoe rack. As soon as he reached the hiding place, bullets punched through the wooden frame and slammed into jackets hanging on the wall behind him. Blaine rolled away along the carpeted floor and didn't stop until he felt cold tiles under him.

Suddenly the three assault rifles were joined by a fourth (*Bobby!*), and Blaine couldn't help but think to himself, *Well, this isn't going well at all.*

He managed to scramble back up to his feet and dart across an aisle, clothes tearing and bullets ricocheting off steel frames around him. It had to be Gerry, trying to take him down. He didn't think Mason would be so single-minded about trying to kill him.

Stupid country yokel.

Blaine fired back blindly as he ran, but he knew the three shots he had just wasted weren't going to hit anything. Or anyone. Not even close. But they did do something, which was make Gerry stop shooting for a while and take cover. Or maybe Gerry was just reloading. Whatever he was doing, Gerry stopped shooting long enough for Blaine to find temporary safety.

He had made it all the way back to where the jewelry cases were. Blaine pushed himself up from the floor and leaned against one of the counters. He looked to his left and saw Maddie reloading her M4 while crouched behind another counter across the store from him. She looked over and grinned, but he saw fear and doubt in her eyes.

Maddie stood back up and fired another three-round burst in Mason's direction before dipping back behind the counter. Blaine heard more windows breaking and glass shattering against floor tiles. He knew she was trying to conserve bullets because they had a limited amount. She was already on her second magazine. Her *last* magazine.

Blaine leaned out from behind the counter to try to find Gerry when two bullets zipped through the wooden counter and almost took his head off. Chipped wood flew inches from his face, spraying the floor and tossing slivers into his hair. He ducked and crawled backward away from the spot, expecting Gerry to keep shooting, but for some reason the man finally stopped.

Maybe he's running out of bullets...

Yeah, right.

He looked over at Maddie again, back behind cover, biding her time. She seemed lost in thought, and he imagined she was probably counting how many shots she had fired. He saw her switching her rifle's fire selector to semi-automatic.

"You still alive over there, Maddie?" Mason shouted from somewhere in the store.

"More alive than Lenny," Maddie shouted back.

"Shit, you killed Lenny?"

"Damn right! We have his weapons, too."

Blaine grinned.

Smart girl.

Someone fired off two quick shots, followed by silence. Bullet casings clattered around on the store tiles in the aftermath.

"You missed, Bobby!" Mason shouted. His voice echoed, and it was hard to pinpoint where it was coming from. "You never could shoot for shit, kid. Frankly, I'm disappointed you joined in on this fun exercise. I expected more from you."

Blaine heard another couple of shots, then two more bullet casings clacking against the floor. Bobby, replying the only way he knew how, with his rifle.

"Miss me, miss me, now you gotta kiss me!" Mason shouted, then laughed hysterically.

The guy's out of his fucking mind.

Blaine was counting how many bullets he had fired (*Five…or six?)* when he heard a loud *crunch* behind him and instantly knew it was boots stepping on broken glass. He shot up like a cannon, raising his gun—

And saw Gerry standing ten feet away, pointing his M4 in his face. Blaine's gun was only halfway up and he knew he was dead. Gerry knew it, too, because he had the mother of all self-satisfied smirks on his face as he stared back at Blaine behind the iron sights of the rifle.

Before Gerry could fire, there was a gunshot and Gerry's right shoulder seemed to explode and blood spurted out. He twisted sideways and as he did, he squeezed the trigger and the M4 raked the store in a series of three-round bursts that blew away mannequins and scarred racks of clothes and shattered counter tops.

Blaine finished raising his gun and shot Gerry twice in the side. This time he didn't miss.

Gerry stumbled into racks of clothes and pulled them down with him to the floor until he was lying still, his body and face covered in pants and shirts.

Blaine hurried over to where the gunshot that had saved his life had come from. He found Sandra leaning against a full-length mirror that covered the door of a fitting room. She slid down to the floor as he rushed over. The Glock—Lenny's Glock—dropped from her fingers.

His eyes widened at the sight of her hands holding her stomach, blood slipping through her fingers in bright red streams.

He kneeled next to her and put his hands over hers. "You'll be fine," he said, trying to smile, trying to convince her. To convince himself. It wasn't working. "You'll be fine. I've seen worse."

"Really?" Her voice was soft and calm and came out almost as a whisper. She was smiling at him as she said it. "Where did you see worse, babe?"

"You're talking to a guy who was shot three times, remember? You just got shot once. This is child's play. You'll be fine."

"He got me pretty good, babe."

"You'll be fine," he said again. "You'll be fine."

He grabbed some clothes draped over a rack and pulled them free. He took her hands and pried them from her stomach. She fought him, but he was stronger and she finally let go. Blood gushed out in the split second it took him to push the shirts over her wound. He wrapped the long sleeves of one of the shirts around her body to keep them in place. Blood instantly soaked the pink fabric and turned it a dark, violent red.

"See?" he said, smiling at her. Or trying to. He couldn't hide the desperation in his voice, and he knew she could hear it, too. "Good as new. I told you. Good as new."

She looked at him through pain and sweat, and she still looked beautiful. Amazingly beautiful. "You're sweet, but you're a lousy liar."

"Who's lying?"

"You are."

"Bullshit. You'll be fine."

"Liar," she whispered, "but I love you anyway."

"I love you too," he said.

The emotions came suddenly, washing over him in waves, and he felt terrified and impotent.

Sandra reached up with one bloodied hand and touched his cheek gently. "Go to Song Island," she said, her voice so soft and weak he had to strain to hear her. "Take Maddie and Bobby. Go to Song Island and try to be happy."

He shook his head. "Not without you. That's the plan, remember?"

"I'm not coming back from this. Not this one. We've used up all our lives, baby. You and me. But you have to keep going. If you love me—if you care about me—you'll keep going. Don't stop. Don't ever stop."

"I—" he started, but stopped.

Sandra closed her eyes, and she wasn't breathing anymore. Her head tilted to one side, and all the life drained from her face. His beautiful Sandra, who had changed his life, given him the best gift anyone had ever given him by loving him back.

She was gone. Just like that, she was gone.

Blaine sat and stared at her. He wasn't sure how long he kept that pose, unable to move, to feel. His brain might have shut down on him, and he wasn't aware of actually breathing or thinking or even being. Even the continued sounds of gunfire behind him didn't shake him loose. He could barely hear them anyway.

He willed Sandra's eyes to open, for her lips to part and start breathing again. It might have been seconds, or minutes, or maybe hours.

The sounds of footsteps invaded his fog, followed by voices. He wasn't sure who they belonged to. Maddie, perhaps, or maybe Mason come to finish what Gerry started. Maybe that was for the best. He couldn't imagine going on without Sandra anyway.

So he waited for the bullet that never came.

Then Maddie was crouching next to him, nudging him on the shoulder, trying to get his attention. "Blaine. Blaine…"

He turned his head slowly to look at her, saw the whiteness of her face, the worry in her eyes, the thin sheet of stinging sweat. He looked back at Sandra, because he was afraid she might disappear if he took his eyes away from her for too long.

Come back, Sandra, come back to me…

"He's gone," Maddie was saying. "Mason. After you killed Gerry, he ran off. It's almost nightfall. We need to get ready for tonight. I don't know how this is going to affect them. The ghouls. We need to get ready, just in case."

Hands grabbed and lifted him from the floor. Blaine wasn't sure if he was supposed to fight them or not. So he did nothing. Bobby was surprisingly strong.

Then he was walking through the store, through the destroyed racks of clothing and bullet-riddled counters. Over shirts and pants and shoes and jewelry. There was glass everywhere. And more jewelry, and even more clothing, and bullet casings sliding under their shoes.

Silver. Take the silver. Make bullets. Silver bullets.

Then he was back inside the employee lounge and sitting on the couch. He didn't know how he got there so quickly.

Bobby locked the door and leaned against it.

Maddie sat on the couch next to him. She wiped at a thick patch of sweat clinging to her face and she had an extra M4 rifle slung over her shoulder. "I don't know what's going to happen next. With the ghouls. I don't know how they're going to respond to the bodies in the store. Lenny's and Gerry's… and Sandra's. So we have to be ready for anything."

He didn't answer. He wasn't sure if he could talk.

"We have to put the suits back on," Maddie said. "Just in case, okay?"

Bobby retrieved their suits from the corner where they had left them. Blaine heard the rustling of clothes and zippers, and a hazmat suit and gas mask somehow ended up in his hands. There was another suit and mask on the floor, like someone had abandoned it.

Sandra's…

"Bobby, you gotta help me put it on him," he heard Maddie say.

Bobby took Blaine's suit and mask from him. They stood him up, directing his actions like he was a two-year-old. They raised his arms and lifted his legs, then someone—Bobby, probably—handed him back the gas mask and patted him lightly on the shoulder, like a father would his wounded son, as if to say, *"You'll be fine, my boy."*

Bobby, in his hazmat suit, walked back to the door and sat down, the rifle resting between his legs, the gas mask draped over one knee. He leaned back against the door and waited. He didn't have to wait very long.

Darkness came quickly, and with it, the ghouls.

For the first time in the last eight months, Blaine discovered he didn't really care that the ghouls were coming, that it was dark outside.

What did any of it matter without Sandra?

CHAPTER 25

JOSH

PROS AND CONS: What were they?

Pros: He was finally safe, on an island the ghouls couldn't get to, and he had never been closer to Gaby. She finally accepted him as more than just a neighbor and a friend, and there were signs she was willing to be more, something he never could have expected just a few days ago.

Cons: There were none. At least, none that he could see. It was hot on the island, but then it was hot everywhere. In Texas. In Louisiana. Where *wasn't* it hot?

Conclusion: Sure, the world had essentially come to an end, but his life was looking pretty bright right about now.

Suck on that, mofos!

After he settled into his room, Josh spent the first few hours on the island exploring, careful to stick to the cobblestone paths that snaked everywhere. He had planned to invite Gaby along, but he could hear the shower running in her room next to his. His face still throbbed, and it felt good to be out in the sun. There was a nice breeze, and it soothed Josh's bruises and seemed to help with the swelling around his eyes.

He had left his gun back in his room. There was something about the island, about the way the islanders walked around without guns—except for the big guy, Tom—that made it seem all right for Josh to do the same. If it was good enough for them…

While everyone stuck to the hotel and the air conditioning, Josh was irresistibly drawn to the Tower, about half a football field from the back of the hotel, perched on the eastern cliff. He stood next to the concrete base of the thick, conical structure, craning his neck to look up at the unfinished glass housing at the top. It was high up, and his neck hurt trying to take in the entire sight.

Josh pulled open the thick wooden door to the Tower. It was a lot heavier than it looked. Or maybe he just needed to work out more. Probably a little of both.

He stepped inside.

There wasn't much of a first floor. There was a chair in a corner and another thick wooden door built into the concrete floor with a ring handle. The basement, he guessed. There was a bookcase with hardcover books, paperbacks, and stacks of yellowing magazines. A spiral cast-iron staircase wrapped around the wall of the Tower's interior like a skeletal snake, gradually extending upward before ending at another wooden door in the first-floor ceiling.

Josh climbed the staircase and was out of breath by the time he reached the door at the end. He pushed at it, felt it giving way grudgingly, and had to put his shoulder into it just to push it all the way up. The damn thing was heavy, and he felt like one of those submariners pushing open the top hatch of the sub in order to step outside. He poked his head through the rectangular opening, not quite sure what to expect.

The second floor was smaller than the first, which made sense since the Tower contracted inward the higher it went up. There was another bookcase across the room, but what really caught his attention were the paintings along one side of the wall. A dog with something in its mouth, a big deer, and a guy peering out from behind some bushes. There was a cot with meticulously folded blankets and sheets. Another section of spiral staircase circled the wall, leading up to yet another thick door in another floor above him.

Josh climbed all the way up and walked to the window across the room. The breeze up here was definitely cooler. There were no curtains on the windows, which were really just big square holes in the wall. He wondered if there were supposed to be more—like window frames with glass, maybe.

Josh leaned out the window and looked around. He could see almost everything on the eastern side of Song Island, including the beach to the south. There was a solar-powered LED floodlight directly above him, hanging just below the windowsill of a third-floor window.

"Nice view, huh?" a voice said behind him.

Josh was startled and turned quickly, surprised to find Tom sitting on the other side of the floor, behind the open door. Tom had apparently been there the whole time, eating what looked like blueberries out of a Ziploc bag; his lips had turned purple from berry juice. The cheap fold-out chair under him looked as if it shouldn't be able to support a man of his weight.

Tom looked pleased at Josh's reaction. "Sorry, kid, didn't mean to scare you. This is sort of my place."

"I didn't know anyone was up here," Josh said. *And how the hell didn't I see you sitting back there all this time?*

"No worries." Tom wiped his hands on his cargo shorts, smearing purple juice over the fabric. "Ugh. Now that's going to stain."

"Baking soda will get that out."

"That right? Baking soda?"

"You can usually rub it out with a wet rag."

"I think we have some baking soda in the kitchen," Tom said, flicking at the stains on his pants. "Josh, right?"

"Yeah."

"What happened to your face?"

Josh flushed a bit. "I ran into this guy."

"Did you at least give as good as you got?"

"Well, he's dead, and I'm not, if that's what you mean."

Tom nodded approvingly. "That's not a bad trade-off." He grinned, showing juice-stained teeth. "You ever been in a lighthouse before?"

"First time. What's up there?" Josh pointed at the third floor above them.

"More of this, but also where the radio message you heard gets sent out into the world. I guess they were planning to run their own radio station or something. Go on up. The view's even better up there."

Josh hesitated. "So you live here?"

"Here, there, everywhere. But I come here for the privacy. Not everyone likes to climb the stairs."

Tom dug out another Ziploc bag filled with more blueberries and began popping them into his mouth. Josh didn't know where he was hiding those bags.

"Got any questions, shoot," Tom said.

"What's with the door?" Josh asked.

Tom looked amused. Apparently he had wondered the same thing. "I guess the guy who designed the place was trying to do something new. It gives the Tower three separate, private floors, so it kinda works. What do you think?"

"The door's a little heavy, but it looks pretty cool."

"That's what I said." Another juice-stained grin. "What do you think of the island so far?"

"It's more than we thought it would be. Which is good. It's really good."

"Wait till dinner. Al cooks a mean fish."

"We're all looking forward to it. We've been eating nothing but canned fruits and stale chips for the last eight months."

Tom chuckled. "Yeah, I can see how fresh fish will taste really good after that." Tom tossed the empty bag into a nearby trash bin. He stood up and glanced down at his stained pants. "I'm gonna go find that baking soda now. Stay as long as you like, kid."

Josh watched Tom come out from behind the door, then start down the stairs. He thought Tom was gone and started to turn back toward the window when the big man stuck his head back up through the opening.

"Hey," Tom said. "That girl. The blonde. She taken?"

"You mean Gaby?"

"I don't know, is that her name? She's a looker, huh? I mean, the other girls, too, but that one. Wow."

"Yeah," Josh said, and thought, *Asshole.*

"How old is she? Seventeen?"

"Eighteen."

"Not that it matters," Tom smiled. "It's not like there are statutory rape laws anymore, am I right?"

AFTER LOITERING AROUND the Tower for a few more minutes, mostly to make sure Tom was gone before he went back down the stairs, Josh continued his tour of the island.

He was still trying to shake off his encounter with Tom. It was unsettling, more so because the man didn't seem to think there was anything wrong with lusting after Gaby in front of him. In Josh's experience, what guys said was usually the least objectionable thing about how they really thought.

What an asshole.

Josh pushed it out of his mind and continued along the cobblestone path.

The Kilbrew Hotel and Resorts was confined almost entirely to the east side of the island, with nearly the entire western half covered in thick vegetation and sprouting trees. Obviously the developers had plans for this half of the island, too, but had never gotten around to it. They weren't really going to leave an entire half unclaimed, were they?

He walked aimlessly for a while, eventually stumbling across a big, gray concrete building. It was an ugly thing, two stories high, with long white poles sticking up along the flat roof like skinny metal limbs. The building was surrounded by hurricane fencing, including a padlocked front gate. Electrical coils extended out from the building, vanishing underground. There was a small, almost insignificant shack next to it with a steel door.

He could hear a persistent humming noise coming from inside the building, and knew right away that this was where the island got its power and where all those solar panels delivered the sunlight they stored all day to be processed into electricity. There was a big generator somewhere inside the building, doing all the work.

A sign read: "Power Station."

Josh walked around the building, taking it all in, until his teeth started chattering from the noise. He found the cobblestone pathway again and followed it south, all the way back down to the beach, where hard rock gave way to soft, mushy sand.

He was about to return to the hotel when he saw Debra farther down the beach. She was pulling a casting net out of the water slowly. When he got closer, he saw that the net was full of fish.

"Wow, that's a lot," he shouted down the beach at her.

Debra gave him a big grin before plopping the net into a big, aluminum bucket. She jerked on the net and the fish fell out, sloshing and thrashing for their lives. Josh didn't know his fish, but it looked like there were at least a dozen different species, most of them as big as his arm.

"This is nothing," Debra said. "Wait until next year. I'm going to need two people just to pull this net out then. Used to be, this lake was full of fishermen, taking fish out of the water as fast as they could spawn. Now, you can't throw a rock in there without conking a dozen fish on the head."

Josh grinned at the image.

"Good for us," Debra continued. "As long as you're a fan of fish, anyway, because we're never going to run out of them. Ever."

Josh did like fish, though he wasn't sure if he liked them that much. He supposed he would have to get used to it. Hell, it beat running around abandoned cities looking for canned goods, anyway.

He caught Debra sneaking a look at his face, but unlike Tom, she was too polite to come right out and say anything about it.

"Is it hard to throw that thing?" he asked, watching as she assembled pieces of the net along her right arm to cast again.

"Nah. It's all in the arms. Here, I'll show you."

She walked back to the water's edge and fluidly tossed the net out. It looked like a spreading spider-web, expanding before falling into the water and dipping underneath the surface.

"The trick is to give it time," Debra said. "Usually you need to know your terrain when you're casting. If you're doing it from the shore and you know there are rocks or other things it could get snagged on nearby, you pull it up faster. Here, though, it's pretty much just sand below, so I'm going to let it sink all the way to the bottom to get maximum coverage."

She started to pull, and once again the net was teeming with fish.

"Voila," Debra said. Instead of throwing the fish into the bucket with the others, Debra pulled a line and the net opened up. Right away, fish began making their escape back into the lake. "We already have more than enough for today, so these lucky suckers get a reprieve."

"We can't just put them all in the freezer for later?" he asked.

"Sure we can, but fish are always better fresh. Besides, they're not going anywhere. As far as I know, the creatures don't like seafood." She hiked the net, now in a tight and neat bundle the size of his head, over her shoulder. "I'm glad you're here. I was wondering how I was going to get all this fish back to the hotel. I usually don't take this many back with me, but since we have a few extra mouths today, I wanted to make sure I got enough."

Josh grabbed one side of the bucket as she took the other, and they headed up the beach toward the cobblestone pathway.

"What happened to your face?" she asked after a while. "If you don't mind me asking."

"Everyone's asking, so why not?" He shrugged. "This guy in Beaumont decided I'd look better with a busted nose."

"Ouch. Did you at least tattoo him back?"

"I didn't, but Gaby did."

"Which one is she?"

"The blonde."

"Young one or older one?"

"Young one. She basically saved my life. Twice now."

"She's pretty."

"Yes, she is."

Debra grinned at him. "You and her…?"

"We're just friends for now."

"'For now.'" Debra laughed. "Teenagers will be teenagers."

Josh felt himself blushing a bit. "Where's Kyle?" he asked, hoping to change the subject.

"Probably in the lobby playing his games. He's like you—not much of an outdoorsy type."

"How do you know I'm not an outdoorsy type?"

She gave him a wry look.

He laughed. "Guilty."

"I've been working out here all my life," Debra said. "I started on fishing boats when I was fourteen, helping crews catch fish and crawdads and you name it, all up and down the Gulf."

"How did you come to Song Island?"

"I fished on the lake on and off. When everything went bad, I figured there were probably worse ways to go than on an island, so I packed Kyle up and came here. I heard they were fixing up the place for a resort and was hoping someone would already be here."

"You found Marcus?"

"Yeah, Kyle and I were actually at the marina about to come over when he showed up in this big SUV. I don't even know how he got out here, but he knew about the resort, too, and was probably thinking the same thing I was. We didn't know it would be the godsend it turned out to be, though."

"So the whole thing with the creatures not liking water, that was an accident?"

"Pretty much."

"When did you guys know for sure they wouldn't—or couldn't—swim over?"

She seemed to think about it. "I'm not sure, really. You'd have to ask Karen. She was here before all of us. She's sort of the leader. We follow her lead."

They walked up the path through the woods, their soft shoes tapping against the stones. They could hear birds fluttering in the air and the wind rustling through the trees around them. Josh hadn't realized how much he had missed nature until now.

"Your parents?" she asked.

He shook his head. "No."

"Sorry."

"Thanks."

"I guess I'm lucky, I still have Kyle." She paused, then added, "At least when he's not vegging out in front of the TV. It's the end of the world, and I still can't get my kid to turn off the TV. Go figure."

"Kids will be kids," Josh smiled back.

AL, THE MAN with the bad comb-over, did most of the cooking, with Sarah, the other single mom, helping out. After delivering the fish, Josh stuck around the kitchen long enough to watch Al take a big meat cleaver and chop off the fishes' heads—some of them were still alive, which made him a bit queasy—before grabbing a long, thin knife and slicing their skin free with the practiced ease of someone who had been doing it forever. Sarah grabbed the fillet strips and washed them, then tossed them into a waiting bowl.

After seeing the fourth fish lose its head, then watching its headless corpse quivering on the cutting board, Josh hurried off. He thought he might have heard Al chuckling behind him as he fled the hotel's kitchen.

He rejoined the others back in the lobby and spent a few minutes watching the girls being girls. Sarah's daughter, Jenny, had gotten over her shyness. Along with Vera and Elise, she ran in and out of the hotel lobby, disappearing down one hallway only to appear out of another one moments later. The adults watched them come and go with smiles on their faces.

Debra's son Kyle was still "vegging" out in front of the same TV, oblivious to everything behind him. The kid had swapped out *Halo* for a *Call of Duty* title, one of the *Modern Warfare* iterations. Josh wondered if he would have stuck himself into a cocoon like Kyle if he were younger. He couldn't blame the kid too much. He was probably like that at Kyle's age, and he hadn't had the end of the world to deal with.

He searched through the smiling faces and finally found Gaby on a couch by herself, looking content to watch the others, living vicariously through their laughter and conversation. Gaby looked cheerful in new clothes, and he had forgotten how bright and shiny her hair could be. Seeing her smile made him smile, too.

Even Will and Danny seemed to have embraced the island. The two ex-Army Rangers still wore their gun belts, while Carly and Lara, like Josh, had put theirs away. Josh had swapped clothes and splashed his face with water before starting his tour of the island. Given his bruises and swelling, he couldn't really get to work scrubbing the dirt and mileage out of his face and hair. In the back of his mind, he was still trying to conserve water, the survivalist in him not quite able to completely let go. He couldn't imagine how much harder it was for Will and Danny.

He walked over to Gaby and sat down next to her. She glanced over and smiled at him. "Where have you been?"

"Exploring the island."

"You've been gone a while. I went to your room and you weren't there."

"It's a big island, and I'm a slow explorer."

Someone had put food on a table in front of the couches. Bags of chips and cold *(cold!)* spring water bottles, the condensation glistening over the plastic labels.

Gaby put her hand over his and squeezed. "Don't wander off too far."

"Okay," he said.

The touch of her hand, despite the fact that he had felt it a dozen times in the last few days, still made him breathless.

IT WASN'T SO much a meal as it was a feast. Al and Sarah served up fish of every kind. Most of them were types Josh had never seen before, but nudged on by Gaby and the others, he dived in and found them all to be universally good. Or maybe it was just the way Al fried and baked and boiled them. He hadn't known there could be so many different kinds of fish in the world or that he could ever eat so much he could barely move. Then another plate with another fish he had never seen before landed, and he ate until he was full, again.

He had forgotten what real food tasted like after living off canned goods and chips and warm bottled water for so long. Or maybe Al was just that great a cook and Josh had never really tasted good cooking before. His mom did her best, but he would never mistake her for a restaurant chef.

They had moved into the dining room next to the lobby. The room was huge, and unlike the lobby, which was mostly finished, the only completed part of the dining room was the floor. The walls and ceiling were still all Sheetrock and wooden frames, dangling wires, and a big hole in the ceiling where chandeliers were supposed to go. Not that the aesthetics mattered. The table was marble and long, and there were plenty of chairs for everyone to sit, so they gathered around and dived into Al's cooking with relish.

Josh ate and mostly listened to the others talking. Amusingly, the seating broke down to Josh and Gaby, along with Will and Danny, Carly and Lara, and the girls sitting on one side, while Marcus and the islanders sat on the other. People were just naturally drawn to those familiar to them, similar to how he ended up sitting next to Gaby without thinking, and Will ended next to Lara, and Danny with Carly.

He stole glances in Gaby's direction every now and then, and couldn't help but smile at how happy she looked.

Around seven in the evening, Sarah and Sienna, Jake's girlfriend, brought out trays of glasses filled with red wine. While they went around the table setting a glass in front of everyone except the girls, Karen stood up and made a toast.

"It's been a while since we had company like this," Karen said. "Drink up, and don't worry about what's out there. We've been here for months, and they've never crossed the water. They're not going to start now, I can promise you that."

"Is there a backup plan in case they do?" Will asked.

"It's not going to happen," Karen smiled.

"Still, better safe than sorry, right?"

"The Tower. It's the strongest building on the island. Of course, you'll have to fight Tom for it. He spends most of his nights there."

Tom grinned. "Everyone's welcome to join me in the Tower. We can have a sleepover and sing songs. Ladies? Any takers?"

"Only if I can take my gun," Carly said.

Everyone laughed…except Josh. He watched Tom closely.

It's a front. The man's got two faces. This is his public face. The one I saw back in the Tower this afternoon was the real Tom.

Next to Josh, Sarah had brought out plastic cups filled with Coca-Cola and ice cubes for the girls. They grabbed at their cups and drank up, spilling the soft drink all over themselves and the table, crunching and savoring the ice cubes like they were the most amazing things in the universe.

Josh didn't have a clue what to do with the red wine in front of him. He looked around the table and saw everyone sipping theirs, so he did the same, sticking his tongue down to taste the liquid. It tasted bitter and unwelcoming, and Josh recoiled and didn't touch it again. Everyone else seemed to like it just fine, even Gaby, who kept drinking until her glass was almost empty thirty minutes later.

They drank and ate and talked well into the night, and Josh caught glimpses of Will and Danny glancing toward the windows every few minutes as it started to get dark outside. The solar-powered lampposts coiled around the island began lighting up one by one, glowing brighter and brighter with every passing second. Someone turned on a light switch, and lights around the dining room walls lit up.

Throughout the night, Will and Danny exchanged silent looks, whole conversations passing between them with a glance or two. Josh wondered what they were thinking and felt a little naked without his gun belt. Whatever had possessed him to give up his weapons so easily? The islanders hadn't even asked him to do it; he had simply left them in his room of his own accord.

It was the electricity. The comfort. The *air conditioner*. The sight of Kyle playing games in the lobby. Tom reading a book, without a care in the world. Everyone was so calm, so oblivious to what was happening out there, that he couldn't help but fall in line.

"Are the lights enough for the entire island?" Will asked Karen.

Karen nodded between spoonfuls of fish. "More than enough. That's how we're able to conserve so much energy generated from the solar panels for things like Kyle's videogames and the AC."

"It's a hell of a setup you guys got here," Danny said.

"It is," Karen nodded. "We were very lucky to find it."

"How can you be sure the ghouls can't cross the water?" Will asked.

"Because we can see them on land, watching us every night, and it's been eight months. Don't you think they would have crossed by now if they could?"

"She's got a point, Will," Lara said.

"I don't blame you for being cautious," Karen said. "I don't have a clue what you've gone through out there just to get here. But tomorrow, when you wake up, you'll feel like it's the first day of your new life."

Maybe the wine was finally doing its job, because Will and Danny stopped sneaking looks toward the windows. They were smiling more, talking more, and had all but stopped noticing the falling night outside.

And when that happened, Josh stopped noticing, too.

It wasn't until around nine that dinner finally wrapped up and the conversation tapered off. Josh could feel the energy sapping from everyone around him, including the islanders. Everyone agreed to call it a night, and Josh was more than happy to finally get up from his chair. It felt like he had been sitting for the last three days instead of hours.

Everyone helped out by taking plates and silverware into the kitchen, then cleaning up the marble table until it was spotless. After that, people began drifting off one by one. Tom had slipped out of the room unnoticed earlier. The man had a real gift for lurking.

Jake and Sienna followed, Sienna leaning tiredly against Jake's shoulder.

Karen excused herself, declaring that she needed a big, hot bath that got a "Hallelujah!" from Carly, who quickly left with Danny.

That left Debra and Marcus talking with Will and Lara about something that, from their expressions, looked important. Josh caught fragments of conversation, bits and pieces about defending the island if something were to happen. Despite the serious topic, Will didn't sound nearly as alert as he had earlier in the day. It reminded Josh of his parents after one of their Date Nights, returning home filled with good food and too much wine.

Will's human after all. Go figure.

Josh and Gaby took their share of the dinner plates into the kitchen. Gaby looked a little wobbly, and at one point he grabbed her arm to keep her from toppling over. "Hey, there, Humpty Dumpty," he said.

She smiled back at him, and he saw mischief glinting in her eyes. "I've never drunk wine before, but I think I really like it."

"Great, you're becoming an alky at the end of the world."

"What better time?"

"Just remember, we don't have AA anymore."

"You're no fun," she said playfully.

Sarah was in the kitchen, wiping down the counters with a wet rag. "Just dump them in the sink, guys. I'll deal with them tomorrow."

There were already piles of plates and silverware in the large industrial sink behind her.

"Are you sure?" Gaby asked. "I can help."

"That's sweet, but the kitchen belongs to Al and me. He cooks, I clean up. Besides, you guys must be tired from the long trip here. I know how it is out there, always running, looking over your shoulder. Go get some rest, and we'll do it all again tomorrow."

"Thanks," Josh said, putting the plates in the sink. "For the food and for everything else, too."

"Don't mention it," Sarah said, smiling back at him. "Go get some sleep. And don't worry about anything. You're safe here."

Josh turned to go, but Gaby paused to embrace Sarah. The other woman looked momentarily embarrassed, but she quickly hugged Gaby back, and he thought both women looked close to tears.

"Thank you," Gaby said. "Thank you for everything."

"You're welcome, you're welcome…God, you're going to make me cry," Sarah said, sniffling.

Gaby wiped at her eyes. "I have something in my eyes."

"Me, too," Sarah said.

They laughed and embraced again.

Josh stood back and watched them awkwardly, not quite sure what to do next.

THEY FINALLY LEFT Sarah in the kitchen, wiping away tears, while Gaby dabbed at her eyes with a napkin. As they were making their way back across the lobby, Josh caught a glimpse of Tom, standing outside on the patio, smoking under the bright halo of the flood-lights.

Tom disturbed Josh, in more ways than one. He was always showing up where you least expected him, like a bogeyman in a horror movie. And Josh still couldn't shake that conversation in the Tower.

"That was a good meal," Gaby said.

"That was a great meal," he nodded.

"I think I'm going to really like it here. What about you?"

"Definitely."

"Even Will and Danny looked pretty happy by the end of the night."

"It must be the wine."

"Probably. I'm still a little light-headed from the wine, too. Did you have some?"

"I tasted a little bit. Not my thing."

"What is your thing?"

"You," he blurted out before he had the chance to stop himself.

"That's sweet. I think."

He did his best to grin away his embarrassment. "I meant that in the best way."

She laughed. "What other way is there?"

They were halfway to their rooms when Gaby stopped in the hallway and reached over and took his hand. She looked him in the eyes and smiled. He was suddenly very nervous, afraid and anticipating where this was going. Maybe she felt his nervousness, or actually saw it on his face, because she said, "Relax."

"I am relaxed," he lied.

They were the only two people in the hallway, and it seemed like they were the only two people in the entire hotel. The hallway had working lightbulbs, and he could see every inch of her lips and the tip of her nose and her light, incandescent green eyes. She was perfect in every way, and he was always reminded of that every time he looked at her.

Compared to her, he was a mess. And that was before the swollen eyes, bruised lips, and cracked nose. What did she even see in him? He had saved her, yes, but she had saved him back. *Twice.* He was the one who owed her, not the other way around. Yet here she was, looking at him with a smile that could make men do just about anything.

What did he ever do that was so right in a past life to deserve this?

"I know we have our own rooms," she said.

"Yeah…"

"But you should come and stay in mine."

"Why?" he was going to say, before he realized why, and said instead, "Are you sure?"

"Yes," she said, then turned and walked up the hallway, leading him by the hand.

He went willingly, floating on air.

THEY WERE SITTING in the middle of her bed when Josh asked the question he hadn't thought he would ever get to ask in this life, much less to the girl of his dreams. "Shouldn't we have some kind of protection?"

"I'm on the patch," Gaby said.

"What's that?"

"The patch. It's a contraceptive. Lara gave it to me, just in case of, well, this."

"How does it work?"

"You stick it to your skin and it keeps you from getting pregnant."

"So it's like a patch? Literally?"

"Yeah. You wanna see it?"

"Where is it?"

"Over my right shoulder."

"Does it have to be there?"

"Not really, but that's where most women put it."

"Oh."

Gaby lifted her arms and pulled off her T-shirt. She tossed it to the floor next to them, then turned back to face him in a white lacy bra. For some reason, he had always expected her to wear lacy white undergarments. "Your turn."

He pulled his shirt off. Or at least tried to. He was trembling so badly she had to reach over and help him. "Sorry."

"For what?"

"I'm nervous."

"I know."

"This is my first time."

"I didn't know that."

He almost laughed. "But I've always loved you," he said, surprised at how earnest the words sounded tumbling out of his mouth.

"I know," she smiled. "We've lived across the street from each other most of our lives, Josh. You don't think I've noticed you watching me from your bedroom window?"

"I didn't think this would ever happen. I mean, I knew it would happen eventually, but I never thought it would happen with you."

"Why?"

"Look at you, Gaby. And look at me."

"It's not as swollen as this morning…"

"I don't mean that. Even before that guy in Beaumont beat the crap out of me, I was still just me, and you were—are—still *you*."

"I don't know what that means, but it sounded sweet." She smiled at him again. "Besides, you probably would've ended up being a millionaire if none of this had happened. I read somewhere that most millionaires who didn't have a lot of luck with girls end up marrying trophy wives who resemble the girls they lusted after back in school."

"Where did you read that?"

"I don't know. *Cosmo* or *US Weekly* or one of those. You think it's true?"

"I don't know. Maybe?"

"Doesn't matter. We're here now."

She leaned forward and kissed him on the lips. Softly, like she was afraid he would crumble against her. Josh leaned into her and kissed her back. When their noses made accidental contact, he felt a stinging sensation but didn't pull away. He was kissing Gaby in bed.

He was kissing Gaby in bed!

He was still repeating that to himself when he felt her fingers against his bare chest and electricity raced through him.

I'M A LOUSY lay, Josh thought, when he heard her sighing with disappointment after it was over, even though he knew she didn't mean for it to come out so loudly, or for him to hear.

"I'm sorry," he whispered against her, out of breath.

"Don't be," she whispered back.

He lay on top of her, feeling useless and lacking, and as manly as a wet paper bag left out in the rain for a month. He wasn't sure if he should move or roll over or stay perfectly still. It wasn't like he had a lot of experience *during,* so his experiences *after* were just as lacking.

"God, I suck at this," he groaned.

"It's okay," she said, and he felt her fingers in his hair. "The night's still young."

"Yeah?" He lifted his head and looked at her beautiful face in the darkness.

"You have someplace else to be?" she said, smiling back at him.

He grinned. "No."

"Good. Lay down on your back."

He did, and she climbed on top of him. The room was dark, except for a night-light in a corner, and they had closed the patio curtains. Still, he could see enough of Gaby in the semidarkness to know that naked, she was even more glorious than clothed.

"Now just relax," she said.

Josh didn't think he could do it again so soon, but when she reached down between them and touched him, he realized he was wrong. Man, was he wrong. She guided him back inside her and he almost died.

This time, he lasted longer, and when she shuddered and lay down on top of him, their bodies slick with sweat despite the cold air pouring from the vents, Josh thought, *Maybe I'm not such a bad lay after all.*

Suck on that, mofos!

JOSH DREAMT OF walks in the park, marrying Gaby, having kids (two or three—that part of the dream was a bit murky) and opening a computer repair shop, of all things. He didn't even like computers that much.

All of that faded when he felt cold, alien fingers around his left calf and something smooth but cold brushing against the back of his head. Josh opened his eyes to find a dark, silhouetted figure moving in front of him. It was a big man, wearing all black, with broad shoulders and dark black hair. And he was *dragging* Josh by the feet along the hotel hallway.

This is such a shitty dream.

He had always assumed post-coital dreams would be better. He had just had sex with the most beautiful girl in the world, and what did he dream about? Some guy dragging him through the hotel hallway.

So Josh lay back and waited to wake up.

And he waited, and waited...

It wasn't until he felt a stinging pain against the back of his head that Josh finally accepted that he was very much awake. He opened his mouth to scream, but no sounds came out. He tried to lift his hands from the polished marble floor, but they wouldn't move. His fingers stared back at him, pliant and useless. The only thing he had control over were his eyes and his mind. The rest was asleep.

He was tilted onto his left cheek, and he couldn't lift his head off the floor. The coldness of marble seeped through his hair and scalp. There was a big bump at the back of his head, and it looked like someone had put his boxers back on him, because he remembered going to sleep with Gaby in his arms, both of them naked.

Oh God, why couldn't this be a bad dream?

The hallway lights stung his eyes, but he couldn't turn his head to look away. At least he had control over his eyelids, so he blinked and allowed himself to slowly become accustomed to the brightness. He didn't know how long they had been moving down the hallway, but it seemed like minutes had flown by. Or maybe it was seconds?

The man turned left, and as he did, Josh's head tilted over onto his right cheek and he saw he wasn't alone. The man was dragging not just him, but Gaby, too. Her long blonde hair streamed behind her like a dirty mop, scooping up dirt and dust from the floor. He was relieved to see Gaby wearing a T-shirt. It looked like his. It was a size too big for her, and it flapped around and sometimes got stuck behind her body as she was dragged, and he caught glimpses of her breasts and lacy panties. Josh flushed with embarrassment for her.

Gaby's eyes were closed, but she didn't look hurt. She actually looked asleep. *Peaceful.* He didn't understand how that was possible, unless she was drugged. But then wouldn't he have been drugged, too? Why had he woken up—well, mostly, anyway—when she hadn't?

There was a soft clicking sound, and Josh heard a female voice, muffled and slightly distorted: "Where are you?"

The man stopped, causing Josh's head to involuntarily flop back onto his left cheek, and he lost sight of Gaby. He felt his leg falling, dropped from the man's grip, then thudding against the floor.

Another clicking sound, and the man's voice: "I'd be there already if you didn't keep calling me."

Tom.

Josh shivered. Or at least, he shivered in his mind. He wasn't sure what his body did, if anything at all.

"Hurry up," the muffled female voice said.

"Yeah, yeah," Tom said, and there was a brief two-second pause before Josh felt Tom's big fingers grip his calf again and lift his leg off the floor, and he was being dragged through the hallway once more.

They turned another corner, and Josh's head returned to his right cheek, and he could see Gaby again. Her hair was now a dirty shade of brown, with dirt and dust and God knew what else from the floor entangled in it.

Finally, Tom stopped again, and Josh heard a door creak open; then they were dragged through. His head was knocked ruthlessly against the side of the door, and pain lanced through his body. He couldn't have let out a scream even if he had wanted to.

The ground under him became gritty and hard, and Josh felt like someone was raking his skull over coarse sandpaper. He glimpsed a concrete floor and knew he was in another unfinished part of the hotel. Josh was suddenly very grateful he had limited control over his body; otherwise he might have kicked out at Tom's grip in an instinctive attempt to escape. That would have gotten Tom's attention, and then what?

When Tom came to a stop again, Josh saw what looked like some kind of ballroom. A big chandelier dangled from the ceiling above him, though it had no lightbulbs. Patches of shadows moved along the ceiling, and it was hard to make out details in the semi-darkness. The wall in front of him was unfinished, and whenever he heard a sound, it echoed back and forth inside the large room.

"About damn time," a male voice said from somewhere across the room. This voice sounded familiar, too, but Josh couldn't quite place it yet.

"Hey, I'm carrying two. You idiots had one apiece," Tom said.

"Excuses, excuses," the other man said.

Tom dropped Josh's leg to the floor again, and Josh quickly closed his eyes. Somehow he was still awake—if not entirely in control of his body—while Gaby wasn't, despite the discomfort of being dragged through the hotel. They were drugged. He was sure of that now. And right now, he needed the islanders to think he was out, too.

"Is that everyone?" a woman asked. It was the same voice he had heard back in the hallway, talking to Tom, only now without the distortion.

"One, two, three…" the second man (who wasn't Tom) counted. "Yeah, except for the two girls. Berg's bringing them now."

"Zip them up," the woman said. "All of them. And make sure they're on tight, I don't want a repeat of what happened with the wrestler. Especially with the two soldiers. They're too dangerous."

"That's why we should just kill them," Tom said. "Put a bullet in their heads and be done with it."

"No," the woman said. There was finality in her voice. "It wants them."

"We can just say we had to, that they fought back," Tom insisted.

"You don't understand. *It wants them.* That means it gets them. It's not up for discussion."

"Whatever," Tom said.

Tom turned, his sneakers squeaking loudly against the concrete floor, and he began walking away. The same door they had come through earlier slammed shut in the background.

Cold fingers (probably the other man's) turned him over onto his side, and what felt like thin, plastic rope tightened around his ankles. Then the rope (no, more like a strip) was pulled tight until his ankles were squeezed against each other. The man grabbed Josh's arms with the same cold fingers and pulled them behind his back, and the same plastic sensation wrapped around his wrists and pulled them tight against one another.

"Karen," the other man said, "maybe Tom's right."

Karen.

The woman was Karen. That's why the voice was so familiar.

Tom and Karen. Then who was the other man?

Marcus.

"Yeah, I know he's right," Karen said. "That still doesn't change the fact that it wants them."

"You mean it's coming here? Personally?" Marcus said. Josh detected more than just a little bit of dread in his voice.

"Yeah."

"That's a first."

"Like I told Tom, it made it very clear it wants the two soldiers intact."

"How long before they show up?"

"I don't know, it didn't say."

"This is stupid."

"Everything about this is stupid, but you should have gotten used to it by now. Go find out what the hell is taking Berg so long with the girls. I don't want that idiot doing something he's not supposed to."

Josh listened to the sounds of Marcus's footsteps fading, then another door—a different one this time—on the other side of the ballroom opening and closing. There was a brief moment of silence while Josh waited to see (hear) what Karen would do next.

Warm fingers touched both his cheeks and turned his head, and he knew it was Karen. What was she doing now? It could have been his imagination, but he thought she might have lingered on his face a bit.

Oh God, does she know?

After a while, she let his head drop, and this time he landed on his right cheek.

He heard footsteps as Karen walked away. Moments later, a door opening and closing.

Josh opened his eyes.

He wasn't alone. Almost all of them, except for Elise and Vera, were here. Will and Lara, lying on their sides next to each other, not too far from him. Will was in his boxers, Lara in a T-shirt that was too big for her. Will's, probably, the same way they had dressed Gaby up in the first shirt they had found, which turned out to be his.

And there, not far from Will and Lara, were Danny and Carly, in the same posture and clothing. Boxers for Danny, T-shirt for Carly. Their eyes were closed, and like Gaby, they looked asleep, blissfully unaware of their surroundings and what was happening to them.

Why am I the only one still awake?

He became frantic, and it only got worse because the only part of his body he could move at all were his eyelids. He still couldn't turn his head, couldn't feel his fingers or toes. But he could feel the coldness of the concrete floor pressing up against his body.

Why am I the only one awake?

Oh God, we're so screwed.

BOOK THREE

SHUDDER ISLAND

CHAPTER 26

JOSH

PROS AND CONS: What were they?

Pros: He was wide awake. He could hear, smell, see, and feel. He had recovered almost complete control over his arms and legs. He could also turn his head and see the rest of the incomplete ballroom.

Cons: Everything else. He was the only one awake and alert and able to do anything about their captivity. He was also bound with zip ties. The kind cops used instead of handcuffs. Strong stuff. His arms were basically glued together behind his back, his legs squeezed tight under him. He wasn't going to break the zip ties. Cops around the world weren't using them because they were easy to break. Besides, he was never the strongest person in the world before The Purge, and that hadn't changed since.

Conclusion: *We're screwed.*

It took an hour before he got all the feeling back in his hands and feet, which allowed him to really feel the tightness of the zip ties, and they hurt. Josh continued lying on his side, opening his eyes only when he was sure there were no islanders in the room. Thank God no one had come back in to check on them in the last hour.

The last person he had seen was Berg, still wearing the same LSU jersey, bringing Elise and Vera in, the girls in their nightgowns. He laid them down on the floor and zip-tied their hands and feet before leaving. After that, Josh only heard voices and footsteps in the hallway, coming and going periodically.

He remembered what Karen had said an hour ago: *"Everything about this is stupid, but you should have gotten used to it by now."*

"Gotten used to it by now," Karen had said.

They had done this before. Lured people to the island. Given them rooms, showers, indoor plumbing, food, air conditioning, and wine.

The wine!

He remembered how they were served during dinner. The trays of glasses already filled with red wine. Sarah and Sienna placing the wineglasses in front of each of them. They knew exactly who was getting which glass. Everyone drinking their wine throughout the night. But Josh only taking a sip or two. Was that why he was awake and everyone else wasn't? Probably. Two and two got you four.

How did that conversation between Karen and Marcus go earlier?

"Karen," Marcus had said, *"maybe Tom's right."*

"Yeah, I know he's right," Karen had answered. *"That still doesn't change the fact that it wants them."*

Then Marcus had sighed and said, *"How long before they show up?"*

"I don't know, it didn't say," Karen had answered.

"It." What was "it"?

Then Marcus had said "they." How long before *"they"* showed up? Who was he referring to?

Whoever they were, Josh had a feeling he wasn't going to like it when *it* and *they* finally showed up on the island.

There were two small windows near the ceiling, but it was too dark outside for him to see much of anything. It had to be midnight now, or just shortly after midnight. Running from darkness for the last eight months had given Josh an intuitive sense of time.

So how long before *it* and *they* arrived?

Josh managed to rock himself into a sitting position. His arms were stiff and tight against his sides and back, making moving difficult. In movies, he had seen people slide their arms under their butts and bring them forward, and it didn't look particularly hard, or as if it required a whole lot of athleticism. Which was a good thing, because he didn't have much athleticism to spare.

He looked down at his legs, at the zip ties wrapped tight against his ankles. So now what? He looked around him. The ballroom was big, and the lack of chairs and tables made it seem even more vast. No wonder every sound echoed in here. He had to be careful about any noises he made.

Sound travels these days.

Josh looked over at Gaby, lying on her side, unconscious, dirty blonde hair splayed behind her like a fan. Behind him, Will and Danny, Carly and Lara, and the girls all still asleep. All zip-tied like him, trussed up like animals waiting for slaughter. The imagery made him shiver, and he instantly regretted it.

Maybe he could wake Will up. Or Danny. They were a hell of a lot stronger than him, and they might have experience with this. Didn't they teach Special Forces guys how to escape in the Army?

"Will," Josh whispered. When that got him nothing, he said again, slightly louder this time, "Will, wake up, for God's sake."

Will remained on his side, eyes closed.

"Danny," Josh said. When he got no reaction, he said again, slightly louder, "Danny, wake up. *Wake up.*"

The last two words echoed slightly in the room.

Shit. Too loud…

On cue, he heard footsteps coming from the door to his left, and quickly threw himself back down to the floor. He grunted as his cheek smacked into the cold concrete and pain shot through his temple.

Josh ignored the pain—or tried to, anyway—and closed his eyes. He willed his heartbeat to slow into a steady rhythm, but it was still chugging along a few seconds later when the door opened.

He braced himself at the sound of soft footsteps approaching. As the figure got closer, Josh realized his heart was still going too fast. He was sure he would be discovered, but the figure walked right past him. As it did, Josh opened his right eye a crack and saw pink tennis shoes flashing by.

The woman stopped a few feet from him, then stopped and walked back toward him—then turned at the last second and stepped out of his peripheral vision.

He couldn't see her without moving, but she was very close, and he heard a soft female voice: "I'm so sorry. Please forgive me."

Sarah.

The single mother with the little girl. The same woman who had recorded the message in the broadcast that lured them to Song Island in the first place. Who, a few hours ago, was fighting back tears as she hugged Gaby in the kitchen. The same woman who had brought out the wineglasses used to drug them.

What the hell was she doing here? And who was she apologizing to?

Josh listened but didn't hear anything else. He was sure Sarah was still there. He could feel her presence nearby. What was she doing? Crouching next to Gaby? The only way to find out for sure was to turn his head and look, but he was afraid she might feel him moving, just as he could feel her presence behind him.

A few seconds later, he heard the soft rustling of clothes, then footsteps as Sarah stood up and hurried off, back toward the door. Josh counted steps, listening to her getting farther and farther away, and his mind was suddenly in a frenzy.

Options. What options did he have? Not a whole damn lot.

Make a choice! You're it! There's no Will! No Danny!

You're it!

So make a damn choice already!

"Sarah," Josh said, and quickly struggled up from the floor into a sitting position.

She whirled around, startled by the sound of his voice. She was wearing the same clothes as last night, and there was shock and horror on her face. "You're awake. *You shouldn't be awake.*"

"Why are you doing this?"

"You can't be awake," she said again, and quickly turned to go.

"Sarah, please wait," Josh said, putting every ounce of desperation he could summon into his voice. He didn't have to dig very deep.

She stopped and looked back at him again. He saw it all in her face—uncertainty, fear, and the thing that gave him the most hope—*conflict.* He was counting on that, on her not wanting to do this. Her apologies to Gaby a few seconds ago, her embarrassment when they had thanked her in the kitchen hours ago, all entered into his equation.

God, please don't let me be wrong about her.

"What's happening here, Sarah?" he asked, looking around, eyes wide. *Sell the desperation. Sell it!* "Please tell me what's happening here?"

"You shouldn't be awake." Then, quickly, her voice falling a bit, "God, I'm sorry, but you shouldn't be awake. I have to tell them."

"No, please don't."

She hesitated. He knew she wanted desperately to go, but something held her back. Something kept her standing there, looking back across the darkened room at him. Probably the same thing that had brought her here in the first place, even knowing Gaby would never know.

"They're going to kill us, aren't they?" he asked softly, keeping his voice low.

Sound travels these days.

"No," she said.

"No?"

"No. We don't…do that." Her voice drifted off.

Josh lifted himself slightly up on his haunches and slid his zip-tied hands under his butt, then kept going along the length of his legs and finally pulled them free. He was shocked it actually worked.

"You shouldn't have done that," she said, even more alarmed than before.

"They're going to kill me if they see me like this, aren't they?"

"No, but they might hurt you."

"Help me, Sarah. Help *us*."

She glanced over at Gaby, then at the others. "I can't…"

"I know you don't want this to happen."

"I have no choice. Jenny…I have to look out for Jenny first."

"Please, Sarah, don't let them do this. I need your help. We all need your help. Gaby needs your help."

"I have to go."

This time she turned completely around and walked the short distance to the door.

"Sarah!" he shouted after her, raising his voice. He had no choice. He had to stop her. "Please! We're going to die unless you help us! Don't let this happen! You can stop this!"

She shook her head, but didn't look back, didn't stop, and before he knew it, she had opened the door and stepped through, closing it sharply behind her.

Wow, that didn't work.

Josh sighed but didn't look away from the door. A part of him expected to see it dramatically open back up and for Sarah to rush back inside.

But the door didn't open.

Defeated, Josh lowered his arms back into his lap and listened to the silence in the ballroom. It was quiet, except for the soft breathing of the others behind him.

Gaby, next to him, soundlessly asleep, peaceful in her heavy, drug-induced slumber. And the girls, Elise and Vera, snoring farther in the back, unaware that the same people who fed them last night, that poured them cold soft drinks, were now plotting their death.

Or something worse than death. He could think of lots of worse things out there right now that didn't involve dying.

"How long before they show up?" Marcus had asked.

Soon. Soon...

HE HAD NO other choice. Maybe Tom and the others had heard him imploring Sarah and were coming right now to make sure he went back to sleep—and this time stayed that way. Even if they weren't, something else was coming for them.

Either way, he was still stuck in the same situation—shit out of luck.

He looked over at Gaby, then looked behind him at the others again. They hadn't stirred, didn't even look as if they had heard anything or were any closer to swimming up from whatever dreams or nightmares they were mired in at the moment. They certainly looked like sweet dreams, judging by the ghost of a smile on Gaby's lips.

It had to be some kind of drug. Roofies, maybe. The date-rape drug he had heard about on the news. But he thought those drugs worked right away, not hours later. Something *like* roofies, maybe?

Whatever it was, it was effective. Except on him, because he was the only one who had barely touched his drink during dinner. Josh felt fully alert and wide awake now, and he tried to concentrate on the problem at hand. It was a hell of a problem, too. But he was a smart guy. He could think his way through this. Right? Of course he could.

We are so screwed.

He looked back at Will and Danny. What would they do in his position? Probably try to break the zip ties. How, though? These things were tough bastards. No. Strength wasn't going to do it here.

Will and Danny would know that. So what would they do if they couldn't break something? How would a pair of ex-Army Rangers get around a problem like this?

God, he wished they would wake up already so he could ask them.

Josh took inventory of the room. It was big, and they had been deposited in the middle. There were no chairs or tables, and the big, expensive-looking chandelier above him wasn't going to be much help. Most of the walls were still just Sheetrock, with electrical wiring sticking out everywhere.

He concentrated on his hands. His wrists were almost pressing against one another except for a half-inch space between the two loops, which were tightened by pulling the ends along a roller-lock system in the middle. The straps themselves were white, but the middle section, where the ends passed through, was solid black and looked like an ice cube.

He tried pulling at the zip tie, but it didn't budge. He gritted his teeth and tried again, this time even harder, but gave up after ten seconds of heavy straining. The zip tie hadn't moved even a little bit. If anything, it felt like the straps had gotten tighter around his wrists. Was that even possible?

Josh stared at them for a moment.

He couldn't break the straps, so maybe there was a way *around* them.

He stared at the plastic device for the longest time, trying to understand how the zip tie itself worked. Everything passed through the block in the center. That much was obvious. But the roller system meant the end of the straps only went one way, pulling the zip inward and around the wrist, and not the other way, which would loosen the straps. Loosening the straps was the goal. But how to achieve it? The retainer block was the key.

He lifted his hands toward him and eyeballed the retainer block up close. Could he break it? How? He could probably smash it with a hammer. If he had a hammer. But why wish for a hammer when he could wish for scissors and just cut the straps? He didn't have a hammer or scissors, so what did he have?

Eureka!

Brawn wasn't going to get him out of this, but brains helped him to see his little sliver of hope. Literally. There was just enough space between the strap and the interior walls of the block that if he had something small enough to insert there, he could loosen the roller and slide the strap back instead of forward. That was the key. Finding something *small enough* to push inside.

Josh glanced around the ballroom again. This time he didn't think about the things the room didn't have, but paid attention to what it did offer.

Plenty of debris. There was dirt and chipped wood and dust everywhere along the concrete floor around him.

Debris. That was where salvation lay.

The chipped wood, though small enough, wouldn't work because the bits weren't strong enough to affect the roller. So it had to be something small *and* strong.

HE FOUND IT almost by accident. He rolled onto his right side and there it was. A nail, lying in a small groove along the concrete floor. It was so small he would have missed it if he hadn't laid his head down just a foot from it. It was brown and rusted over, but nails were nails, and they were usually strong.

Josh scrambled back up to a sitting position and picked up the nail. It was so small it almost slipped from his fingers.

He looked at the nail, then at the retainer block of the zip tie, before cautiously positioning the sharp point between the strap and the interior wall of the retainer block. With the ball of his forefinger, he pushed the nail in and felt both strap and block resisting. He pushed harder and felt pain against his finger. He kept pushing, almost willing the nail through the slot, and was finally rewarded when the nail sank a full quarter of the way down.

From there, it was easier to get the nail down another half inch. Then three quarters. With the nail now firmly lodged between the strap and the retainer block, Josh pushed his right wrist downward against the strap.

The strap didn't move at first—then slowly but surely, it went down half an inch. That was enough for Josh to slip his right hand free, and he had to restrain himself from shouting out in triumph.

Suck on that, mofos!

He hurriedly pulled the nail out of the retainer block and used it to free his left hand. He did the same to the zip tie around his ankles, then pushed himself to his feet. He did it too fast and stumbled, almost fell, but caught himself on his knees just in time. He got up again, this time more slowly.

Nail in hand, Josh hurried over to Will. He thought about freeing Gaby first, but that was the soft, gooey part of him talking. The tough, hardened part of him knew he needed help. Freed or not, he wasn't going to be able to take on Tom or Marcus—or hell, even Karen—by himself if they showed up now. Not wearing boxers and armed only with a nail, anyway.

Josh checked the doors again, in case all of his rolling around had attracted attention. Still good to go.

Will was where Josh had last seen him, resting on his side in his boxers, hands zip-tied behind his back. "Will," Josh said, crouching over him. When that didn't work, he said louder, "Will, wake up."

That didn't work, either.

Josh thought about it, then tapped Will lightly on the cheek. "Will, wake up."

Nothing. Josh really thought about it this time, then slapped Will across the cheek. He was prepared to jump back if Will woke up and swung at him. But he didn't have to because the slap did nothing.

Will didn't even stir.

Josh felt for Will's pulse, just to be sure, and found it. There. He really was just asleep, and Josh had no idea how to wake him up. In the movies, all you had to do to wake someone who had been drugged was tap them on the cheeks. Or say their name loud enough. That wasn't going to happen here. He had done both those things, even the slapping part, which had terrified him.

So now what? Maybe if he could splash water on Will's face. That usually worked in the movies, too. Of course, he didn't have any water…

Josh was trying to find ways around this new problem when he heard noises.

Footsteps!

He scrambled up and darted across the room toward the door the footsteps were approaching. He was suddenly very glad he was barefoot, because he made almost no noise as he ran. He flattened his back against the wall next to the door and held his breath.

He listened to the footsteps getting closer. Was it his imagination or did it sound like the person was moving fast, almost urgently? Or maybe it was just his heart racing, making his entire body vibrate against the wall, all the way down to the cold floor.

The floor was so cold. Why was it so cold? Oh, right, he wasn't wearing shoes.

The doorknob jingled and began turning clockwise. It looked like it was moving in slow-motion, rotating barely an inch per second, but that was just his mind playing tricks on him. The doorknob opened at the same speed that all doorknobs opened, but at that moment, standing there pressed against the door in his boxers, trying to remember to breathe, everything looked like it took forever to process, even the delicate, thin flakes of dust floating through the moonlight in front of him.

Then the door was opening and Josh saw a flash of skin and shirt and pants and before he knew it, Josh had thrown himself forward and into the figure, catching the person around the waist. They both went sprawling to the floor, and Josh heard the sound of something metallic clattering. He managed to look up and saw a small knife spinning along the floor, away from them.

Josh scrambled up on top of the person, raising himself slightly, and he thought, *I'm about to hit someone. Oh God, I hope I'm doing this right*, and cocked back his right hand as far as it would go.

He was ready to deliver the blow, to smash down with righteous indignation, when the person under him looked over their shoulder and Josh heard a female voice through the adrenaline flowing through him like a loud, rushing river.

"Josh, stop!"

Josh froze and looked down at Sarah's frightened face. "Sarah?"

"It's just me," she said, looking up at him, trying to catch her breath.

Josh's right hand remained cocked. Sarah was one of them, one of the people who had lured them here and fed them and laughed with them and drugged them. She was the one who had brought out the glasses with the wine.

She was reading his face, terrified at what she was seeing. "I came back to help, Josh! Please, I only came back to help!"

He glanced over at the knife.

She followed his gaze, understood. "I was going to cut you free.

And then the others. I swear, Josh, I only came back to help."

He hesitated. Was she telling the truth? Could he even trust her? He had pleaded with her earlier because he'd had no choice. But he had the upper hand this time…

So this is what it feels like to be on top for once.

"Why?" he asked, keeping his body on top of her. She hadn't tried to get away, so that was encouraging.

"I thought about what you said. I can't keep doing this anymore. It's not right."

"We're not the first ones…"

"No." He could hear sadness in her voice. It was genuine. Either that, or Sarah was the greatest actress who ever lived.

Make a choice!

He did, and climbed off her. Sarah looked relieved and picked herself up from the floor. Josh offered his hand and she took it. "Are the others coming?"

"No, they're asleep. Except Tom. He doesn't sleep very much. He's up in the Tower, where he always is."

"Can he see us from there?"

"No, I don't think so. The ballroom is toward the other side of the hotel." She paused, then said, "How did you get out of the zip ties?"

"I used a nail."

"A nail?"

"Yeah."

"Wow."

"Why?"

"No one's ever gotten out of those zip ties before. But then no one's ever woken up before, either. Are you…immune to it or something?"

"That depends. What is 'it'?"

"It's a form of Rohypnol."

"I don't know what that is."

"What?"

"Rohyp-what?"

"Rohypnol," Sarah said. "People call it roofies."

"I knew it. The date-rape drug thing."

"It's not pure Rohypnol," she said, almost defensively. "I adjusted it a bit."

"Whatever." He walked over to the knife and picked it up. "Whose idea was the drug in the wine bit?"

She gave him a sheepish look. "Mine. It was either that, or do it Tom and Karen's way, and that…wouldn't have been good for any of you."

"So you're doing us a favor?" he said, the doubt plain in his voice.

"Yes." She looked embarrassed again, her cheeks appearing slightly red even in the semi-darkness of the room. "I'm sorry."

He shook it off. She had a lot to answer for, she and the others, but this wasn't the time. Not even close. He looked up at the moonlight coming in through the high windows above them. "How long before whoever is supposed to come here for us actually comes for us?"

"I don't know," Sarah said. She rubbed her shoulders as if she were cold. He thought that was amusing, since he was the one walking around barefoot in his boxers. "Only Karen knows when they're coming. She says it could be soon, or later, or tomorrow night. I don't know for sure. Karen, Tom, and Marcus are the ones who really take care of things. We mostly just stay out of their way."

"Who are 'they'?" Josh asked. The question had been on his mind for a while now. "The people that are coming. Who are *'they'?"*

Josh saw the color drain from her face, and he suddenly knew the answer before she said it.

"*Them*," she said. "The creatures. They're the ones coming for you…"

CHAPTER 27

WILL

"HE WANTS YOU, Will."

He was back in Deussen Park, watching an idiot in a fast boat going back and forth on the lake ten meters from where the pier ended. The man was annoying a small group of fishermen along the shore of Lake Houston, and every now and then, one of the fishermen would flip the boater off, but the man was oblivious. Either that, or he didn't care.

"'He?'" Will said.

"The blue-eyed ghoul," Kate said. "The first one you saw, outside the bank in Cleveland. His name is Mabry."

"They have names?"

She laughed. It was melodic and feminine, and he was struck again by how much more human and womanly she sounded and looked in these dream encounters, compared to the way she had when he had actually known her. Back when she was still human.

That was a long time ago…

"We all have names, Will," Kate said. "Most of us just don't use them anymore."

"What about you? Do you still use 'Kate'?"

"I do. I find it helps me stand out from the crowd. And when there are billions of your species out there, and everyone kind of looks like everyone else, it's a little hard to stand out." She smiled. He wondered if that was a joke. "Mabry doesn't mind. After all, he's keeping his."

She leaned against the railing along the walkway that rose three meters from the calm water below. At least, it was calm for the few seconds it took the man in the fast boat to come back around.

He was wearing slacks and a white dress shirt for some reason. Kate wore a pink Sunday dress. It was simple and elegant, and it looked fantastic on her. She always did have a beautiful body. A woman's body. Curves in all the right places, as they say. Breasts pressing out at all the right angles.

She smiled. "I'm glad you like it. I made some improvements for you."

"This would go better if you stopped reading my mind."

She laughed again. "Sorry."

"No, you're not."

"No, I'm not."

They continued up the walkway, passing an angry fisherman in mud boots and a straw hat throwing the finger at the fast boater.

"Why does he want me?" Will asked. "This Mabry?"

"At first, he was angry at you. But then after you survived the siege at Harold Campbell's facility, I think he became infatuated."

"That's a disturbing thought."

"It's a compliment."

"I don't take compliments from undead ghouls."

"Be a little more open-minded, Will," she said, sounding like a mother chastising her son.

"What does he want with me?"

"He wants you to join us. Come over."

"I thought you just wanted me to kill myself. Get it over with."

She shrugged. "He's changed his mind. Now he wants you to become one of us. It's not like you have much choice, Will. When you wake up from this, you'll realize that Song Island isn't the sanctuary you thought it was. Far from it, in fact."

"I never thought it was a sanctuary."

"No, but you led the others there. You might not have believed it, but you *hoped* for it."

Maybe…

What the hell was going on out there? Back in the real world? He remembered going to sleep. And then dreaming, which had brought him here to Deussen Park. And Kate was here, as if she had been waiting for him to return since the last time.

"Why does he want to recruit me?" Will asked. "I thought humanity was a lost cause. That we can't win this war."

"You can't."

"So why?"

She sighed, as if he were testing her patience. "Because Texas isn't the only place where people like you are still fighting, Will. You should see how much trouble those idiots in New York are giving Mabry. That's why he's left me in charge of this area. He has to deal with them. California's a mess, too. And Alaska. Well, it's Alaska. It's cold out there, and Mabry isn't sure he even wants it."

"Sounds like you have your hands full."

"Humanity can't win this war, but you're capable of making it difficult for us to move forward. Mabry wants to deal with the troublemakers, nip it in the bud, if you will. Leave it alone for too long, ignore the problem, and it will fester and grow. That's why he wants you. You're a soldier. Mabry is smart, but he's not a soldier, and a part of being smart is understanding your limitations. He wants both you and Danny, but he'll settle for just you."

California? New York? How many other places?

"They can't help you, Will," she said. "They're in worse shape than you are, they just don't know it."

"They don't know about the silver."

She shrugged. "It doesn't matter. What matters is that it's all over for you and Lara and the others. Arriving at Song Island was the end of the road."

"What's happening on Song Island?"

"Oh, you'll find out soon enough." She smiled mischievously at him. "It was my idea, you know. It's why Mabry turned me. He's been planning this for years, decades—God, I don't know, maybe centuries. But he's no longer human enough to think outside the box. I am. But then again, I was always good at selling dreams to desperate people."

The man on the fast boat went by again, and the sound of his outboard motor had somehow gotten louder. Will didn't know how that was possible.

"I can give you Lara," Kate said. Will looked over at her and she nodded. "I can give Carly to Danny, too. And the little girls, Elise and Vera, if you want. We don't need them. We have all that we need. But we'll have to turn the two of you. It's the only way we can be sure."

"There must be millions of soldiers out there. Why do you need us?"

"Once you're turned, become what you call 'ghouls,' it's impossible to reverse the transformation. You lose more than your humanity, you lose your experiences, everything that makes you, you. That's what Mabry wants. You'll still be you, Will, only...*more*."

"And Lara?"

"She doesn't have to be turned. We'll leave her alone if you want. Let you have her to go home to in the day." She looked amused by the idea. "Maybe she'll grow to love you—the new you—all over again."

"I don't believe you."

"Have I lied to you before, Will?"

He didn't answer.

"I'm not lying to you now," she continued. "Help us put an end to this ridiculous troublemaking. I know you want to. You're tired. Lara's tired. Danny, Carly... They're all tired. Isn't that why you fell for Song Island so easily? Even you and Danny. You *wanted* what it promised so badly, you couldn't wait to give in."

What the hell is happening on Song Island?

"Aren't you tired of the constant fear, the constant running?" she asked, moving closer to him, the heat of her breath against his skin. "It can all end. It will anyway. But this way, it'll be your choice. And you'll have Lara. And Danny will have Carly. You're saving them from the misery. Don't you want to save them, Will?"

"What's happening on Song Island?" he asked.

She smiled. "You'll see. Just know this. I'm coming for you, Will. I'm coming for you..."

The fast boat was now almost right next to him, flying by so fast and so close the waves rose into the air a good four meters. Will braced himself as the water came crashing down right on top of him with the force of a Mack truck.

HE WOKE UP to the sight of Josh, eyes closed and right hand wound back like he was preparing to deliver the mother of all curveballs. As the kid's hand came down, Will grabbed his wrist and held it in the air.

Josh's eyes snapped open in shock.

"Okay, I'm up," Will said.

"Oh, God, please don't kill me," Josh said, and stumbled back when Will let go of his hand.

Will sat up on a hard concrete floor in his boxers. A pair of zip ties lay at his feet, the straps slit in half. His head was spinning, but he managed to swim through the thick mud to look around him at a large, unfinished room. Lara, Danny, and the others lay scattered around him. Lara lay on her side, wearing his T-shirt. Danny snored lightly on his side as a woman kneeled next to him, lightly tapping his cheek. There were more recently cut zip ties on the floor.

The woman was saying over and over, "Wake up. Danny, wake up," to no real effect. Danny continued to snore. When the woman looked over her shoulder, Will saw that it was Sarah. The single mother with the little girl. The voice on the broadcast.

"What's going on, Josh?" Will asked.

Josh gathered himself, and Will saw he was wearing his boxers, too. "You want the long story or the short story?"

"Get on with it," Will said impatiently.

Josh nodded and told him everything. Waking up while he was being dragged through the hallway by Tom. Escaping from his bindings with, of all things, a nail. Sarah deciding to help. Rohypnol in their wineglasses during dinner. The true purpose of the island.

"It's not like you have much choice, Will," Kate had said in his dream. *"When you wake up from this, you'll realize that Song Island isn't the sanctuary you thought it was. Far from it, in fact."*

He crouched next to Lara and felt her pulse. It was steady, and she looked blissfully asleep. He brushed at a strand of blonde hair and watched her for a brief moment before standing up. His legs were wobbly, and it took a while to get blood circulating to all the correct parts.

Will said, "Tom and the others. Where are they now?"

"Tom's in the Tower," Sarah said. "The others are asleep. It was a lot of work, getting you guys here. I guess they're tired."

Will nodded. He had plenty of choice words for Sarah, but he didn't say any of them at the moment. She was here, helping them. For now, that made her an ally. He would circle back to the topic when this was all over. Right now, he had a hard time just staying upright.

"Rohypnol?" he said.

"Not in its pure form," Sarah said. "I made some changes to it."

She's done this before.

"You're a chemist?" he asked.

"I worked at a pharmacy."

He nodded. He would circle back to that one later, too. "Our clothes?"

"There's a room we've been using for storage at the very back of the hotel. Berg is going over your stuff now, looking for valuables or something we can use. Tom has your weapons."

They've definitely done this before.

"Tom's alone in the Tower?"

"Yeah. I don't know where he keeps the weapons, though."

"There are three floors," Josh said. "First floor, with a staircase that goes up to the second floor, in the middle. Then a final third floor."

"What about a basement?" Will asked.

"I saw a door in the first floor. Could have been it."

Will nodded, absorbing all the information as best he could through a plume of sleep that clung persistently. He looked over at Danny, asleep on the hard concrete floor. "Hit him harder."

"What if…" she started.

"He's drugged. You need to hit him harder, or he's never going to wake up."

"Okay," she said, but she sounded unconvinced. Or maybe she was just afraid.

"I need that knife," Will said, and picked up a knife someone had laid down on the floor nearby. "Stay here and wake the adults up. But not the girls. It's better if they stay asleep through this." He sighed, blinked a couple of times, then added, "I'll be back."

"Where are you going?" Josh asked, sounding alarmed.

"To get some clothes and then our weapons. Tell Danny where I'm going and what's happened as soon as he wakes up. And both of you, stay here until I come back. Don't wander out of this room."

"What if you don't come back?"

"I'll come back."

"Okay," Josh said, but like Sarah, he didn't sound completely convinced.

Will couldn't be bothered with their reluctance right now. He felt naked without his weapons, and wearing nothing but his boxers didn't help. He walked across the big room and pushed through the door and into the dimly lit hallway. He found that if he kept moving, the fog cleared up faster.

The lights were working at half their normal brightness, and Will picked his way up the hallway, stepping around anything suspicious lurking on the floor. He listened for the slightest noise, hearing only silence around him. Of course Karen and Marcus were asleep. Why not? They had done this before.

Will thought back to the dream. To Kate. What had she said to him, with that beaming, proud smile of hers?

"I was always good at selling dreams to desperate people."

She had sold them the dream that was Song Island. Not just them, but other people before them. How many other victims? How many times had Sarah spiked the wine during a feast of fish and friendly chatter and talks about what they used to do back in the old days?

It was all so damn perfect. The island. The food. The AC. The working indoor plumbing. He had done his best to stay wary, to look for the hidden troubles, but in the end, even he had been suckered in. He and Danny both.

Fuck.

Will forced himself to keep moving, push aside his failure. It hung over him like a black cloud, fouling up his mood. At least he was still alive. So there was that. And Lara, too, along with the others. He had failed them, but it hadn't cost them. *Yet.* That could change in a heartbeat, unless he made sure it didn't.

As he kept moving through the hallway, he thought about something else Kate had said to him in the dream. It was part of her sales pitch, and it stuck with him:

"Because Texas isn't the only place where people like you are still fighting."

It was always at the back of his mind that there had to be others out there, still fighting, still surviving. Now he knew for sure. There were people in New York, California, and who knew where else across the United States. In the heartland. The mountains. The hills and valleys and small towns. Possibly in other countries. That made him feel better. It even chipped a bit at the self-recriminations running through his mind.

A bit, anyway.

Soon, the hallway became more hazardous, and he had to actively skirt around nails, stray strands of duct tape, and broken two-by-fours on the floor.

He turned a final corner and saw a plastic see-through sheet hanging across a doorway. On the other side was darkness, though he detected the small glow of a soft light somewhere in the back and a shadowy figure moving in front of it.

Berg.

Will changed his grip on the knife and hid it behind his back. He pushed quietly through the plastic covering, slipping into the dark room unnoticed.

The room was supposed to be some kind of office. There was only a bright night-light in the corner, creating a halo effect around a two-meter area. In the middle was Berg, crouched in front of boxes, rifling through their contents. He wore a gun belt, with a Glock in a hip holster.

Will walked into the room. He was quiet. He was always good at being quiet when he had to be. It helped that he had honed the skill while weighed down with weapons and heavy equipment, so keeping silent in his bare feet and boxers was almost no challenge.

Berg didn't know he was coming until Will was just a meter away. When he finally sensed danger, Berg stood up and started to turn, right hand reaching for the Glock. Berg might have even managed to brush his fingers against the handgun's grip before Will slapped his left hand over Berg's mouth. At the same time, Will drove Berg back and into the unfinished wall and jammed the sharp point of the knife against his left eyeball.

Berg might have screamed against Will's hand, or he might have just let out a low wheezing sound. Either way, nothing came out while his eyes darted to the cold, slightly dented steel pressing dangerously close to his eye. In the glow of the night-light, the sharp edge probably looked extra menacing.

"It's going to hurt," Will said, keeping his voice low, but not so low Berg couldn't hear the venom dripping from every word. "Do you understand? It will hurt. A lot."

Berg nodded. Or tried to. It was mostly a slight tremble.

"Stand very still," Will said. "My hand's been asleep for the last few hours. It could slip very easily."

Will took his hand away from Berg's mouth. Berg snapped his mouth shut willingly, perhaps afraid he would involuntarily make a sound. His eyeballs were focused on the knife, and he might not even have noticed when Will slipped the Glock out of the holster before taking a step back.

Berg let out a loud sigh of relief. "Please don't kill me," were the first words out of his mouth.

"That depends."

"On what?" Berg seemed to regret the question as soon as it came out of his mouth.

"Zip ties. Where are they?"

"In one of my pouches."

"Let's see them."

Berg took out a handful. "Here," he said, and offered them to Will with a shaking hand.

Will tossed the knife away and saw Berg's eyes, predictably, following its path. Will smashed the Glock into Berg's temple as he was looking and the man crumpled to the floor in a heap. Will crouched and picked up the fallen zip ties and looped them around Berg's feet and hands. He pulled them tight while Berg groaned on the floor. He wasn't sure if Berg was too stunned to attempt anything or too scared to try. Not that it mattered.

Will grabbed a pair of silk panties and stuffed them into Berg's mouth. Berg tried to spit them out but was unable to. There was already blood along his temple, dripping down to his cheek.

It took Will a few minutes to find a crate with his clothes. Or at least they looked like his clothes in the soft light. They could very well have been Danny's since they were about the same size. Will pulled on cargo pants and a T-shirt, then socks, but had to hunt around for some boots that would fit. He slipped them on, then took a moment to re-orient himself with the hotel's layout.

Will glanced down at his left hand, expecting to find his watch, but it wasn't there. He spent another few minutes looking for it among the crates, but couldn't find it anywhere. He gave up after about four minutes and headed for the back door instead.

Maybe Tom had a watch he could take off his dead body…

WILL STEPPED OUT of the hotel and into the night with the Glock. He saw the Tower right away. It was hard to miss. LED floodlights below the third-floor windowsills lit the structure like the beacon it was supposed to be, even with the unfinished top. He had initially pegged the Tower at forty meters high, and now that he was closer, it looked more like forty-five, give or take.

The island itself was surprisingly bright, thanks to the strategically placed lampposts covering the hotel grounds. Karen was right when she said you could see the lights from the shores. There were more floodlights jutting out of the sides of the hotel, creating a halo effect around the structure.

Will stuck to the shadows. Eventually he was able to use the palm trees for cover. He slowed down, then stopped completely when he was ten meters from the Tower and sat on his haunches in the darkness next to some shrubbery. He couldn't see any lights coming from the second floor of the building, but there were soft lights coming from one of the third-floor windows.

He counted to one hundred, then began jogging toward the Tower, keeping as low as possible, though he didn't think it was necessary as long as Tom didn't peer out the window at that exact moment. Even then, Tom would have to look down. Will was still thinking about those possibilities when he reached the structure and leaned against the fat, curving concrete base.

He was close enough to the door that he didn't have to reach very far to touch the lever. He gripped it and spent a second wondering if Tom had alarms on the door, but he hadn't even finished that thought before he cranked the lever down, pulled the door open, and slipped through, the Glock rising to chest level.

A split second later, he was inside the first floor of the Tower.

A soft yellow light above the door made the interior look claustrophobic, despite being the biggest section of the structure. It was the size of a small studio apartment, with shelves in one corner filled with books, trinkets, and what looked like a stack of board games. Tom hadn't struck him as the board-game-playing type. A spiral cast-iron staircase along the wall led upward. Will spotted the door in the floor Josh had mentioned. It had a ring handle and a padlock.

He glanced up toward the second floor and stopped breathing for a few seconds and listened, but couldn't hear anything moving around above him.

Will walked over to where the staircase started. The steps looked solid enough. He put one foot on the stairs and heard a slight creak, but it wasn't loud enough to wake someone from sleep. At least, he hoped not. Will took a second step, then a third, and was halfway to the second floor a few seconds later.

He kept the gun aimed at the thick wooden door above and across the room from him. Because the stairs arced along the wall, he started at one side of the Tower and ended up on the other side by the time he was halfway up the stairs. He wouldn't be directly below the door until he had gone another full revolution.

Halfway up, he stopped and listened again, but still couldn't hear anything from above him. It was much darker up here, as the small lightbulb below didn't reach this far. The door had no locks, which meant it opened upward and could only be locked from the other side.

He started up again and stopped only when he was directly under the door. It was more like a hatch.

Who the hell designed this thing?

He had no real choice. Tom was too dangerous to take slowly. The faster he could get up there and confront the man, the better.

Will positioned himself below the door. He gripped the ring handle with his left hand, careful not to jingle the metal base. He adjusted his stance on the steps so his left shoulder was just barely touching the door. With the Glock in his right hand lifted up to chest level, Will took a deep breath, then a second one, then finally a third before shoving his body upward, driving everything he had not into the door, but *through* it.

He emerged through the hole in the second floor and into darkness and knew instinctively he had screwed up.

His eyes hadn't adjusted to the pitch blackness yet when he heard movement behind him.

There was no choice now. Will lunged all the way out of the door and onto the floor and spun around just as Tom attacked, throwing his full weight into Will's chest like the brawler Will knew he was.

The Glock flew from Will's grip as Tom crashed into him, driving his shoulder straight into Will's chest, his entire bulk crashing down like a sledgehammer. Then Tom's arms wrapped around Will's waist and the man carried both of them across the room and right into the wall, smashing Will hard against the concrete, the impact sending something clattering to the floor next to them in the dark.

Tom didn't waste a second. He pressed his attack, and Will felt one, two—*four* quick uppercuts connecting with his ribcage, pounding on his kidneys in the darkness. Before he could fully absorb the pain from those blows, Tom's left fist caught him in the right cheek and Will staggered sideways, the world suddenly exploding in a burst of pain and colors and sound.

Will fought for breath, trying to get control of his legs, forcing them to stop moving. It wasn't working. He felt the air inside the room shift as Tom followed, stalking him like a hunter after wounded prey.

He raised his arms in a weak attempt at making a shield, unable to find Tom in the darkness. Tom punched through his defenses and connected again, and Will heard his nose breaking, the skin tearing, and blood spraying the cool air of the second floor. Will fell face-first onto something soft (thankfully soft).

Will pushed himself up just as he heard a soft *click* and an LED lightbulb on the ceiling buzzed to life, illuminating the room and the cot he had been lying on, bleeding onto a white pillow.

He spun around and saw Tom in cargo pants and T-shirt, picking up the Glock from the floor. Will sat down on the bed and wiped at the blood dripping from his nose. There was a break on the bridge, with some blood there, too, but he didn't worry about that at the moment. Instead, he tried to catch his breath and watched Tom turning the Glock over in his hands.

"Nice gun," Tom said. "Looks familiar. Berg's? That stupid kid. I knew we shouldn't have given him a gun." Tom reached behind his back and pulled out a second Glock. He grinned at Will, and the only thing missing was him shouting, *"Ta-da!"* Instead, Tom said, "I could have shot you when you stuck your head through the door, you know. I was waiting in the back, where you couldn't see me. No one ever looks behind them when they come through the door. See, this is basically my house. I know where all the blind spots are."

"So why didn't you?" Will asked. His voice sounded muffled for some reason.

"Too easy. Way, *way* too easy. Besides, you're the leader, right?"

Will didn't answer. He took the respite to slow his breathing down and gather himself.

"I'm actually kind of disappointed," Tom said. He tossed Will's Glock back on the floor and it slid into a corner, next to a bookcase filled with hardcover books, magazines, and more board games. "I thought you'd be tougher. But I guess toughness is defined by the people you hang out with. I bet those girls and that other soldier boy think you're pretty hot shit."

"You gonna shoot me or talk me to death?" Will said, and spat a mouthful of blood out onto the floor.

Tom laughed. "Don't be in such a hurry. This is the best time I've had in months. This probably won't come as too much of a surprise, but it's hard to find someone decent to go a few rounds with on this island. Marcus can barely throw a punch. And Berg, well, you know kids these days. Hell, Karen gives me a better fight in the sack. She likes it rough, you know."

"I really couldn't care less."

"Hah, yeah. I guess she's not your type." He grinned, as if he had just thought of something wonderful. "Lara, that her name? A little too skinny for my taste, but hey, I might give it a try anyway. You gotta spice life up every now and then, right? Otherwise it's not worth living."

"She'd eat you for dinner."

"We'll see. She looks like she might be ready for a trade-up. What do you think?"

"I think you should shoot me now, because it's going to hurt if we go round two."

Tom grinned at him. "You think so?"

"I know so."

"Prove it."

Tom tossed his Glock away, and it skidded along the floor and landed a few inches from the other one.

Will grinned at him.

Tom saw the grin and returned it. "I like the confidence. So show me, tough guy. Show me what the Rangers taught you."

Will stood up from the cot and began walking toward him. Tom stood his ground and watched him come.

The man didn't move. Didn't blink. Didn't fidget at all.

Tom had three to four inches on him and a good, solid fifty pounds. Tom was bigger, stronger, and a hand-to-hand fight was probably not in Will's favor. He didn't think a guy like Tom had ever lost a fight in his life. Definitely not in a one-on-one situation. And he probably wasn't going to lose this one, either, so his confidence was justified.

Bigger, stronger, but maybe not smarter.

Maybe.

Will went right at him.

He faked a right punch that made Tom lift his left with the intention of blocking, but instead of going through with the punch, Will launched himself forward and rammed his shoulder into Tom's gut. He caught the big man by surprise, but Tom quickly gathered himself and smashed down with two huge elbows into Will's back. Will ignored the pain, tried to pretend he didn't even feel the blows connecting, though that was damn difficult. They were connecting, all right, and each blow was like a boulder crunching down on him from on high, driving him to the floor, trying to bury him.

Ignore it!

Will used his leverage and momentum to lift Tom off his feet, grunting, shouting, screaming with the effort because Tom was heavy (*Too heavy!*). But somehow he managed to lift the big man off his feet, however slightly, but enough to carry both of them across the room.

Will kept going long after he ran out of breath, long after every inch of his body began aching. Pushing his legs to keep churning, his arms to keep their grip around Tom's body, even as Tom continued to slam down with his elbows. Maybe Tom realized what was happening, what Will was planning, because his blows started to come down faster and stronger. Will wondered if you could possibly break a man's spine with just your elbows, because that was exactly what it felt like Tom was trying to do.

Then, mercifully, Will reached his destination and slammed Tom, back first, into the bookcase on the other side of the floor. Two of the shelves gave way as Tom's back smashed into them, and books and magazines and board games tumbled down on top of their heads. Not that either of them noticed.

Will heard the breath expelling from Tom's lungs in surprised gasps, but he didn't spend even a single second wallowing in the minor victory. He untangled himself from Tom and stepped back, then spun to his right and grabbed the bookcase from behind and pulled it with everything he had, until the thick wood furniture careened forward, crashing into Tom's back and plunging to the floor, taking Tom along with it.

Will didn't have any illusions that the bookcase was going to hold Tom down for long. In fact, Tom was already halfway off the floor, the bookcase sliding off his back, when Will smashed his right knee into Tom's left temple. That forced the big man back down, the bookcase crashing on top of him for the second time in the last ten seconds.

This time, Tom didn't get up quite as fast. But get back up he did, pushing the bookcase off him as he slowly rose from the floor.

"That all you got?" Tom shouted, though Will didn't detect the same level of boisterous bravado as before.

"Not by a long shot," Will said.

Will walked over to where the Glocks were and picked one up. He checked the slide to make sure there was a bullet in the pipe.

Tom had risen from the floor behind him, and he stood like a hulking giant. A hurt but still hulking giant slightly bent at the waist, his breath coming out in ragged gasps. He eyeballed Will like a predator. "It's not over yet, soldier boy. There's still round three."

"It's over."

Tom's eyes went to the Glock in Will's hand, but he managed to grin through a mouthful of blood anyway. "Bullshit. I know guys like you. We're cut from the same cloth."

"You don't know me."

"The hell I don't. You were a cop, too, right? After the Army?"

"Yeah."

"See." He spat out a thick gob of blood. "I know guys like you. I went to work eight hours a day, five days a week with guys like you. Gung-ho motherfuckers to the very end. Just like me. That's how I know you're not going to use that gun."

Will was tired and hurt and his back felt like it had been crushed into a thousand different sections. He stood across from Tom, watching the man breathing in a lungful of air with every gasp. "You don't think so?"

"Fuck no," Tom said, brimming with confidence. "You're going to end this the only way guys like us know how. With our fists." He held up his hands, balling them into fists for effect. "Round three, motherfucker. Show me what you got."

Tom had on a nice, dull black watch with what looked like a polycarbonate frame. Will glimpsed a digital readout and compass and backlighting functions.

"I like your watch," Will said.

Tom looked confused. "What?"

"Your watch. What's that go for? Three hundred?"

"How the fuck should I know."

"I need a watch," Will said, and he shot Tom in the forehead.

CHAPTER 28

LARA

SHE WAS SIMULTANEOUSLY trying to reach the surface of a swimming pool filled with dense, sticky mud and process what Josh was telling her and ignore the flaring of pain in her left arm. The bullet wound had suddenly re-manifested itself after taking a leave of absence for most of yesterday. That led to her wondering if her painkillers were still in her hotel room. The Tramadol would be nice about now, maybe even a Percocet, or a Vicodin…

Lara could tell from the looks on Carly's and Gaby's faces as they sat next to her that they were having the same difficulties—but minus an old gunshot wound, lucky them. The fact that she was wearing panties and one of Will's shirts didn't help her to adjust quickly to the situation. The shirt was about two sizes too big, though the most disturbing part was realizing *someone* had dressed her. She had been nude when she had fallen asleep in Will's arms last night.

She shivered a bit as she tried to push the repulsive idea of someone molesting her while she was in bed out of her head.

She was also barefoot, and the floor was hard and cold and pricking against her feet and legs and butt, despite the air around her feeling heavy and humid. How was that possible? And the itchy sensation in her left arm was getting more intense, and it was all she could do to grit her teeth and force herself to ignore the urgent desire to rake at the scabbing wound under the bandages.

"Where's Will?" were the first coherent words out of her mouth.

"He went to look for some clothes and weapons," Josh said. "That was about five minutes ago."

"Figures," Danny said, yawning behind them.

Danny was wearing boxers covered in leaping dolphins. Unlike Lara and the others, he didn't look like he was having very much difficulty accepting what Josh had told them. But that was Danny. Army Ranger. Ex-SWAT commando. Flippant comedian. Like Will, he adjusted amazingly well to almost any situation.

"He's always going off and having fun without me," Danny said. "I really need to start putting bells around that boy's neck."

"What about the girls?" Carly asked, looking back at Elise and Vera, still asleep on the floor behind them. Elise had curled up into a ball, her hands under the side of her head as makeshift pillows. Vera was snoring lightly with the strangest smile on her face. Lara wondered if she had looked like that while she was under, too.

Rohypnol, Josh had told them. Or roofies, the date-rape drug. She had known right away they had slipped it to her and the others during dinner, in the red wine, before Josh had even filled her in on that part.

"Will says to let the girls sleep," Josh said.

Lara nodded. "There's no point in waking them up." She looked over at Sarah, standing nearby, not saying a word. Lara thought the other woman looked scared.

She should be.

"Sarah," she said, "the wine last night. That was you."

"I had no choice," Sarah said.

"Of course you did," Carly snapped. "We all have a choice. Don't stand there and tell me you didn't have a fucking choice. You decided to go along with this."

"You don't understand," Sarah said. She sounded close to tears. "I came here with Jenny, hoping to get away from those things out there just like the rest of you. Karen and Tom and the others were just dragging people out of their rooms by gunpoint back then. People got hurt, some got killed. A boy we came with got shot because he fought back. I convinced them they could use Rohypnol instead so that wouldn't happen again. It was safer. That was how I saved my family. I had no choice."

"How many times did you have to tell yourself that before you started to believe it?" Carly asked. The hard edge in her voice hadn't softened a bit.

"Carly," Josh said, "she came back here to help us."

"So what's the new angle, Sarah?" Carly's eyes were still zeroed in on Sarah.

"There is no new angle," Sarah said, almost offended by the suggestion.

"Bullshit. Spit it out. What angle are you playing now?"

Lara watched Sarah's face carefully, and she thought she understood. What would she do for Will? For Elise? Or for Carly?

Lara walked over and got between the two women. "Not now. We'll have plenty of time to talk about this later." Before Carly could respond, Lara looked over at Josh and said, "What else did Will say? When is he coming back?"

"He didn't say," Josh said. "Just that we should stay here until he comes back with the weapons."

"So where are they?" Danny asked Sarah. "The party people?"

"Karen, Marcus, Tom, and Berg are usually the only ones involved," Sarah said. "The rest stay in their rooms until morning. Tom is in the lighthouse—the Tower. Berg is in the unfinished part of the hotel, going through the things we brought out of your rooms. He's kind of odd; he spends a lot of time doing things the rest of us find a little disturbing. Karen and Marcus are probably asleep."

"What about guns? I didn't see them wear any all day except for Tom."

"It's part of the façade. It's how they get people to let their guard down. Once you're convinced the island really is as safe as they say it is, then it's easier…later, with the Rohypnol during the feast."

"Clever buggers. But they have guns?"

"Yes. Karen and Marcus have weapons in their rooms. The others don't. Al, Jake and Sienna, myself—we're not armed. I don't know, I don't think they really trust us that much. We came here because of the broadcast, like you did. They let us stay because we could contribute something."

"Can't blame them. A good cook's hard to find in the apocalypse."

"How many?" Lara asked. "How many have come before us? Not counting you and the others still here?"

Lara watched her reaction to the question. It wasn't that Sarah had to think about it, because Lara thought she knew the number *exactly*—it was more that the answer was not going to be well received.

"How many?" Carly pressed, when Sarah didn't answer fast enough.

"I only know of twenty-one," Sarah said. "I don't know how many there were before I got here."

"Jesus Christ. *Twenty-one?*" Carly's voice had risen noticeably, the menace coming through loud and clear. "You sentenced twenty-one people to their deaths, and you stand there trying to justify it?"

Sarah started to respond, but thought better of it and said nothing instead. It was smart of her, because it would only have encouraged Carly to wade into her even further. After that, Sarah seemed to drift away, even though Carly continued to stare daggers at her.

"I need clothes," Danny said, casually breaking the thick tension in the air. "You said Will already went for them?"

"Yeah," Josh said. "About five—well, ten minutes ago now."

"So that means whoever's watching over our stuff is either dead or dead-ish. That saves me the trouble. You stay here with the girls. I'll be back soon, preferably dressed and with boots on." He started off in his bare feet, looking absurd in his dolphin-covered boxers. "In the meantime, try not to kill each other until I get back, ladies. I love me a good ol' fashioned chick fight. Carly, that means you."

"No promises," Carly said back through gritted teeth.

THEY SPENT THE next ten minutes waiting for something to happen, and when nothing did, it only added to the already conflicted atmosphere in the room. The island itself went on as if nothing had occurred, the silence outside the hotel matched only by the silence inside what was supposed to be a ballroom, but was, at the moment, really just one big unfinished hall with concrete floors.

Lara kept busy by making sure the girls were fine. The Rohypnol had put them both into a deep slumber, as it had done to the adults. If Josh and Sarah hadn't been tapping on their faces and nudging them awake, they would probably have slept through the entire night and most of the day. She still felt the grogginess lingering, but it wasn't nearly as bad as it had been in the first few minutes after opening her eyes.

Josh stood near one of the doors with Gaby, the two of them whispering softly to each other. It wasn't hard to tell they had become more than just friends. Watching the two of them made her smile.

"I noticed they turned off the AC," Carly said. "It's getting swampy in here."

"I guess they don't need the façade anymore," Lara said.

They stood quietly in the dark, listening to the silence. Beads of sweat appeared along Lara's neck and temple, despite the odd chill from the floor under their bare feet.

"He's taking too long," Carly said after a while. She looked toward the door. "I should go after him, in case he's in trouble."

"Carly, the last thing he wants is for you to go after him. If he's in trouble, there's not going to be a lot you can do. Danny is an Army Ranger. Remember?"

Carly nodded, but she didn't look any less concerned. Knowing didn't keep away the fear, something Lara knew all too well. She felt the same nagging anxiousness whenever Will left her side. She knew he could take care of himself, that if anyone was equipped to survive in this new world, it was him and Danny. Knowing and accepting weren't the same, though.

Lara looked over at Sarah, standing by herself against the other door into the ballroom. Lara felt sorry for the other woman, and her thoughts flashed back to Kevin, a young man who had sold them out to the ghouls back in Dansby, Texas. Will had killed him. Or at least she assumed he had. One moment Kevin had been there, the next he was gone. So why didn't Will do the same to Sarah? Maybe he knew Sarah had a better reason to do what she did. Maybe he was thinking about her daughter, Jenny.

She came back to the present when the door next to Josh opened, and Josh stiffened, preparing to fight. He didn't have to because Danny walked in, wearing cargo pants and a T-shirt and carrying one of their supply crates.

"Santa has brought clothes," Danny announced.

They swarmed the box—all except Sarah, who was already dressed. They pulled out shirts and pants and shoes like eager kids given early Christmas gifts.

"I stuffed in as many as I could find that would fit you guys," Danny said. "But I'm no fashionista, so if there's something that doesn't match, or God forbid, clashes, you'll have to make do for now."

Lara found a pair of cargo pants and a T-shirt that actually fit her and pulled them on. She expected to feel embarrassed stripping down to her panties in front of everyone, but the need to get some clothes on easily overwhelmed that silly notion of modesty.

The others dressed just as quickly around her, pulling on clothes and shoes and socks.

"Did you find Will?" Lara asked Danny.

"He was already gone. Went out the back door from the looks of it." He took a knife out from behind his back. "I found this, though."

"That's the knife I brought over from the kitchen to cut you guys loose," Sarah said.

"Why did he leave it behind?" Lara asked.

"Probably because he found something better," Danny said. "Berg had a gun belt on him with an empty holster."

"What happened to Berg?" Sarah asked.

"He's alive. Will zip-tied him and left him gagged on the floor. I would say that's his idea of irony, but I know for a fact Will doesn't know what irony means."

Lara rolled her eyes at him and got a grin back in response. "Maybe it's time we go looking for him."

"Now why would we want to do a fool thing like that?"

"You'd rather we just wait for him in here?"

"I don't *want* to wait for him in here. I'm not a waiting around kinda guy, in case you haven't noticed. But it's the smart move. Right now, the rest of the island doesn't know we're free and footloose. We have the advantage. As long as they stay clueless—"

A loud gunshot from outside the hotel cut Danny off.

"Or not," Danny finished.

"What now?" Carly asked.

Danny looked back at the others, saw that they were all dressed—or close enough, anyway—then scanned the room. "Everyone move away from the open." He pointed to the two doors. "Stick to the walls, make like darkness so they can't see you from the doors. Carly and Lara, get the girls."

Carly picked up Vera while Lara picked up Elise. Lara couldn't help but notice the girl had packed on a few pounds since the last time she had held her. They moved toward the wall, into the patch of darkness, and laid the girls back down on the floor.

Gaby and Josh slinked back against the wall a few yards from them, melting into the shadows, hands finding each other in the semidarkness.

Danny, knife in hand, moved back to the door he had come through. He didn't say a word, only pressed his back against the wall and stood perfectly still.

There had been no sounds after the gunshot.

Lara waited to hear some kind of commotion, either from outside the hotel where the gunshot had come from, or inside, as Karen and the others woke up. Instead, there was just the silence. It was suffocating and quiet and so damn still, and Lara's left arm was still itching like it was on fire. She rubbed against the bandages with the palm of her right hand, fighting the urge to tear the bandages free and swipe at the scabbing wound.

They waited.

Five minutes went by. Then ten.

Lara looked over at Carly and saw the other woman looking back at her. She was thinking the same thing. *What now?*

After a while, Lara started to think maybe the rest of the island hadn't heard the gunshot after all. Maybe Danny was wrong. She had almost convinced herself when the door to her left opened and Marcus stepped inside with a silver automatic in his fist.

Lara's head snapped in Danny's direction and she opened her mouth to scream, but she didn't have to. Danny had either heard or seen Marcus coming through the other door and was already sprinting across the room. She had never seen him move so fast, and hadn't known he was even capable of that kind of speed.

Marcus fired at Danny—*too fast.*

Either adrenaline or fear had gotten the best of him and Marcus's first shot went wide, slamming into the wall behind Danny, at least three feet off its mark. Realizing his mistake, Marcus took careful aim with his second shot.

"No!" Lara screamed.

Marcus jumped at the sound of her voice. He swung the gun in her direction, but he quickly got over the shock and turned back toward Danny, who was halfway across the room by now.

Marcus shot again—*and missed again.* Though this time he came closer to hitting Danny, and Lara swore Danny flinched as the bullet zipped past his head.

Danny, still running, threw the knife while in mid-stride and the sharp blade flashed across the room and embedded itself into the side of Marcus's neck. Marcus let out a wheezing sound and dropped the gun and stumbled sideways.

Lara scrambled forward and snatched the gun from the floor even as Marcus moved around in front of her on wobbly legs like some hopeless drunk. He grabbed the handle of the knife in his throat and Lara thought, *No, don't do that, don't pull the knife out. Jesus, don't pull the knife out.*

But he did—and blood gushed out in a thick stream and Marcus collapsed to the floor, already slick with his blood. He seemed to convulse, his arms and legs like fish out of water, while blood kept pumping out of the ghastly wound in his throat.

Lara heard another door opening, and she looked up and saw Sarah running out of the room, the door slamming shut behind her.

"Should we go after her?" she asked Danny, who was crouched next to Marcus, watching the other man flopping in a pool of his own blood. Marcus's fingers looked like ants dancing in a thick sludge of Hawaiian punch.

"Let her go," Danny said. "She's probably just going to get her daughter."

"What if she's gone to warn them?"

"They already know. Besides, she's already committed to us."

He was right. There was no way back for Sarah now, and Lara was reminded again of what a hard choice it must have been for the woman to risk everything to help them. To turn her back on a sure thing. She was risking not just her life, but her daughter's, too.

She's a lot braver than I gave her credit for.

"Danny," Lara said, and handed him Marcus's gun.

Danny took the Smith and Wesson and checked the magazine.

"What now?" Carly asked, coming over.

"Karen, Tom, and Marcus are the ringleaders," Danny said. "Tom is probably dead, and Marcus is dead. That leaves Karen."

"What about the others?" Lara asked. "Jake and Sienna. Debra and her son…"

"Cut off the head of the snake, and the body slithers away. Or something to that effect."

"Sounds about right to me," a voice said behind them.

They looked back at Will, coming through the same door Marcus had left open. He had his M4A1 slung over his shoulder and was carrying two familiar-looking duffel bags. And more importantly, he was alive, and when he stepped into a pool of moonlight, she saw a fresh cut over the bridge of his nose. He had cracked lips and bruises along his temple and chin.

"You don't look so hot, Kemosabe," Danny said.

"It's my disguise," Will said.

"I can see it. Lon Chaney, right?"

Will smirked, then looked down at Marcus's still body. "What did he do, kill himself so he wouldn't have to listen to your jokes?"

Danny grunted. "Those for me?"

Will dropped the bags on the floor. They clattered loudly. He pulled back the zipper on one, reached in, and pulled out a Remington shotgun that he tossed over to Danny. Will also pulled out a pouch full of shotgun shells.

"Sweet, you always bring me such nice things," Danny said. "Where'd you find them?"

"Tower basement. They've been storing things down there for a while now."

Danny opened the pouch and pulled out one of the shells. "Silver buckshot?" He held up the shell. It had a white "X" written on the side. "You see something out there besides some backstabbing humans?"

"It's night. Better safe than sorry."

"Sarah told us there have been twenty-one people before us that she knows of," Lara said.

Will pulled out four Motorola radios—theirs—from the bag and handed one each to Danny, Josh, and Carly, keeping the last one for himself. "Where's Sarah now?"

"She ran off," Josh said.

"Tom?" Danny asked.

"He's taking a nap," Will said. "So how many are left?"

"Karen."

"What about the others?"

"According to Sarah, we don't have to worry about them."

"Good."

"So now what?" Lara asked.

"Let's go find Karen," Will said.

"Maybe she's still asleep in her room," Danny said.

"Captain Optimism," Carly smirked.

Danny grinned back at her. "Just doing my part, babe."

Will handed Lara another one of the Remingtons. "How's the arm?"

"Itchy," she sighed.

He leaned in and kissed her. He caught her off guard, but she quickly got over it and kissed him back. When he pulled away, she touched the bridge of his nose, then ran her fingers across the cuts on his lips and felt the swelling along his cheeks and temple.

"My hero," she whispered, smiling at him.

"You should see the other guy," he smiled back.

"Get a fucking room," Danny said behind them. "Better yet, let's go get Karen's. I'm sure that bitch won't mind."

THEY DIDN'T FIND Karen in her room. The door was open, but there was no one inside. There were signs she had left in a hurry, though it was unclear how long ago. Maybe she had sent Marcus over while she snuck out of the hotel.

Just like a politician.

As they came out of Karen's room and back into Hallway A, they spotted Al farther down the hallway, coming out of his own room. He saw them, and for an instant Lara thought he might run back inside.

They know. They're all in on it, just like Sarah said. They've all been expecting—dreading—the night when their actions come back to haunt them.

Al stood frozen in the hallway as Will and Danny reflexively swung their rifles in his direction. Lara could imagine how intimidating the sight of them must have been. They were wearing the no-frills version of their urban assault vests, M4A1s in their hands and the Remingtons slung over their backs. Their pouches were brimming with magazines and shotgun shells, and they had those very distinctive cross-knives of theirs on their left hips. Will had found all their gear conveniently stacked near the basement door, not yet tossed in with the rest already down there.

Lara had the Remington and a Glock in a hip holster, and even with just those two weapons, she was already sweating profusely in the hot hallway.

"Where's Karen?" Will asked Al.

"I don't know," Al said, shaking his head. He was wearing Winnie-the-Pooh pajamas, and his big belly poked out noticeably from underneath a yellow nightshirt. "Please don't kill me. I only did what they told me."

The men walked toward Al, their weapons lowered a bit. Lara still expected Al to flee back into his room at any moment, but he didn't. She didn't know if it was bravery or stupidity on his part.

"Please, I only did what they told me," Al said. His voice sounded like it was about to crack. "I even tried to talk them out of it, but they wouldn't listen to me."

"Where are the others?" Will asked, ignoring Al's protests.

"I don't know. In their rooms, I guess."

"Go back into your room and stay there."

Al nodded anxiously and hurried back inside. Locks snapped into place, then heavy footsteps faded.

They continued moving up the hallway, toward the lobby.

Farther up Hallway A, another door opened and Danny and Will swung their weapons up. Debra came out of her room and froze at the sight of them. She had put on jeans and a T-shirt.

"What's going on?" Debra asked. "I heard gunshots. Why is everyone armed?"

"Where's Karen?" Will asked.

"I don't know. She's not in her room?"

Lara couldn't tell if Debra was playing a role or if she really didn't know.

Bullshit. She knows.

"Go back into your room and stay inside," Will said.

"What's going on?" Debra asked again.

"Go back into your room."

"Not until you tell me what's going on—"

Danny fired into the wall above her door, the sound of the gunshot thunderous in the narrow hallway. Debra crouched and clung to the open door with both hands. She looked at them, all pretenses of defiance vanished from her face, replaced by terror.

"Go back in your room and stay inside," Will said. Calmly, without any menace whatsoever.

Debra nodded and disappeared into her room without another word.

They walked past Jake and Sienna's door. It was closed, but Lara thought she heard movement inside. Maybe someone was even looking through the peephole as they went by.

"I got two donuts that say the bitch bugged out," Danny said.

"Probably," Will nodded.

"It's a big island."

"Yup." Will keyed the radio Velcroed to his assault vest. "Josh, what do you see up there?"

"Nothing," Josh said through the radio.

The others were back in the Tower—Josh, Gaby, and Carly, along with the girls. According to Will, the Tower was the most secure building on the entire island. It was probably the only thing Karen hadn't lied about. It had strong doors, and there were two extra floors that could be defended.

"What about the beach?" Will asked.

"Nothing, no movements at all," Josh said. "Where are you now?"

"Hallway A, moving toward the lobby."

"Karen?"

"Nowhere in sight. Keep an eye out and let me know if you see anything on or off the island."

"Will do," Josh said.

They were coming up to the lobby now.

Will and Danny flattened against each side of the hallway while Lara stood back. She felt odd being with the two of them. They were so good together, moving without even talking—at times, without even looking at one another. They just *knew* what they were supposed to do and what the other was going to do in turn.

Will glanced back at her. "Stay back."

She nodded and took a step backward.

They moved out into the lobby, Will sweeping right, while Danny, slightly behind him, swept left. They covered the large room, constantly in motion behind their weapons. They looked almost poetic, and a part of her envied Danny for being so in sync with Will.

"Lara," Will said.

She hurried out after them.

The lobby was empty. Someone had opened the windows, and a nice breeze flooded inside. The doors were also open, and the big solar-powered floodlights outside illuminated the black marble patio.

Danny came out of the kitchen to their right. "She's gone, but at least she didn't take the spatula. That would have really sucked."

"She couldn't have gone far," Lara said. "Where would she go if she didn't head straight for the beach and one of the boats?"

Will's and Danny's radios squawked, and they heard Josh's excited voice: "Will, I see her. She's on the west side of the island."

"What's over there?" Will asked.

"Nothing, except for the power station."

"Where is she now?"

"Halfway to the building. She's moving slowly, too." Josh paused for a moment. "Guys, I think she's wearing one of those hazmat suits. The Level B kind."

"She's got a hell of a head start on us," Danny said.

"Is she alone, Josh?" Will asked into the radio.

"She's alone," Josh said.

"All right. Keep an eye on her."

"Will do."

"Why the power station?" Lara asked. "And why the hazmat suit? The last time we saw those…"

She didn't have to finish. They all remembered Dansby.

"Let's find out," Will said.

He jogged out of the hotel, Danny right behind him. Lara followed them out onto the patio, then down the steps, and they were racing across the lawn toward the western side of the island, leaving the cobblestone pathway behind quickly.

Will and Danny were moving fast, and she had to push herself to keep up.

She heard Josh's voice through Will's and Danny's radios ahead of her: "She's at the power station fence. I think she has a key, she's opening the padlock…"

They had been running for about thirty seconds when the number of lampposts started dwindling, and soon they were moving through darkness, with only the moonlight to guide their way. She glanced down at her watch as she ran, but there was nothing around her wrist.

Dammit, I liked that watch, too.

Even without lights, she could see they were racing across open ground now. Tree branches and dirt crunched under her shoes, and the Remington in her hands felt like it had doubled in weight in the last few seconds.

"She's inside," Josh said through the radios.

Will and Danny hadn't said a word. They kept running, even gaining speed and starting to slowly pull away from her. She resisted the urge to yell at them to slow down, to let her catch up. She could feel the urgency in their pace, because they knew, just like she did, there was a reason Karen was wearing a hazmat suit. And there had to be a damn good reason why Karen was retreating to the power station, of all places.

Finally, Lara burst through a wall of trees and saw the power station dead ahead. It was a big, gray brick building, two stories high, surrounded by hurricane fencing and ringed by LED floodlights. It was ugly and squat, poles jutting out from its roof. The building was designed for one purpose—to generate the power that ran the island. There was a reason it was hidden all the way on this side of the island, among the woods. The tourists were never supposed to see how the sausages were made.

Will and Danny were halfway across the fifty yards that separated the trees and the power station. They were making a beeline toward the open front gate. Karen was nowhere in sight. Lara could just make out a smaller, shack-like building next to the big gray structure where all the humming noise was coming from. The air around her crackled like every particle was heavily charged and ready to burst.

Will and Danny were at the gate when she saw them come to a sudden stop. For a split second, anyway. Then she heard the almost simultaneous loud booms of shotguns firing, their flames stabbing the night air, searing the area around the gate in hot flashes of orange light.

She slid to a stop forty yards away from them and saw Will turning and running back as Danny stayed behind and fired again—and again—into the power station. Danny finally stopped shooting, turned and ran about the same time Will stopped and turned back and began firing back into the darkness—once, twice, three times—as Danny jogged past him, feeding shells into the shotgun as he ran.

"Go go go!" Danny shouted at her.

Lara backpedaled, but she couldn't turn and run. Not yet. She had to see what was happening. What they were shooting at? She couldn't help herself, curiosity gnawing at every fiber of her being.

As Danny got closer to her, Lara heard Josh's voice through Danny's radio, alarmed, "What's going on, guys? I can't see a damn thing down there. What's going on? What are you shooting at? Is everyone all right?"

Danny didn't answer. He didn't have time to answer. He was too busy feeding shells into his shotgun and running at the same time. Lara looked past Danny's running form and saw Will turning and running, feeding shells into his own shotgun as he did.

Behind him, the darkness seemed to shift and move, as if alive.

Because it was alive.

It wasn't the darkness, or the night. It was something else. Something familiar.

Ghouls.

A wave of them, pouring out of the power station gate, moving so fast and crashing so indiscriminately against each other, against everything, that the fence shook and threatened to collapse under their charge. But the fencing didn't fall fast enough, so they began vaulting it, leaping over each other to get to the other side, until finally there were too many of them clinging to the fence at one time and the whole thing careened forward and buried itself into the ground with a loud, grinding squeal, like nails on a chalkboard.

She had forgotten how fast they were, how thin and skeletal, and how inhumanly dark their eyes were. It was like staring into the abyss and seeing the blackness staring back.

Danny was almost on top of her. He grabbed her arm and dragged her with him, shouting, "Go go go!"

She turned and ran alongside him. "What about Will?"

"Keep going!"

Danny stopped and turned around just as Will flashed past him.

Will reached for her arm, found her wrist, and pulled her along with him, even as she heard Danny's shotgun firing behind them.

Guys, I'm not a baton, she thought to herself, but her thoughts were interrupted by Danny's shotgun blasts.

Once, twice, three shots.

Then four, five, six, and seven shots.

Seven shots. The Remingtons have a limit of seven shots.

Will released her hand and stopped and turned.

She looked back and saw Danny coming, passing Will, who had begun firing back at the moving, surging wall of ghouls, each one of his blasts sending a wave of flaming death that shredded the creatures. They were still far off, the closest one thirty yards away, but they were close enough she could see the silver buckshot ripping into them, searing flesh—or what little they had left—from bone. They fell in a row, but it didn't matter, because one, two—a *dozen*—were soon leaping over the fallen ones, coming in a relentless deluge across the open ground.

She felt her heart sink at the sight of them.

Where the hell did they all come from?

"Go go go!" Danny was shouting, grabbing her wrist and pulling her with him. She thought her arm might snap out of its socket, but it didn't.

Lara ran as fast as she could, and suddenly the pain in her left arm came screaming back like a roaring train, engulfing her in a firestorm. The Remington seemed to have tripled in weight, and it was all she could do to hold desperately to it, too afraid to let go. She gritted through the pain and kept running, her legs pumping hard under her.

Behind her, she heard Will's shotgun roaring, firing again, and again…and again.

And each shot got closer, and closer…and closer still.

We'll never make it. We'll never make it…

CHAPTER 29

JOSH

PROS AND CONS: What were they?

Pros: They had taken the island from Tom, Karen, and Marcus. Tom was dead, which was a major plus. Josh didn't ever want to deal with that asshole again, and stumbling across his body on the second floor of the Tower hadn't disturbed him nearly as much as he had thought it would. Marcus was also dead, which to a lesser extent Josh supposed was a good thing. The others, like Sarah, had just gone along in order to survive. Josh could understand that. Hell, he might have done the same thing if Gaby's life were at stake.

Cons: Karen was unaccounted for. Which was disturbing, because Karen was, to hear Sarah tell it, the real brains of the operation. Josh didn't doubt that at all. Karen looked like the kind of woman who would barter and trade for what she needed, and survival was a hell of a need. So he didn't like having her out there, running around in the dark. Who knew what she was up to?

Conclusion: It could be worse.

He was up on the third floor of the Tower, along with Gaby. Carly and the girls were below them on the second floor, with the girls still sound asleep on the cot Tom used as his bed. The second floor had been a mess when they had arrived, with a small pool of blood where Tom lay, a neat hole in his forehead. The real mess was on the wall, where his brain had splattered when Will had shot him.

Will had ordered them to toss Tom's body out the window to save them the trouble of carrying it down the narrow spiral staircase.

Josh thought he would feel a little queasy about just tossing Tom out the window, but he felt strangely okay with it as he watched the corpse tumble down the side of the Tower to land in a bush. Well, after it bounced off the bulging base of the Tower.

Instead of cleaning up the blood, they threw a towel over it and picked up the bookcase and tossed the books and Playboy magazines and board games back on the shelves. You could tell there had been a fight, but it wasn't like Elise or Vera noticed as they snored. Carly, for her part, sat and watched them sleep with a shotgun leaning against the wall next to her. She looked too tired to care that someone had been shot in the room not all that long ago.

The radio broadcast that had lured them to Song Island came from a simple setup that looked like something he could have put together back in his bedroom in Ridley with parts from the local Radio Shack. A thirty-inch LED monitor sat in front of a tower hard drive and keyboard, with a broadcasting microphone hanging from a thin metal arm bracket. There was a pile of black cords under the table, hooked into multiple jacks along the wall. The monitor showed a program running over a Windows 7 desktop.

Microsoft. End of the world or bust.

Will radioed them right away, asking if they had seen Karen from the windows. They hadn't.

"Keep an eye out and let me know if you see anything on or off the island," Will said.

"Will do," Josh said.

Gaby looked over at the computer setup, then grinned at him. "Didn't you used to have something like this at home?"

"Something like this, yeah. Wait, when were you in my room?"

"Wouldn't you like to know," she said, and gave him a mischievous wink.

Like on the second floor, there were four windows around them, spaced out to give them an excellent, all-encompassing view of the island and beyond. They were both armed with night-vision binoculars that were hanging from hooks along the wall when they arrived. Gaby was over on the south window, which faced the beach. She leaned the Remington shotgun against the wall next to her and tossed two ammo pouches filled with shells on the floor.

"Have you ever fired that shotgun before?" he asked.

"No," Gaby said, "but it can't be that hard. Just point and shoot, right?"

"I guess."

"Danny says there's supposed to be a big kick."

She looked comfortable with the shotgun. He hadn't even wanted to touch the thing. It looked dangerous, like it could go off in his hands by accident if he touched it the wrong way. The Glock, by comparison, looked innocuous.

Josh turned back to the west window and began scanning the trees in the distance with his binoculars. This side was mostly dark forest, with only the occasional glint of moonlight against the solar panels ringing the island.

"See anything?" he asked.

"Water," Gaby said.

"I got more water on this side."

"This is not a competition, Josh."

"I win."

She laughed.

He was thinking about how much he liked the sound of her laughter when he saw a strangely bright, colored figure darting through the trees in the pitch-darkness.

Karen.

"GHOULS," GABY SAID breathlessly. "Oh my God, there are ghouls on the island."

Josh didn't believe her at first, because it was absurd. Wasn't it? They had seen night fall, and there were no ghouls. Even if Song Island was a trap, he had seen night come with his own eyes and *there hadn't been any ghouls.*

So why would there be ghouls now? It didn't make any sense.

But there they were, flowing across the open grass, dark black shapes rendered clear as day in the fluorescent green neon of his night-vision binoculars.

Ghouls!

There were so many they swallowed up the ground underneath them, dark figures merging perfectly with the surrounding night. They crashed out of the power station and across the clearing and smashed into the wall of trees and seemed to stampede anything and everything in their path.

The radio in Josh's hand squawked, and he heard Will's voice shouting (but somehow calm, though Josh didn't know how that was even *possible)*: "We're taking them through the hotel to slow them down! Let anyone into the Tower who isn't undead!"

"Roger that," Josh said, though he wasn't sure if what he actually said was *"Roger that"* or something else. He might have even babbled something unintelligible. It was hard to tell because his heart was pounding and his fingers were numb.

There are ghouls on the island!

Song Island isn't safe!

He heard movement behind him and looked back and saw that Carly was standing behind them. When did she even come up here? Then she was moving across the room, snatching up the Remington shotgun Gaby had leaned against the wall. She picked up the pouches of ammo as well and walked back to them.

He watched helplessly as Carly took the radio out of his hand and replaced it with the shotgun and ammo, handing the radio to Gaby. "Gaby, you stay up here and keep in communication with Will and Danny. They might need a spotter. That's you." She looked over at him, eyes hard, in full command. "Josh, you come downstairs with me. Understand?"

He heard Gaby, surprisingly calm, reply, "Okay, go."

Then he was moving, following Carly to the door in the floor and hurrying down the narrow spiral staircase to the second floor. The girls were up and sitting on the cot, rubbing at their eyes, looking disoriented.

"Stay up here, girls, and don't move," Carly said. "Don't go near the windows. Don't move from that cot. Understand?"

They nodded back and didn't argue. Josh knew how they felt. At that moment, Carly sounded like the voice of God.

Carly snatched up her shotgun from the wall, then disappeared through the door. He heard her moving down the spiral staircase. "Josh, come on!"

He hurried after her. The new set of metal steps under him felt flimsy and undependable all of a sudden. Carly was in front, moving downward with purpose.

"Hurry, Josh," Carly said between breaths.

He followed her down to the first floor, surprised he didn't trip or fall to his death on the way down. He could barely feel his legs moving. It didn't help that he could hear gunshots the whole time. Booming gunshots. Shotguns.

They're getting closer, leading them right to us…

"Stay calm," Carly said.

He nodded. He didn't trust himself to speak.

She opened the heavy wooden door and stepped outside. Josh followed obediently, fumbling with the shotgun in his hands.

He knew how a shotgun worked. You pulled the slide back to load a shell into the chamber and you squeezed the trigger. It wasn't all that hard. Even the dumbest person alive could pull it off. All you needed was the strength to work the slide—or whatever it was called—because the trigger was easy. He had fired a gun before. A shotgun wouldn't really be that much harder, would it?

They stepped outside, into the night air. It had gotten more humid. How was that possible? It had felt almost chilly back on the third floor. Maybe it was the altitude?

The crash of gunshots snapped Josh back to the present. They were even closer now, coming from within the hotel, less than fifty yards from their position. When Josh looked in the direction of the building, he saw a dark figure emerge from the blackness.

A familiar voice, shouting at them, "Don't shoot! Please don't shoot!"

Sarah appeared in a circle of bright LED lights. She was holding Jenny in her arms, the girl clutching her mother's neck, small face buried in Sarah's chest. Sarah was running as fast as she could, but to Josh it looked like she was moving in quicksand. Why was she running so slowly? Didn't she know what was *coming?*

Josh didn't remember exactly when he made the decision, but he was suddenly racing toward Sarah, the shotgun slung over his back, the big heavy barrel tapping him over and over again.

Sarah ran straight to him.

"Give her to me!" Josh shouted.

Sarah pried Jenny loose and handed the girl to him. Josh took her, could feel the girl wiggling in his arms, fighting, but he ignored her resistance and began racing back toward the Tower, Sarah running next to him. He was actually running faster than her, even with Jenny and the shotgun, and had to slow down for her to catch up. She was tired and out of breath, but she pushed forward until they finally reached Carly and the Tower.

"Where are the others?" Carly shouted at them.

"I don't know!" Sarah shouted back.

"Get inside!"

Josh handed Jenny back to her mother and Sarah gave him a grateful nod before she disappeared into the Tower. Josh wished he were right behind her instead of standing out here in the dark. Even with the LED floodlights pouring down from the third-floor windows, he still felt like he was swimming blind.

Josh looked back toward the hotel, then suddenly heard a new sound.

Rifles.

Will and Danny were using their assault rifles now. What did that mean?

He didn't have to wait long to find out. They heard Gaby's voice from directly above them. She was leaning out the window, radio in one hand. "They're coming! Get ready!"

Josh was going to ask *"Who?"* when he saw them.

"The roof!" Gaby shouted above them.

He thought he was prepared for it, but he was wrong. He stopped breathing at the sight of them racing across the rooftop of the hotel, almost gliding, dodging and leaping and weaving around parts of the construction that had never—and would never—be finished. He had forgotten how sickly they looked, how amazingly fast and preternatural their movements were. They seemed to come out of nowhere, spat out by the night. One second there was nothing, and then the next, the island was bristling with them.

My God, there's so many...

Then they weren't just on the roof anymore. They were all over the hotel grounds, too, swarming around the big building in their path. There were so many that at first he had trouble separating them from the bushes and grass and trees. But then it became easier as they began darting in and out of the LED lights. They were converging on the hotel, almost as if they hadn't noticed the Tower existed yet. The continuous, smashing sounds of gunfire were drawing them like moths to flame.

Will and the others are still in there.

"Get ready!" Carly shouted.

Josh lifted the shotgun up to his shoulder. What was that Gaby had said? *"There's supposed to be a big kick."*

Okay. No problem. He was smart. Smarter than most people his age. Smarter than most people older than him. He could handle the recoil of a shotgun as long as he knew it was coming. And he knew it was coming.

"Josh," Carly said, her voice strangely clear despite the fog dominating his brain at the moment. "Don't shoot until you see the black of their eyes. The shotgun has a limited range. Understand?"

"Yes," he said hoarsely.

The sound of gunfire was constant, a steady stream of shots that sounded closer and closer with every passing second. Were Danny and Will even reloading? Every second seemed to be filled with gunfire. How was that even possible?

"Back exit!" Gaby shouted from above.

Josh looked toward the back of the hotel and saw figures racing through the inky blackness, then the stabbing flames of a gun firing backward. Handguns. They were down to handguns now.

That's not good. That's not good at all.

Will and Lara emerged out of the shadows, running as fast as they could. Will was loading his Glock as he ran, the M4A1 bouncing wildly behind his back. Lara was trying desperately to keep up, but falling behind. Each time she fell too far back, Will slowed down and turned and shot into the darkness.

Josh saw ghouls leaping off the rooftop behind them.

"Oh, fuck," Carly whispered.

Josh pried his eyes away from the back of the hotel. They were moving so fast, and there were so many of them, it was hard *not* to see them, rampaging across the hotel grounds. They darted in and out of the halos of the scattered lampposts, the lights flickering off their smooth, hairless, and malformed bodies. They were still far away, but getting closer. Josh was reminded of a stampeding herd of cattle.

Is the ground trembling? I swear the ground is trembling.

There was a loud boom next to him. It was so close he thought he had gone instantly deaf, but that proved false when he heard a second boom and turned to see Carly firing into the shadows to her left. Josh watched with odd fascination as two ghouls emerging from the darkness evaporated before his eyes, their skin ripped free from shiny white bone as Carly's shotgun blasts tore into them.

Oh God, how did they get so close?

Then he heard them coming from his right. He turned and saw hollow black eyes moving quickly across the darkness and into the light.

Two eyes—no, four—no, six—

Josh lifted the shotgun and thought, *There's going to be a kick, prepare for the kick*, and pulled the trigger.

Immediately he was sure his shoulder was dislocated. He grunted through the pain and saw the first ghoul come unglued under the onslaught of buckshot. He hadn't fully grasped what had happened to the creature—it was there one second and gone the next—when two more instantly appeared and sprinted across the distance at him.

He worked the slide and fired again and watched buckshot catch both ghouls in mid-stride and exploding chunks of skin scattering into the night air. The creatures didn't make a sound, not even a squeak, as they fell, but the sight of them dying (*Dying!*) was something to behold. He recalled the ghoul in the back of the store in Lancing where Matt was bitten, watching them with its head hanging off its shoulder, refusing to die.

Not here. Not this time. Not against silver.

Suck on that, mofos!

Suddenly the pain in his shoulder didn't hurt so much anymore, and the shotgun felt lighter in his hands.

Carly shouted next to him, "Hurry up!"

Will and Lara were twenty yards away and getting closer. As Will neared them, Josh saw that his clothes were covered in thick clumps of black goo. Lara was running next to Will, trying to keep up. Will was purposely staying with her, never straying too far ahead.

There was another figure behind Will and Lara. Sienna, Jake's girlfriend. She wore pajamas and a T-shirt and there was a horrified expression on her face as she ran. Josh wasn't sure if she was laughing or crying. It might have been both, or neither.

"Where's Danny?" Carly shouted.

As soon as she said it, Danny appeared behind Sienna. He was running calmly but fast, loading his Glock at the same time. Like Will, Danny's clothes and parts of his face were covered in the black, gooey substance. Danny reached up and wiped a thick slab of the goop off his face, flicking it into the grass as he ran.

"Go go go!" Danny shouted, to no one in particular.

"Shotgun!" Will yelled.

Carly tossed the shotgun at him and Will snatched it out of the air. He immediately stopped and spun and fired, erasing a wall of ghouls emerging out of the night to his left. Josh hadn't even seen them until Will fired, the flames from the shotgun lighting them up in the half-second it took the buckshot to rip into them.

Then Lara was there, and Sienna, and they ran into the open Tower door behind him.

Then Danny, ten yards away, shouting, "Shotgun!"

Josh didn't think, he just reacted, and tossed the shotgun at Danny. But he must have had too much adrenaline pumping through him, because the weapon sailed right over Danny's head. Danny glanced back, following the trajectory of the shotgun as it landed and disappeared into the grass behind him.

Will was backing up toward them, firing into the darkness. "Go go go!"

Danny didn't go back for the shotgun. He kept coming, grabbed Carly with one hand, and lunged for the door. Josh followed, heard Will firing one last time before he, too, was suddenly behind Josh and pushing him inside.

Josh lost his balance and sprawled on the hard concrete floor and rolled over, saw Danny slamming the door shut behind them, shoving the deadbolt into place just as *bang!* something crashed into the thick wood on the other side.

"Josh," Carly said, standing next to him.

She grabbed his arm and pulled him up. Josh felt tired and heavy, but somehow she managed to get him up anyway. Carly led him away from the door as Will and Danny carried the heavy bookcase over, grunting with the effort. Lara hurried over to help, flinching noticeably with pain, and they slammed it down against the door, even as the pounding increased in volume and urgency.

"Second floor," Will said calmly. "Go go go."

They hurried up the flight of stairs, moving in a train. Squeezed in between Carly behind him and Sienna in front of him, Josh felt his feet moving on automatic pilot. Sienna was crying, tears flooding down her cheeks, though he couldn't hear her over the pounding noise from below and the loud roaring in his ears.

"Keep moving, Josh," Carly said behind him.

Farther up the staircase, he glanced down and saw Danny crouched next to the open basement door, reaching down and pulling out weapons and boxes of ammo that Will was passing up to him from somewhere inside the opening. The beam of a flashlight flickered back and forth from inside the basement.

"Hurry," a voice said above them. Josh looked up and saw Gaby leaning through the open second-floor door.

The others were waiting, with Elise and Vera peering down from the third-floor door above them. Sienna had found the cot and was sitting on it, crying quietly to herself. Lara walked over and put her arms around the other woman and Sienna broke down, tears splashing across Lara's already sweat-stained shirt.

"Where're Danny and Will?" Gaby asked.

"They're coming," Carly said. "Where's Sarah?"

"Third floor. That's where we should all be."

"Go. I'll wait for them."

"You sure?"

"Yes, go," Carly said.

Lara took Sienna up first, the other woman stumbling, shell-shocked, every step of the way.

Gaby was also on her way up when she realized Josh hadn't moved and looked back. "Josh, come on."

"I'll be right up," he said.

"Hurry," she said, and climbed the stairs.

Josh stayed behind. He wasn't sure why, but the idea of abandoning Carly now didn't seem right. So he didn't move and waited alongside her.

The pounding from below them went on and on. Relentless.

"Can they climb?" he asked nervously.

"Yes," she said, "but not if there's nothing to hang onto. Is there anything to hang onto out there?"

He shook his head. The Tower was a smooth conical structure that got smaller as it got taller. And it went pretty tall. But he didn't recall anything that could be used as handholds.

Carly smiled at him. "You did good out there."

"Thanks."

"For a kid."

He managed a decent grin back at her.

Will and Danny finally arrived, climbing through the door in the floor. They were carrying duffel bags that looked heavy.

Josh's eyes went to the front door. It was still closed, and the bookcase was still pressed against it, but he could see the thick oak shelves trembling each time the ghouls smashed into the door. It had begun to slide half an inch at a time with each impact, moving back a little every time…

Will slammed the floor door shut, so loudly Josh jumped a bit. Will and Danny picked up the bookcase and moved it over, then laid it on top of the door. They took a step back and exchanged a look.

"That's not going to hold," Danny said.

"Probably not," Will nodded. "What else we got?"

"The computers on the third floor," Josh said quickly.

"What else?"

Danny looked over at Josh and grinned through the mask of dripping black ghoul blood and flesh. "Hey, kid, how much do you weigh?"

THE FIRST-FLOOR door gave way ten minutes later, but by then they had reinforced the second-floor door with the bookcase and about twenty pounds of computer equipment from the third floor, including the desk. Everything else that wasn't nailed down went on top of the door, including paintings, pieces of the cot, and all the hardcover books.

While they were stacking books on top of the door, Danny said, "We should have kept Tom around. He's what, a good 250?"

"About that," Will said.

"Definitely should have kept him around. Make the big lug useful for once."

The ghouls began pounding on the second-floor door almost immediately, but there was no leverage for them to break the deadbolt. Still, they continued at it, banging away, pouring an unrelenting torrent of force that did little good. Even though the door held, and didn't look to be in danger of giving any time soon, Josh couldn't shake the disconcerting feeling of so many of the creatures below them, salivating at the thought of coming through.

The island isn't safe. It was all a lie…

Josh crouched next to the open third-floor door and looked down through the opening at Will and Danny, sitting calmly on top of the bookcase. They had wiped the black clumps of dead ghoul flesh and blood off their faces and gotten as much out of their clothes and hair as they could manage. They still looked like homeless soldiers wearing camouflage face paint that refused to wash off. They had transferred most of the weapons they had taken out of the basement up to the third floor, leaving just enough on the second floor. They were loading a couple of shotguns with shells that didn't have an "X" on them.

We're out of silver bullets.

The third floor was crowded, but they made do. The girls, Elise and Vera, sat in a corner together, holding hands, and eventually dozed off. Lara sat with Sienna, doing her best to calm the other woman. Josh didn't have to ask what had happened to Jake, Sienna's boyfriend. Or Al. Or Debra and her son. At least Sarah and her daughter, Jenny, had made it, and mother and daughter sat on their own side of the wall, the girl asleep in her mother's lap. Sarah stroked Jenny's hair, staring off at nothing in particular.

Gaby and Carly had shotguns, and the two women guarded the windows around them. He was feeling pretty useless sitting next to the open door in case Will or Danny needed anything. The continuous banging against the door below didn't help.

"Hey, kid," Danny said below him. "Nice throw for a computer nerd. I didn't think you had it in you."

Josh gave him an embarrassed grin. "I'm not a computer nerd."

"Nothing to be ashamed of. Nerds rule the world. Well, used to, anyway. We all know who rules the world now, don't we?"

"Ghouls?"

"No, guys with shotguns."

There was a thunderous boom behind Josh that made him jump. He looked back at Carly, who was leaning out one of the windows. She racked her shotgun and fired down the side of the Tower a second time.

"What's going on?" Will asked from below.

"I don't know," Josh said.

"They're trying to climb the walls," Carly shouted.

Will stood up and walked to one of the second-floor windows. He glanced out, then Josh saw him fire two shots down the side of the Tower.

"They're climbing the walls?" Danny asked.

"Yeah, they're climbing the walls," Will said.

"How the hell they doing that?"

"They're standing on top of one another. Like pyramids."

"No shit?"

"No shit."

"I gotta see this." Danny walked over to another window and looked down. "Wow. They're climbing the walls."

Danny fired down the side of the Tower with his shotgun. He paused, then racked and fired a second time.

"Did that stop them?" Josh asked. He couldn't see anything from his position.

"No, but it's slowing them down," Danny said. "Hard to climb with a face full of buckshot, silver or no." He stuck his shotgun out the window and fired two more times. "Come on, I got all day."

"We don't need all day," Will said. "We only need two hours."

Will was right. Josh didn't have his watch, but his instinctive internal clock told him it was going to be sunup soon. All they had to do was wait a little longer.

Behind him, Carly fired down the side of the Tower again, and then Gaby did the same thing on her side. Carly had the south side, Gaby the north, while Will and Danny took the east and west windows. Between the four of them, they had all four sides of the Tower covered.

It went like that throughout the night.

Will and Danny fired, then stopped. Then Gaby and Carly fired while Will and Danny reloaded below them. When they were done, Will and Danny went back to shooting, and Gaby and Carly reloaded.

Somehow, despite the tumultuous crash of shotgun blasts all around and below them, Sienna managed to fall asleep against Lara's shoulder. Lara was wide awake, though Josh could tell she was struggling to stay that way. Sarah had already fallen asleep nearby, her daughter still lying with her head in her mother's lap.

Josh's eyelids started to become heavy, and after a while he stood up and paced the floor to keep his feet moving and his blood flowing.

Gaby held the shotgun out to him. "Your turn. My arms are

about to fall off."

Josh took the shotgun gratefully and went to the window and looked down.

He thought he was prepared for the sight of ghouls below them, but that couldn't be further from the truth. There were so many of them that he couldn't see the grass anymore. They stretched across the hotel grounds, and there weren't nearly enough lights to illuminate them all. They moved around restlessly, climbing over each other to be the next creature at the bottom of the pyramids amassed around the base of the Tower. And they were climbing, using each other as stepping stones.

But they never got very far up the side of the Tower—at least not far enough to grab onto the windows on the second floor—before a shotgun blast tore through the closest ghoul. The force of the blasts knocked it free from the squirming, living pyramid and sent it tumbling back down.

But each time that happened, another ghoul was there to take its place.

Josh fired straight down the side of the Tower. Some of the buckshot scraped against the building's side, tearing off chunks of concrete, but most found their target. He watched a ghoul's face disappear, revealing a deformed but polished skull underneath, and the ghoul lost its footing and dropped ten yards into the pile below. Then the ghoul got back up and started climbing again, scarred bones glaring up at Josh from under sheared flesh.

Josh worked the slide of the shotgun and fired again, knocking another handful of ghouls free from the swaying hill of black flesh. Like the last ones, these picked themselves up and got back in line to climb as if nothing had happened.

"Ammo," Gaby said, and passed him a handful of shells.

He loaded the shotgun, stopping momentarily to look up at Gaby, smiling at him. He smiled back.

Then she picked up another shotgun and leaned out the window and fired down at the ghouls below. The giddiness with which she did it made him grin.

Who would have thought? He and Gaby, at the end of the world, standing on the third floor of a lighthouse, shooting ghouls in the face while trying to wait out the night.

Suck on that, mofos!

CHAPTER 30

BLAINE

BLAINE HEARD THEM moving all around him. Something was different tonight. They sounded more active, and their footsteps were heavier somehow. The ghouls were always amazingly light on their feet, a result of their dwindling muscles and the fact that they were mostly skin and bones because that was all they needed.

And the blood. They needed the blood most of all.

But tonight was different, and looking across the employee lounge at Maddie, sitting on the dirty orange couch in her hazmat suit, the gas mask in her lap, trying not to fall asleep, he could tell she knew it, too. Even mute Bobby, leaning a few inches from the fridge pushed against the door, seemed aware of it also.

The room was pitch-dark, with only a few strands of moonlight finding their way through the high window. They sat silently in the Sortys employee lounge and listened. Blaine listened without interest. He was still numbed, still empty. Still trying to decide whether it was even worth it to keep going without Sandra.

The ghouls were indifferent to his pain, and their activity went on for hours. It started as soon as darkness fell, and it didn't stop. He heard footsteps throughout the early morning hours, racing across the rooftops, outside in the parking lot. But they never strayed into the hallway outside the lounge. Maybe they knew there was nothing for them there from their previous forays into the mall. Or maybe they were all assigned other duties. Blaine knew from experience the creatures weren't stupid. Far from it. They were disciplined, and they did as they were told.

The blue-eyed ghoul…

He didn't care. They could come through the door. It didn't make any difference to him.

After what seemed like hours of sitting in silence in the darkness, Maddie finally whispered across the room at him. "What are they doing?"

He shook his head. He didn't know what she expected him to say. Blaine wasn't even sure he could talk. Or if he wanted to.

"I've never seen this before," she whispered. "They've never been this…active."

Bobby pointed up at the ceiling. Maddie nodded.

"The second floor," Maddie said. "He's saying most of the activity is on the second floor. Where the sleepers are." She shook her head again. "This is something new. I've never seen anything like this before in all the months I've been here."

He didn't care. His mind was elsewhere.

"If you love me—if you care about me—you'll keep going," Sandra had said as she died in front of him.

But how could he keep going? Without her?

Blaine laid the Glock down on the floor next to him and leaned back against the wall and closed his eyes.

"If you love me—if you care about me—you'll keep going."

Impossible. How could she tell him that? How could he keep going without her? All of this was *for* her. Blaine would have been happy to spend the rest of his life in someone's dark basement, running from town to town. As long as she was with him.

He had wanted Song Island for her. What was the point of going there now?

Not without you, baby. Not without you…

Blaine closed his eyes. He didn't even remember when he fell asleep, but he welcomed the darkness for the very first time in a long time.

WHEN HE OPENED his eyes it was morning, and sunlight was splashed across the room. Blaine pulled himself up from the floor where he had slid during the night. His neck hurt and there was silence around him, reminding him how quiet it could be in the mornings when most of the planet was dead.

Like Sandra…

Maddie wasn't on the sofa, and the fridge lay on its side. Bobby wasn't anywhere in the room, either, and Blaine couldn't find signs of a battle. The door was open, and it looked to be in good shape. The ghouls hadn't attacked last night.

He sucked in air for a moment.

"If you love me—if you care about me—you'll keep going."

He looked down at the Glock in his hand. He didn't remember when he had picked it up from the floor.

"Don't stop. Don't ever stop…"

He didn't recall when he had started to lift the gun, but it was suddenly up to his chest when he heard footsteps and looked over as Maddie walked into the lounge.

She had her M4 rifle over one shoulder and a backpack over the other. She saw him and gave him a brief, awkward smile. "You're up."

Blaine consciously lowered the gun and glanced at his watch. Already 10:16 A.M.? He had slept through most of the morning. "You should have woken me."

She shrugged. "You looked like you needed the rest. Besides, there wasn't a lot to do."

"The others…?"

"Gerry's gone. Lenny, too."

"What about Sandra?"

"I'm sorry. She's gone, too."

Of course they would take Sandra, too. Why would the world allow him to grieve properly?

She walked over to the couch and sat down. Her eyes went to the gun in his hand. "No signs of Mason, but I have Bobby on the roof just in case he comes back."

"Is that safe?"

"Safer than all of us sitting in here where he can sneak up on us."

Blaine looked down at the Glock in his hand. It looked foreign, and the feel of it against his palm was unnatural.

"Blaine," Maddie said, "put the gun away."

He looked up at her, momentarily taken aback by the hardness in her voice. What did she think he was going to do with the gun? Kill himself? He wasn't going to kill himself.

Right?

Blaine slipped the Glock into its holster and sat back down on the floor. Maddie unzipped her backpack and took out a bottle of water and tossed it over to him. He took a big gulp and was halfway through when he started spilling some on his shirt and slowed down.

"So what now?" she asked.

"What do you mean?" He set the bottle between his legs.

"I mean, what now? They're gone, you know."

"Lenny, Gerry, and Sandra, I know."

"No, not just them. The others, too. All the sleepers on the second floor."

Blaine gave her a surprised look.

"Yeah, all of them," she nodded. "That was all the commotion last night. They were carrying away the sleepers en masse. There isn't a single soul left up there. You'd think there might be one or two or a dozen that they would leave behind, who might have died; but no, they took them all."

"*All* of them?"

"It doesn't make any sense. Nothing about last night makes sense."

"Where would they take the sleepers?"

"I don't know."

"How many were up there? Thousands?"

"At least."

"That's a lot of people to move in one night."

"There were a hell of a *lot* of them last night, Blaine."

He nodded. He had to remind himself this was their world now. They—he and her and Bobby—were the anomalies, running around trying to survive, to avoid being stamped out of existence. One nightfall at a time.

So this is what being a cockroach feels like.

"So what now?" Maddie asked again. "Do we follow your friends to Beaufont Lake?"

"Go to Song Island," Sandra had said. *"Take Maddie and Bobby. Go to Song Island and try to be happy. If you love me—if you care about me—you'll keep going."*

"Blaine?"

He looked up at her. She was watching him closely. "What?"

"Do we follow your friends to Beaufont Lake?"

He thought about it. It was hard to concentrate on any one thing. He still felt numbed—not just physically, but mentally as well. "Will and the others would have reached the island by now."

"You think so?"

"Yeah. Probably."

"So we should go, too. Take what we can from here—the food, water, weapons, and clothing—and start off now." She glanced at her watch. "We could be on the road by noon. If we push it, we can be in Louisiana and on our way to Song Island well before nightfall."

"It's a plan," he nodded quietly.

"But is it a good plan? Is it doable?"

"What does Bobby say?"

She grinned at him.

"You know what I mean," he added.

"He's good to go. We have vehicles. Gas. And it wouldn't be hard to shoot out the lock in the security room and gather up the weapons."

"We need silver."

"What for?"

"Silver kills the ghouls."

"Since when?"

He told her about Will and Danny discovering silver. About his own use of silver at the house with Sandra.

Sandra...

"Jesus," Maddie said. "When were you going to tell us this?"

"After we killed Mason."

"Fair enough. We have more silver than we know what to do with in the department stores. The question is: you know how to turn them into bullets?"

"I don't have a clue. You?"

"None."

"Didn't you say you used to hunt as a kid with your dad?"

She gave him a wry smirk. "Yeah, but we bought bullets from the store like normal people."

HE HAD TO see it for himself, so he went up to the second floor. He expected to see the rows and rows of sleeping bodies. Instead, there was just emptiness.

It didn't seem possible the ghouls could remove thousands of people in one night, but they had. Even so, he walked along the second-floor walkways just to be sure, spaces once filled up with frail, sleeping bodies hanging between life and death. He could see outlines of where they had lain, created by dust and dirt and spilt blood, like obscene police chalk outlines. There wasn't nearly as much blood on the floor as he had expected.

They don't waste a single drop.

After a while, Maddie joined him. "Not even one night. They did all this in half a night. I guess I shouldn't be surprised. They took over the damn planet in one night."

"How many buildings in Beaumont are as big as the Willowstone Mall?"

"I don't know. I haven't exactly explored the city since I got here. That was Mason's job, and he gave me mostly guard duty. Why?"

"They had to have taken the bodies somewhere."

"You're assuming they're going to keep them in the city."

"You're right," he nodded. "They wouldn't have gone through all this trouble just to swap one building for another in the same city. Not because of us. I don't think they're afraid of us at all."

"Hardly. There are what, millions of them out there? Billions? How many of us are left? A few hundred in the state? A few thousand across the country? The planet?"

One less without Sandra…

"We should start getting ready," Maddie said. "I think we need to be gone from here by noon. Just to give ourselves enough time to get to Song Island in case we run into trouble along the way. Besides, I'm not fond of the idea of Mason waiting out there for us."

They walked back to the escalator.

He knew she was watching him closely, trying to gauge his state of mind. "I'm fine."

"I didn't say anything."

"Yeah, well…"

He walked past her and down the escalator, trying to pretend like he really was fine, and failing miserably.

"If you love me—if you care about me—you'll keep going..."

BLAINE AND MADDIE went down to the security room for their weapons. Maddie shot the lock with her M4, and Blaine collected his Remington shotgun and handgun while Maddie grabbed as much as she could carry.

They took the weapons to a Jeep parked outside Sortys, with Bobby standing sentry on the roof. It took them three trips, using two shopping baskets, to carry all the ammo outside. They stuck to the M4 rifles and shotguns and left behind a stack of weapons for whoever came after.

He didn't speak as he gathered up the weapons, then the ammo, then the silver from the cases around the department stores. Maddie didn't seem to mind the silence, and Bobby, well, he was Bobby.

They amassed an impressive amount of silver within the hour—two baskets full of cutlery, pens, ornaments, candleholders, and things Blaine didn't even know came in silver. Maddie seemed to be able to pick out the real silver from the fake easily enough, but Blaine had to take a second and sometimes a third look just to make sure.

By the time they were done, it was almost noon, and Bobby came down from the roof with his weapons and a backpack stuffed with food and water. He climbed in, squeezing wordlessly between the crates of silver and weapons latched onto the back of the Jeep with bungee cords.

Maddie slipped behind the wheel and tossed a quick look back at Bobby. "How you doing back there?"

Bobby gave her the "OK" with his fingers.

"How about you?" she asked Blaine.

"Okay," he said.

"Up I-10 and into Louisiana, right?"

"Straight shot, yeah."

"Keep an eye out for Mason. That asshole's out there somewhere. I wouldn't be surprised if he tried to take a pot shot at us somewhere along the way."

Blaine had the Remington in his lap. He checked to make sure it was loaded, then gave her a nod.

"Okay, then," she said. "Let's get outta here."

She turned the engine and the Jeep hummed to life without a problem. Maddie drove through the parking lot. Blaine expected to hear gunfire at any second—Mason, hidden somewhere out there, getting in one last goodbye before it was too late.

But there was nothing except the quiet purr of the Jeep as Maddie maneuvered them out of the Willowstone Mall parking lot and onto the feeder road. They were on their way, and Blaine couldn't help but wonder what Sandra would say right about now. Probably something positive, something to lift their spirits. Maybe a joke, or a smile. All it usually took was a smile from her.

"Don't stop. Don't ever stop..."

EVENTUALLY, THEY STOPPED at a Shell gas station in the Louisiana city of Salvani, hoping to grab some food and drinks. It was 3:13 P.M., and they had made good progress out of Texas and into Louisiana. It took them longer than Blaine would have liked, but slow and steady meant no disasters on the road. He knew all about disasters on the road.

Sandra did, too.

He spent the entire drive trying to decide whether he could go on without her. She had told him she wanted him to, but he hadn't made any promises. He couldn't make any promises. Every now and then he sneaked a glance at Maddie behind the wheel, and Bobby in the back, his face turned into the wind.

They're so young...

This was all because of him, he realized. He had introduced the idea of Song Island to Maddie. He was the one who had convinced her to betray Mason. Without him, Maddie and Bobby would be blissfully moving on with their lives in the mall. So what did that mean?

They were his responsibility. It was his fault they were here. Could he just abandon them now?

"Go to Song Island. Take Maddie and Bobby. Go to Song Island and try to be happy. If you love me—if you care about me—you'll keep going."

He didn't know if he could be happy without Sandra, but he

could at least take Maddie and Bobby to Song Island. He owed them that much. After that? He didn't know. It was a big world still, and it wasn't likely it was going to miss him.

Song Island first…

They found what they needed either in the pungent-smelling freezers in the back of the Shell or scattered along the floors. A couple of bottles of warm Gatorade, another three bottles of Powerade, and some boxes of snacks the rats and animals hadn't gone through yet. From the looks of the footprints in the well-tread aisles, there had been plenty of creatures big and small looking over the Shell's shelves in the past eight months.

Blaine looked up when he heard the chime over the front door jingle as Maddie came in.

"Anything?" he asked.

"Town's dead. Big surprise." She pulled a folded map out of her back pocket. "I did find a map of the area, though. You find anything good?"

"Drinks, junk food, the usual."

Bobby came out from the back with BBQ-flavored Pringles he was popping into his mouth from a can. Blaine thought with some amusement that this was the most sound he had ever heard come out of Bobby's mouth.

Maddie sat down on an ice cream freezer near the window. She looked tired as she fixed him with a querying look. "Still Song Island or bust, right?"

She's still worried. Afraid I'll off myself when she's not looking.

Maybe she's not so wrong…

"Unless you've changed your mind," he nodded.

"Got nowhere else to go. No job interviews or anything." Maddie looked over at Bobby. "How about you? You think we should turn back now or keep going to Song Island?"

Bobby gave her a thumbs up without hesitation.

"He's good to go," Maddie said.

Blaine picked up the bag of drinks and took out a warm blue bottle of Powerade and tossed it over to Maddie.

"Ugh. Warm Powerade," she said.

"Better than warm nothing."

"Just barely—" she started to say, but was interrupted by the familiar drone of car engines coming down the road outside.

"Down!"

Maddie dropped behind the big ice cream freezer while Blaine went down behind the counter. He looked out the window and saw a black Toyota Tacoma truck racing down Ruth Street, swerving around an old red pickup sitting half on the curb and half on the road. Blaine caught a glimpse of two guys in the front seat and shadows in the back, though he couldn't be sure if they were more guys or supplies.

His eyes darted to their Jeep parked outside the front door of the Shell. If the Tacoma had been moving slower and someone had bothered to look in their direction, they might have noticed the Jeep. It was hard to miss, with the big pile of crates in the back. Fortunately there were two big gas pumps between the Jeep and the road, so even if someone had looked over, there was a chance their view might have been slightly obstructed.

The Tacoma kept going, disappearing down the road.

I guess they didn't see us.

He was about to stand back up when two more trucks appeared off the I-10 feeder—a white Ford F-150 and a silver Chevy Silverado, similar to the one he and Sandra had entered Beaumont in. For a second, he thought it might be the same truck, but as the Silverado flashed by, he saw white stripes along the side. He glimpsed two men in the front seat of the truck. He was so focused on the Silverado that by the time the F-150 went by, it was just a white blur.

For a moment Blaine thought the last two cars were chasing the first one, but he soon concluded that wasn't the case. They were together. Or at least, going in the same direction. He watched them disappear down Ruth Street, the sound of their engines lingering in the air for a long time. They could still hear the trucks for minutes afterward.

He stood up from behind the counter and exchanged a look with Maddie.

"More survivors headed to Song Island?" she asked.

"Has to be. What else is down there?"

"How many you figure were in those three trucks?"

"I saw two in the front seats of the Tacoma, two more in the front seats of the Silverado, but I didn't catch the F-150."

"At least two, I think." She looked back at Bobby. "How many did you see, Bobby?"

He shrugged and put up two fingers. Then shrugged again.

"He's not sure," Maddie translated. She looked back at Blaine, saw the look on his face. "What is it?"

"They were in a hurry," he said.

"And?"

"There's no reason to be moving that fast." He glanced at his watch. "We're still a good five hours away from sundown. It's not going to take more than an hour max to reach Song Island. There's no traffic on the road, at least not out here. So what's the hurry?"

She seemed to think about it, but didn't have any answers for him.

Behind them, Bobby popped another BBQ-flavored Pringle into his mouth and crunched loudly.

"IT SHOULD BE ahead of us," Maddie said, consulting the map in her lap.

"How far?"

"There should be a right bend in about a mile. Route 27 keeps going around the lake's western cove for another two miles."

"Anything about a marina?"

"No, but there should be one or two before the two miles are up."

"Why do you say that?"

"Because coves make for good fishing spots. I'd be surprised if there weren't at least two launches around here."

"If you say so."

"You don't sound convinced."

"I'm more concerned about those trucks," Blaine said.

He was unable to forget about the trucks. Three trucks, with at least two men in each one. The farther he went down south, the more convinced he was they were headed to Beaufont Lake. But it was the way they were traveling—fast, with purpose—that stuck with him. Even though he had only seen them from a distance, something in the way they drove didn't seemed right for survivors looking for safety. It was too aggressive.

It was hard to explain, and there was always a chance he was being overly paranoid. Then again, if only he had been more paranoid about entering Beaumont, taken precautions, maybe Sandra would still be here…

The right turn Maddie had predicted came up, and Blaine slowed down and took it without any problems.

"There," Maddie said, pointing.

Blaine slowed down some more, heard Bobby moving excitedly behind them. Bobby made so little noise that whenever Blaine did hear him, it always startled him just a little bit until he realized who it was. He didn't think he would ever get used to having someone around him who didn't speak.

Maddie pointed at a faded sign along the side of the road. The only thing Blaine could make out was the word "marina," and he didn't have to wait long before the marina itself appeared in the distance. He glimpsed the tip of a gazebo and the sun sparkling off the aluminum roof of a garage-like building.

Blaine stopped the Jeep about fifty yards away, putting the vehicle into park along the side of the road out of sheer habit.

"Why are we stopping so far away?" Maddie asked.

"Just to be safe."

"The trucks?"

"Yeah."

The trucks. If they were heading for Song Island—and he was fully convinced they were—then they would have seen the marina and pulled in. Unfortunately, fifty yards was too far away to pick out the three trucks from the dozen or so vehicles at the marina at the moment.

Behind them, Bobby stood up and peered through a pair of binoculars.

"See anything?" Blaine asked.

Bobby handed him the binoculars and pointed forward. Blaine stood up in the driver's seat and peered through them.

The gazebo to the left of the marina, a storage garage farther in. None of the vehicles looked like the ones he had seen passing the Shell earlier. There was an inlet next to the marina, and on the other side, a sprawling, white two-story house surrounded by hurricane fencing. He couldn't see signs of movement around the property, but it was hard to tell from this distance.

"Anything?" Maddie asked.

"House across from the marina," Blaine said.

He handed her the binoculars. She stood up and looked for herself, and after a moment, lowered them. "I don't see anyone."

"Neither do I. And that's the problem. There are no other places for those three trucks to have stopped but here. At least, if they want to get to Song Island."

"You're assuming they were headed there."

"What else is down here?"

She looked around at the emptiness for a moment. "Maybe they already took a boat to Song Island. I saw a boathouse on the property."

"Can you see the island?"

"I see a patch of dirt," she said, peering through the binoculars again. "Way, way in the distance. And something that looks like a lighthouse, but I can't be sure." She lowered the binoculars. "So what do we do now? There aren't any boats at the marina, and there might be people at the house who may not be friendly. This has gotten a lot more complicated."

Blaine glanced at his watch. They were pushing up against five in the evening. They had, at best, just over three hours of sunlight left.

Suddenly there was the loud *crack* of gunfire in the distance.

A second shot followed, then a third. Not a burst, or a three-shot burst, but carefully squeezed-off shots. They came from the water, though Blaine couldn't tell from which direction, or how far away.

Then the loud rattle of return fire, like fireworks, rolling across the lake surface for a good five seconds. More than one assault rifle firing, unloading on something. That, or someone was wasting a lot of bullets answering the first three shots.

They heard the *crack* of another gunshot, then a fifth and sixth shot followed.

Then there was silence.

They waited to hear something else—more returning fire—but whatever had happened seemed to have run its course. The quiet settled back over the lake as if nothing had happened.

"That's not a good sign, right?" Maddie said. It wasn't a question. "Gunfire from Song Island. If that is Song Island out there."

He shook his head. "I don't know what to think."

"What about your friends? You think they're on the island right now?"

"They must have arrived a full day ahead of us, so it's possible." Then he heard something else. It was a grinding sound, gradually growing in intensity. "You hear that? What is that?"

"Outboard motors," Maddie said. "Boats."

IT DIDN'T TAKE the boats long to reach the shore, but by then Blaine had moved the Jeep out of the road and into the side of the ditch. The Jeep wasn't completely hidden, at least not from anyone with eyes traveling along the road. From a distance, it had a chance of going unseen, though that was probably a stretch, too.

They crouched along the edge of the ditch, watching with binoculars as the boats—there were two—chugged down the inlet between the marina and the house, then turned left and headed toward the boathouse on the property. Blaine saw four men in one boat and four more in the other. He couldn't make out faces, but it wasn't hard to see they were all heavily armed.

"One of them's hurt," Maddie said beside him.

"Which one?" Blaine asked.

"First boat."

Blaine looked again and saw that she was right. One of the men was sitting down, slightly slumped over, holding his shoulder.

"The second boat's motor is damaged," Maddie said.

"How can you tell?"

"It's coughing up smoke. Too much smoke."

Blaine saw that, too, though he didn't know what a damaged boat motor looked like. She was right, though, the motor on the second boat was definitely putting out more smoke than the first one.

The boats pulled up to the boathouse, which had three slots, the third slot empty. A man appeared from the side of the binoculars' field of view and guided the boats in. The men climbed out, two of them helping the injured one up.

"Make that two injured," Maddie said.

"Which one?"

"Second boat. Looks like his right leg."

Blaine focused on the second boat as the men climbed onto the dock. And yes, one of them was limping badly. One of the limping man's comrades reached over and helped him up the wooden deck. They left the boathouse, arguing and gesturing wildly. He followed them to the two-story house as far as he could, glimpsing trucks parked in front of the house, and was sure one of them was the Silverado from earlier. Another vehicle might have been the blue Tundra.

"That's a lot of firepower," Maddie said. "You think they were attacking the island?"

"If they were, it didn't go well." Blaine lowered his binoculars. "I only heard six shots in all, not counting the loud free-for-all in the middle. What about you?"

"Six."

"What about you, Bobby?"

Bobby held up one hand and one finger on his second hand.

"So six shots in all," Blaine said. "That's not a lot. But it might be enough for a pair of Army Rangers to put the hurt on a couple of boats trying to land on their beach. The question is, why are they even attacking the island? What's going on over there?"

"So you think your friends took the island?" Maddie asked.

"I think they're on it, yeah. I've seen them shoot. They wouldn't need more than six shots to repel an attack by boat. Even a couple of boats with four guys apiece."

"Are they that good?"

"They're really well-prepared, and they know what they're doing."

They settled back down into the ditch.

Maddie wiped at a bead of sweat along her forehead. "So what now? We can't just stay here forever. Sooner or later it's going to get dark, and we're going to need shelter."

He didn't have any good answers for her. They could attack the house from the front, but he flashed back to the gunfight at the mall. What happened that day was forever etched into his brain. He reminded himself that he, Maddie, Bobby, and Sandra could barely take on two men they had the drop on. Which made it unlikely they were going to take on at least eight heavily armed people in a two-story house, even if two of them were already hurting. That still left six.

Six too many…

Blaine glanced down at his watch: 4:16 P.M.

"Well?" Maddie said, watching his face carefully. "Should we attack the house?"

"That wouldn't be a very good idea," a voice said behind them.

Blaine shot up and spun around—and found himself staring into the barrel of an assault rifle.

CHAPTER 31

WILL

MORNING BROUGHT SALVATION and sent the ghouls back to their point of origin. It wasn't hard to figure out where that was. All they had to do was follow the jagged lines of white bones scattered across the island, the flesh seared off completely by the sun's rays. The unnatural mist of evaporated, tainted flesh and ghoul blood lingered in the air long afterward. Thank God for the wind that appeared out of the north to help drive the smell away.

The sight of so many dead ghouls in one place took Will back to the bank outside of Cleveland, Texas, all those many months ago. That was the day he had lost Kate. He didn't know it until much later, but that was when she had started to slip away. His failure to notice cost them Harold Campbell's facility and forced them on this journey to Song Island. Maybe, in the long run, it would all work out.

If they could hold the island…

Less than thirty minutes after sunup, Will and Danny emerged from the Tower. Instead of a cobblestone pathway, they followed the bones from the eastern cliff back to the power station in the west. They bypassed the hotel. There wasn't anything in there they hadn't already seen last night. The dead would be gone, including Al, Jake, Debra and her son, and Berg. Will didn't know if Berg had ever made it out of the zip ties before the ghouls had invaded the hotel, and he didn't particularly care.

He did care just a little bit about the others, especially Al, whose screams were one of the last things Will had heard before the cook had vanished under a sea of swarming creatures. He hadn't seen what happened to Debra or her son Kyle, though he had seen Jake swinging a golf club when the ghouls had entered through the windows around them. He remembered grabbing Sienna and dragging her away. She had fought him, trying to get back to Jake, and Will had been half a second from letting her go when she had decided to finally stop fighting and run.

That was last night. This morning, they were alive. Most of them, anyway.

Gaby and Josh, armed with shotguns and radios, stayed behind in the Tower. As soon as the sun rose, they could see everything for miles from the windows. The south and east directions gave them a clear line of sight of the lake's shorelines, including the marina and the two-story house. The Tower, as Will had predicted, made for a brilliant sniper's perch.

Now all he needed to do was turn Gaby into a shooter…

The others had begun clearing bones out of the hotel and the grounds around it. The light bones were easy to pick up, stack in wheelbarrows, and roll away. They gathered the remains of the dead in a pile along the north side of the island, next to the cliff.

Will and Danny reached the power station and stepped over the trampled hurricane fencing, still half-buried in the dirt. The big gray building hadn't been touched, but there was a clear path from where the front gate used to be to the small shack. As he got closer, Will noticed it wasn't really a shack. It was a stand-alone brick building with a steel door that opened inward, revealing very little on the other side. He thought he could hear rustling wind through the opening, though most of it was lost in the loud, rumbling hum of the generator next door.

Will turned on the flashlight duct-taped to the side of the Benelli shotgun and aimed it at the door. Four pairs of charcoal eyes stared back at him before quickly shrinking back into the darkness, trying to escape the probing light.

"Hellooooo, nurse," Danny said.

They were squeezed inside the building, just beyond the reach of sunlight, simultaneously salivating at the sight of them and morbidly afraid of the brightness splayed across the open metal door. It was hard to tell how many of them were actually in there. Will guessed the building had a flight of stairs that angled downward and under the island. Where the stairs went after that, and where the ghouls came from, were questions that played themselves over and over in his head. The only way to find out was to go into the shack—or find where the tunnel ended, which had to be somewhere on land, along the western cove. Neither option was particularly viable at the moment.

Will walked around the shack to get a better look at what he was dealing with. It wasn't any bigger than anything he would have found in someone's backyard. The front was about two meters wide, the length around three and a half. It was concrete from top to bottom, with a flat, unremarkable roof and a metal door.

When he circled all the way back to the front, he took a quick step toward the door and fired with the Benelli. Regular buckshot ripped through a ghoul standing defiantly in front of him. The creature was thrown back by the impact, half of its side shorn off, revealing bone and flesh underneath. It picked itself up and glared at him, gaunt cheeks flickering in the flashlight beam.

"I don't think it likes you," Danny said.

Will fired again, taking off the top half of the creature's head, where its brain would have been if it still had one. The creature stumbled back into the wall of ghouls crowding behind it before picking itself up and looking back at him through its remaining right eye.

"You got any silver on you?" Will asked.

"Just the knife. You wanna reach in there and stab it?"

"Not particularly." He tried to get a better look at the interior of the shack, but he couldn't see anything past the squirming black mass of prune flesh. "Basement?"

"Has to be, right?"

"Must be a big-ass basement. How many came out of it last night? A thousand?"

"Don't exaggerate. A few hundred, at the most."

"Looked like a lot more than a few hundred to me."

"Okay, maybe just a shade under a thousand."

"So where are they coming from? A tunnel at the end of the basement? Connected to the shore? That would explain where Karen went."

"What do I look like, an island tunnel expert?"

Will took a step back. "How many you think are in there now?"

"Lots."

"Not very scientific."

"Bunches."

"Better."

"I found my C4 in the Tower's basement this morning while I was poking around."

"How many were left?"

"Bundles."

"That a lot?"

"Better than bundle. See, the plural?"

Will smirked. "So you wanna blow it up, is that what you're telling me?"

Danny shrugged. "That would seal the tunnel, wouldn't it? Cave it in on itself?"

"Well, there's a problem with that. We don't know how far or deep the tunnel goes. What if we rupture it, but don't cave it in completely? Water's gotta go somewhere once they get inside the tunnel. Like up here on the island."

"So, no C4, then?"

"We'll save them for later. I didn't get farther than the stairs where he stacked our stuff last night. What else did you find down there?"

"There was a pretty sweet tritium ACOG scope in a case. Four-by-thirty-two."

"Nice."

"Ol' Tom's got some expensive gun habits. I'm mounting it on my rifle."

"You're definitely getting sentry duty."

"Figures."

"What else did you find?"

"That place is huge. Like a friggin' pawnshop. Who knows what's down there? Another ACOG, maybe, if we're lucky. Maybe a bazooka or a tank, possibly even Jimmy Hoffa."

"Tom's been collecting for a while…"

"Yeah. Tom was a real hoarder. A back-stabbing, hoarding piece of crap." He looked back at the door. "So we can't blow it up. How do we seal it, keep those pesky buggers from coming out later tonight? This door might not hold forever. Remember that sorry incident with the car back at the bank? That was pretty out-of-the-box thinking for a bunch of undead prune faces."

Will thought about it. "I have an idea, but we need to close the door first."

"Sounds simple enough. Not."

"Can you reach the door?"

Danny studied the angles for a moment, then shook his head. "Not before they're all over me."

He was right. The ghouls were less than a meter inside the open door frame, about the same length it would take to reach in and grasp the lever. Then there was the extra second or two to actually swing the door. More than enough time for a creature to latch onto an extended arm. The only positive was the key, still stuck in a lock four inches above the lever. Of course, in order to lock the door, they would have to close it first.

"We need to close that door," Will said again.

"Do we?"

"Yes."

"I'm open to suggestions," Danny said.

SARAH WAS THE one who told them about the concrete mix and unused concrete blocks stored in one of the unfinished rooms of the hotel.

"We never could figure out what to do with them," Sarah said. "It wasn't like anyone had ever built anything before. Though I guess Tom had, when he was younger. Can we use them? I mean, if we can't destroy them, or push them back, what if we just sealed them inside the shack?"

They found the Quikrete concrete mix bags where Sarah said they would be. There were enough blocks stacked on top of one another in a row to put together a small house. All the building equipment was also in the same room.

Will called Josh down from the Tower to help carry everything over to the power station. It took them two hours of trudging back and forth, hauling bags of easy-to-mix and block after block of concrete, before they were even ready to start. It was almost ten in the morning when they were finally able to break their first bag of

Quikrete over the mixer, pour water inside with a hose, and create usable mortar. Both Will and Danny had worked construction before, and Will had done his share of mixing and slapping mortar on concrete blocks with trowels when he used to work with his father in the summers.

Lara took a break from bone duty, as the others had begun calling it, and came over with food and cold bottles of water, something they couldn't get enough of. You could only drink so much warm water before the taste of something cold was like a miracle drug.

"So we're just going to cover it up?" Lara said, staring at the darkness inside the open shack door, at the unblinking eyes peering back out at her. She shivered a bit.

"That's the plan," Will said.

"They can't break through?"

"Probably not."

"That's not very reassuring."

"Mostly not."

"So you're Danny now, is that it?" She smirked at him. "Bad jokes and all?"

"I'm right here," Danny said.

"It'll hold," Will said, doing his best to sound convincing.

The truth was, he didn't know if it would actually hold. Or if it proved effective now, how long that would last. The ghouls had proven themselves to be resourceful creatures, and they had unlimited numbers and time on their hands.

Dead, not stupid.

Lara nodded, but looked only partially convinced. "We're almost done clearing out the bones. I can't believe they all came out of that one building. Do you think Karen is one of those things staring at us right now?"

"I think she knew she'd survive," Will said. "It explains the hazmat suit."

"Like Kevin…"

"Yeah."

"Then that means there's a tunnel down there. She would need a way off the island. Plus a way for these things to reach the island without having to swim. And if they need the tunnel, that means the water really does keep them back."

"Looks that way."

"Well, at least the island's safe. Sort of." Lara shivered again. "Hurry up. I hate the idea of that door open like that, with those things inside."

She left them, clutching her shotgun as she went.

Will looked over at Danny. "Ready?"

Danny grunted. "No."

"Good."

Will picked up the shotgun and took two quick steps toward the open door and fired. The buckshot ripped the faces off the two closest ghouls and they stumbled back into the others behind them. Even before the rest of the creatures had a chance to respond, Will fired again and kept firing until he had emptied the entire weapon. Each blast shoved the creatures back little by little. It wasn't much, but it was just *enough*.

As soon as Will fired his last shot, he stepped aside as Danny lunged forward and grabbed the door by the lever. The closest ghoul started forward, but before it could get close, Danny slammed the door shut and held on. Almost immediately, ghouls crashed into the door on the other side, banging relentlessly against the steel. The lever moved under Danny's grip, but he held on while Will grabbed the key, turned it, and heard the deadbolt latching into place.

They both stepped back and listened to the ghouls continue to rain blows against the door.

Danny sucked in a big breath. "Let's not do that again. Ever."

"It's all in the wrists," Will said, pocketing the key.

"That's what she said," Danny grinned.

It took them the rest of the morning to put up a concrete wall directly over the steel door, covering up the entire front of the shack just to be safe. By the time they were done, they were covered in flakes of concrete and rivers of sweat. Will didn't know what smelled worse—the state he was in this morning, or the way he had been last night while he was running with ghoul flesh and blood stuck to his face.

At ten minutes past noon, they tossed the trowels to the ground and gave the shack a long look.

"You think it'll hold?" Danny asked.

"They'd need a tank to get through that," Will said.

"Need I remind you about that unfortunate incident with a car?"

"I doubt that tunnel's big enough for a car."

They paused for a moment.

"Has to be a tunnel down there, right?" Danny said.

"Has to be," Will said.

"Which means it comes out on the other side, on land."

"Sounds logical."

"We should find out where that is and close it up like a virgin's legs."

"We should, yeah. But not yet. This should hold for a while."

"You got a hot date I don't know about?"

Will was about to answer when his radio, sitting on one of the unused concrete blocks, squawked and they heard Gaby's voice: "Will, Danny, I see movement on land."

Will snatched up the radio. "Where?"

"At the marina."

"Cars?"

"Trucks. More than one."

"Stay with them."

"Will do."

They picked up their shotguns and gun belts and began jogging back toward the hotel.

"And here I thought it was going to be a quiet morning," Danny said.

THE DOOR TO the Tower was gone, shattered from last night's assault. They hadn't bothered to fix it yet, so Will and Danny ran through it and up the spiral staircase to the second floor, then kept going all the way up to the third floor.

Gaby was at the south window, peering through binoculars. "Two trucks."

"Marina?" Will asked.

"No. They drove past it and went straight to the house."

Will walked to the window and picked up a second pair of binoculars dangling from a hook on the wall. He peered through them at the house and spotted two new trucks parked in the front yard, like toys left out in the sun.

He lowered the binoculars and glanced down at his watch:

12:36 P.M.

Danny was peering through Gaby's binoculars. "More of us, or more like Karen?"

Will looked over at the computer station behind them. Josh had put it back together earlier, but it looked turned off. "Is that thing still broadcasting?"

"No," Gaby said. "Josh said you told him not to turn it back on yet."

"Maybe Karen's in that house," Danny said. "If we're lucky, we should start hearing gunshots any time now." He put down his binoculars and waited silently. Then, after about ten seconds, "Or not."

"You're assuming she made it off the island," Gaby said.

"Of course she did," Danny said.

"How can you be so sure?"

"She's a bitch. They don't die that easily."

Lara climbed up the stairs behind them. "I heard more survivors showed up?"

"Maybe," Will said.

She walked over and he handed her his binoculars. She peered through them for a moment. "What could they be, then?"

"That's the question," Will said.

"More collaborators?" Danny said.

"There's always that."

"God, how many of them are out there?" Lara said. She sounded exasperated.

"Probably as many as the ghouls need," Will said.

He had once tried to imagine how many blood farms were out there just to feed the millions (*billions*) of ghouls roaming the planet at the moment, but he had given up after the number became too incomprehensible. It was something he didn't want to waste too much of his time thinking about. The truth was, it didn't matter, because it didn't factor into keeping everyone alive *right now*.

Will looked over at Danny. "Grab the ACOG. You've got sentry duty."

"You sure you don't need me out there?" Danny asked.

"I'll take Josh. Where is Josh, anyway?"

"He went to the hotel to get us something to eat," Gaby said. She looked over at them, and added, "Can I stay here in the Tower with Danny? I want him to teach me how to shoot."

"You noticed that she didn't ask you?" Danny grinned at Will. "That's because she recognizes skill when she sees it."

"I just thought because Will was leaving," Gaby said.

"Ouch," Danny said.

HE WALKED BACK to the beach with Josh and Lara in tow, their shoes clacking against the cobblestone pathway. Will had washed off the grime from this morning's labor and put on his urban assault vest and comm gear. He carried his M4A1 and was thankful there was plenty of 5.56x45mm ammo in the basement underneath the Tower, enough to feed his and Danny's rifles for weeks to come. Finding ammo at the end of the world was always the easy part; turning it into silver was the challenge. It was also the priority.

"I'm not sure you should be leaving us right now," Lara said. "At least take Danny with you."

"I need Danny's rifle in the Tower," Will said.

"Then wait for tomorrow. The marina will still be there in twenty-four hours."

"We need silver, Lara. Everything we need to make that happen is back in the marina."

Lara wasn't convinced. Neither was Josh, who walked quietly next to them. Will imagined the kid must feel caught up in a parental spat. He had given Josh a stripped-down version of their urban assault vest and hadn't realized how awkward the kid looked until he had strapped it on. Besides his gun belt, Josh carried the Remington over his shoulder. Will didn't expect the kid to use the shotgun. Fact was, if Josh started shooting at all, they were already in deep trouble.

"You already sealed the power station," Lara said. "They're not getting back on the island, so we don't need silver yet."

"We don't know what other kind of access they have, and I don't want to take the chance."

"Sarah doesn't think there are any other ways onto the island."

"Sarah didn't know about the power station, either." He glanced down at his watch: 2:10 P.M. "Josh is coming with me, Lara. We'll be fine."

"Be serious, Will," Lara said, exasperated. Then she quickly glanced over at Josh. "No offense."

"Hey, I agree with you," Josh said. "I'll let you guys hash it out."

He walked on ahead, leaving them on the beach.

"That wasn't very nice," Will smiled at her. "Now you've hurt his feelings."

"Will, this isn't the time to leave," she said, undeterred.

"It's the only time. We're stuck here on this island. We need something to defend ourselves with. We need silver."

"Okay, let me rephrase that. After last night, *I* don't want you to leave."

He brushed a strand of hair out of her eyes. "I'm not doing this because I want to. I'm doing this because I have to. You know that."

"I hate you," she said, and pulled him to her and kissed him deeply.

Will slipped his arms around her and held her against him, lingering against her lips. She tasted warm, like the sun. Kissing her was always like coming home.

After a while, he had to pull free. "I have to go."

"Then go," she said. "And come back. Promise me."

"I promise."

"Do you mean it?"

He looked deeply into her blue eyes. "Nothing in this world can keep me from you. Face it, you're stuck with me, lady."

She smiled, then leaned in close and whispered, "I love you."

"I love you, too," he whispered back.

He left her on the beach and joined Josh, who was on one of the piers, staring off at the water. The kid looked scared even from a distance.

"That was sweet," Danny said through the earbud in Will's right ear. "Make that goodbye a little bit longer and I was ready to call the *Guinness Book of World Records*. That, or barf into my binoculars. Either/or."

"You can see me from the Tower?" Will asked.

"The ACOG's got four-by-thirty-two magnification. I can see the mole on the back of your neck from here. Want me to shoot it off?"

"Maybe later."

The Advanced Combat Optical Gunsight—or ACOG—

mounted on Danny's M4A1 was a rifle scope that made the red dot sights they had been using up till now look like kids' toys. It could shoot targets at a much longer range and with more accuracy, with an optimal distance of 800 meters. At over $1,500 apiece—if you could get one for cheap—the ACOG was a luxury.

Will heard Gaby's voice in his earbud, cutting in on Danny: "Don't listen to him, Will. That was very sweet."

"Kids these days," Danny said.

When Will reached him, Josh tossed him a key attached to a round fishing float. "You know how to drive a boat, right?"

"Just like driving a car."

There were five boats still tied along the three piers, but they could only find keys to one of them in the boat shack. Will made a mental note to look for the rest of the keys when they had time.

"What if they're friendlies?" Josh asked. "The people at the house. Why do we have to go around them?"

"We can't take the chance. Not now. Not after last night."

"And everything we need is stored in the garage at the marina?"

"Should be."

"Should be?" Josh frowned. "What if it's gone when we get there? What if the people at the house raided the garage and took it?"

"They didn't."

"But how can you be sure?"

"Because it's not valuable to anyone but us."

The boat was a slightly beat-up Carver that didn't look like much, but it was in one piece and it ran. It had a one-person seat in the middle and an outboard motor at the back that had worked reasonably well when Will had tried it earlier. They were fortunate Debra kept all the boats in good working shape, with plenty of oil to mix and gasoline stored in the boat shack, along with batteries that were being trickle-charged using the solar panels.

"Get in," Will said.

Josh climbed gingerly into the docked boat, stumbling a bit as the craft shifted in the water under him.

"Relax," Will said.

Josh gave him a pursed smile as if to say, *"I would if I could,"* and continued fumbling his way to the seat in the center.

Will untied the anchor rope and tossed it into the boat, then climbed in. He set up the small trolling motor in the back, connecting it to a reserve battery. The trolling motor looked like a long, skinny paddle with propellers at one end and a small hand-held motor on the other. It was battery-powered, which meant it was slower than the main outboard motor. But it was also quiet, especially when the propellers were under water. The purpose of a trolling motor wasn't to go fast, it was simply to go while making as few waves and as little noise as possible.

Will put his rifle on the floor and sat down on the bench at the back. He flicked the switch and the trolling motor powered up with a slow whine. When Will dipped the propellers into the water, the whine became a quiet hum that vibrated through the thin fiberglass of the boat. They heard and felt it because they were connected to it.

Will pressed his radio's PTT. "Can you hear us?"

"Not a peep," Danny said through his earbud.

"All right, we're heading out."

"*Vaya con dios.* And tell Josh to relax. I can see the kid through the ACOG, and he looks like he's about to shit a brick. Or a dozen."

Will looked over at Lara, watching him from the beach. She hadn't moved from the spot where he had left her a few minutes ago. She waved tentatively, and he waved back.

"I'll see you when I see you," Will said. "Watch Lara for me."

"Okay, but Carly's already a handful. I'm not sure I can add another hot babe to my harem. But I'll give it a shot. What are friends for?"

Will maneuvered the Carver from the pier, then turned completely around and aimed it west, away from the marina and the house.

They hadn't gone very far before Josh glanced back at him. "Is this the fastest this thing can go?"

"It's a trolling motor, Josh. It's not meant to go fast. It's meant to go quietly."

"Yeah, but this is it?"

"This is it. What's on your mind?"

He hesitated, then said, "It seems awfully slow, that's all."

"You got somewhere else to be?"

"Nah, not really," Josh said, and turned back around.

Will's earbud clicked and he heard Danny's voice again: "Hey, old-timer, you left your turn signal blinking."

Will smiled.

He looked at the wide-open lake in front of him and for a moment allowed himself to enjoy the picturesque surroundings. There was a slight breeze, but not enough to rock the Carver. Pelicans flew overhead. A big striped fish showed itself a few meters to his right, only to dive back into the water a second later. If Will closed his eyes, he could almost believe there was absolutely nothing wrong with the world.

AFTER A WHILe, Will decided they had gone out far enough and began angling the Carver back toward land. He could see Route 27 in the distance, flat and empty. The inlet connecting the lake to the marina was also visible.

"I didn't think we would ever turn back around," Josh said.

"You play a lot of videogames, Josh?"

"Yeah, how'd you know?"

"Just a lucky guess."

They traveled for another long stretch, the trolling motor doing its job, barely creating any ripples in their wake. Will eyed the inlet entrance in the distance, though that wasn't his destination. The inlet was too close to the house, easily visible, especially from the house's second floor. He would have preferred to do the work under the cover of night, the way he was trained, but darkness had ceased to be his friend months ago.

Adapt or perish.

Will heard them before he saw the sun glinting off their roofs. They were moving fast down Route 27, which ran parallel to the shoreline.

He reached back and flicked off the trolling motor and said, "Down, Josh."

Josh looked back, confused. Will lowered himself to the bottom of the boat, making himself small. Josh got the hint and almost leaped to the floor of the Carver as the trucks flashed by on the road.

Will counted one, two…*three.*

They were moving fast. Too fast.

Fifty miles per hour. At least.

He took it as a good sign when none of the vehicles slowed down, because that would have meant they had spotted the boat adrift in the lake to their left. All three vehicles eventually slowed down before turning into the yard of the two-story house.

Will heard his right ear click, and Danny said, "You see that?"

"Yeah," Will said.

"I counted three from a distance."

"Three. All trucks."

"Did you see how many per?"

"No, too far."

"Where are you now? I can't see you through the binoculars."

"Southwest from your position. About 1,500 meters from the mouth of the inlet, 500 meters from the shoreline."

After a moment, Danny said, "Ah, there you are. A tiny, unremarkable speck. Is Josh still there? I can't tell if that's another person in the boat with you or a pelican."

Will smiled. "He's here."

Josh, who had picked himself back up from the floor of the boat, glanced back anxiously. "Is something wrong?"

"Relax," Will said. "We're almost there. No one's seen us yet."

"Yet," Josh said, flashing Will a nervous smile.

"Stay low, just in case."

Josh got into an uncomfortable-looking crouch next to the seat. Will wanted to tell him to relax again, but that probably wasn't going to help. It was liable to just wind the kid up even more.

Will turned the trolling motor back on and eased the Carver forward. He angled the boat southeast, making a beeline for the shore. The ridgelines of the lake were raised high enough that if he could get the boat there without being seen, they could then travel south, closer to the marina, without being spotted the rest of the way.

Eventually, as Will turned the Carver to run parallel to the raised shoreline, he heard the unmistakable sound of outboard motors roaring to life from the house. Not one, but two. Will remembered seeing a boathouse across the inlet and two boats inside when they had arrived at the marina yesterday.

His right ear clicked, and he heard Danny's voice: "I must be hearing things. Are those motors?"

"Those are motors," Will said.

"What do you see?"

"Squat."

From his angle, Will couldn't see anything but the water in front of him and the raised shore immediately to his right, the wall of dirt and high, swaying grass less than a meter from the Carver's starboard.

"Okay, I see them," Danny said.

"What's going on?" Josh said, looking back at him again.

Will shook his head. "What do you see?" he said into his throat mic.

"Two boats," Danny said. "They're moving down the inlet. Fast. They should be coming into your view…now."

Two fast-moving boats blasted out of the mouth of the inlet, multiple silhouetted figures in each craft. Just as fast as they appeared, they were gone, shooting up the lake toward Song Island as fast as their powerful outboard motors could carry them. At that rate, it wouldn't be long before they arrived at the island.

"What do you see?" Will asked.

"I don't know yet," Danny said. "They're still too far away. All I see right now are stick figures on two boats coming toward us at full speed. I don't think they're following boating regulations, either. Someone call the Game Wardens."

Then Danny went quiet.

Will waited, listening to the loud screams of motors racing across the lake.

After a while, Will said, "Danny, what do you see?"

"Four to a boat," Danny said. "They're definitely coming full bore. Looks like you were right to skirt the house on your approach. I told Carly you weren't nearly as dumb as you look."

"Good to know. What are you dealing with?"

"Assault rifles. A pair of AK-47s. M4s. The good stuff."

"Can you take them?"

Will saw Josh looking worriedly back at him again, but the kid somehow managed to restrain himself from blurting something out.

"Do fish shit in the lake?" Danny asked.

"I don't know," Will said, playing along. "Do they?"

"Last time I checked. Anyway, you should get to the marina as fast as you can. It should be relatively clear at the moment. Or clearish."

"We're there now."

Will aimed the Carver toward shore until the starboard side was pressing up against the dirt and flicking at branches sticking out of the ground. Will let the boat drift for a bit before they finally reached an area where he could drive the boat up onto the muddy beach.

He instantly cut the trolling motor and hopped out of the boat, landing in a hard patch of dirt and mud, with the anchor rope in hand. He saw a tree trunk nearby and wrapped the rope around it, then pulled it tight before dragging the boat farther up until he was satisfied it wouldn't drift off on its own.

Josh stumbled out after him, cradling the Remington like it was a precious baby. Will resisted the urge to tell the kid to sling the weapon instead. The last thing he needed was for Josh to trip and accidentally blow his own head off. Besides alerting whoever was still at the house, it was going to cost him valuable manpower. Neither one of those things were acceptable losses at the moment.

Will poked his head above the ridgeline and took inventory of their position. The tall, uncut grass was both an ally and a hindrance. On the one hand, it kept him hidden, but it was hard to see through it. Fortunately, the sun had baked enough of the grass that it kept the height reasonably in check.

He was surprised to see they weren't that far from the marina. Will could make out the high-raised roof of the gazebo about 200 meters to his left. And slightly behind that was the back of the garage. He did the math in his head and concluded that carrying the supplies over the distance was going to involve a lot of sweating and grunting, but it was doable.

Will was still gauging the distances when he heard gunfire from Song Island. He knew instantly it was Danny's M4A1. He waited to hear return fire, but instead he heard the M4A1 fire a second, then a third time.

Josh crouched silently next to Will near the ridge as they heard loud returning fire from multiple weapons. There was a volley, shattering the calm air in a loud, reckless downpour. Then Will heard three more shots. The M4A1 again. Calm and unhurried shots.

Then there was silence.

"What happened?" Josh asked, looking over at Will.

"I don't know," Will said.

His right ear clicked and he heard Danny's voice: "They're heading back to you now, tails stuck firmly between what are no doubt very wobbly legs. Looked like weekend warriors to me. I might have clipped two. Definitely got one of the motors."

"Good work."

"Have Tower, will snipe. Good luck."

"Roger that." Will looked over at Josh. "They're fine. You ready?"

Josh shook his head, but said, "Yeah, okay, sure."

"You'll do fine. Let's go."

He climbed up first and raced across the flat ground, thankful there were enough tall blades of grass to hide most of him, if not the top of his head. He stopped ten meters from the ridge and looked back and saw Josh following, hunkered down in that same uncomfortable pose he'd had back in the boat. At least he was low to the ground, and anyone looking from the house probably couldn't see him.

Probably.

Will gave him a nod, hoping to give the kid some confidence. It might have worked, or it might not have. It was hard to read anything beyond Josh's absolutely terrified expression.

Will looked forward and started moving through the grass again. He could see the garage and gazebo coming up, still a good 280 meters away, give or take.

But then something else caught his eye, and he went into a crouch. Josh, not anticipating the sudden stop, bumped into him from behind. Will grunted a bit as the barrel of the Remington Josh was carrying dug into his back.

"Sorry," Josh said.

"You're doing good," Will lied.

He looked across the field and to his left at a Jeep buried in the ditch along the road. It was parked about forty-five meters from the marina, give or take, and Will could make out three figures crouched next to the vehicle, looking in the direction of the house. Two of them had binoculars.

Will slipped the M4A1 from his shoulder. He lifted the rifle and looked through the sight. He was still too far to make out any details, but there was enough for him to know two of the three were men, the third a woman. The biggest one was up front, and Will set the red dot against the side of the man's head.

It was a fine target. Big and juicy and oblivious, just the way he liked it.

CHAPTER 32

LARA

LARA HID AMONG the trees that lined the beach, one hand holding the radio, the other gripping the Benelli shotgun so tightly that her fingers were white. She watched them coming from a distance. They had been coming for a while, the sounds of their loud boat motors reaching the island well before they did.

They looked like toy boats from this distance, and she could see men clinging to the sides—the starboard, or port, or whatever they called those sections. The boats were moving so fast they looked like they were about to take off into the sky at any second, the front half literally hopping over the surface of the lake only to smash back down again, then going right back up. She was amazed none of the men had been tossed into the water already.

She heard Will and Danny talking back and forth on the radio. She fought the urge to butt in, reminding herself this was what they did—they cracked jokes in the middle of a crisis. She had learned a long time ago to give them their space.

Finally, the boats were close enough Lara could actually see with the naked eye that the men onboard were coming fully armed. That was when she heard the crack of Danny's rifle, and the boats seemed to slow down all of a sudden.

Danny shot again, then a third time.

Warning shots. If Danny wanted to hit them, he would have hit them. Of course, the men on the boats didn't know that, and they started firing back. Or firing, anyway, but not necessarily back at anything, especially Danny, high up in the Tower across the island.

Will would never waste bullets like that.

Then Danny shot again, and one of the men in the first boat doubled over and grabbed his leg. A second shot, and another man doubled over in the second boat. Danny's third and final shot sent black smoke billowing from the first boat's motor.

Damn, he's good.

She knew full well Danny could have killed everyone on the boats if he wanted to, especially with that new scope mounted on his rifle. These men were getting a second chance, and the irony was that they didn't even know it. But they did get the hint that their attack wasn't going well and began to turn around.

Lara watched the boats heading back to the marina.

Well, at least they're not total idiots.

CARLY WAS WAITING for her at the hotel patio. They had both changed clothes at least three times today.

Clearing out the bones from the hotel grounds was easier than cleaning out the hotel hallways. Not all of the ghouls had been exposed to sunlight, and they were forced to wear respirator masks that Sarah brought out from a supply closet just to keep down what little breakfast they had managed earlier in the morning.

Dragging the twisted, pruned, and blackened bodies into the sunlight and watching them turn to fine white mist was the kind of experience Lara didn't think she would ever forget. It was both fascinating and soul-destroying, and she remembered thinking, *This is what the human race has become. Nothing more than dust in the wind.*

Scrubbing the blood and flesh from the hotel hallways and lobby had taken even more effort. By the time they had wiped down the tiles with bleach and scraped the disgusting remains of dead ghouls from the walls, she wasn't sure if she could even smell anymore. They decided to leave all the bullet holes for Will and Danny to deal with later, since the two men were responsible for most of them in the first place.

They hadn't decided what to do with the bones yet. Burying them was one option. The other was to throw them into the lake.

Lara preferred the second option. An ocean of bones sounded better than bones buried in their backyard. Bones in the lake might drift away eventually, whereas burying them would always mean living right next to a graveyard. The human bone, depending on the condition, could last for thousands of years in the ground before it dissolved completely. She wasn't prepared to live with that kind of timetable.

"Eight guys?" Carly said, as Lara climbed up the front steps of the patio.

Carly handed her a bottle of cold water. Lara took it gratefully and drained it. She hadn't realized how much she missed something as simple as a cold bottle of water until she finally tasted it again yesterday.

"Eight guys, give or take," Lara said.

"Are we sure they weren't just survivors responding to the message? Like us?"

"They didn't look very friendly."

"I guess it doesn't matter now. How many did Danny kill?"

"He wounded two."

"Lucky them. He's a pretty good shot."

Lara sniffed the air. The smell of fried fish was strong and thankfully horned in on the still-lingering acidic aroma of evaporated dead ghouls still clinging to parts of the island. "Are you frying fish?"

"I'm trying to overwhelm this morning's disgusting smell in fish, yeah. Al left plenty in the freezer."

"No wonder I smell something burning."

Carly made a face. "It's all part of my master plan to convince Sarah to take over the kitchen."

"Are you two getting along now?"

"I guess," Carly said, and shrugged. "I should probably apologize for trying to devour her soul last night."

"I'm sure she'd appreciate it."

"Yeah, well, I'm still working up the courage to actually do it."

Lara looked around. "Have you seen Sienna?"

"No. Why?"

"I haven't seen her since this morning."

Sienna had helped with the bones that morning. She had worked quietly, almost robotically, and the half-dozen times Lara had stopped to check on her, the other woman had simply smiled back mutely. Once, she had nodded, but that was it.

"She'll come around," Carly said. "We all have to adapt. What's that saying you and Will came up with? Adapt or perish?"

"Yeah."

"That should be our motto from now on. We should make a big banner and hang it right there—" she made an imaginary banner with her hands "—in big bold letters: 'Adapt Or Perish.'"

"Capital letters?"

"Of course. Gotta be capital letters. Maybe different colors, too."

"Now you're just being silly."

Carly laughed. "We could get the girls to help."

They headed back into the hotel lobby. The AC was turned off, and it was hot again, even with the windows and doors open all night and this morning to help cleanse the place of the smell of dead ghouls.

Sarah told them the AC was never something Karen and the others kept on at all times. All the luxuries they were shown yesterday were to impress them. Them, and everyone who had come before them, whose clothes, weapons, and other personal belongings were buried in the unfinished sections of the hotel and in the Tower's basement. Even Kyle's games weren't something he was normally allowed.

No wonder the kid could barely pull himself away from them. He only got to play them when one of us showed up.

"God, I miss air conditioning," Carly sighed. "When did Will say we can turn it back on?"

"When he's sure there's enough juice in the generators to power the island."

"That doesn't sound very hopeful."

"It's not."

"Ugh."

They were halfway across the lobby when Lara's radio squawked and Will's voice came through: "Heads up. I just made contact with Blaine."

"He's still alive?" Danny asked through the radio. "Talk about beating the odds. That guy just refuses to die."

Lara keyed her radio. "Will, what about Sandra?"

"That's a negative on Sandra," Will said. "They made it into

Beaumont while we were there yesterday morning, but they got into trouble with some collaborators. Probably the same ones Gaby shot. Sandra died while they were trying to escape."

"Tell him I'm sorry," Lara said.

She had never met the woman, but she had been looking forward to it ever since meeting Blaine. She remembered when they had found him, lying half-dead on the road with three bullets in him. He was still alive *because* of Sandra. Any woman special enough to make a man give death the middle finger had to be pretty special.

Now she would never know, and a part of her felt sad at the missed opportunity.

"I will," Will said.

"Back to the matter at hand," Danny said. "Are we making silver bullets tonight or what?"

"We'll be heading back as soon as we can," Will answered. "If all goes well, we'll be back within the hour."

"See you then," Lara said into the radio.

"Later, alligator," Danny added.

IT WAS 2:12 P.M. and the sun had settled into the sky when Lara went back to the Tower, where Danny and Sarah were putting up a new door to replace the one the ghouls had obliterated the night before. It was essentially two doors from two unused rooms in the hotel, nailed together into one big slab of thick, dull wood. It was overly heavy (which was the point) and took a lot of grunting and grimacing to carry over from the hotel where Danny had put it together.

Lara helped them raise the door into position, then held it in place with Sarah while Danny grabbed an electric drill and fired large screws through makeshift hinges into the concrete wall one by one. By the time he was done, they were out of breath and their clothes were drenched in sweat—again.

The door didn't look like much. In fact, it was ugly, but it could open and close and was locked in place with an iron bar that fell into a latch drilled into the side. More importantly, it would not fall as easily as the last door. They had gotten by last night thanks to the Tower's rather oddball design, but Will and Danny wanted to make sure the ghouls never made it *inside* next time.

When they were done, Lara said, "Anyone seen Sienna?"

"She was in the hotel the last time I saw her," Sarah said. "About thirty minutes ago."

"What was she doing?"

"I don't know. She was in her room."

"She'll come around," Danny said.

Lara left the two of them to finish up. She headed up to the second floor, where they kept a couple of crates with emergency supplies, including one with clothes. She grabbed a new undershirt and pulled it on, tossing her drenched one into a waste basket. Laundry had become unnecessary with clothes lying around everywhere, though she thought they might have to revisit that now that they were going to be staying on the island.

The idea made her smile. The island could become a home, something they hadn't had since Harold Campbell's facility. This was what she had wanted when they had set off in search of Song Island months ago. Even after the horrors of last night, the very real possibility of having a place to call home made her almost giddy.

She traveled up to the third floor, where Gaby stood watch along the windows. The teenager was moving from window to window, peering through binoculars for about thirty seconds at each spot. She looked the part of a sentry, and Lara understood why Will was so high on her.

"Anything?" Lara asked.

"Nothing," Gaby said.

"Can you see Will and Josh?"

"If by 'see' you mean noticed two tiny specks in the distance that could very well be Will and Josh—or bird poop—then yes."

Lara walked to the south window, picked up another pair of binoculars hanging from a hook, and looked through them. She could see the shoreline in the distance, along with the house and marina. The gazebo, the tallest structure in the marina, blinked under the glare of sunlight. She made out the garage, with its aluminum rooftop, and the black asphalt parking lot with the dozen or so vehicles inside, including the Ridgeline and Frontier they had parked there yesterday.

"They went into the garage about ten minutes ago," Gaby said. "I haven't seen them come out yet."

"Is Blaine with them?"

"I can't be sure, but I saw five dots moving around out there at one point."

"Anything from the house?"

"I saw a couple of them walking around the front yard. Do we know who they are yet?"

"Not yet."

Lara turned the binoculars back to the house, picking up a lone figure moving around the yard. Or at least, it looked like a figure. It could have been a balloon blowing in the breeze for all she knew.

"They finished with the door down there?" Gaby asked.

"Pretty much."

"Heavy?"

"Like a stone."

"I guess that's good. Hard to break down stone."

"That's the idea." Lara looked back at the marina and focused on the garage, but she couldn't see anything inside, outside, or around the building. "They're taking their time," she said softly.

"Maybe you can contact Will on the radio."

Lara unclipped the radio from her hip and pressed the transmit lever. "Will, can you hear me?"

She didn't get a response right away.

Five seconds went by, then ten.

She was about to press the transmit lever again when the radio squawked and she heard Will's voice, whispering, "Yes."

Why is he whispering?

"Is everything all right over there?" she asked.

"Everything's fine," he said, still whispering. "We're about to head back now."

"Be careful."

"Will do."

Gaby glanced over. "I guess he's okay."

"I guess so."

She fought the urge to call him back.

No. He said he was fine. Why would he lie?

But why was he whispering?

SHE WAS HALFWAY back to the hotel when she heard the gunshot. It came from the hotel lobby, and she knew instantly it was a handgun.

Glock. That's a Glock.

Lara dashed across the grounds, aiming for the side door. She had become more acquainted with the hotel's layout since this morning, while coming and going with arms full of ghoul bones.

As she ran, Lara unsnapped the radio from her hip and shouted into it: "Danny!"

"I heard," Danny said calmly.

"Hurry!"

She was halfway to the side door when she heard another shot.

Lara threw open the door and darted inside. Her sneakers slipped on the freshly bleached tiles, but she regained her footing and raced through the short hallway until she reached Hallway A that led into the lobby.

As she made the turn, she heard two more gunshots, very close together.

"Danny!" she shouted into the radio again.

"I'm coming," Danny said calmly.

She heard voices as soon as she neared the lobby. Female voices, almost conversational, which seemed impossible. She saw a pair of bullet casings scattered on the floor in front of her and almost slipped on one as she burst into the large sun-drenched room, drawing her sidearm at the same time.

The smell of frying fish from the kitchen overwhelmed her senses, but they were quickly overcome by the sight in front of her.

Lara was prepared for the worst, but she was still shocked to see Carly sitting on the floor with her back against one of the lobby walls, bleeding badly from the left side of her neck. Blood trickled out between the fingers of Carly's left hand, which she had pressed over the wound to stem the flow. There was a Glock on the floor nearby, just out of Carly's reach, and her eyes were focused on the woman standing in front of her, about five feet away.

Sienna.

She was holding a Glock aimed at Carly's head and her back was to Lara, but as soon as she heard Lara's footsteps, Sienna looked over her shoulder. Lara didn't recognize the young woman from last night. The same one who had screamed when Jake was swallowed up by the flood of ghouls in the hallway, who had cried into her shoulder all night as they sat on the third floor of the Tower and waited out the horror.

This woman looked different. She looked angry, and Lara heard all that fury come out in a scream that paralyzed her: "Stay back!"

Lara slid to a stop ten yards away, and her gun snapped up and she took aim at Sienna's head, and in a split-second she wondered if she could do it, if she could pull the trigger.

Jack Sunday. That man in the church. I've killed before. I can do it again.

Please, please, let me be able to do it again, for Carly's sake…

But maybe she didn't have to. Maybe she could talk her way out of this. Maybe…

"Sienna, what are you doing?"

Lara's eyes moved briefly back to Carly. She looked awful, all the color drained from her face. There was a thin trail of blood stretching from the kitchen to the wall where Carly sat. Carly looked back at her, and her friend blinked, as if she didn't quite have the strength to keep her eyes open, and was fighting, fighting just to do that much.

She's losing too much blood…

"This is the natural order of things," Sienna was saying. She sounded rational, calm again. "Jake's dead. Everyone's dead."

"Not everyone," Lara said.

"Everyone that matters to me!" Sienna shouted.

"Don't, please…"

She wasn't sure if she was actually pleading. Maybe she was. All she could focus on was Carly, bleeding on the floor, and how heavy the Glock felt in her hands, how strong the trigger was against her forefinger, and the smell of fish, not just frying, but burning now…

"You can't stop me," Sienna said, smiling. "I—"

She never finished. There was a loud gunshot from across the lobby and Sienna's forehead exploded and blood (*brain*) splattered the floor. Sienna's body crumpled like used skin and bones, the Glock that was gripped so tightly, so insistently in her hand mere seconds ago fell and clattered against the floor even before what was left of Sienna's head did.

Lara looked over at Danny, entering the hotel lobby through the front doors, holstering his Glock. He ran the rest of the way, reaching Carly about the same time Lara did.

"Dammit, babe, I told you not to get shot," he said, crouching next to her.

Carly looked at him and somehow managed to smile. “My hero,” she said, her voice soft, barely a whisper.

“What happened?” Lara asked. “Why did she shoot you?”

“I don’t know.” Carly shook her head. She looked even paler up close. How was that possible? “I was in the kitchen, doing woman’s work—”

Danny grinned.

“—and I saw her come in. She looked at me and then shot me without saying anything. God, she shot me. I’ve never been shot before. It hurts.”

“I wouldn’t know, I’ve never been shot,” Danny said.

“I hate you,” Carly said, then closed her eyes.

Danny glanced at Lara and she saw all the boyish charm disappear, replaced by worry and love and, for the very first time, very real fear.

“She’s lost a lot of blood, but it’s not a fatal wound,” Lara said. “She’ll be fine.”

Please let me be right. Just this one time, God, let me be right. You owe me that much, don’t you?

“Help me get her to the table,” Lara said. “And keep her upright.”

Danny lifted Carly in his arms as if she weighed nothing, with her head resting against his chest instead of dangling off his arms, and carried her to a big table in the middle of the lobby. Lara walked alongside him, her hand pressed against Carly’s neck, the blood squirting through her fingers. She pressed harder and Carly moaned but didn’t open her eyes. They had to step over Sienna’s still body, twisted awkwardly on the floor.

“She’s really bleeding,” Danny said.

“She’ll be fine…”

Sarah arrived in the lobby when they were halfway to the table. She saw Sienna, then Carly, and ran over. “My God, what happened?”

“Sienna shot Carly, then I shot Sienna,” Danny said, like he was discussing the weather.

“Oh my God…” Sarah said, putting one hand over her mouth.

“Where are the girls?” Lara asked Sarah.

She didn’t want Vera to see this. Didn’t want Elise or Sarah’s daughter, Jenny, to see it, either. But especially not Vera. The girl had already been through too much; Lara didn't think she could—or *should*—see this, too.

"They're at the Tower," Sarah said. "I sent them to stay with Gaby when I heard the gunshots."

"Good, good," Lara said, grateful for that, at least. "Clear the table, Sarah."

Sarah ran over to the table ahead of them and with two hands brushed the surface clean except for the linen sheet on top. Danny sat Carly down gently, with all the care and love in the world, but kept her head leaning against his chest, upright.

"Sarah, I need your hand," Lara said. Sarah rushed over to her side and Lara showed her where to put her hand against Carly's neck. "Here. Push hard. Don't worry, you're not going to hurt her. Whatever you do, don't let her lay her head down on the table."

Sarah gave her a reluctant look but pushed on the wound the way Lara showed her. Lara stepped back. She looked down at her hands, covered in blood up to the wrists.

She's lost so much blood…

She looked back at Sarah. "Keep it pressed as hard as you can, understand?"

Sarah nodded, but she looked queasy, especially every time blood squirted through her fingers and peppered the thick tabletop.

"I'll be back," Lara said, and jogged off quickly.

She ran back to her room, trying to wipe the blood off on her pant legs, but only succeeded in bloodying them up, too.

The black bag was in the corner of her room, on the armchair where she had put it this morning. She snatched it up and hurried back out, rushing down the hallway. For some reason, it seemed to take her much longer to get back to the lobby.

Somewhere between her room and the lobby, she heard the soft, echoing reports of gunfire.

For an instant, her mind conjured up images of Sienna, risen from the dead, engaging in a gun battle with Danny. But no, the gunfire wasn't from the lobby. It was distant, reaching them from across the lake.

She hurried into the lobby, where Sarah and Danny were still standing over Carly. Lara was afraid Carly wasn't breathing, but as she drew near, she saw Carly's chest rising and falling slightly, if labored.

"Will," Lara said, catching Danny's eyes.

"He can take care of himself," Danny said. "I need you to focus on Carly right now, okay?"

She nodded, and willed herself to ignore the soft, echoing *pop-pop-pop* of assault rifles firing in the background.

Instead, she pried back Sarah's hand to reveal the bullet wound in Carly's neck.

The bullet had gone clean through, taking a big chunk of muscle with it. It was an ugly sight, made impossibly uglier by the sheer amount of blood loss. But it wasn't fatal, and the carotid artery was intact. All she had to do was stop the bleeding, and Carly would live.

Let me be right. Please, let me be right.

She became aware of Danny's voice, as if from a distance: "Lara? How is it? How does it look? Tell me she's going to live. Please, tell me she's going to live."

"She's going to live," Lara said.

Please, God, I beg you, don't make a liar out of me.

In the background, far away, the *pop-pop-pop* of assault rifles continued unabated…

CHAPTER 33

JOSH

PROS AND CONS: What were they?

Pros: He was with Will. That was a hell of a pro right there. When there were men with guns around, he preferred to have the guy next to him be an ex-Army Ranger. Then Blaine had showed up. Josh hadn't really gotten to know Blaine except for that brief time in Lancing, but he seemed like a good enough guy. And he was huge. As someone who had spent his fair share of time learning to escape bullies, Josh appreciated size in his friends. Blaine probably didn't consider him a friend yet, but they were on the same side, so it was all good.

Cons: They were on enemy soil. Or close to it, anyway. Behind enemy lines would probably be the better description. Either way, there were people across the inlet with guns who probably wouldn't like it if they discovered Josh and the others were in the marina. Never mind that they were only taking what was theirs. The men in the house had tried to attack the island and gotten repelled. They were probably not very happy about that, either.

Conclusion: As long as they stayed invisible, got what they came for, and left with no one the wiser, Josh had nothing to complain about. But that was the trick, wasn't it?

Josh was hiding on the right side of the garage at the end of the marina, next to a side door. He watched Will and the others jog over to him, keeping low and sticking to the four-foot-tall grass. He wouldn't have spotted them if he didn't already know they were there.

Just to be sure, Josh leaned out from behind the garage and looked toward the house. There was no one on the roof or looking out from any of the second-floor windows, but he was alarmed at the sight of two men walking around the front yard of the house. By the time Will, Blaine, and the other two reached him, the two men had walked from one end of the yard to the other and were now moving up the driveway toward the road.

Where the hell are they going?

Then Will was next to him. "Josh, you remember Blaine."

"Hey," Josh said, and exchanged a nod with Blaine.

"Hey, kid," Blaine said. He indicated a short woman with dark hair and a guy in his twenties next to him. "This is Maddie and Bobby."

"Hey, Josh," the woman named Maddie said.

Bobby just nodded at him.

"Bobby doesn't speak," Maddie said.

"Oh," Josh said.

Wait, where's Sandra?

The last time he had seen Blaine, he was going in search of Sandra, the woman who had helped Josh and Gaby escape from Folger. He remembered Sandra—tall, beautiful, and hell on wheels when the chips were down. They would never have escaped Folger without her help. He also remembered how desperate Blaine had been to find her.

So where was Sandra now?

Something about Blaine's face told him this was probably not the right time to ask. Blaine could be intimidating. No, Blaine *was* intimidating. Josh decided to save his questions for later. Maybe he could find out about Sandra through Will.

Will spared him the awkwardness by tapping his shoulder. Josh moved back and Will took his place. He leaned out and scanned the house for a moment.

Blaine moved to stand alongside Will. "Trouble?"

"Probably not," Will said. He looked back at the rest of them. "The priority is the equipment inside the garage. We'll come back for your stuff the first chance we get. For now, we have enough to work with."

"I hate the idea of leaving all that silver and guns out there,"

Blaine said.

"Can't be helped."

Will walked over to the garage door and opened it soundlessly, then slipped inside. They followed him in, Josh falling in behind Maddie, with Bobby coming up behind him.

The garage was mostly dark, with a few spots brightened by shafts of light poking in through holes in the walls and roof. Will flicked on his flashlight, using a wide beam to illuminate where the sunlight couldn't reach. Over the months, rainwater had seeped inside, leaving patches of wetness under their shoes as they walked across. The whole room had that aroma of abandonment and occasional flooding. It made Josh gag a bit.

The old boat they had seen parked inside when they had first arrived was still there, parked across half of the available space. The crates of food, water, and supplies were also where they had left them, stacked along one corner of the warehouse.

"There," Will said, pointing at the crates. "We'll take what we can in the first run and come back for the rest later."

The equipment Will and Danny had been using to melt down and recast bullets was stored in separate crates at the very bottom of the stack. They had to remove the others—filled with food, water, and clothes—first before they could get to the ones they were after.

Josh had to admit, Will had the right idea. Anyone raiding the garage would definitely poach the food, water, and clothing first, and when they finally got to the bottom and saw the smelting pot, the pairs of rubber mallets, the dies and presses, the urge would be to leave them. Who wanted to drag around someone else's heavy tools? Josh hadn't even known what these things were when he had first seen them. But then again, he hadn't known people even made their own bullets.

The silverware and jewelry were all bundled up in another crate, also at the very bottom of the pile. More things that your average raider wouldn't have bothered with, not with jewelry and gold and other precious metals waiting to be taken in almost every house and building you went into. There was a time when Josh was awestruck by the sight of gold lying around. He got over that real quick. Gold was less valuable these days than a bag of chips that hadn't yet gone stale. Plus, bags of chips didn't weigh a ton.

Will pointed at the crate with the silver. "Maddie and Bobby, that's yours. We'll follow you with the tools. Head northwest for 200 meters and the boat should be below the ridgeline."

Maddie and Bobby slung their weapons and picked up the crate. Josh could tell it was heavy by the way they were straining. The crate was stuffed with so much silverware that, in the old world, it would probably have fetched a few hundred thousand. Now, though, it was only useful to people who understood its significance.

Maddie and Bobby grunted as they moved the crate over to the door one foot at a time. Josh hurried past them and opened the side door for them.

"Thanks, kid," Maddie said.

Josh nodded back. "We'll be right behind you."

"Take your time," she grinned back.

Maddie stuck her head out the door first before leading Bobby out. Josh watched them lug the heavy crate between them through the grass, keeping as low as possible. It wasn't easy, but they seemed to be managing well enough.

He closed the door and hurried back over to the other side of the garage, where Will and Blaine were re-stacking the crates into an orderly pile against the wall, having removed the one they needed.

Will picked up a small box of canned food and gave it to Josh. "This should come in handy."

"Any fruit in there?"

"Pretty much all of them."

"Awesome. Gaby'll be happy."

"I know, that's why you're taking it back to the island."

Josh grinned appreciatively at him.

Will positioned himself on one side of a large crate opposite Blaine. "How are the bullet holes?" he asked Blaine.

"Duct tape's working miracles," Blaine said. "But I could use a refill on those painkillers."

"Lara can take care of that. Ready?"

"Try not to drop it on my foot."

"No promises."

They clutched their respective ends of the crate and lifted with a loud grunt. Blaine's face almost instantly turned pale and sweat popped all along his forehead. Josh thought the big man was going to faint, but somehow he didn't.

"Lead the way, Josh," Will said, his voice straining a bit.

Josh nodded and hurried across the garage again, this time with the box of canned fruits in his arms. He skated around the big, dilapidated boat and was almost at the side door when he heard shuffling noises outside.

Josh froze, and so did Will and Blaine behind him.

Footsteps moved outside the front doors. He looked down, where the doors met the ground, and saw a pair of shadows moving on the other side. The voices of two men drifted through the small opening, and Josh knew instantly it was the same two he had spotted at the house, walking toward the road.

"What did you see?" a man asked.

"Something," a second man said.

"You brought me here because you saw 'something'?" The first man laughed. "You're a fucking idiot."

"I saw something," the second man insisted.

"Birds. Geeses. Whatever those things are that's flying around the lake."

"Pelicans. And the plural for goose is geese. Not geeses, idiot."

"Whatever," the first man said dismissively. "Let's go back. It's too fucking hot out here to be going for a walk."

"I told you, I saw something."

Josh watched the shadows moving up the length of the garage doors, toward…

The side door.

Josh looked back and was surprised to see Will and Blaine had already put the crate down. Blaine drew his sidearm while Will put a finger to his lips, signaling for Josh to be silent, and moved forward, passing Josh, until he was almost pressed up against the wall next to the side door. He beckoned, and Josh, realizing he was just standing in the middle of the garage like an idiot, hurried over to stand next to him. Josh forgot he still had the box of canned fruits in his arms until Will gave him an amused look.

Josh returned a nervous smile and watched Will reach down and soundlessly slip a knife out of a sheath fastened to his left hip. Josh had seen that knife before, but he had never seen Will use it. The handle of the knife looked more like a cross that had been sanded down, like something a holy person would fashion, which surprised him because Will wasn't even remotely religious.

Blaine moved toward the back of the garage, slipping behind an old metal shelf filled with plastic oil cartons and rusted metal tools. The crate sat in the middle of the garage.

Shouldn't we move that?

Josh listened to the footsteps looping around the garage, shuffling lazily from the front to the side. The men were still talking, oblivious to how much noise they were making.

"There's nothing here," the second man was saying.

"I told you, I saw something," the first man insisted.

"From the house?"

"Yeah."

"You have bionic eyes or something? I can barely make out this building from over there."

"You should get your eyes checked."

"You know any good optometrists?"

The first man chuckled, and the second man joined in.

They sounded like good friends. Or at least, that's what he envisioned buddies sounding like. He and Matt were kind of like that once they got to know each other.

Josh jumped slightly when he heard Will whisper, "Yes," next to him.

Josh glanced over, expecting Will to be looking at him, but Will's eyes were fixed on the door two feet to his left, and he was talking to himself. No, not to himself. He remembered the earbud dangling from Will's right ear and the plastic mic wrapped around his throat.

"Hi, I can't take your call right now, I'm in the middle of a life-and-death situation."

Josh sucked in his breath when he heard the doorknob on the side door move as someone touched it on the other side. He didn't have to look around Will's body to see the doorknob moving because the big, metallic motor hanging from the back of the boat in front of him was reflecting the side door like a mirror. Sunlight splashed across the image, giving Josh an even better view of what was happening next to him.

Josh might have stopped breathing entirely when the door opened and one of the men stepped cautiously inside. Josh heard the crunch of a boot on the soft ground and saw the man's reflection as he looked down, and Josh knew he had seen the tracks they had left behind when they first entered the garage.

The man might have opened his mouth to say something, but

then Will was suddenly moving and Josh saw Will's form spinning away from the wall and something sharp flickering, and he heard what might have been a gurgling noise, like someone spitting water.

Josh stumbled away from the wall, barely holding on to the box of canned fruits. He looked back toward the door and saw a man with long, dirty blond hair and a beard falling through the door, into the garage, his hands grabbing frantically at his neck, where blood was spurting out in thick, shiny streams. There was so much blood. Josh didn't know how one man could bleed so much, so fast.

The man stumbled to his knees a few feet inside the warehouse, but Will was already moving past him, slipping outside.

Josh heard a voice say loudly, "What—" But the man never got the chance to finish. Instead, there was the sound of a body falling to the ground.

And then silence.

A second later, Will reappeared in the open doorway with the cross-knife, its double-edged blade slicked with blood. He looked calm, like he had just been out for a Sunday stroll and had somehow ended up with a bloody knife in his possession.

"Everything's fine," Will said, not to Josh or Blaine, but into the throat mic.

Who is he talking to?

Will walked inside, crouched, and wiped the knife clean on the jeans of the man with long blond hair. "We're about to head back now," he said into the mic. Will picked the man up by the legs and dragged him over to a corner, where he deposited the body in the darkness. "Will do."

Will walked back to the crate and nodded at Blaine. "You good?"

"Yeah," Blaine said, grimacing a bit. He didn't really look "good" at all, and if anything had gotten paler. "Let's get this show on the road."

They picked up the crate and started toward the door again.

Josh hurried out after them, almost tripping over the second man, who was lying on his back outside the door, his hands positioned out at his sides like he was enjoying the sun splashed across his face. He had short black hair and there was a big, old scar along his left cheek that was mostly hidden by a full beard. There was a big, red bloody circle over his chest, where his heart was. The man's face looked almost pleasant, like dying hadn't hurt at all.

"Josh," a voice called patiently.

Josh looked up at Will and Blaine, waiting for him about ten feet away.

"Come on," Will said. "We're burning daylight. Let's get those canned fruits to Gaby."

Gaby!

Her name snapped him back to the present, and Josh nodded and walked around the dead man. There was no blood on the ground, so at least he didn't get any on his shoes.

They moved steadily across the tall grass, back toward the ridge-line and the boat waiting on the beach. Josh caught sight of Maddie and Bobby, crouching across the field, waiting for them with weapons in their hands.

Josh glanced up briefly at the sun. Still high. Still plenty of time.

There was no one else around them, and they moved at an almost leisurely pace. They were halfway to Maddie and Bobby when Will and Blaine suddenly stopped and looked back at him. No, not at him, but *past* him. Josh turned around and looked back at the marina and saw the sunlight glinting off the hood of a huge, bright red truck barreling into the parking lot. There was a man standing in the back of the truck and there were two more inside, one driving, the other leaning forward, hands on the dashboard, like he was afraid he might go flying through the windshield.

The man in the back of the truck was peering through binoculars, holding them with one hand while clutching the side of the truck with the other to keep from falling off. The man must have spotted them because he lowered his binoculars and began banging on the roof of the truck and pointing right at them.

Oh, shit.

"Josh, go," Will said behind him.

Josh turned and began running. He passed Will and Blaine, who were unslinging their rifles and moving into a crouching position. Josh kept going even as he heard the first sounds of gunfire from the marina and the ground exploded around him, chunks of dirt kicking into the air and what sounded like bees screaming past his head.

Don't look back! Whatever you do, don't look back!

Then he heard more gunfire, this time closer. Will and Blaine, returning fire. He didn't know for sure. That would mean looking back as he ran. That would slow him down, and he didn't want to be slowed down at the moment.

So he ran, clutching the box of canned fruit in his arms. It had really gotten much, much heavier since he had taken it from Will. The equally heavy Remington shotgun thumped freely against his back as he ran, and it hurt. He thought about swiveling the shotgun around, but that was impossible with the box in his arms.

Can't drop the canned fruit. Gaby will love it. She loves this stuff.

He had to get back on the boat. He had to go back to the island. Back to Gaby. That was the most important thing.

Maddie and Bobby were in front of him, frantically waving him over, their faces twisted into that odd expression people have when they're trying to hurry other people along. He wondered what they thought he was doing.

Gee, thanks for the advice, guys. I couldn't have done it without you.

He almost cracked a smile until he felt a sudden stinging sensation in his left leg. He stopped running before he even knew what was happening, and the box of canned fruit went flying out of his hands and he was tumbling forward like an acrobat. He saw the ground coming up and quickly tucked in his shoulders, the way he remembered seeing action heroes do in movies.

The Remington smashed into his back as he landed on the ground and rolled over, tall grass slapping at his face and arms. He thought his spine might have snapped on impact, paralyzing him. But no, he was still in one piece. Mostly, anyway. He found that he could still roll over and sit up in the grass, even as dirt splashed into the air and he heard the sound of more screaming bees trying to sting him.

Get away, bees!

Someone screamed his name. "Josh!"

He wasn't sure if it was Will or someone else. It sounded like it was coming from in front of him, and when Josh looked up he saw Maddie running back toward him, Bobby moving alongside her and firing into the distance with his rifle.

Maddie grabbed him and pulled him up with one jerk of her hands. She was deceptively strong for such a little thing. He looked down and saw that he was bleeding and there was a neat hole in the front leg of his cargo pants.

Oh, shit, I've been shot.

He was surprised it didn't really hurt all that much. But maybe that was the adrenaline pumping through him. Maybe it would hurt later. Probably.

"Hold on to me!" Maddie shouted at him.

She didn't have to shout. He was right next to her. Maybe she felt like she needed to shout because of all the gunfire around them. There was a lot of it, especially with Bobby standing right next to them firing one shot at a time. Josh wondered why he wasn't firing the whole magazine. Wasn't that what people did in action movies? Unleash the whole magazine on the enemy?

He heard another voice behind him. "How is he?"

"He's shot in his left leg," Maddie said.

"Go go go," the voice said.

Josh felt another pair of hands grab him around the waist, and he was suddenly lifted up like he didn't weigh anything and dragged forward. Bobby, moving on his right, holding him around the waist. They were running. Or a combination of walking and running, with Bobby holding him on one side and Maddie on the other. They were making pretty good time, the ridgeline coming up fast.

Finally, his curiosity got the better of him, and Josh risked a glance backward.

Will and Blaine were jogging casually after them, the big, heavy crate swinging dangerously back and forth between them. Well, Will looked casual. Blaine's face was locked in a tight, pained grimace. Josh wondered if Blaine had gotten shot, too.

Back at the marina behind them, the red truck had driven into the grass until it couldn't go any farther. The man in the back of the truck was firing at them with a rifle. A second truck had shown up and three men were climbing out of it. They were armed and were running, joining others already rushing through the tall grassy field.

Bullets zipped through the air and burrowed into the ground to their left and right, but Josh guessed they had a good 100 yards on their pursuers, and it was hard to hit a moving target from that distance. Or at least, that's what he had heard.

Will and Blaine suddenly stopped and turned, then began firing back. One of the men chasing them stumbled on something and pitched forward into the grass and didn't get back up.

The others kept coming.

I guess 100 yards isn't that great of a distance to shoot someone after all.

Will and Blaine snatched up the crate once again and started running after them. Josh was certain the heavy crate was going to spill its contents all over the grass at any moment. Then what would they do? Pick them back up, probably.

Amazingly, it never happened, but Josh couldn't help but hold his breath anyway every time the crate swung forward, then swung back, then forward again....

Then Will and Blaine were suddenly running next to them, and Josh didn't know how they had caught up with Bobby and Maddie so effortlessly.

"Look on the bright side," Will shouted at him, "now there'll be a reason for Gaby to spend all that time in your room!"

Josh grinned back at him. He had a point there.

"Hold on!" Maddie shouted.

Josh looked forward just in time to see Bobby and Maddie, with him hoisted like a child between them, jumping down the ridge and landing on the wet ground below. Mud splashed, some spraying the boat. The crate full of silverware was already inside, in front of the steering wheel in the middle.

Josh heard heavy grunting and looked over to see Blaine landing beside him. The big man instantly turned around and grabbed his end of the crate—dangling dangerously off the ridge above them—just as Will hopped down after him. The crate came down with Will, slamming into the ground and sending thick patches of mud in every direction.

"Go go go!" Will shouted.

Maddie and Bobby stumbled forward, dragging Josh between them. They practically threw him into the boat, and he grabbed at the silverware crate as it came rushing up at him. He managed to get his hands on the edge at the last second, then somehow got himself turned around to sit down on it. The crate was hard and uncomfortable, but it was better than sitting on the floor.

Josh unslung the Remington shotgun and looked up at the ridgeline, expecting the men with guns to show up at any second. He thought he could hear them coming by the heavy trembling around him, but after a second he realized it was just his body shaking uncontrollably.

Will and Blaine almost tossed their crate into the boat, and it slammed home behind the steering wheel. The boat dipped dangerously under the sudden added weight, but the Carver somehow stayed afloat anyway.

Thank God.

He was still looking at the ridge, the shotgun at the ready, when he heard the big outboard motor fire up in the back, the sound so much louder than the trolling motor that it made him jump.

Then they were moving away from the beach, thanks to Blaine, who pushed off with a paddle. He was grunting with the effort of moving five people in a boat designed for four, not counting the two unwieldy crates between them.

They were twenty yards from the beach when Josh saw the first man appear along the ridgeline. He was short and stocky and wearing an old, faded Houston Astros cap with the five-sided star on the brim. The man was holding one of those AK-47 assault rifles that even a gun virgin like Josh recognized instantly.

Josh saw the man and the man saw Josh at almost the exact same time. The man lifted the AK-47 to aim and Josh pulled the trigger on the Remington purely on instinct. He thought he was prepared for the recoil, unlike last night, but the blast still knocked him loose from the crate. Even as he fell backward, Josh saw bright red wetness spread across the man's chest before he vanished from the ridgeline as if by magic.

Josh continued falling, slamming into the floor of the boat when he heard someone—probably Will—yelling, "Covering fire!"

Gunfire exploded around him, so much louder than before. Something small and hot fell on Josh's head. It burned his scalp, but before he could get out a scream and swat at it, the spent bullet casing fell away and clattered to the boat floor next to him. Other casings were falling around him and on the crates, the *click-clack* sounds almost melodic.

Josh struggled back up into a sitting position while Maddie and Bobby shot back at the beach. The boat was moving fast now, the speed of the outboard motor making Josh completely forget about the snail-like pace of the trolling motor. Despite the burden they were putting on it, the boat was moving smoothly, with Will driving in the center, keeping just low enough to not get his head shot off.

By the time Blaine, Bobby, and Maddie stopped shooting in order to reload, the boat was almost a full 150 yards away from the beach. Far enough that when the men chasing them finally got the courage to stand up and shoot back, their bullets harmlessly sank into the water around them, the *plop-plop-plop* of bullets disappearing into the lake.

"Look," Maddie said, pointing toward the mouth of the inlet.

A boat appeared out of the inlet, hitting the main lake at full speed. It immediately turned left, pointing in their direction. It slowed down real fast when Blaine, Maddie, and Bobby all unleashed a torrent of bullets in its direction. Josh saw men on the boat diving to the floor and the boat seemed to jerk off-target.

There was a loud *ping!* and Josh jumped. One of the bullets fired from the ridgeline had actually hit the side of the boat, kept going, and almost put a hole in Josh's right sneaker, missing only by a few inches. The bullet punched through the bottom of the boat and water sprang inside.

But the bullet had surprised him, and Josh stood up without thinking, ignoring the electric pain in his left leg.

Oh, there's the pain.

He looked down and saw a thin trickle of blood from the earlier gunshot. He was still marveling at how little blood there was when he heard one of those bees screaming right next to his ear. He looked up and saw one of the men on the ridgeline taking careful aim with a rifle. Josh couldn't tell if it was an AK-47, but he did remember that AK-47s were notoriously bad for long-distance shooting. Or at least, that's what he had once read on the Internet.

Josh grinned at the man.

Give it up. You're not going to hit anything, dude.

Behind him, he heard Will's voice: "Josh, sit the fuck down!"

Josh looked back at Will and smiled. "He's too far away to hit anything," he said, when he heard that loud, screaming bee coming back for another pass, but this time instead of zipping by harmlessly, the bee actually *hit him in the side of the head.*

Josh stumbled across the boat, suddenly very light-headed. His legs didn't seem to be doing what he was telling them *(Stop, you idiots, stop!)*, which was annoying.

He caught sight of Will, who for some reason looked like he was moving sideways, lunging at him from across the boat, his hand reaching out, screaming, "Josh!"

Oh, shit.

Josh reached out for Will's hand—but missed it by inches.

Then he was falling, falling, and there was water all around him and he knew he was in the lake.

And he was sinking.

Sinking…

CHAPTER 34

WILL

GOOD NEWS AND bad news. The good news is, we got what we went back to the marina for. The bad news? I got the kid shot up and now he's at the bottom of the lake.

Of course, he didn't say that when Lara and Sarah came out to greet them at the pier. It didn't take Lara very long to notice Josh wasn't in the boat with them, though, but he thought her face looked pale even before that.

"What happened?" he asked.

"Sienna shot Carly," Lara said.

"Is she okay?"

"She lost a lot of blood. I won't know for sure until tomorrow, and maybe not even then."

"Where's Sienna now?"

"Danny shot her." She looked at the boat, at the faces that were climbing out, and looked back at him. "Where's Josh?"

"He got shot and fell into the water. I had to leave him behind."

"You left him behind?"

He couldn't tell if she sounded incredulous, angry, or confused. Maybe none of the above. Possibly all three. "I had to leave him behind," Will said again.

Lara looked at him blankly. He could tell she was still traumatized by what had happened with Carly and Sienna and wasn't quite sure how to process what he had just told her about Josh.

After a while, she nodded. "Let me tell Gaby."

Will nodded back. He felt relief and guilt, but mostly relief. He had lost men in combat before, but it wasn't the same as losing the kid. Josh wasn't a soldier, and Will hadn't expected him to contribute much in a firefight. But he was a decent enough kid, and that counted for something when there were so few decent people still around these days.

They transferred the crates from the boat to the pier, then carried them back to the hotel. Will and Blaine took the tools to one of the unfinished rooms in the back where there were plenty of walls without windows for ventilation. Maddie and Bobby followed inside with the crate of silver.

Danny showed up later to shake hands with Blaine. "Good to see you back in one piece."

"Good to be in one piece," Blaine said. "Mostly, anyway."

"Sorry about Sandra."

"Yeah," Blaine said. "I hope Carly's okay."

"She will be," Danny said, with absolute certainty.

"This is Maddie and Bobby. Bobby doesn't speak."

"Yeah? I bet the girls go crazy for that," Danny said.

Bobby grinned sheepishly back at him.

"Don't worry, I make up for his lack of speaking," Maddie said.

"Welcome to Song Island," Danny said. "Unlike the previous landlords, we're not going to feed you to the ghouls."

Maddie, Blaine, and Bobby exchanged a confused look.

Blaine looked over at Will. "Wanna fill us in? There seems to be an awful lot of shooting around this place. I didn't quite expect that."

"I know you thought you came here to get away from the fighting," Will said, "but it's more complicated than that."

"How complicated?" Maddie asked.

WILL AND DANNY gave them a brief, half-assed tour of the island, filling them in on Karen, Tom, and Marcus along the way. They told them about the previous night, about the ghouls, and ended the tour at the power station, where they stood in front of the concrete wall they had built over the door of the shack.

"Are you serious?" Blaine said. "They're in there *right now?*"

"Yeah," Will nodded.

"How many?" Maddie asked.

"A few hundred," Danny said. "Give or take. If by 'take' you mean possibly lots of hundreds. Or thousands."

"The only way to tell is to go in there," Will said.

"We're taking volunteers," Danny added.

"Where do they come from?" Maddie asked.

"We think there's a tunnel under there," Will said. "We don't know where it goes, or how far it runs under the lake. Eventually, we'll have to figure it out, but that's for later."

"But the island is safe, though? They can't swim over?"

"We don't think so. As far as we know, this tunnel seems to be their only access to the island."

"As far as you know?" Blaine said doubtfully.

"We can't be sure," Will said. "But as far as we know, yeah."

"So they're stuck in there?" Maddie asked, exchanging a private look with Bobby.

"That's the going assumption," Will said.

"And you know what happens when you assume," Danny said.

"They've been down there all day?" Blaine asked.

"Since last night, yeah," Will nodded.

"Jesus Christ."

Danny chuckled. "Get to the island, it'll be safe. No more ghouls to worry about. Except for the few thousand already waiting underneath it. Hey, it beats running around out there, right?"

Blaine, Maddie, and Bobby exchanged a look that said they weren't entirely sure about that anymore.

"It's not too late," Will said. "They want the island, but you don't have to be here when they try to take it. If you decide to leave before they come back, we'll give you everything you can carry—food, ammo, weapons, and supplies—and we'll give you a boat and help you get back on land, avoid the people at the house. There are other places to dock that don't involve the marina, and we'll do everything we can to help you move on. No hard feelings."

They listened quietly, not saying a word. He could see their minds reeling, then gathering, then trying to sift through the pros and cons.

"But if you want to stay here," he continued, "you'll have to fight for the privilege. That may sound like a shitty deal, but it's all I have to give you at the moment."

Maddie and Bobby exchanged another private look that didn't involve Blaine.

Then Maddie said, "One question."

"Shoot," Will said.

"Who the hell are those guys at the house?"

"Ghoul collaborators," Danny said. "Assholes working with the creatures in exchange for their hides. Like Song Island's previous tenants."

The three of them exchanged another series of quick looks, and he wondered if they believed Danny. The concept of collaborators, human survivors throwing in their lot with the ghouls, was a hard pill to swallow. He might not have believed it himself if he hadn't seen it with his own eyes twice now.

Blaine said to Maddie and Bobby, "If you guys want to go, I'll go with you."

"You were the one who wanted to come here," Maddie said. There was no accusation in her voice, it was just a statement of fact. She even sounded a bit confused by his offer.

"I know, but Sandra's death changed things for me. My priorities have changed." He seemed to struggle with his thoughts. "Let's face it, it's no better out there. Hell, it's probably worse. Here, at least, there's a chance at something approaching a normal life for you and Bobby. So we'll have to fight for it. So what else is new?"

Maddie glanced over at Bobby again. The mute boy nodded and gave her the "OK" sign with his fingers.

"Why the hell not," Maddie said. She looked over at Will. "So, silver bullets?"

SO THEY MADE silver bullets.

A lot of them.

Maddie and Bobby proved to be good workers. Neither one had made bullets before, but Maddie knew her way around a rubber mallet, and Bobby took instructions easily. Blaine wanted to help, but Will sent him to Lara to see to his wounds instead. The gunfight at the marina hadn't done Blaine any favors, even if he insisted otherwise.

Will also decided Danny should go back to the Tower to keep overwatch with the ACOG.

"You think they'll hit us back this quickly?" Danny asked.

"I would," Will said. "They lost a few people back there."

"Man, you're just going around the end of the world making friends, aren't you?"

After Danny left, Sarah and the girls chipped in, bringing more silver from around the island, even raiding the kitchen and closets and racing through all the rooms.

They didn't stop until they had melted all the silver and pounded out as many 5.56x45mm and 9mm bullets and as much buckshot as possible. There was enough ammo from the Tower's basement, collected over months from all the poor souls lured to the island before them, that they ran out of silver long before they ran out of bullets to recast.

At one point, Maddie said, "If I knew I'd be working this hard, I would have stayed behind in Beaumont."

Bobby, drenched in sweat next to her, grunted his agreement.

The acrid fumes of smelting metal, iron, and brass, mixed with silver, lingered over the island long after they were done. Will didn't let them stop until they were literally walking around in puddles of their own perspiration.

"Load up with what you can carry," he told them. "Silver and regular ammo. The rest goes into the Tower."

"And these will actually work?" Maddie said, holding up one of the silver bullets.

"They work," Will said. "Shotguns for close quarters. You'll need to keep all three types of ammo with you at all times. There are two more Benellis in the Tower. When in doubt, load the silver. They'll kill a man just as easily as a ghoul."

Bobby tapped Maddie's shoulder excitedly and nodded at Will.

"He wants to know if you have any more assault vests," Maddie translated.

BEFORE SIX IN the evening, he took away the M4s that Maddie, Bobby, and Blaine had arrived with and gave them new ones from the Tower's basement. The new M4s had fully automatic capabilities, which would come in handy in a frenzied firefight. Amazingly, the more they searched the Tower's basement, the more useful things they found, including assault vests and more radios.

Later, they ate in the lobby, loading up on calories and proteins from fish and MREs. Blaine had rejoined them, looking better. Or at least, not walking with nearly the same noticeable limp as earlier. Bobby took to the MREs, and that got a chuckle out of Will and Danny, who had never really seen anyone who wasn't ex-military take a liking to the bagged food the U.S. military was known for. The MREs were designed for maximum efficiency, supplying nutrients and over a thousand calories per bag. The taste, on the other hand, left a lot to be desired.

Afterward, he got them set up along the beach, where he expected to need them to repel the coming attack on the island. If they were lucky, the people at the house would wait for tomorrow, and all of the preparation would be a waste of time.

If they were lucky.

Yeah, right.

Lara was waiting for him on the hotel patio, arms folded across her chest as if she was cold. "You really think they're going to attack?"

"I would."

"But they've already lost too many men. Why would they attack again so soon?"

"Who says that's all they have? There could be more coming."

She frowned. "That's a terrible thought."

"Hope for the best, prepare for the worst. Isn't that our motto?"

She gave him a wry smile. "You'll have to fight with Carly about that. She likes the 'Adapt or Perish' one better."

"How's she doing?"

"She's stable. That's the good news."

"The bad news?"

"She lost a lot of blood, Will."

Will nodded. He put his arms around her, and she sighed into his chest. "She'll be fine," Will whispered. "She's a tough kid. Remember before The Purge? It was just Carly and her sister, and she got through it. She's a fighter."

"I know," Lara whispered back, though he wasn't sure if she actually believed it.

WILL WALKED WITH Lara back to the Tower. Carly had been moved to the second floor and was lying unconscious on a bed Danny had brought over from the hotel. They had dumped Tom's old cot and most of Tom's stuff out the window. Lara had set up an IV drip, and there were fresh flowers in vases. The place reminded him of a patient recovery room, minus the suffocating, cold, and sterile feel of a hospital.

Carly looked like she was in a deep slumber, which wasn't far from the truth. Lara had given her enough sedatives that he wondered if even an attack on the island would wake her up. Probably not. He had seen wounded soldiers sleeping through firefights before.

"How's Vera taking it?" Will asked.

"She's worried. She wouldn't leave Carly's side after it happened. Danny and I had to practically drag her out. Elise is taking care of her."

"Elise?"

"Yes, Elise." Lara smiled. "They're more than sisters now, you know. They pick each other up when the other is down. It's amazing how fast kids adapt."

Will looked out the window. He could see the marina and the house from here. Well, silhouettes of the buildings, anyway. It was quiet, and he couldn't detect any activity across the lake.

He stuck his head out of the window and looked up, and wondered if Gaby was up there looking at the marina, too.

When he pulled his head back in, Lara was watching him. "You should go up there. I talked to her, but it's not the same. I think she needs to hear it from you."

He nodded reluctantly.

GABY WAS AT the south window, looking at the shoreline with binoculars. She stood very quietly, almost relaxed, when he opened the third-floor door and climbed up. She looked over and smiled a bit, though he could tell she had been crying, and her eyes were still slightly red.

He understood why Josh had been so head-over-heels about her. Gaby was a pretty girl. In a lot of ways, she reminded him a bit of Lara. A younger, taller Lara. In a few more years, she would have men tripping over themselves to get her attention. Not that they wouldn't be tripping over themselves already, given the option.

"Anything?" he asked.

"Nothing yet." She walked back to the east window and peered out at the house and marina.

He walked over and stood silently next to her.

Say something, you idiot.

"They kept a boat outside the mouth of the inlet for a few hours after the shoot-out," she said, "but then they pulled it back and I haven't seen them move again since."

Her voice sounded normal, but what did he know? He was never that good at reading women. Even worse at comforting them.

"I'm sorry about Josh," he said.

She didn't say anything for the longest time, or seem to react at all, and Will wondered if she had actually heard him.

After a few excruciating seconds that felt more like minutes (or hours), she said, "I know you did your best to save him. I don't blame you, if that's what you're worried about."

"I know."

"You and Danny always do your best to keep everyone safe. I know that. We all do."

"He was a good kid."

"He was a pretty good guy. Funny thing is, it took the end of the world for me to realize that."

"You guys…" He started to say, but stopped himself. What the hell was he doing? Jesus, he was bad at this. "I'm sorry," he said instead.

"Thanks."

He didn't know what else to say, so Will said nothing. Thankfully, she seemed just as willing to let the rest go unsaid.

There was a fair breeze, and he could feel the coming night despite the heat coating the island like a thick wool blanket. He didn't dread the night. He never did. He anticipated, expected, and prepared. That was how he lived his life, how he had survived The Purge.

"Can anyone learn to shoot?" she asked, finally breaking the silence.

He was surprised by the question. "Anyone can learn to shoot, yeah."

"I mean, shoot like you and Danny. I was watching Danny earlier today, when those two boats came over. He could have hit every single one of them from this Tower, but he didn't. I know that rifle scope he was using helps, but I don't think just anyone can use it, especially on moving targets."

"No, you're right. Danny's the best shooter on the island, by far."

"That's what I figured. Anyways, after Danny shot at them—those warning shots—the people on the boat shot back. They were just shooting at anything, like they didn't know what they were doing. The difference was so obvious. Can anyone learn to shoot like that? Like you and Danny?"

"Anyone can learn to shoot, but not everyone can shoot."

"What's the difference?"

"Have you thought about that man in Beaumont? The one you shot to save Josh? Or the one in the semitrailer. What was his name?"

"Betts."

"Have you thought about them since?"

"Yes."

"How do you feel? Thinking back on those moments?"

"I'm not happy about what I did, if that's what you mean. I did it because there was no other choice."

"Would you do it again, if put in the same situations? Knowing what you know now? How it made you feel afterward?"

"Yes," she said without hesitation. "To save Josh, or to save any one of you guys. I'd do it again."

He nodded. "To answer your question, anyone can learn to shoot. Not everyone has the will to shoot. You did. Twice. The first time wasn't with a gun, but it's the same thing. So yes, you can learn to shoot like Danny and me. We'll teach you when this is over."

"Thanks."

"It won't be easy."

"I know."

"You'll want to quit."

"I won't."

"You'll want to."

"I won't," she said.

They said nothing for a while.

"I'm sorry about Josh," he finally said.

"I don't want to talk about that anymore," she said.

WILL STOOD AT the western cliff, beyond a large swath of untapped forest taking up nearly half the island, looking down at the ten-meter drop from the ridgeline to the water below. He had circled the entire island on foot, making sure there was no other way onto it except through the south side using the beach.

He kicked at a pebble and watched it drop into the water below. Climbing a cliff took skill. Someone had to come up first, then throw ropes down to pull the rest up. He and Danny could do it, given time and cover, but it would be a hell of a stretch for weekend warriors like the ones Danny had sent away earlier.

It was doable, but unlikely.

The beach. They'd have to storm the beach to get onto the island.

He was emerging out of the wall of trees when his earbud clicked, and Danny's voice: "You hear that?"

Danny was back in the Tower with Gaby. They had decided Danny would be on the third floor for the entire night with the ACOG. Not that he could have pried Danny away anyway, with Carly on the floor just below him.

"No, what?" Will said.

"Vehicles. I think they just got more reinforcements."

"How many?"

"Looks like three… No, make that four trucks. It's always gotta be trucks, doesn't it? You gotta love the South. Throw a rock on the road and you're liable to hit a dozen trucks before you get to the first sedan. Yee haw."

Will jogged back to the hotel through the grass. "I'm on my way back."

"Oh, and you won't believe this..."

"More good news?"

"Depends. You like fishing?"

"Not really, no."

"Then not so much good news."

"What're you seeing?"

"They're bringing over more boats."

"How many?"

"I count two. That gives them four that we know of. I put a bullet through one of the boat motors, so maybe three and a half, depending on whether they have a mechanic who knows boats or not."

"Keep an eye on them."

"I was going to go bowling, but okay, just this once."

Will met Blaine as he was coming out of the hotel with MRE bags.

"How're the stitches?" Will asked.

"I'm not bleeding to death, so that's good. Lara gave me some kind of pill cocktail that seems to be doing the job. I've lost all feeling except for my tongue."

Will grinned. "You heard on the radio?"

"Yeah." Blaine fell in next to him as they moved toward the beach. "Four more trucks. Assuming two to a truck, that's eight people. And that's lowballing it. It's probably more like three to a truck, maybe four if you really want to get pessimistic about it."

"Sounds about right."

"All collaborators, too? Why are they converging here? The ones I met in Beaumont didn't have any contact with any of the others. I got the feeling they didn't even know the others existed the whole time I was with them."

Will had considered the question, and he had always come back to the same answer: *Kate.*

"There's a blue-eyed ghoul," Will said. "She's in charge of the blood farms and pretty much everything that happens in Texas as far as I can tell. Maybe Louisiana, too. My guess is, she's the one calling them over here."

She wants me. No, not her. The other *blue-eyed ghoul. She said his name was Mabry...*

Blaine didn't respond right away. Will wondered if the other man thought he was nuts.

But no, that wasn't it. He saw something else in Blaine's eyes. *Recognition.*

"You've seen it," Will said.

Blaine nodded. "A few nights ago, when Sandra and I were hiding in that house you patched me up in. I saw one. Then later, in Beaumont, Maddie told me she saw a blue-eyed ghoul talking to the guy in charge of the collaborators there. She thought it was a woman, but she wasn't sure."

Damn, Kate, you get around, don't you?

"How many collaborators were there? In Beaumont?" Will asked.

"Five. You guys killed one of them, so they were desperate to recruit us."

"You, Sandra, Maddie, and Bobby?"

Blaine nodded.

"So she's bringing them from a lot of places," Will said.

"You talk about this blue-eyed ghoul like you know her. Or it." He shook his head. "Whatever it is now."

"I did. Once upon a time."

"How's that?"

"I slept with her," Will said.

AT 7:14 P.M., with nightfall an hour away and sunset spraying the horizon in a picturesque red and orange glow, he expected them to attack.

But they didn't.

He waited in the relative darkness of the woods, watching the beach and the piers extending out into the lake in front of him, calm under solar-powered LED lampposts flickering on around the island. He couldn't see Blaine, who was somewhere to his left, or Maddie, farther up the beach to his right. Bobby was somewhere between the hotel and the Tower, watching their backs in case they had to retreat.

Danny and Gaby had the Tower, with Lara and the girls on the second floor of the structure, watching over Carly. Sarah was on the first floor, manning the door. Everyone had a radio.

Finally, he heard what he had been expecting for the last half hour, coming from land. It was a low rumbling sound.

His right ear clicked, and Danny's voice: "Hear that?"

"I hear it," Will said.

"Are those engines?" Blaine asked through the radio.

"Outboard motors," Maddie said.

Just as quickly as they heard them, the motors stopped.

For a while, anyway.

Then they heard the noise again, starting up, loud despite the distance. Then it went away again.

It went on like that for a while. One minute, two—five.

"They're testing out the motors," Maddie said. "They must be making sure the new boats they brought over are working."

He glanced down at his watch. "It'll be dark soon. Everyone stay frosty."

"Maybe they got tired of playing with their motors and decided to take the night off," Danny said.

"Captain Optimism," Will smirked.

THE SOLAR-POWERED lampposts did their jobs around them while darkness fell over the calm lake surface. There was no fanfare, just the exchange of day for night. Such a simple transition, but so monumental these days.

Will hadn't moved from his spot in the last hour, the M4A1 on the ground next to him, the Remington slung over his back. With the blanketing darkness, he could make out lights from the shoreline with the naked eye. Straining his ears a bit, he heard what sounded like the hum of generators.

By nine, there was still no attack, but Will didn't move from his position.

Neither did Blaine or Maddie, or Bobby behind them. Danny and Gaby didn't wander very far from the four windows on the Tower's third floor, either.

No one was going anywhere tonight.

Not by a long shot.

MIDNIGHT CAME AND went, and Will was starting to think the collaborators weren't going to attack after all. He didn't move from his position, but he did sit down and dig out a bag of MRE and laid the M4A1 on the ground next to him.

"I don't think they're coming, Kemosabe," Danny said in his right ear.

"We'll wait until the hour of the wolf," Will said.

"What's that?" Maddie asked.

"Three in the morning," Danny said. "Otherwise known as the time when anyone with half a brain should be asleep, but the wicked are up thinking about their evil deeds. Or more affectionately known as the best time to attack a sleeping enemy because they're at their lowest point of the day."

"This MRE is good," Blaine said through the radio.

"What are you eating?" Maddie asked.

"Turkey and mashed potatoes. Or it's supposed to be turkey and mashed potatoes. Looks like something someone threw up, but it actually tastes like turkey and mashed potatoes. Sorta."

"Welcome to the glamorous world of professional soldiering," Danny said. "Don't forget to grab some T-shirts at the gift shop on your way out."

Will heard movement behind him and was about to reach for his rifle when he got a whiff of her scent and relaxed. She pushed her way through the branches and sat down next to him, laying a Benelli shotgun on the ground.

"Thought you wouldn't mind some company," she said quietly.

"I never mind your company."

She smiled. "Wow. That's the most romantic thing you've ever said to me. And that's...kind of sad."

He chuckled. "Sorry about that."

"Eh, I didn't fall in love with you for your ability to romance me off my feet. It was more the whole shooting undead creatures thing."

"Have gun, will shoot."

Her face grew a bit more serious. "How did the talk with Gaby go?"

"As could be expected. She's a tough girl."

"She really liked him. Josh. You want to talk about it?"

"About what?"

"What happened with Josh."

"He got shot and fell off the boat. That's about it."

"Will…"

"Lara, I'm not sure what you want me to say. I'm sorry about the kid. I liked him. But there was nothing I could do."

She watched him intently, trying to read his face. "All right," she said after a while. "You can talk to me about anything. Anytime."

"I know. That's why I love you."

She climbed up on his lap and sought out his mouth in the semidarkness of the woods. Will tossed the MRE bag away and wrapped his arms around her. After a moment, she pulled slightly back and looked down at him as if trying to memorize every inch of his face. She looked beautiful in the moonlight, and he found himself wanting to become lost in the crystal blue of her eyes.

"You take me to the best places," she smiled.

"Nothing but the best for my gal."

"Now that's the kind of sweet nothings guaranteed to get a girl's pants off."

She kissed him again and put her hands on his chest before trailing down. She started to unbuckle his belt.

"Lara," he managed to say, pulling away from her for just a moment, "I want this. God, I want this. But this is probably not the time or place—"

"Oh, shut up," she said. "This is exactly the right time and place. We could die in a few hours. Or tomorrow. After Josh and Carly… I want to make the most of every minute and every hour with you, Will. Don't deny me that, please?"

He nodded. "Okay."

She kissed him again, and he slipped his hands under the warm cotton fabric of her shirt. She sighed when he cupped her breasts. She wasn't wearing a bra, and she felt soft against his rough palms, her nipples hardening instantly. It never ceased to amaze him how sensitive she was there.

She had already unbuckled his belt and was slipping her hand into his pants when he heard the soft, familiar sound in the distance.

It came almost lazily, wafting through the night air, like something out of a dream. He wasn't even sure how he managed to hear it with his chest pumping and other parts of him enflamed with Lara's mouth and breasts and heated body pressed up against him.

He didn't think Lara had heard it because she was about to pull his pants off when he put his hands on her shoulders and stopped her. "Wait."

Lara was out of breath and flustered. "Are you kidding me?"

"No, I hear something."

She lifted her head and listened. "I don't hear anything."

"You don't hear that?"

"No." She gave him a wry look. "Is this your way of saying you'd rather not have sex with me on the beach?"

"No. God, no."

"Good answer."

She climbed off him and he scanned the sky. There wasn't enough light to really see anything beyond the halos of the lampposts around the island.

He pressed his radio's PTT. "Danny, do you hear that?"

"I hear it," Danny said through his right ear.

"Hear what?" Lara asked.

"I don't hear anything," Blaine said through the radio.

"Me neither," Maddie added.

Will snatched up his rifle and went into a crouch. He looked southeast, toward the marina.

There.

He could hear it again, getting louder. The gradual but familiar *whup-whup* that was such a constant during his tours of duty in Afghanistan. It was so common that the only days he had felt something was wrong, that something wasn't quite right with the world, was when he *didn't* hear it.

Whup-whup-whup-whup.

Lara was frantically shoving her shirt back into her pants next to him. "Will, I don't hear anything."

"There," he said, pointing.

She squinted her eyes at the dark skies. "What is it?"

"You don't see it?"

"No, I—" She stopped, and he saw her mouth open slightly. "Holy shit."

"You see it?" Will said into his mic.

"I see it," Blaine said.

"Fuck me," Maddie whispered.

The helicopter came in low, gliding at a smooth, unhurried pace. It had a spotlight in front, under its cockpit, and the light skipped along the water's surface and flashed across the beach, lighting up the piers and the boats tied to them.

"Danny, do you have a shot?" Will said into his throat mic.

"I have a shot," Danny said.

"What do you see?"

"Squat. Spotlight's doing its job. I can't even make out if it's military or civilian."

"Any guns on the side? Armaments?"

"None. But like I said, it's like staring into the sun. I can put some holes in it, but forget about details."

"Hold your shot."

"Ah, you're no fun."

"They could be friendlies."

"Now who's Captain Optimism?"

They watched the helicopter keep going, swooping high above them, running its light over the woods, before raking the side of the Tower. Then it was gone, passing over the island's eastern section.

For a moment, Will thought it would keep going, but then the helicopter began to turn, coming back for a second pass…

CHAPTER 35

JOSH

PROS AND CONS: What were they?

Pros: He was alive!

Cons: He had no idea where he was or why he wasn't dead. His body hurt. His arms hurt. His left leg was numb, but not so much he didn't notice the sudden surge of electricity shooting from it every time he tried to move even a little bit. His head felt heavy, and each time he breathed, he thought it was going to explode.

Conclusion: *I'm alive!*

He had woken up in a bedroom, lying on a small bed under sheets covered in Transformers characters. It took him a while before he realized the bed was in the shape of a racing car, and it was at least half a foot too short for him. His legs were draped over the end, which didn't help the pain in his left leg any.

Josh pulled his legs back until he was almost curled on the bed. It was cold. Very cold. Which didn't make sense because it was hot outside, rays of sunlight flitting in through white blinds over the window to his right.

Josh pulled his head off the fluffy pillow and tried to sit up. It hurt, so he decided the smart thing to do was lie back down to catch his breath.

I'm alive!

He didn't know how that was possible. He remembered standing up (*That was stupid*), then getting shot (*Served me right for doing something so stupid during a gun battle)*, then falling. He remembered Will reaching for him, but Will must not have been fast enough, because soon Josh was in the water. Josh had never been a good swimmer, so he didn't fool himself into thinking he had swum back to the island on his own and just didn't remember it.

So how did he get here? Wherever "here" was?

Wet clothes clung to his body. Someone had slashed open his left pant leg and wrapped bandages around where he had been shot. That was nice of them. He saw blood on the bandages, but not as much as he thought being shot would have produced.

Josh tried to sit up again. Slowly, this time, without any sudden movements. He managed to stay upright and looked around him. Transformers posters on the walls. Toys scattered about the floor. Transformers action figures. Fluffy dinosaurs. A plastic baseball bat and a small football designed for a kid's hands.

There was a sudden spark from his temple, and Josh lifted his hand to touch the wound. He felt gauze tape instead. Jesus. He remembered getting shot in the head. Okay, not really *in* the head, but close. It was just a crease. Still, it hurt like a bastard, so he stopped touching it.

He went completely still when he heard the door across the room open. A lone figure entered and stood in the doorway, but there was too much shadow and Josh couldn't make out a face or very many details. The figure looked in at him, as if trying to figure him out. Josh stared back, unsure about what to do.

He was stuck here. In this room. This house. He could barely walk, much less run. And where was he going to go? Plus, he had to keep reminding himself that someone had saved him from the lake, so it didn't make sense for them to hurt him now. Unless, of course, they had saved him only because they intended to do something unimaginable to him. He had seen plenty of movies like that.

The figure walked over to the window and flipped the blinds all the way open. Josh saw the outline of a woman. She was looking out at a group of men gathered in the front yard of the house. The view outside looked familiar, but Josh couldn't quite place it. There had to be two, maybe three dozen men out there, milling around a half-dozen trucks. The *click-clack-snap* of weapons being loaded, even though he couldn't quite tell what they were arming themselves with from his angle.

"Thirty men," the woman said, looking over at him. "In case you were wondering. There are thirty men out there, waiting to kill your friends."

The voice sounded familiar. Josh tried to focus on the face, half-hidden in the shadows.

Karen.

He was in the two-story house, the one across from the marina. In one of the rooms along the first floor. The house looked different from the inside; it was darker, more cramped, and less inviting. Even with sunlight flooding through the window, it was too dark in here.

"You're alive," he said. "How is that possible?"

Karen gave him an amused look. "The tunnel underneath the island comes out on the cove. They were going to run a rail system to ferry supplies and vacationers back and forth, like a nature drive underneath the lake. You should see some of the blueprints. They were going to turn Song Island into a real attraction for the rich and spoiled. Not so much now."

So Will was right after all. The tunnel underneath the power station really did run all the way back to shore, and that was how the ghouls got on the island last night. He wondered how many of them were there now, hiding underneath the lake, waiting for their chance to come up again.

Gaby. Gaby's still on the island...

"Josh, right?" Karen said. "I thought you looked familiar."

"You saved me?"

"You sound surprised."

You tried to kill me last night.

"A little," he said instead.

"Information is power. End of the world, post-end of the world. Still the same. Information is still king."

"Information about what?"

"The island. More specifically, the people currently inhabiting it. The new ones that just showed up. Everything."

"I don't know anything."

"Of course you don't," she said, with that same amused expression that told him she was two, three steps ahead of him every time he opened his mouth. "Your girlfriend. What's her name. Gaby?"

"What about her?" He didn't like the way Karen said Gaby's name.

"I'll let her live," Karen said.

Gaby…

"I don't understand," Josh said.

"The island, Josh. It's mine. I want it back. It's been good to me, and I don't like the idea of losing it. Call me a sore loser. Do you see those guys out there, the thirty men with assault rifles?"

"You're going to attack the island again?"

"Again? No." She almost laughed. "The first time wasn't my idea. A couple of idiots thought they could just ride their boats over and Will would just let them land on the beach. That didn't work out too well. I've convinced them to try it my way this time. The smarter way. It's what I do well. I solve problems, Josh."

Gaby's still on the island…

"It's going to cost me half those guys out there," Karen continued. "Maybe more. But hey, you can't make omelettes without breaking eggs." She looked back outside at the men standing around the yard. "It's going to work, too. The question is, when it does work, is Gaby going to be one of the people I have to kill in order to retake the island? Or one of the people I hand over to the creatures after it's all over?"

"No," he blurted out, instantly regretting it.

"So tell me what I need to know."

I can't…

"And save Gaby's life."

Gaby…

"You love her, don't you?"

"Yes," he answered quickly.

"You don't think she wants to live?"

"Of course she wants to live."

"So why are you hesitating? You have to actually think about saving her life?"

"What about me?"

"What about you?"

"If I tell you, and you spare Gaby, what happens to me?"

"I don't care about you. You and Gaby both. You're just kids. Will and Danny are the ones I'm worried about. They're the ones *she* wants."

"She?"

"The rest?" Karen continued. "Neither one of us could care less about what happens to them. I just want the island back, and she just wants the soldiers. As for you and Gaby?" She shrugged indifferently. "You could stay on the island with us, or go on your merry way and see how long you last out there. I really don't care. And neither does she. One or two more won't make a whole lot of difference to them. They have bigger fish to fry, and they apparently need—want—Will and Danny for that."

He looked past her, at the men milling outside.

Thirty heavily armed men…

That was a lot. Will and Danny were soldiers. Great soldiers, from what he had seen. But could they really fight thirty heavily armed men? That was a lot to ask of them. Even with Blaine and his two friends there. That was what, five people total?

Thirty against five…

He liked Will and Danny. He liked Carly, Lara, even the girls. But he liked Gaby more. No, he didn't like Gaby, he *loved* her. He had known her for most of his life. Worshipped her from across the street. And now, after all this time, she felt the same way about him. It was more than he could have hoped for, and it was real. It was tangible. She had proved it last night when they made love.

Thirty against five…

Who were Will and Danny and the others, anyway? He only knew them for a few days. It wasn't like he grew up with them, the way he grew up with Gaby. He liked them, but he didn't *love* them, the way he loved Gaby.

I have to protect Gaby…

SHE ASKED HIM what happened to Tom.

"Will killed him," Josh said. "That night."

She nodded. He wasn't sure if he detected sadness or just acceptance. Maybe indifference. It was hard to read Karen, especially since she stood next to the window and was somehow still mostly hidden in shadows.

She asked about Marcus.

"Danny killed him. The same night."

Again, the slight nod that he couldn't figure out.

Then she asked him about Sarah, about Berg, about the others.

He told her what he knew.

Then about the shack at the power station, the one connected to the tunnel with the ghouls inside. He told her about the concrete wall Will and Danny had put over the door.

Then, to his surprise, she smiled and said, "Ghouls? Will calls them ghouls?"

"Yes."

"Why?"

"I don't know. I guess they just looked like ghouls to him."

"It's not a bad description, actually. I should probably start calling them that, too. Just not to their faces." She smiled, almost as if she expected him to return it. When he didn't, she continued. "Who is this Blaine guy?"

"I don't really know. He's just some guy we met in Lancing, Texas. Then he showed up here later."

"And the two with him?"

"Maddie and Bobby."

"Are they soldiers, too?"

"They didn't look like soldiers. The guy is a mute."

"What does that mean?"

"He doesn't talk."

"Doesn't talk or can't talk?"

"I don't know for sure. Maddie just said he doesn't talk."

Karen nodded. "What about the women? Carly and Lara. How good are they with weapons?"

"They can shoot."

"Anyone can shoot," Karen said impatiently, like he was trying to pull one over her. "The question is, how *good* are they with weapons?"

He flashed back to last night, standing side by side with Carly as she calmly defended the Tower with a shotgun. He knew Lara had killed before. That man in the church back in Lancing, for one.

"They're good with weapons," he said.

"So that's seven."

"I guess, yeah."

"But it'll probably just be the five defending the beach. Lara and Carly will most likely be back in the Tower with the kids. Speaking of the Tower…Who is up there? The one shooting this afternoon?"

"Danny."

"What does he have on that rifle? Some kind of high-magnification scope?"

"I don't know. Will called it an ACOG."

"What the hell is that?"

"I don't know. Something Tom had in the basement. It lets him shoot farther and straighter."

"Tom had a lot of things in that basement, most of which he didn't know how to use." She waved a dismissive hand. "So they have a sniper. Danny. Four at the beach, because Will knows that's the only place for boats to land. He'll commit everyone there. It's the smart thing to do. The obvious thing to do."

I should stop now…

"What did you come back for?" she asked. "What was in the garage in the marina that was so important?"

I shouldn't tell her…

"Tools," he said.

"Tools?" She gave him a sharp, suspicious look. "Tools for what?"

"For making bullets."

"Bullets? There are plenty of bullets on the island, underneath the Tower."

Don't tell her…

"Silver bullets," he said.

Shit.

"Silver bullets?" she repeated, narrowing her eyes at him, trying to decide if he was lying to her again.

"Yes."

"Why does he need silver bullets?"

"The ghouls. Silver bullets kill them."

Her eyes widened and her suspicion grew. "How do you know this?"

"I've seen it. Will discovered it months ago, when all of this started. He and Danny have been making silver bullets whenever they could ever since. They left the tools in the garage when we arrived because there was no room on the boat."

Karen seemed to mull it over. She didn't know about the silver, that much was obvious. Josh wondered if that affected how she looked at the ghouls. Would she still work for them if she knew she could actually *kill* them?

"Smart guys," Karen said finally. "Too smart for a couple of jarheads."

Jarheads are Marines. Will and Danny are soldiers. Even I know that.

But he didn't say it out loud. He was too busy trying to justify himself to the traitorous feelings washing over him like some sick, disgusting bile rising from the very pit of his stomach and forcing its way out of his mouth, onto his tongue. The taste was hideous and made him want to gag.

He watched Karen standing beside the window. She was looking off into a corner, and he could almost see her mind working, crunching the numbers. What was that Sarah had said about Karen? She was a politician; she bartered and made deals to save her own skin because that was who she was. She was the one who had struck the deal with the ghouls—with the blue-eyed ghoul in particular—to turn the island into a honey trap.

"All right," Karen said after a while.

"So what happens now?"

"Now I take back my island."

"What about me, I mean?"

"You stay here. I might have more questions for you if this doesn't go well. It will," she added quickly, "but you can never be too sure. I always like to have a backup plan. Like the tunnel at the power station. I was going to wait for the blue-eyed creature—the blue-eyed *ghoul*—to show up before I let them in. My big *ta-da!* moment, to prove to her that I could be trusted with bigger things."

Jesus, she was using the island as a job application for a promotion. What a bitch.

"You guys spoiled that," Karen said, with a slight frown. "But that's all right. Nothing worth having ever comes without a little hard work." She walked across the room, opened the door, but then stopped and looked back at him. "One last question. I'm really curious."

"About what?"

"Sarah woke you guys up, right? She was the one who betrayed us?"

"No."

"No?"

"I mean, yes, she betrayed you, but she wasn't the one who woke us up. I did. I woke up first, then I convinced Sarah to help us."

Karen stared at him for a moment, again trying to gauge his trustworthiness. "You woke up first? How? No one's ever woken up before."

"I barely touched the wine during the feast."

"Shit," she said, and almost laughed. "I should have kept an eye on you. I told Marcus to pour you the Coke instead, that you'd probably never drunk wine in your life. But you looked older, and..." She shook her head. "Sonofabitch."

She turned back to the door.

"What about me?" he asked. "Do I just...sit here?"

"There'll be someone outside. Try to escape and he has orders to shoot you dead. Got it?"

He nodded mutely.

"Good boy," she said, and left, slamming the door behind her.

HE MANAGED TO get up and walk over to the window in his wet clothes. The pain seemed to be easing the more he moved, which was unexpected. Still, he unconsciously favored his left leg, but even when he put pressure on it, it didn't really hurt that much. Josh couldn't wrap his mind around that, but quickly decided he didn't care enough to keep thinking about it.

He peered through the blinds at the men outside. They seemed to be waiting for something, sitting on open tail gates and leaning against trucks, talking quietly, almost nervously, among themselves. There were open cases of weapons around them and in the backs of the trucks. A dozen or so of the men seemed to be drinking beer. Warm beer, of course. The island probably had cold beers. But not out here. Out here, it was go warm or go home.

Thirty against seven.

They can't win. How can they win against all those men with all those guns?

Josh looked up at the sky and right into the bright sun. What time was it? It had to be almost evening by now. He had left the island with Will in the afternoon, and God knew how long he had been asleep before Karen showed up.

The door opened behind him, and a short man with a bad haircut came in.

The man wore cargo jeans and Army boots. He had a gun belt and a rifle slung over his back. Despite that, he looked innocuous, especially since he was eating an apple when he gave Josh a bored look. "You hungry?"

"Yes," Josh said quickly. He was famished. He hadn't realized how famished until his stomach growled.

The man took another apple from a pouch around his waist and tossed it across the room. Josh clumsily caught it. "I found a whole tree on my way here. But don't tell the others. They don't know."

"Thanks," Josh said.

"I was the one who fished you out of the lake, you know," the man said. He grinned at Josh, showing off a big gap where he was missing a front tooth. "Literally. There was this big pole—" he mimed it for Josh's benefit "—with a hook at the end. I guess they used it to grab nets or some shit. I was never much of a fisherman. Never cared for the water, to be perfectly honest with you."

"Thanks. For saving my life."

"Sure. Happy to do it."

"Was I…dead when you pulled me up? I don't remember anything after I fell in."

"Nah, you were still breathing. Mostly, anyway. I pumped on your chest a few times and you spat all the lake water out. Then you lost consciousness."

"Thanks," Josh said again.

"No biggie. Try the apple."

Josh bit into the fruit. It was warm, but the juices tasted good just the same. He took another bite and savored the flavor.

"Not bad, right?" the man said. "I ate a dozen of them before I got to this place. The name's Mason, by the way."

"Josh."

"Yeah, I know. The bitch told me." Mason grinned at him. "Or, ahem, excuse me, Karen, as she likes to be called. But still a royal bitch, right?"

Josh grinned back. He couldn't disagree with that assessment.

"Exactly," Mason said. "I would totally still hit that, don't get me wrong."

Josh couldn't imagine Mason "hitting" Karen. She had to have at least five inches on him. The last person who had "hit" it when it came to Karen was Tom, who had been a hulk of a man. Compared to Tom, Mason looked like someone's kid trying to puff up his chest to look bigger than he really was.

But Josh didn't say any of that out loud. The guy had given him an apple. Hell, he had even fished Josh out of the lake. That counted for something.

"She's got a real mouth on her," Mason was saying. "But hey, politicians, right? They can talk and talk and talk."

"I guess."

Mason turned to go. "Anyway, you stay in here. I'll go outside and 'guard'—" he made air quotes with his fingers "—you."

"Thanks," Josh said again. "For everything."

"Don't mention it, kid. Hey, we're all in the same boat, right? Just trying to survive another day."

Josh nodded. He couldn't have put it better himself.

JOSH FINISHED OFF the apple but continued to spend his time at the window, peering out, careful not to be seen, as the men continued to get ready in the front yard. It didn't take a genius to know what they were getting ready for. They were going to attack the island, except this time there were more men and more guns, and they weren't going to be chased away by Danny shooting at them from the Tower.

It was going to be a massacre. People would die. He just hoped Gaby wasn't one of them.

Every now and then, he saw Karen outside, sending one of the men here and there. They seemed to listen to her. Karen was tall and imposing, sure, but there were men out there who looked rough and dangerous. There were some big ones with no necks who filled out their camo pants and hunting vests like they were born to them. But they all obeyed Karen just the same. He wondered why.

Josh had seen trucks arriving with boats. First just two, then three, then four. From his vantage point inside the kid's room, he tracked them heading down the driveway and toward the boathouse at the back, where he lost sight of them.

He glanced up at the sky. It was still bright, but it looked like the heat was letting up. He didn't have his watch with him, and the clock on the wall had died a while back. But if he had to guess, it was probably evening. Six or seven o'clock. That meant darkness wasn't too far away.

So was that it, then? Was Karen's big plan to attack the island at night? He supposed that was probably better than driving their boats right up to the beach in daylight. The last time they had tried that, Danny had shot them up. And he was just one man. Now Will was back there, and he had three more guns with him in Blaine, Maddie, and the mute guy, Bobby.

Whatever Karen's plans, Josh hoped Gaby stayed out of the way. He didn't want to have done all this for nothing.

Just thinking about what he had done made him feel physically sick. He wanted to heave it out, that troubling, agitating feeling deep inside him, but when he opened his mouth, only breath that still smelled like filthy lake water puffed out.

I'm sorry, Carly. I'm sorry, Will. I'm sorry, Danny.

I'm sorry, everyone...

HE WASN'T SURE how long he stood at the window. Eventually he got bored and hobbled around the room, heavily favoring his left leg. He kicked at a yellow toy car and it went skating across the room and under the bed. Josh eventually ended back at the car bed, sitting down and staring at a giant poster of Optimus Prime.

That was when he noticed that the slits of sunlight coming into his room had started to taper off. He glanced toward the window and saw that it was darkening fast.

He stood back up, alarmed, his natural instincts reacting to the coming darkness. He moved quickly back to the window and looked out, and he could tell the men outside were getting a little nervous, too. They began collecting their things, picking up their weapons, as if preparing for something. Their eyes darted around and their voices became muted whispers, if they talked at all. Most of them pretended they weren't looking around. All of them were, though.

Josh heard a generator start up. It was a low, rumbling noise at first, then got louder as tall spotlights strategically placed around the property began snapping to life. The men in the yard grimaced at the sudden brightness.

He glimpsed the first one from the corner of his right eye. It came out of nowhere, sliding around the trucks, moving into one of the spotlights, then quickly out again. He thought the men were going to start shooting it. A man in a camo hunting cap actually started to lift his rifle a bit.

Then there were two more—before two became a dozen—and before Josh knew it, the yard was filled with them.

Hundreds.

They came out of the grass beyond the road, gliding into the space around the house, swarming the men in the yard but ignoring them, as if the men didn't exist, didn't have the blood the ghouls so desperately desired. Even so, Josh could see the men watching, eyes darting, terror washing across their faces.

The ghouls kept going, moving toward the edge of the lake, spreading out in a long jagged line. They looked across the water, craning their necks, leaning their bodies, all toward one object.

Song Island.

He could see the island's lights in the distance. The solar-powered lampposts and floodlights had trickled on one by one. The easiest feature to pick up with the naked eye was the Tower in the east. There were four floodlights up there under the third-floor windows, and they lit up the tall structure like the beacon that was never completed.

Josh knew, though he didn't know how, that Gaby was in the Tower right that moment.

I did this for you, Gaby. I hope you'll understand…

HE MUST HAVE wandered back to the bed and dozed off, because when he opened his eyes again, he could tell it was much later in the night. He wasn't sure how much later, but there was a thickness in the room, a heaviness in the air that hadn't been there before.

Josh yawned and climbed off the bed and gimped his way back to the window. His clothes had started to dry, but he could still feel his boxers clinging to his butt.

He peered out the window. Most of the men loitering around the yard were gone. There were just five left, but they seemed busy with their vehicles. Seeing men outside at night, without a care in the world struck Josh as unnatural somehow. Didn't they know there were creatures out there?

But of course they knew. They were collaborators…just like him. And collaborators didn't need to fear the night.

He wondered if the others were on their way to Song Island. He tried to listen for the sounds of boat motors or gunfire, but the only thing he heard was the stillness in the room and the occasional *clinking* sound of the men outside tinkering with their vehicles. There was also the hum of the generators around them.

Josh jumped when something appeared in front of him on the other side of the window. He took a couple of steps back as the creature pressed its pruned black face into the glass pane and seemed to sneer at him. Black eyes stared through the blinds, but there wasn't the rabid hunger he usually saw in them.

This one just looked…curious.

Josh didn't know whether to run out of the room or leap to the floor or race to hide beside the window. So he did nothing. The ghoul looked back at him with cold, detached eyes. Then it seemed to lose interest and moved on, leaving an impression of its deformed face on the glass.

"Freaky, huh?" a voice said behind him.

Josh looked over at Mason, leaning in the doorway, grinning at him over another apple.

"You think you're used to them, and then one of them goes and does something like that," Mason said casually. "Then you remember they're not really your friends after all. Don't worry, we're safe in here. Boss lady's given them the order not to mess with the house."

"Karen?"

"Not even close. Skin and bones. Blue eyes. That boss lady."

"Oh."

"You ever seen it before?"

"No."

"You think those little fuckers are freaky? Wait till you meet the boss lady. Nothing about it feels right. The way it talks, the way it looks…" He shivered. "Creeps me out every time."

"What's going on out there?" Josh asked, hoping to steer the conversation somewhere else, somewhere less likely to raise the hairs on the back of his neck.

"Boys are getting ready to take back the island." Mason walked over to the window and peered out. "Or at least, that's the plan."

"You don't think it's going to work?"

"I don't give a shit if it works or not. I just care that those little bastards don't come in here tonight."

Mason looked toward the part of the yard still covered in darkness, safe from the spotlights powered by the generator. It occurred to Josh that he was actually taller than Mason by almost two inches.

"She's out there, you know," Mason said.

"Who?"

"You know. *It.*"

The real boss lady.

"How do you know?" Josh asked.

"Because we're not wearing hazmat suits. We have to wear those things when it's not around, just to be safe. But when it's nearby, it has full command of the little buggers. It's some kind of psychic link, right out of the comic books. The link is stronger the closer it is to its soldiers."

"Soldiers?"

"Foot soldiers. It's a war, you know. A war between humanity and these undead fucks."

He hates them. He works for them, but he hates them.

"When's the attack?" Josh asked.

"Around midnight, I think."

"Why not now?"

Mason shrugged. "I didn't bother to get all the details."

"Are you going, too?"

Mason grinned, and they were so close this time that Mason's missing front tooth looked like a big black stain in an otherwise white sea of pearls. "Nah. I got babysitting duty, remember? I gotta thank you for that."

"Sorry."

He chuckled. "For what? Keeping me from storming that beach and getting my nuts shot off? No, I mean it. *Thanks*, man."

Josh smiled awkwardly back at him. "You're welcome, I guess."

"In fact," Mason said, "I was going to—"

He stopped in mid-sentence and went back to the window. He

looked out for a moment before pulling the blinds up, exposing the two of them to the yard and the men milling outside.

"What is it?" Josh asked.

"You see that?" Mason pointed up at the sky.

Josh looked out, following Mason's finger. He didn't see anything at first, but then slowly it came into view.

It was a bright light in the sky, getting bigger every second.

Even the ghouls seemed to notice the quickly approaching light, and Josh saw stirring among the shadows. The men also stopped what they were doing and stared up at the sky.

After all, it wasn't like you saw *that* every day. At least, not since The Purge.

"Is that what I think it is?" Josh asked, straining to see details against the black sky.

"Holy shit," Mason said. "That's a helicopter, kid."

CHAPTER 36

LARA

THEY STARTED THE attack thirty minutes after midnight.

Lara could hear them coming from a distance, even through the thick concrete walls of the Tower, where she was staying on the second floor standing watch over Carly and the girls. It was the sound of their boat motors. They were loud and screeching, announcing their arrival well in advance. As Will had predicted, they were making a beeline for the beach.

It's a beach landing. Like something out of World War II.

How did we come to this?

At first, Lara had thought they might not attack at all tonight, especially after the helicopter had shown up out of nowhere. Her fear that the helicopter was part of the attack quickly gave way to curiosity when it circled them twice before turning and heading off, vanishing into the distance, never to be seen again. She would have chalked it up to an overactive imagination, except everyone on the island had seen it, too.

About twenty minutes after the helicopter appeared and flew away, the people from the house attacked.

"They're coming, aren't they?" Sarah asked from the first floor.

Lara stood at the south window, and she could see the tiny dots of light dancing across the water in the distance. They were still too far away for her to make out any details, even through the binoculars. They could have been anything. Fireflies, small campfires in the distance. Except she knew better.

"It's the water," Will had told her. *"Sound travels better away from shore."*

That, and it was night, and there were no other sounds at all. There was hardly any wind, and the waters were calm, the waves pushing tirelessly against the beach. It was like the night knew what was coming and didn't want to interrupt, didn't want to interject its own soundtrack into the furious violence to come.

Lara walked back to the open door in the floor and looked down at Sarah, standing anxiously below her. "Yes, I think so."

"I can hear them," Sarah said. "I don't know how, but I can hear them. Boat motors. Can you see how many?"

"I can't be sure. Four, I think. But I can't be sure."

"What does Will say?"

"He's not going to see a lot from his vantage point. Danny should know more soon."

Sarah nodded and put on a brave face, but Lara saw fear in her eyes. She didn't blame the other woman. Sarah, like the rest of them, hadn't gotten much sleep in the last couple of days, and it was beginning to show on all of their faces.

Lara looked over at the three girls, trying bravely to ignore everything happening around them. They sat in a corner on the floor, at the foot of Carly's bed. Vera was the ringleader and sat in the middle holding both girls' hands. The eight-year-old caught Lara's eyes and smiled. Lara found the strength to smile back, hoping to comfort her, but she realized, ironically, that it was the eight-year-old who was comforting her.

Always the brave soldier. Carly would be proud.

Lara walked back to Carly to check her vitals. She was still pale, but she looked much better than she had that afternoon. She had lost a lot of blood, but Lara had been prudent enough during their stay at Harold Campbell's facility to get everyone's blood type. Carly was B negative, which was bad, because B negative was rare. Fortunately for them, Danny was O negative, which made him a universal blood donor. He had sat patiently for two hours cracking one bad joke after another as she had transfused his blood into Carly.

Lara watched her best friend, who looked strangely at peace. And why not? This was probably the most sleep Carly had gotten in the last few weeks. She wasn't going to wake up for anything, even if the world ended tonight. The sedatives would make sure of that.

Get all the sleep you can, girl. You might not get another chance after tonight.

The radio clipped to Lara's hip squawked, and she heard Will's voice, utterly calm in the face of what she knew he could see coming right at him: "I count four."

"So do I," Danny said through the radio.

Danny was up on the third floor with Gaby at his side, providing what Will called "overwatch" with his ACOG-mounted rifle. Gaby was on her night-vision binoculars next to him, and her job was to search out targets for Danny to shoot. Lara didn't know how she felt about using Gaby that way, but the teenager had agreed so quickly that Lara didn't know how to argue against it.

They're all growing so fast. Her, the girls…

Adapt or perish.

"There should be more than that," Will said. "Six. You saw four new boats this afternoon."

"That's an affirmative," Danny said.

"So there should be six. Where are the other two?"

"Maybe they couldn't fix the motor I shot?"

"That still leaves five."

"Dammit, you and your counting."

She went to the window and picked up her binoculars and peered through them. She picked up the four boats she had seen earlier. They were closer and their lights looked bigger. Each boat had headlights and additional lights along its sides. The boats were coming in a horizontal line, spread out four wide, moving side by side. It was easy to tell how far apart they were from each other—about twenty yards each—because of their lights. And they were so loud. It was amazing how loud and obnoxious they were being as they approached the beach.

So loud…and so bright…

And so obvious…

She unclipped the radio and pressed the transmit lever: "Will. Something's wrong."

"I know," Will said. "Two boats are missing."

"No. I mean, yes, two boats are missing. But it's not just that. Something else is wrong."

"What do you see?"

"They're making it too obvious. Look at them. Why do they even have lights on? They don't need them. They know exactly where we are. Song Island is covered in lights. So is the beach."

"So they don't crash into each other?" Blaine said through the radio.

"No, it's not that," Lara insisted. "They're too far apart to start ramming each other now."

"She's right," Will said. "It's a diversion."

"Yes," Lara said quickly. "It's got to be some kind of diversion, right?"

"Danny," Will said, "keep an eye on the incoming four. Gaby, start scanning the rest of the approaches to the island. Concentrate on our six."

"Our what?" Gaby said through the radio.

"Behind us," Will said.

"Oh. I'm doing it now."

"Nice call, Lara," Will said. She could hear the pride in his voice, and she found herself strangely exhilarated by the compliment, mostly because he gave them out so rarely.

"Thanks," she said.

"Get a fucking room," Danny said.

"After this," Will said.

Lara smiled, then hurried over to the other windows and peered out. The solar-powered lampposts only reached so far, and there were whole sections of the western part of the island that were pitch-black. Lara found it difficult to separate the water from the island. She wondered if Gaby was having better luck.

"Anything?" Will asked through the radio.

"Nothing so far," Gaby said.

"Keep looking. If they're going to try to sneak onto the island, it'll be either from the north or the west."

"Will do," Gaby said.

"Can they climb up the other sides of the island?" Lara asked into the radio.

"It's difficult," Will said, "but it's doable."

After a while, Lara went back to the south window. The girls watched her with curious eyes, following her movements without a word. Jenny was already half asleep, but Vera and Elise looked awake, even alert.

"Anything?" Sarah called from the door.

"Nothing yet," Lara said back.

Lara picked up the four boats coming toward the beach again. It didn't look like they were trying anything fancy—four boats flying across the lake's surface, side by side, bright spotlights shining ahead of them.

She couldn't tell how many men were in each boat. There had already been at least eight of them at the house before reinforcements had come. If there were even just two to a truck among the newcomers—they had counted six trucks in all earlier today—then that was already twenty people. Lara thought there had to be more. She remembered the ghoul collaborators in Dansby, Texas. There were ten of them just there alone. If Will was right, and Kate was calling in people from around the area, then there would be more than ten.

Probably more than twenty...

Lara lowered the binoculars for a minute and glanced down at the Benelli leaning against the wall next to the window to remind herself it was still there. Behind her was a second shotgun, and two pouches of shotgun shells loaded with silver buckshot sat next to each weapon. It had been Lara's idea to go with the shotguns. She was going to be in the Tower for most of the night, and if she had to shoot, it would mean there were ghouls or human attackers very near the Tower. In that kind of close-range situation, the shotguns were most effective.

The sight of the weapons reassured her, and she thought, amused, *Mother would never approve.*

The loud *crack* of a gunshot from above startled her. She glanced up briefly and saw the barrel of Danny's M4A1 poking out of the Tower window just as he fired two more times.

Lara peered through her binoculars and saw that one of the boats was now moving in darkness, its lights shot out.

Danny fired again, and Lara thought she saw a man topple from one of the boats.

Then a long string of unrelenting gunfire exploded, shattering the calm night with such massive velocity and force that she almost jumped.

My God, is this what being at war sounds like?

There was a jagged line of fire stabbing toward the beach from the water. The men on the boats were shooting as they neared the island. For a moment, Lara expected to see tracer bullets like in the movies—brightly lit "laser" lines following the path of gunfire—but there was none of that.

The boats were clearly starting to slow down as they neared the beach. Lara wasn't even sure if Will, Blaine, and Maddie, waiting on the beach, were firing back yet, or if they were biding their time, waiting for the attackers to get closer.

Above her, Danny was firing nonstop now. Single shots. Calmly, with precision. She knew the M4A1s had only two fire settings—semi-automatic and full-auto. Danny was squeezing off one shot after another.

One of the boats burst out of the water and slid up the beach. Men scrambled to climb over the boat's railing even before it had stopped moving, but it was hard to make out how many of them there were exactly. Then one of the men stumbled and fell face-down on the beach and didn't move again.

The gunfire didn't stop. If anything, it got louder and faster and more intense.

She saw bodies falling on the beach as another boat came in, but it was moving too fast and didn't stop in time. Or maybe that was the point. The boat slashed across the sand, traveling up even farther than the first boat. The men inside were shooting as they scrambled out, raking fire in every direction. She didn't know if they saw what they were shooting at or if it was just desperation. Hoping to hit something while praying they didn't get hit.

She knew Will was somewhere in the center of the beach, hidden in the trees, with Blaine to his left and Maddie to his right at opposite ends of the long stretch of sand. They would be firing into the center of the beach, into what Will called a "kill zone."

And above her, Danny was still firing. Calmly, one shot at a time. Over and over again. She didn't remember if he had even reloaded yet.

Lara continued looking through the binoculars, swinging left and right and center, watching men stumbling away from boats beached haphazardly on the sand, only to fall. She could already see bodies in the sand. Maybe a dozen. Maybe more. It seemed unreal, and it wasn't even much of a fight. They were dying. Just dying. What did they think they were doing? Whose plan was this, to send men to die? Did they really think they were going to take the island just by boating up to it?

This is a suicide mission.

She lowered her binoculars. She didn't want to see any more. There wasn't really a fight on the beach. Will had set it up perfectly, and with Danny firing from a high position, there was no way they were going to lose the beach. No way—

One of the lampposts in the yard between the Tower and the hotel glinted off something metallic below her. Lara saw it out of the corner of her eye and looked down. The first thought that raced through her head was, *Oh God*, just before she pulled her head back—a half-second before the man standing below her window fired and a big chunk of concrete above the window frame exploded and showered her as she fell to the floor.

Lara scrambled away from the window as fast as she could, ignoring the sudden stabbing sensations from her tailbone, where she had slammed into the hardwood floor after falling. She backpedaled with her feet like a turtle on its back, sucking in air.

She frantically reached down and snatched the radio off her hip and screamed into it: "They're here! They're at the Tower!"

"Where?" someone asked through the radio. It might have been Will, or Danny, but she couldn't be sure.

A second later she heard an ear-splitting explosion directly above her. The floor that separated the second and third floors shook so violently that dust and splinters came loose and fell down on top of her and the girls and Carly. She thought she saw brick and mortar falling down across the window in front of her, like sheets of rain.

Jenny began to cry and Vera grabbed the girl and held her, while Elise pressed her hands against her ears and squeezed her eyes shut.

Brave girls, stay brave.

"What was that?" someone shouted through the radio. Male. It might have been Will. "What the hell was that?"

No. Not Will. The voice was too panicked, too loud, and too out of control.

She heard gunfire outside the Tower, and it was very close.

They're outside! How did they get on the island?

Will had to be coming. Will or Blaine or Maddie. There were collaborators on the island.

They're on the island!

But she could still hear gunfire from the beach. How many were left? Hadn't Will and the others already killed everyone trying to land?

And the third floor was silent. That was the most disturbing part. Danny wasn't shooting anymore. He had stopped shooting as soon as she had heard the explosion above her.

Oh, God, Danny...Gaby...

Lara scrambled to the other side of the floor. She grabbed the Benelli, which was still leaning against the wall, and struggled to her feet. She leaned out the west window and looked down and saw two figures racing by below her, appearing in the large pool of floodlights. One of the men stopped and looked up. She saw some kind of green-and-black camouflage paint over his face, but his eyes were wide and blue, and they zeroed in on her just before he lifted his rifle and fired.

Lara flinched as the bullet buzzed past her right ear. It wasn't courage that kept her standing at the window—she had simply frozen and didn't pull her head back as she should have. But the man fired too quickly, shocked by her appearance, and *missed.*

Lara shoved the Benelli outside the window and pointed it down and squeezed the trigger without aiming. The man's legs buckled under him; then he seemed to vanish into a thick shrubbery.

She was in the middle of pulling the weapon back when the second man suddenly reappeared and began firing a shotgun up at her window. His first shot scattered buckshot along the window frame, and Lara screamed as some caught her left arm and she lost her grip on the Benelli. The shotgun fell through the window and the man, thinking it was some kind of attack, scrambled out of the way.

Lara stumbled away from the window. Her right arm was bleeding, but she knew it wasn't serious. Shotguns didn't kill unless you got most of the fire into center mass, and the man had gotten her with stray buckshot. It still hurt, and she was trickling blood on the floor as she moved.

Somehow, Lara managed to block out the pain. She ran across the floor and grabbed the other shotgun from under the south window. It had fallen down, and she thought she must have tripped or kicked it when she was scrambling away from the window during the initial attack.

She grabbed the shotgun and ran to the closest window; that was when she saw it. It looked like a bullet, but it was much bigger than a bullet—at least ten times bigger, and the bulbous tip looked golden. It slammed into the top of the window frame above her head and chipped concrete with the impact. Lara threw herself to the floor, looking back just in time to see the bullet-like object ricocheting out of view.

What the hell was that?

She heard a male voice say, "Oh, fuck," just before a loud explosion erupted below her, outside the building. The explosion was so close that the entire length of the Tower trembled like it had been wracked by an earthquake.

Lara stood up and slipped alongside the window and looked down and saw what used to be a man lying at the base of the Tower. Parts of him were scattered among a crater of blackened and charred grass, as if he had taken a direct hit from a meteorite. She couldn't begin to fathom what had happened, or what the huge bullet object she had seen earlier was. Was that what had caused the explosion below her and killed the man? Was it a grenade? It didn't look like a grenade, but it wasn't like she had seen every grenade ever invented by man.

Lara looked above her and gasped in horror at the sight of the third floor. Or what was left of it. The entire top of the building looked like it had been sheared off, exposed to the night sky. The windows were somehow still intact, along with the floodlights underneath them, but the roof and parts of the unfinished beacon housing were gone.

Oh, Danny…

She heard screaming from her floor and turned, saw Elise looking at her, large eyes focused on Lara's right arm. The girl had a horrified look on her face, and it was all Lara could do to smile at her and fumble her way over to the eight-year-old, kneel in front of her, and take her head in her hands. Elise's eyes darted to the blood trickling to the floor from Lara's arm.

"I'm all right," Lara said, as gently and forcefully as she could manage. "I'm all right. It's just a scratch. See? I'm fine, sweetheart."

Her head snapped up when she heard gunfire outside, very close to the Tower. Almost right *next* to the Tower. She knew immediately someone was shooting at the door on the first floor.

Will. Where the hell are you?

"Sarah!" Lara screamed.

Lara waited for an answer from Sarah, but didn't get one.

She looked back at Elise one last time, smiled, kissed the girl on the forehead, then hurried over to the open door. She looked down and saw Sarah standing in front of the thick double door, the Remington shotgun in her hands.

"Sarah," Lara called down.

Sarah glanced up, wide-eyed. "Is everyone okay up there? Jenny…?"

"Everyone's fine, Jenny's fine."

"You're bleeding!"

"It's just a flesh wound." *I hope.*

They had stopped shooting at the door, probably after realizing it wasn't going to buckle. She heard gunfire from farther away instead. Not as far as the beach, but maybe between the beach and the Tower.

Will. Please let it be Will.

Lara unclipped the radio and pressed the transmit lever: "Will. Anyone. Are you out there? They're attacking the Tower. Will?"

She didn't get a response. Lara pressed the transmit lever again and was about to repeat herself when she realized it hadn't made any sounds. Usually there was a squawk, a signal for her to start talking. Lara turned the radio over in her hand and saw two big holes in the back. Buckshot. It had cracked the radio's shell and damaged whatever was inside.

"Lara," Sarah said from below the door.

Lara looked back down at her. "What?"

"Listen."

"Listen to what?"

"*That.*"

Lara stopped moving and listened.

Silence.

She didn't hear another gunshot. Or voices. Or any sounds at all. It was perfectly quiet inside and outside the Tower.

It was suddenly silent all across the island.

"I think it's over," Sarah said.

God, please let it be over.

Lara looked up at the wooden floor above her. She thought she could almost smell the smoke and destruction drifting down from the top floor.

Danny…Gaby…

She rushed up the stairs, doing the best she could to pretend she wasn't dripping blood with every step. She told herself they were minor cuts, remembering how badly Carly had been bleeding earlier today. Compared to that, this was a flesh wound.

She grabbed the door and pushed it open. Or tried to. It budged, but it didn't fling open the way it was supposed to. She knew the door was unlocked, because it opened an inch for her, but that was it.

Lara braced herself against the metal step below, then put her entire body into the door. It finally moved, though grudgingly, and with a great effort she was able to throw the door open.

Her senses were immediately overwhelmed by thick, acrid smoke that stung her eyes and made her nostrils flare. She squeezed her mouth shut so she wouldn't suck in the smoke and powdered concrete floating everywhere on the third floor.

The open night sky above her instantly came into view.

She had thought it looked bad from the second-floor window, but that hadn't revealed the whole truth. She could see that a great big chunk of the ceiling was missing, along with most of the north side, where the explosion had originated. The floor was covered in debris, big stacks of concrete blocks and brick. The computer setup was buried, and tiny blocks with letters from the keyboard were scattered everywhere.

Gaby sat on the floor with her back against the wall. She looked dazed but alive, blood flowing down the side of her face from a big gash on her left temple. Her right cheek was pockmarked with superficial cuts, and Lara noticed, oddly, that the teenager wasn't wearing her shirt, just her bra.

She looked down at Gaby's lap, which was cradling Danny's head. One entire side of Danny's face was covered in blood, and his right arm was wrapped in some kind of sling made from a shirt. Gaby's shirt.

Gaby somehow managed to smile across the smoke at Lara. "I don't hear any more shooting. Does that mean we won?"

"I think so," Lara said.

She climbed all the way up and stumbled over the pile in the middle of the room. She crouched next to Gaby and Danny.

"Your arm's bleeding," Gaby said, almost casually.

"I know. It's just a scratch."

"Lots of scratches."

"Where else are you hurt?"

"What you see is what you get, doc."

"Third-year medical student," she smiled.

"Good enough for me. Check if Danny's still alive. I can't tell."

Lara felt his pulse. It was weak, but it was still there. "He's alive."

"Good. He promised to teach me how to shoot, and I'm not letting him off this easy."

Lara wiped as much of the blood from Danny's face as she could before finding the source of his bleeding—a couple of gashes along his temple. Not life-threatening, though the amount of blood made it look much worse. He would scar, as they all would, but he wasn't going anywhere just yet.

"You did this?" Lara asked, looking at the sling.

"Sucks, huh?"

"I've seen worse."

"Yeah, where?"

"I dunno, let me think about it for a moment."

Gaby chuckled, prompting Lara to smile.

She pulled aside Gaby's shirt and peered at the wound underneath. There was a big piece of shrapnel buried near Danny's shoulder blade. She would have to remove that as soon as she could, or Danny might lose the use of his arm completely by morning.

"What happened?" Lara asked. "I heard an explosion."

"Some kind of grenade launcher," Gaby said. "Blew up the ceiling. Well, blew up everything else, too, I guess. Danny must have seen the guy. He grabbed me and pushed me down to the floor and covered me with his body. Saved my life. It's almost enough to make me forgive him for all the crappy jokes I've had to listen to for the last two days."

"Sounds like Danny," a voice said behind them.

Lara looked over at Will, climbing up through the door in the floor. He had his Remington slung over his back, and his left arm hung loosely at his side, a field tourniquet tied around it. There was blood on his arm and shirt.

"You've been shot," she said.

She remembered how he had teased her about getting shot in Lancing. He had been through wars. He and Danny. And neither one of them had ever gotten shot. For a while, she had thought of them as invincible. That night in the Cleveland bank, the siege on Harold Campbell's facility… They were always untouchable. Until tonight.

"It's fine," he said. "Take care of Danny and Gaby."

She gave him a long look to see if he was lying to her. He wasn't. "How are the others?"

"We stopped them at the beach. Bobby's dead." He sat down on the floor and leaned back against the wall across from them. "Maddie was shot."

"Come here and let me take a look at that arm."

"Only if you let me take a look at yours first," he said.

"Get a room," Gaby said, rolling her eyes.

CHAPTER 37

WILL

A SHOT RANG out from behind them. Danny, firing from the Tower.

Will saw one of the spotlights on the incoming boats blink out of existence. Then another shot, and another light went out.

A third shot took out the final light.

The boats were close enough now that when Will looked through his night-vision binoculars, he could see four figures scrambling around on the darkened boat. He couldn't tell if they were panicking or getting ready to land. They were heavily armed, he saw that much. Weapons swung around with their bodies.

He moved the binoculars over to his right and picked up four more men in another boat. The spotlights of the second boat were still shining, too bright, and made watching them difficult with the lights directly in his eyes.

Will heard another shot and looked back at the first boat just in time to see a man pitching off the side. The remaining three men were in full panic mode now, and suddenly he saw the man behind the steering wheel shove the throttle forward. The boat began pushing across the calm water at full speed. Will lost track of it for a moment before picking it up again, just in time to see a second man stumbled over the side of the boat, almost as if the wind had caught him by the shirt and jerked him free. He fell into the water and disappeared into the blackness.

Then they were suddenly there and Will dropped the binoculars, picked up the M4A1, and opened fire. His first shot hit the driver of the second boat in the chest, the bullet smashing through the clear screen guard. The man's body jerked violently and he fell forward, his hand hitting the throttle. The boat took off, leaving the others behind.

Will pulled his eye back from the rifle's sight to watch the boats coming. They were almost on top of them.

Thirty meters...

Twenty-five meters...

Blaine and Maddie took his cue and opened fire on the incoming boats. They were close enough now that Will could see bullets smashing into the sides and chopping off chunks of wood and fiberglass. The collaborators were firing back, but they were firing blind, trying in vain to gauge where the bullets were coming from.

Amateurs.

Then the first boat hit the beach and kept coming.

For a moment, Will thought it would continue to rake its way across the beach and right into the woods, but it stopped five meters up the sand and its occupants (three left) jumped out. Will shot the first one just as he landed—a tall man with a mustache and a Dallas Cowboys cap. The man fell face-first into the sand.

The other two opened fire in Will's direction. He calmly lowered himself to the ground as tree bark above him cracked and snapped loose. The AK-47 fire continued for a while, joining the other gunfire erupting all over the beach. Will saw one of the men clutch at his chest and go down.

Nice shot, Danny.

Will, still on his stomach, shot the third man in the side. The man stumbled but didn't go down. Another shot from the Tower and the man collapsed.

Then the second boat hit the beach and this time it really did keep going. Will was about to pick up the Remington and run for his life when the boat finally stopped halfway up the beach and the three men inside scrambled out. Will heard a hellacious torrent of fire from his left *(Blaine)* firing on full-auto. He watched chunks of the boat's side splinter and one of the men fall, try to get back up, then fall again. The remaining two returned fire into the woods in Blaine's direction.

Will took the momentary distraction to sit up and shoot the closest man in the chest. The man fell, and as the third and last man turned toward him, Will shot him in the chest, too.

He heard intense gunfire from the right side of the beach and looked over, saw that the other two boats had made landfall and men were spilling out, kicking up sand as they scrambled forward, desperately trying to escape the beach. There were four in one boat and five in the other, and Will watched one of them stagger and fall as Maddie razed them from her hiding spot. In response, nearly all of the men turned in her direction and fired back.

Shit.

Will quickly switched the M4A1 to full-auto and unleashed a volley into the group of men. He caught one of them square in the chest, hit another one in the thigh, and dropped a third man with a lucky shot to the head.

They turned away from Maddie and toward him and sent their own fusillade his way, forcing him to snatch up the Remington and dart farther back into the woods. Behind him, the trees where he had been crouched were torn and reduced to green mist in the black night.

He was still moving through the woods, picking his way toward the cobblestone pathways to his left with the Remington in his hand, the M4A1 slung over his back, when he heard Lara's voice, screaming into his right ear: "They're here! They're at the Tower!"

The Tower!

He reached for his PTT, but Blaine beat him to it: "Where?"

Will looked back toward the beach when a new round of gunfire drew his attention. He stopped, went back down into a crouch, and listened. He heard M4 rifle fire coming from his left, then responding AK-47 fire from his right, very close to him.

Blaine. Or Maddie. Engaging on the beach.

Will jumped the last few meters out of the woods and onto the cobblestone pathway. He didn't expect them to be there, but they were. *Right in front of him.*

There were three of them, two looking back toward the beach at the sudden massive exchange of fire. They were big men in boots and camouflaged hunting clothes. The man directly in front of Will, who had a look of total surprise on his face when he saw Will leaping out of the woods, was wearing an assault vest with a radio in one pouch.

The man's eyes widened as far as Will had ever seen in his life and the guy lifted his AR-15. Will shot him first from almost point-blank range with the Remington. The distance between them was nonexistent, and Will didn't even have to lift the shotgun to aim. The man's body seemed to sink right into the stones under his boots, exposing his two comrades standing behind him.

The two men were turning, lifting their weapons, when Will racked the Remington and shot one, then the other.

He didn't even have time to ponder the bloody mess smeared across the cobblestones before he heard a thunderous *boom!* from behind him.

Will knew instantly what that meant. He spun around just in time to see thick white smoke sprouting up from the Tower's third floor like chaotic smoke signals, while brick and concrete tumbled down all around the building like hail.

"What was that?" someone shouted in Will's ear. Blaine again. "What the hell was that?"

Will began running up the cobblestone road, back to the hotel grounds, back to the Tower.

Bobby, where the hell are you?

He saw them moving across the grounds of the hotel almost as soon as he burst out of the woods and into the clearing. They were fanning out. Dark figures, looking for targets. They were smart enough to keep away from the LED lampposts, and he saw one of them randomly shooting at the solar-powered lamps scattered about the area. There might have been five, maybe more. A couple were already circling the Tower, while one was trying to kick in the front door.

Will slung the shotgun as he ran, pulling the M4A1 free. He could still hear gunfire behind him, from the beach. Blaine and Maddie, still slugging it out.

My amateurs are better than your amateurs, Kate.

He looked up at the Tower in the distance, his gut sinking. The initial explosion had sent most of the Tower's roof down into the surrounding area around the base of the structure. The third-floor windows that he could see, amazingly enough, remained intact, along with the floodlights under them. Where there used to be a cap at the top, there was now only a jagged opening with smoke still rising lazily out of it as if it were a chimney.

His attention snapped back to the grounds around the Tower

when he heard a series of gunshots. Rifles, then shotguns, firing back and forth. He looked up just in time to see sections around one of the Tower's second-floor windows breaking free from a shotgun blast.

Will was halfway across the grounds when he caught sight of one of the attackers stepping into a pool of light. The man had on black face paint and was wearing a knit cap. Will shot the man in the back of the head from thirty meters away. The man crumpled into the grass as if he had simply been swallowed up.

A figure in front of Will turned and opened fire. Will saw flames stabbing out of the man's weapon from forty meters away and felt bullets slashing past his head. Then something hit him in the left arm and for an instant he was tossed to one side.

He darted behind a big palm tree as the man kept firing. Tree bark shredded and bullets *zip-zip-zip* around him harmlessly. His left arm was bleeding and had gone numb, but he could still hold the rifle and shoot, so it couldn't have been that bad.

When the man finally stopped shooting, Will stepped out from behind the tree and calmly shot him in the chest while he was struggling to reload.

Then he continued running toward the Tower.

He arrived in time to see a man armed with an M16 rifle feeding something into a tube attached to the bottom of the barrel. He recognized the M203 grenade launcher attached underneath the rifle. That was what had taken off the top of the Tower's third floor.

Will glanced up and saw Lara appear in the second-floor window directly above the man loading the M203. The man saw her and took aim.

Will screamed, "No!"

That got the man's attention. He looked over at Will, momentarily distracted, but quickly turned back to the window and fired. Will's gut sank at the *ploompt!* sound as the M203 launched, and Will watched, horrified, as the grenade round smashed into the window frame just above Lara's head—*then ricocheted back down.*

It didn't arm!

The M203 fired impact grenades that needed to travel a certain distance before they armed themselves. The third floor had been far enough, but not the second-floor window. When Will saw the grenade hit the top of the window frame above Lara's head, sending her stumbling back in shock, he knew it hadn't achieved the proper distance.

As the grenade fell back down to earth, Will watched the man who had fired it scrambling to get away. But the man had misjudged the trajectory of the grenade and was going in the wrong direction. When the grenade landed two meters in front of him, the man shouted out a curse that was quickly swallowed up by an explosion that ripped out a piece of the Tower's base along with it. Any closer, and it would have punched a hole in the Tower itself.

He caught a glimpse of Lara, alive and well, looking out the same window at the remains of the man below her. He wanted to laugh and run to her, grab her, and kiss her.

Instead, he crouched in the darkness and scanned the area. He didn't see anything. Or anyone. Where had they come from? Probably the west side of the island, past the power station. It was the lowest point on the island other than the beach in the south.

Will got up and moved toward the Tower. He was ten meters away when he almost stepped over a body in the grass. He crouched next to it and looked down at the young face.

Bobby.

There was a big bloody spot on his chest where he had been shot at close range. His M4 rifle lay nearby, along with a man with camouflage on his face and a bullet hole in his left cheek. Will imagined the kid heard the attackers coming and ran over to intercept.

He looked up at the realization that the gunfire behind him, from the beach, had stopped, and the island had become ghostly quiet.

He clicked his PTT. "Situation report."

"Beach is cleared," Blaine said in his right ear. "Maddie's hurt."

"How bad?"

"She's been shot a couple of times. Thigh and arm. The arm looks like a flesh wound. She wants to know if anyone's seen Bobby."

"Tell her I'm sorry. Bobby's dead."

"Fuck." Blaine was silent for a moment. Then, "What about the Tower? What was that explosion I heard?"

"One of the attackers had an M203 grenade launcher. He took out the roof. I'm checking on it now."

Will jogged the final distance to the Tower. He looked up at the smoke still puffing out of the remains of the third floor. It didn't look like the grenade had gotten inside the building itself, which would have been catastrophic.

He pressed the PTT again as he neared the Tower. "Lara, can you hear me? Lara."

There was no reply.

"Sarah. Danny. Gaby. Anyone in the Tower. Give me a situation report."

Nothing.

Will reached the door and banged on it. There were more than twenty bullets embedded in the thick mahogany wood. But it had held.

"Open the door!" he shouted. "Whoever's in there, if you can hear me, open the door!"

Mercifully, the door began to open, an inch at a time…

BLAINE LOOKED LIKE week-old shit under the morning sun. And frankly, so did he, if he were to look in a mirror. They were operating almost entirely on fumes and painkillers. Even so, Will's body protested every movement, and he could only imagine how Blaine was feeling at the moment. The big man didn't complain, though.

They glided swiftly across the lake in the same boat they had used yesterday. The Carver had proven itself sturdy, even with a dozen bullet holes in various parts of its frame, including five on the bottom that he had patched with caulk and spackling from the boat shack. Blaine steered from the middle while Will crouched at the bow with the M4A1, scanning the horizon for targets. He wanted to see someone, notice a head poking out from the ridgelines in front of him. He wanted to shoot something. Someone.

Anything, dammit.

The two-story house across from the marina looked dead and abandoned, even from a distance. Will scanned the yards and could find no one. The boathouse was empty—of people and boats. If there were people still at the house, they would be inside. They could certainly hear the Carver coming because Will hadn't done anything to disguise their approach, with the outboard motor roaring in the still morning.

So where were they?

He didn't believe for a second they had killed every single collaborator in last night's attack. Twenty-five men, in all. The storming of the beach had been a diversion to keep them occupied as two other boats came along the west side and the men scaled the cliff. They had found ropes and hooks there this morning, the boats themselves drifting at anchor in the water. Three of the men who had tried to climb hadn't made it. Two had fallen to their deaths against the rocks below and a third was floating nearby.

Twenty-five dead men...

Including Bobby.

Of everyone on the island, he and Blaine were the most mobile. The bullet wound in his left arm was easy to ignore with painkillers. He felt like sleeping for a week, but that wasn't anything new. And like all the other times when he was tired and could barely walk, he soldiered through it. It wasn't like he had any choice.

They went up the inlet, outboard motor piercing the clear morning air. Will expected to see the sun glinting off rifle barrels at any moment.

Any second now...

But it never happened.

He knew they were gone as soon as he jumped from the boat and set foot on the patch of land the house sat on. Blaine struggled with the boat for a moment but finally jumped out with a rope and tied it around a nearby tree.

They scanned the house. Will shot one of the windows just to let anyone inside know they were coming, then waited for a figure to appear so he could shoot it.

He saw no one.

"Gone?" Blaine asked, keeping his voice low.

Blaine gripped his M4, and like Will, he had a shotgun slung over his back. They had brought enough ammo with them to last a while in a stand-up firefight. Will was hoping he got to use all of it. Or most of it, at least.

"Let's check the house," Will said.

THERE WAS NO one in the house. The place looked heavily lived-in, and there was food in the kitchen and living room and cases of bottled water left on couches. Boxes of clothing, ammo, and guns lay scattered everywhere. The bedrooms were similarly used and abandoned.

There were trucks in the yard, parked in a kind of semi-circle, the grass around them trampled by heavy boots and bare feet. He saw a generator near the back of the house, and portable spotlights lined the yard.

They had been here last night. Gathering, waiting for the call to attack. And when the call came, they boarded their boats and charged.

A suicide run. Why would they do that?

Because they didn't have a choice.

She was here. Kate. She sacrificed the collaborators to get to us.

"What now?" Blaine asked.

"Grab the ammo and guns from the house."

Will siphoned gas out of the trucks into containers he found in the boathouse. When Blaine came back outside, Will handed him two of the containers.

"We're going to burn the house?" Blaine asked.

"Yup."

"Why not save it? In case we need it later?"

"We don't need it. We have the island. The next time they come back, they should be as uncomfortable as possible."

They doused the house with gas inside and out, added fuel to the boathouse and the big storage building across the yard, then lit a match and stood back and watched it all burn under the sun. The heat quickly became suffocating.

With the fire gutting the house behind them, Will and Blaine checked the garage in the marina. The crates they had left behind were still there, but they had been strafed with automatic gunfire. Perforated water bottles had leaked onto the ground.

"Anything we can salvage?" Blaine asked.

"Clothes, shoes…"

"Got holes in them."

"Probably."

They filled a crate with all the undamaged supplies they could find, then doused the garage with the remaining gas and lit it. For good measure, they burned down the gazebo, too.

Will noticed that the bodies were gone. The two men he had killed around the garage, and the three or so they had shot during the gunfight afterward.

Blaine noticed, too. "They took the bodies. They did that at the Willowstone Mall in Beaumont, too. Sandra's body was gone the next morning. They can't turn the dead, can they?"

"Not that I've seen."

"So why did they take them?"

Will shook his head. Just another mystery to add to the pile of mysteries. Eight months had gone by, and they hardly knew anything about the creatures.

They walked to Blaine's Jeep, parked in the ditch farther up the road. It wasn't there anymore, though they did find a couple of silver candle holders lying in the grass nearby.

"Sonofabitch," Blaine said. "That's the second Jeep I've lost."

"Should have known better than to leave your car unlocked on the side of the road," Will said.

"Rub it in."

They climbed back into the Carver and rode back to the island.

Will watched the house burning, half of the two-story structure already consumed by the large flames. The trucks in the yard had become blackened wrecks and some caught fire, their tanks adding more fuel to the bonfire raging next to them. The small boathouse had gone quickly, along with the garage and gazebo at the marina.

Will turned back toward Song Island and settled down in the stern of the boat, Blaine steering in front of him. He could feel the heat flaring against his back, even from a distance. It felt even warmer than the sun above them.

HE WAS SHORT on manpower, so he gave Maddie first watch, positioning her in what remained of the Tower's third floor. She was wounded, but she could still shoot, and the painkillers helped. Blaine walked the island, circling it every few hours. Will didn't know how he was even still up and about after last night, much less still moving. Danny was already conscious, but he wasn't going to be useful for a while.

The next few days and weeks would be dangerous ones if the collaborators decided to attack again. His only hope was that they didn't know how much he had lost last night. If Kate decided to risk more of her humans, their ownership of Song Island would prove short-lived.

Will located Danny's remaining bundles of C4 in the basement underneath the Tower where Tom had left them. He planted them along the beach and kept the detonator with him at all times.

Hope for the best, prepare for the worst.

Tonight. He would find out how much Kate wanted the island, how much she was willing to sacrifice.

He was lucky he still had Sarah around. Along with the girls, he and Sarah were able to keep an eye on the wounded—Carly, Danny, and Gaby, now lying side by side on the second floor of the Tower. It was still the safest and easiest-to-defend location on the entire island, even after last night's grenade launcher attack.

An hour later, Will found Lara asleep in their room.

She was exhausted and slept in the same clothes from last night. Her right arm was covered in bandages she had put on herself—both of her arms were now covered in bandages—and her face was blackened and bruised, as were her legs and, he knew, most of her body.

She was curled up on her side on the bed, sleeping in a pool of sunlight pouring in from the open patio window. There was a light morning breeze, and the room felt strangely cool despite the oppressive heat outside.

He sat down on a chair next to the bed and watched her sleep. It was quiet. So quiet. The only sounds were the birds outside, water lapping against the island, and her soft breathing. He could look at her forever, he realized.

After a while, she stirred and opened her eyes.

She saw him immediately, and a ghost of a smile appeared across her bruised lips. "You're back."

"I'm back."

"How did it go?"

"They were gone by the time we got there."

"Figures."

"Yeah."

"Any signs of where they went?"

"No."

"What about Blaine's Jeep?"

"Gone."

"Thieves."

"Yeah."

She lay still, and they were content to look at each other in silence for a moment.

"Carly woke up for a bit while you were gone," she said. "She should be back on her feet soon, though she won't be very chatty for a while. Danny's and Gaby's wounds aren't too bad. Nothing life-threatening. And Maddie's going to be gimpy for a few days."

He nodded.

"How's your arm?" she asked.

"It's fine."

"Are you sure?"

"Yes."

She reached out and stroked his cheek with her fingers. "You look like shit."

"Thanks."

"But I still love you."

"You just love me for my body."

"Who told you?"

"It's obvious."

She was quiet again.

"What is it?" he asked.

"What happens now?"

If they attack tonight, we're probably all going to die, he thought, but he said instead, "We gave up a lot for this island, so we're going to make the best of it. They might have lured us here on false pretenses, but they weren't completely lying. Song Island is a haven, and it has everything we need to live out the rest of our lives."

"Are you saying you want to grow old with me?" she said, smiling at him.

"I would like to see you with gray hair."

She laughed. "It's called Clairol Perfect 10, babe. The first sign of gray hair, and I'm sending you out there to fetch me a box."

"The things I do for love."

She took his hands in hers and pulled him onto the bed with her. "Come here."

"You're still hurt."

"So are you. We'll make it work. Adapt or perish, remember?"

"Adapt or perish," he repeated, and lay down on the bed next to her.

She slipped comfortably against him and Will wrapped his arms around her and held her tight. He ignored the stabbing pain in his arm. It was a small price to pay for this moment with her, which could very well be their last.

"Will?" she whispered.

"Yeah?"

"If you dream about Kate again, I'm going to kick your ass."

"Fair enough."

EPILOGUE

"WE'RE GOING TO need a new leader," Mason said, grinning through that big black hole in his front teeth.

It was dark outside the kid's room. Very dark, despite the fact that there was moonlight and the spotlights, and the sound of the generator humming in the background could be heard. But it was very dark in the front yard, though Josh thought that might have been because of the ghouls.

They were everywhere, spread out across the yard, spilling over the driveway, flattening the grass as far as he could see. Their dark skin looked like black oceans of tar swaying slowly back and forth under the window. He wondered how terrified he would be if they turned and looked at him all at once.

He pushed the thought out of his head. They weren't going to turn. They were focused on what was happening in the middle of the yard.

Josh felt a strange sense of fascination mixed with dread at the sight of *it* moving through the crowd of ghouls. It stood out because the other ghouls were homogenous, devoid of identity. But this ghoul was different. He could tell, even from a distance, that it was female. It walked straight, and if not for the supernatural fluidity with which it moved, he might have believed it was human.

No one had returned from the island. There had been a gun battle the likes of which he had never heard before. At one point he swore he even heard an explosion or two, and all he could think was, *Gaby, please be safe, please be safe…*

The gun battle seemed like it went on and on for hours, and it sounded like the end of the world all over again. He wasn't sure how long it really lasted. Maybe twenty minutes, maybe ten minutes, maybe even less than that. It was hard to tell. He was so far away that the *pop-pop-pop* of gunfire sounded surreal, like listening to a movie. Not even watching a movie, just hearing the echoes of one playing in the theater next door.

She lied to me. Karen lied to me. She didn't go there to save Gaby. She's throwing everything at the island.

Lying bitch!

And when it was over and no one returned, he heard the loud rustling of movement outside his window and looked out and saw Karen on her knees, waiting, as ghouls appeared out of the darkness and surrounded her. They came from nowhere and everywhere, and he had forgotten momentarily that they were hiding in the night all around him.

No, that wasn't true. They didn't really "hide" anymore. It was where they lived. Where they dwelled. It was *their home.* He was the one hiding in a kid's room. *They*, the humans, were the ones who didn't belong anymore.

"What's happening?" Josh asked.

"Karen didn't follow orders. It told her not to attack the island, but she did it anyway." Mason smirked. "See, kid, this is what happens when you overestimate your abilities, not to mention your importance in the larger scheme of things. When it's all said and done, we're just cogs in the machine. Remember that."

The female ghoul stood over Karen, and Josh could see *bright blue eyes* piercing the darkness, almost glowing. The blue-eyed ghoul touched Karen's hair, seemed to brush it like a mother would her child's.

Karen was talking now. Talking fast.

The blue-eyed ghoul seemed to nod, then it put a hand under Karen's chin, and Karen stood up slowly. Karen smiled, but it didn't last long because suddenly the blue-eyed ghoul's head was pressed against the side of Karen's throat and Karen's mouth opened in a wide, surprised O.

The ferocity and speed with which it happened made Josh take an involuntary step away from the window.

"Relax, kid," Mason said. "If they wanted us dead, they'd have come in and gotten us already. Front door's not locked."

Josh didn't know how to answer that. Was that supposed to

make him feel better?

He walked over to the bed and sat down. The mattress underneath him was still damp from his wet clothes, but he hardly felt it. His whole body was numb. Jesus, was he even still breathing?

"Relax," Mason said again. "You're going to hyperventilate yourself to death, kid."

"What if we run?" Josh asked suddenly.

"Run?"

"Sneak out the back door. Run away before they notice we're in here."

Mason laughed. "Have you looked outside? There are thousands of those things out there. Where do you think we're going to run *to*? You got a Batmobile I don't know about? We wouldn't last a second outside this house."

"But we can't just stay here."

"Of course we can, and we are. We're not doing shit—"

He stopped suddenly.

Josh stared at him, wondering why he had stopped.

Mason's eyes left Josh's, and he turned his head back toward the door.

Josh felt something seize his chest, punch its way through flesh and bone, and wrap around where he thought his soul was. Josh didn't use to think souls actually existed, but as he stared at the door, he realized how wrong he was.

We all have souls, because it's staring straight into mine.

The blue-eyed ghoul stood in the doorway, its long, lean body covered in black prune skin like the thousands of others outside. It was the same, but different. He knew, without a doubt, that this creature—this *thing*—was more.

So much more.

It stood tall, and he could see the womanly curves of its hips, see where its breasts used to be when it had still possessed—and cared about—gender. And when it smiled at him, Josh thought it looked pleased with his response to its presence.

Something inside Josh died.

"Josh," it said, in a soft, almost feminine voice that traveled across the small bedroom and seized him by the soul and refused to let go. "Josh… We have a lot of work to do, you and I. We're going to change the world. Are you ready?"

21362760R00315

Made in the USA
Middletown, DE
26 June 2015